Prais

Any story that has the ability to keep the reader up until five am in the morning, after a whole night of reading, is a masterpiece in my mind. And this story certainly did not disappoint.

From the very first chapters I found myself being completely sucked into the world of Sophie and Elliot.

The author does a fabulous job and through the tone and descriptiveness of the writing, has your feeling such strong emotions for each of the characters that you can't help but to fall in love with them, despite their histories and flaws. In fact, personally, I think that is what made me fall in love with them and the story even more. The fact that each character is so human, and at some stage or another, you find yourself being able to relate to them or their situation.

I absolutely loved this story, from start to end. It had me smiling and laughing out-loud, but at times had the tears free-flowing down my cheeks and had me feeling such strong feelings of empathy and sadness that I thought it would swallow me whole. Such an emotional, but moving story.

I definitely see myself reading this story many more times, and I am very much looking forward to book two. Absolutely brilliant.

Amy West - The Review Lounge

N.K. Smith

Old Wounds

First published by The Writer's Coffee Shop, 2010

The Writer's Coffee Shop
(Australia) PO Box 2013 Hornsby Westfield NSW 1635
(USA) PO Box 2116 Waxahachie TX 75168

Paperback ISBN- 978-1-61213-004-0
E-book ISBN-978-1-61213-005-7

A CIP catalogue record for this book is available from the US Congress Library.

Cover image by: Konstantin Sutyagin
Cover design by: Jennifer McGuire

www.thewriterscoffeeshop.com/nsmith

N K. Smith has been writing in some fashion since the early age of 10 years old. Her first short story, written in fifth grade, was a summer camp mystery. Now, N.K. is realizing her childhood dreams with her first novel Old Wounds.

Having lived several places throughout the northeast United States, N.K. has returned to her native Indiana where she lives with her husband, two children, and three cats. N.K. has an avid interest in natural, organic, and sustainable living and lives a vegan lifestyle.

Dedicated To

First of all I have to thank my family. My strong and passionate husband, Josh, and my two smart, witty, and gorgeous children are wonderful and help me find my way through the world.

I don't know where I'd be if it weren't for my mother. She's quite honestly one of the best people I know and has helped, encouraged, and guided me during every stage of my life.

I'd like to thank the editors Lea Dimovski, Caryn Stevens, Roberta Curry. Many thanks go to Donna Huber my marketing agent, and Amanda Hayward, the publisher, for giving me this opportunity and extending such consideration and kindness.

This story would not be without the help, love, and support of a few of my favorite women in the world. The following people have left lasting fingerprints on this story: First Brittany Larson guided and championed this endeavor for no other reason than she is my friend. She gave so much of herself and asked questions that helped me flesh out the story. I am forever grateful for her. Jennifer Ebbing, Debbie Matlock, and Amanda Webb provided a massive amount of detailed feedback as well as love and support. Without these four ladies, nothing would be the same. I orbit them.

Chapter 1

New Town, New Life

Sophie

This was exactly what my life needed right now. The stupid hospital bed creaked and groaned and I just knew it was the herald of bad things. As if on cue, some young doctor came in, her hair perfect in that 'I make more money in a week than you'll make in a year' kind of way, and smiled at me.

I looked away.

"Miss Young?"

"Sophie," I croaked. I always hated it when people addressed me formally like that.

The doctor checked a few things, running her fingers over my bruises. When I looked back up, I saw that smile. Doctors all wore the same one, but this chick made me wonder if she knew more than what the police had told her. Maybe she knew more than just about the accident.

"There are a couple of people outside waiting to talk to you."

I swallowed hard as if I could push back the dread and panic with the action. Who was outside? I assumed the cops, but had they already called Helen? She was going to be angry. Really, *really* angry. And I was already in so much pain.

Trying to sit up, I groaned and then gave up.

"You're pretty beat up, so I told them all they couldn't see you for a while."

Even though my ribs felt broken, I'd been told that they were just bruised, but they still hurt like hell when I tried say more than a few words at a time. "Is my mother out there?"

The doctor's expression remained neutral for the most part, but I thought I saw something flicker across her face. It was hard to interpret. "Is your mother a short little lady with a mouth like a hardened sailor?"

I assumed she was talking about my mother's eloquent manner of speaking, not that I was much better. If it was a four-letter word, it was used about three times in every spoken sentence. "Yes."

"Do you want to see her?"

"No."

The doctor tapped on one of the machines with her index finger and pursed her lips. "How are you feeling?"

"My head hurts."

"You have a concussion."

No wonder the room wouldn't stay still. "Did I break anything?" Broken bones hurt and more than that, they made it next to impossible to get around. Even a broken arm messed up everything.

I didn't need my life to suck any more.

"There's a shadow on the film of your left hand." I curled my fingers and rotated my wrist. It hurt, but didn't feel broken. "It could be a hairline fracture, but the radiologist won't say for sure."

She didn't seem overly stressed about my medical condition, so I switched to an equally important topic. "Am I in a shitload of trouble?"

Her expression softened. "I would say you're in a bit of trouble, yes."

My sigh said it all. She checked the chart at the end of my bed, replaced it, went to the dry-erase board next to the door and wrote down a few numbers. Then very slowly, she returned to my bed and sat down in the uncomfortable-looking chair next to it.

"There's going to be a social worker coming in soon, but I want you to know that if you don't feel comfortable talking to her, you can talk to me."

My gaze drifted away again. It was always the same. They always said stuff like this, but no one *really* wanted to listen. No one *really* wanted to help and I didn't think they ever could.

I was sure this woman, and the social worker, were fine people with good intentions, but intentions counted for shit in my world, so once again, it was time to protect myself. The cops waiting outside weren't as scary as some of the other things awaiting me, so there was no reason to cooperate.

I'd botched it all up and made a bigger mess than before.

"What the hell do you want me to talk to you about?" I asked in an intentionally snotty voice.

"Your medical history is not a mystery, Sophie."

As much as it hurt, I folded my arms over my chest and rolled my eyes. "I'm clumsy."

The pity never left her eyes, but I could tell she had only a little more patience left. Then she'd give up and let the social worker "do her job," so I stepped up my game.

"Don't strain your overworked brain too much over this. I'm sure you have some patient in worse condition to give false hope to."

"Hope isn't always false. Take your situation for instance. All you need to do is—"

"Shut the fuck up, will you? My head hurts."

It wasn't long after using what most adults thought was "strong" language that she left me alone. I gave the same treatment to the fiftyish woman who came in with her grandmother smile and her out-of-style clothing.

I'd gone that route one time and there was nothing they could say or do to convince me that telling anyone about any of this shit would ever "help." The cops could come in, intimidate me, process me, and I would take my punishment, because nothing they could do would be any worse than what Helen had planned for me.

❧ • ❧

I was sitting at the kitchen table, listening as Helen called him.

"She stole a car, Tom. It's fairly obvious I can't handle her anymore, isn't it?" Helen's voice shrilled at her ex. "Look, it's your turn. She's only got a year and a half left until she can..."

I sighed, trying to imagine Tom's side of the conversation, and wondering if he was really going to let himself get bulldozed by Helen yet again. I wondered how he could even be a firefighter when he lacked enough testicular fortitude to stand up to one miserable woman.

"Her choices are slim. Either she goes to jail, goes to live in some kind of group home for troubled kids, or she lives with you. You can straighten her out, Tom, I know you can."

Another pause, her eyes flicking to me.

"Don't you dare pull that bullshit about me just not wanting her anymore!"

The drive from Dulles International airport in Washington, D.C. to the small town of Damascus with my biological father Tom was nearly unbearable. I didn't speak more than two words, which consisted of "hi" and "fine."

It wasn't like he was very good at talking to me either. As usual he had no clue what to say, so after he asked how I was, he was silent too. Not that I minded that shit. It meant I didn't have to constantly think of ways to avoid ridiculous questions.

Nestled close to the Blue Ridge Mountains, in the heart of Maryland, Damascus was an almost equal distance between Baltimore and Washington. It had a population of around eleven thousand people compared to my old hometown of Tampa that was home to four million at least.

The town was just as I remembered it. Small. Nothing exciting ever really happened here. It was where Tom's Fire and Rescue Company was based. Most of the houses we passed looked fairly old and I wondered if there were enough kids in this little town to actually supply a high school. I supposed there were worst places to be stuck, but this was…

The car stopped and I looked out of my window and up at the house Tom had always lived in. It was old, but I could tell he cared about it. The paint was chipping, but it'd been repainted within the last five years, and the windows had obviously been replaced recently. His house backed up against a bit of woods which seemed common in this part of Maryland. The trees were just beginning to turn and even though I hated it, there was some part of me that was excited about getting to experience the change in seasons. The weather was always the same in Tampa; hot and muggy. Everything stayed green. I would miss the Gulf, but living someplace colorful where leaves fell and snow drifted would at least be unique.

I stared at the second floor window on the right, and I already knew what my bedroom would look like. I had spent summer after summer in this house. It was one of the few times

Helen actually smiled in my presence; when she knew she'd have three whole months without me. I was sure she was happy now, knowing that she was officially free of me and my messed up life. Or rather, me messing up *her* life.

"Here we go, Sophie," Tom said, false happiness apparent in his voice. I rolled my eyes, wondering why he allowed himself to be manipulated into taking me. I knew he didn't want me. Hell, he hadn't even wanted me years ago during those short summer months. He worked a lot and rarely requested time off when I visited. He was a firefighter and paramedic, so his shifts consisted of entire days. I would watch TV or roam the far-too-safe streets, and in the evenings we'd eat pizza or take-out Chinese without talking about much of anything. If he was working, I had to go to my grandmother's or whoever else he could pawn me off on. Some days I had to accompany him while he hiked or climbed rocks. When I had potential to be good at both, I had to intentionally make him believe I was bad at it. I would let go of rocks, or trip over small branches; anything to perpetuate the "clumsy" cover. When I grew older, he let me stay home during the day, where I shamelessly went through his things, snickering at the bad porn stashed in his closet.

I got out of the car and waited for him to pop the trunk. As soon as he did, I loaded myself down with my things, leaving only one small bag for him. The look on his face said he thought he should be carrying my things, but I didn't need him. I was perfectly happy lugging them myself. My bags contained my stuff and I didn't like other people touching the few things I actually owned.

I also didn't like people in my room, so I was thankful when Tom acknowledged this and stopped in the doorway as I pushed the old door open and looked upon my new/old room for the first time in years. I dropped the bags on the floor as I looked around, feeling nauseated at the sight. It was a kid's room, complete with childish crayon drawings of the sun and trees. I hadn't been here since I was fourteen, but how could I have possibly been happy being in this room during the summers of junior high?

Tom cleared his throat behind me and I turned to see him set my bag down on the floor and run a hand through his hair, while smoothing down his goatee with the other. "I made an appointment with Dr. Dalton for you. It's tomorrow at ten."

Great. Just what I needed. "I'm in perfect health, Tom." I was sure he wanted me to call him "dad" or some shit, but he said nothing.

"You're enrolled in school, but you can't start without a complete physical and you know just as well as I do that you're required to go to the doctor for your diabetes at least twice a year, and I figured you were due."

Dammit. Helen never took me to the doctor, and I couldn't have given less of a shit about a physical for school, but I supposed that it was better than a group home or jail. "Fine."

"I leave at a quarter to seven, but I'll be back at nine-thirty to pick you up."

"So, what? You'll leave me at the hospital by myself if you get called back?" I asked. His twenty-four on, twenty-four off shifts could work to my advantage, but he could also wind up annoying the hell out of me on his off days.

"I won't just up and leave you there, Soph. I doubt I'll get called during that short time, but if I do, we'll figure it out." He looked at me like he thought I was weird.

After barricading the door and spending a few hours taking down all of the silly little girl drawings and taped-up pictures of rainbows and unicorns, I tried to sleep. I slept like shit though. The house felt foreign and despite the new windows, there was a cold draft. I didn't usually sleep much anyway. I spent a few hours sitting by my window, watching the breeze sweep leaves from the trees. I liked watching them dance in the air. They seemed light and free. Everything I've never felt I was.

The next day, Tom took me to the doctor. Dr. Stephen Dalton's practice was attached to the hospital. I hated hospitals, but I had to go, so I found myself alone in a little examination room when in walked the most gorgeous man I'd ever seen. He had dark, barely-peppered-with-gray hair and looked youngish, but dignified with his professional hair style and well-cared-for fingernails. If this man was Dr. Dalton, he could examine me any day.

"Miss Young?"

I plastered on my best smile. "Sophie," I corrected him. He smiled at me and my heart thumped like I just finished running a marathon.

"Sophie," he said, my name sounding even better coming from his mouth. He motioned behind him and a mousey little nurse came through the door. "This is Tracy." Dammit. Stupid hospital rules about male doctors examining females alone.

The exam was going perfectly fine until he started running his hands over various bones. While I wanted to pretend he was giving me a much more intimate examination than necessary, I couldn't. My brain froze, hoping that his good looks made him an incompetent physician.

"Hmm."

I swallowed hard, looking at the ceiling, ignoring his exploring fingers on my collarbone. "What?"

"Have you broken your clavicle before?"

Shit. Taking in a deep breath, I nodded. "Yeah."

"What about your humerus?" He squeezed my upper arm and I nodded again. "Did no one set it?" He pulled the top of the gown up slightly, covering my collarbone again and then gently helped me into a sitting position, his hands moving to explore my back.

"Um, no." I could feel my skin flush as I tried to figure out how to get around the truth on this one.

"A few ribs too?"

"I was stupid and I didn't go to the hospital." I saw his perfect eyebrow arch in question. "Skateboarding." It was a lie. I'd never been on a skateboard in all my life.

"Hmm," he said again, but then he removed his hands and sat down on his little stool, scribbling notes into a chart. "So, how is your diabetes, Sophie?"

I shrugged. "Fine."

"Are you eating right? Counting your carbs?"

I let out an exasperated sigh. "Yes."

"Exercising?"

"Yes," I said, even though I really wasn't.

"Monitoring your blood-sugar levels?"

God dammit, of course I was. "Yes. Four times a day at least."

"What about insulin?"

I shrugged again. "What *about* insulin?"

"Are you still taking it?"

Didn't these guys ever get tired of asking the same damn thing over and over? "Whenever I need it."

"So daily?"

"Yes," I sighed, highly annoyed.

He smiled at me and all of my annoyance fled my body. Dumb good-looking doctor. "Well, all we need to do is take a few X-Rays and we'll be all finished here."

"X-Rays?" X-Rays had never been a part of the physical exam experience before.

Smiling again, Dr. Dalton nodded. "There are just a few things I'm curious about."

~ • ~

I was sitting outside of Dr. Dalton's office, waiting for him and my father to finish up their discussion. We'd been at the hospital for nearly three hours and I was sick of it. The door to the office was slightly ajar, so I could hear their voices as they discussed random things. Dr. Dalton had already filled out the evaluation form that would allow me to go to school, and then they had a ten minute conversation about some sporting event, so I was quite bored with eavesdropping until I heard Dr. Dalton ask, "How well do you know your ex-wife, Tom?"

It took my father a moment to answer. "Well, we were together for a little less than six years, two of them in high school." He paused. "Why do you ask?"

"How much interaction have you had with her over the years?"

"Not much. Her mother took her when she was four. Sophie's come out here several times, but Helen's never come back. Why?"

Dr. Dalton paused, I supposed, for dramatic effect. I held my breath, already sensing where this was going. "Sophie has an incredible amount of old, healed contusions and also more healed broken bones than your average teenager."

"Well, Helen always said that Sophie's a klutz."

"Tom," Dr. Dalton said with a sigh, "these aren't the types of injuries one gets from falling down. Is it possible that Sophie's mother…"

Shit. Shit. Shit. I stopped listening at that point. He was going to say it and Tom would have to think about it. Then Tom would know and he'd probably force me into some kind of conversation about it.

My mind drifted. I could see my reflection in the framed picture of a sailboat across from where I sat. I looked little, tired, and bored, but there was nothing special about me. Well, except for the combination of my hair and eyes. I was sort of a genetic freak of nature with those. Brown hair and crystal blue eyes; two traits that didn't usually go together, and usually garnered a fair amount of attention, but apart from that I was thin with ugly freckles from the sun.

Tom finally exited the office. "Sophie," he said, much softer and more careful than ever before. Damn, he knew. "You ready?"

"Yeah. Everything okay?" I couldn't help but ask.

Tom nodded and gave me a tight-lipped smile, holding up a piece of paper. "You're free and clear to go to school tomorrow."

Much to my surprise and eternal gratefulness, Tom didn't say a word about the information he received from the incredible Dr. Dalton. He simply dropped me off at home, told me to make sure to eat, and then went back to work. I hoped that he would continue this laissez-faire style of parenting.

My day went by quickly as I continued to shift my room into something more suitable. Tom wasn't much of a housekeeper, so after I finished with my room, I scrubbed the small bathroom upstairs. Cleaning was easy and it kept my mind off of things I usually tried to avoid thinking about. Soon, the upstairs was so sparkling clean I almost didn't recognize it. I didn't do Tom's room, but I went downstairs to clean the living room, bathroom, dining room and kitchen.

The hum of the vacuum lulled my mind into a numb state, allowing me to remember exactly how my collarbone had been broken. Of course, Helen hadn't taken me to the hospital then, or for any of my other numerous broken bones for that matter. There would have been questions and poorly-concealed dirty looks as the medical professionals made their silent judgments and decided if calling the Department of Children and Families would be necessary.

Looking at Helen and her tiny little five-foot-five frame, one wouldn't think that she'd be able to inflict such damage, but I knew from experience that she was a force to be reckoned with. It wasn't that she was so physically strong; it was that she had a lot of fiery passion and aggression within her.

I shook my head as I flipped the vacuum off. I hadn't had any weed since I'd left Tampa and I was in desperate need of it. Getting some was going to be one of my top priorities at school tomorrow. There had to be some killer bud around and all I needed to do was find the person at Damascus High who could hook me up. I didn't have much money saved, but I could easily get a job. Besides, in the past it was fairly easy to *hook up* with my hook up. Not that I was a pot whore or anything. It was just easy to find mutual pleasures and typically, when you're banging someone, they don't charge you for the shit you smoke when you're with them. It's also easy to get them to break you off some for when you're not.

It was nearing five o'clock when I finally starting hunting around in Tom's cabinets and refrigerator to see what I could make for dinner. I wasn't trying to be domestic, but cooking and cleaning were just some of my responsibilities at Helen's so it wasn't as if I was stepping outside the realm of traditional Sophie roles.

Tom had next to no food in his house. His fridge was filled with random condiments and a shitload of beer. Damn. If only beer was my preferred method of getting fucked up. It looked as though he had enough to not even miss a few. Well, perhaps I'd be able to stumble across some hidden bottles of the good stuff. The harder stuff. Where only a few shots would leave me warm and peaceful.

I needed to stop fantasizing about getting wasted. Dinner was the most important thing right now. Finally, I found some frozen hamburger and a box of that shitty Helper stuff, so I went to work. It was incredibly unappealing and I would have to talk to Tom about getting actual food into the house.

I ate, watched TV, and went to sleep. The house was quiet, but I still felt better when I barricaded my bedroom door with the wooden computer chair, wedging it up under the doorknob.

The next morning, I was taking my blood sugar as Tom walked in the front door. I watched him as I sat at the dining room table. He kicked off his boots, and some of the mud splattered on the newly-cleaned tile. He looked around, eyeing the state of his house. He must have forgotten I lived with him now. "Sophie?" he called.

"Right here, Tom."

He looked up and gave me a small smile. "You didn't have to clean the house."

"I'm sorry." My reaction was immediate and I hated myself for apologizing. I would clean if I wanted to.

"What's that smell?"

"Breakfast, but it's probably pretty shitty. You need more food."

He cocked his head. "Watch your language." I bit my tongue and looked back down at the monitor, picking up my pen to record my results. "Everything okay there?"

"111. Perfectly normal, Tom."

The rest of breakfast was silent, except for when he said it was good, to which I responded with silence. He handed me a hundred bucks to go shopping for the week before I went upstairs. It would definitely make scoring easier and seeing how well he stocked his pantry, I knew he would have no clue how much money was actually spent on food.

I grabbed my bag and waited for him by the door. I was ready to get the show on the road and be finished with the awkwardness of changing schools mid-year.

I wasn't exactly nervous about my first day. To be honest, I really didn't give a shit if I fit in or made friends, or any of that nonsense. I disliked being driven to school by my father. My license had been taken away and I had no vehicle of my own, so my other priority was to find someone who would give me rides to and from school.

Tom made what I figured were typical "Dad" comments before I got out of the car. I was happy to be out of such a confined space with him. He was an okay guy, but being strapped into a moving vehicle mere inches from the man put me on edge.

My first stop was the administration office where I picked up a stupid map of the school and my class schedule. I took a moment before heading back out to peruse it. At least Tom made sure they gave me some of the classes I wanted. I got into Photography, although it was a basic level class and I was already beyond that. U.S. History, blah, Calculus, whatever, Physical Education, was this a joke? British Literature. Okay, I could handle that, even though I doubted the reading list covered anything that would be new to me. Spanish. Tal vez yo pueda excavar mi cerebro con una cuchara. Horticulture. I was in it back in Tampa, so at least I could breeze through this class, and most of my others, with only minimal effort. Yes! My personal favorite, Study Hall.

I located all my classes quite easily on the map and went back out into the hall. Students passed me left and right, casting me curious looks, their eyes moving from my feet to the top of my head. Apparently I was endlessly fascinating to the kids of Damascus. As long as none of them talked to me, I'd be okay.

"You must be Sophia!" I cringed as I turned to the dark-haired guy with pimples and braces. "I'm Connor." Good for you. Now what do you want?

"It's Sophie, actually," I corrected, deciding that being nice, or at least not being so shitty to everyone, would help with my two priorities of scoring a little weed and finding rides to and from school.

"Do you need help finding your classes?"

I gave him a tight-lipped smile and did my best to calm myself. After all, it was probably fairly irrational to be upset with someone offering me help. "I think I can manage."

"I can fill you in about Damascus High if you want."

Seriously? What did I need to be *filled in* about? It was high school, right? There were cheerleaders and jocks, nerds and geeks, thugs and punks, loners and delinquents. I could pick them out all out by myself and certainly didn't need a pimply puppy following me around. I sighed. "My first class is English."

Connor peered at my paper in a totally intrusive way, scanning all of my classes, teachers, and room numbers. "Right this way," he said, as he started to lead me down the same path I'd already been on.

"Hamill! Finally get a girlfriend?"

Again, I cringed. Two minutes standing with this fool and already I was his girlfriend? Scowling, I turned to look at the other boy who came running up. Obviously a jock, but not a first-string jock. Looking at his expensive clothing, I deduced that he probably only made it onto the varsity teams because his daddy was some local Big Name Guy. He had shaggy brown hair that looked like he worked *really* hard to make it look that unruly.

"Oh," he said, as he took me in, his eyes scanning every part of my body, making me feel like I'd just been visually violated. "Hi. I'm Chris. You're Sophia the new girl, aren't you?"

Before I could correct him or even sigh in annoyance over the use of my proper name, Connor smiled at Chris and said, "It's actually Sophie, and I'm taking her to her first class."

Chris smirked and took the paper from my hands. My jaw clenched. I hated when people touched my things. "I have English with you. Hamill has Econ, but it's in the other direction. Come on, I'll show you." He scanned the list again. "Oh, we have Horticulture and P.E. together too. Too bad about Reese's class though, the only open seat is next to—"

"Chris," the other guy began, "Sophie and I were involved in a very personal conversation which you very rudely interrupted."

The sleaze smiled at me.

With a frown on my face, I grabbed my schedule back from the idiot named Chris, rolled my eyes at Connor the brainless wonder, and started toward my class. This was exactly what I needed; a dork and a jock already fighting over who could walk me to class.

Neither of them would have a hook up, and even if they drove, I didn't think I would be able to stand two minutes alone with either one of them.

They both trailed after me, trying to engage me in some form of conversation or another, but I ignored them. It wasn't until someone ran into me, knocking my bag off my shoulder and my schedule out of my hands, that I stopped and let them catch up.

"Jesus Christ, D-D-Dalton. Can't you watch where the fuck you're going?" Chris snarled at the boy who bent down to pick up my fallen bag while Connor ran after my floating schedule. I wondered briefly why Chris had drawn out the kid's name like that.

The boy looked up, first at Chris and then at me, and froze for a moment. "S-sorry," he mumbled.

He stood up straight, holding out my bag to me. What the hell was *this* guy doing in Podunk, Maryland? And why the hell did he take shit from the likes of this Chris guy? The Dalton kid was obviously so far superior in every way. His dark, rusty-red hair fell naturally over his eyes like a shield, but managed *not* to look messy. I felt the urge to run my fingers through it just to dishevel it. He had a perfect face, all straight lines, hazel eyes, and long lashes. And he was tall. I was only five foot five, so it wasn't hard to beat that.

"Why you gotta be such a freak?" Chris kept up, roughly grabbing my bag from Dalton and handing it back to me.

I was just about to tell Chris to knock it the hell off when the biggest high school kid I'd ever seen came around the corner. My eyes widened as I took in the anger etched on his face. He stopped right next to the rusty-haired god with low self-esteem and shot daggers at Chris. Instantly, Chris's body conveyed his nervousness. On instinct, I stepped away from the three boys, suddenly realizing that Connor had frozen in place behind me.

"What is your problem, Anderson?"

"Um, hey, David," he said, carefully, his voice quivering as he spoke. "Nothing. Your, uh, your brother just nearly knocked the new girl over and I…"

"Thought calling him a freak would be an appropriate response?" David took another step closer to Chris. This was kind of interesting. The big guy was the rusty guy's brother, and while Chris seemed to enjoy being a prick to the rusty guy, he was absolutely terrified of the big guy.

I hoped Chris pissed his pants.

I shook my head. What the hell was I doing? Why did I give two shits about the happenings between these people? I had to remember my priorities. The rusty guy seemed absolutely too weak to give me a ride anywhere and I wouldn't be in a confined space with the big one if someone paid me loads of money *and* weed. Also, neither of them could be dope smokers. I could tell.

Grabbing my schedule from Connor, I walked away, not missing Rusty Dalton's eyes carefully following my actions.

God, his eyes. They were the most beautiful hazel eyes I'd ever seen.

࿐ • ࿐

Thank the Flying Spaghetti Monster for Study Hall. I enjoyed Photography a little, but everyone had nicer cameras than I did and it made me jones for some pot even more. I got to the library and took a seat at a vacant table. No one else seemed to be here yet. I was hungry, so I quickly checked my blood sugar, trying to be discreet about it, before I pulled out my bottle of water and Pop-Tart. Ah, the snack of champions.

Before I knew what was happening, the empty table I was sitting at filled up with people I had seen in various classes. If that didn't sour my mood, Chris sitting down next to me surely took my mood from sour to unbelievably tart and acidic.

Suddenly a girl started whispering, "Oh my God, Sophie, I cannot believe that we haven't had a chance to talk yet. You're in my English and Calc classes. I'm Megan. Connor said you like Sophie rather than Sophia, and I totally agree; there's something just so beautiful about the name Sophie and something so stuffy about Sophia."

I turned to the girl sitting on the other side of Chris. Jesus, she could talk, but I couldn't remember her from even one of my morning classes, let alone two. "Hi."

Her eyes widened as if she was shocked that I acknowledged her. "So, how do you like Damascus? Are you getting around okay? It must suck to have your dad drive you around. If you want, I can take you. I have a Honda. It kind of sucks, but I think my parents are planning to get me something new when I graduate. Too bad that's a year and a half away, right?"

I smiled, but scanned the other people in the library. I stopped at the table where Rusty Dalton was sitting with Big Dalton. There were several other people sitting with them: A beautiful strawberry-blonde, obviously a cheerleader, hanging all over Big Dalton. Another girl who looked like one of those waifish models. She wasn't short, but not really tall either; thin, but not skinny. She had about six earrings in each lobe, and an industrial piercing through the cartilage of her right ear. I couldn't see if she had any other piercings, but she definitely seemed edgy for Damascus. Also, I liked her hair. It was so different for this little town, with big white frosted streaks cutting through the jet black. She was holding hands with a tall, lean boy who was laughing at something. There were two other cheerleaders and three more jocks sitting with them.

Rusty looked so uncomfortable.

"I see you've discovered the Daltons and their entourage. Everyone loves David and David only loves Rebecca. The weirdo with the crazy hair's Jane. She's spastic. They say her name's Jane because she's a Jane Doe. You know, like, she doesn't have a real family or whatever. David and Elliott are her adopted brothers. Someone said she was rescued, or whatever, from some hill-billy family up in the mountains, but I don't think that's true. That's her boyfriend next to her, Trent Cooper. He is like, *so* hot, but a total hellion. His mother works with my father and he says that 'he cannot be controlled,' and goes on and on about how horrible it is for a single woman to have to deal with that. The guy next to him is Christian and let me tell you, he's anything *but* a Christian. The girl next to him is Kelly and she tells *everyone everything* he does with her. Like I said, positively sinful. See the black guy with the green eyes? Yeah, contacts, but he's *totally* fine, don't you think?"

I had no time to answer because she kept right on going.

"Then there's Jackie," she said, her voice dropped to a conspiratorial whisper now, "She's *real* friendly with everyone on the football team, if you know what I mean. And there's Luke, so sexy, but he got Heather McCormick pregnant last year, so he's kinda, sorta on the outs with most of the girls. He said it wasn't his, but everyone can see those blue eyes on that baby."

There was one person Megan didn't even mention. "Who's the redhead?"

A strange smile spread over her features. "Oh, that's Elliott. He's—"

"The freakiest one in a big bunch of freaks," a blonde-haired girl next to Megan interrupted. Instantly, I didn't like her.

"Thank you!" Chris exclaimed. "They're all crazy or messed up in some way. That's why they flock together like that."

"Didn't you and Elliott have a *thing*?" the blonde asked Megan.

Megan immediately blushed. "Oh yeah. For being a big freak, he's very skilled. It must be those musician's hands. Jackie says that Becca says whenever she's over, he's always playing music in his room." My eyes trailed down Rusty Dalton's body until they reached his hands. They weren't overly large, yet the fingers were long and slender. I supposed they would be good for playing instruments. "No need for him to talk when there's so many more interesting things to do with his mouth."

Chris rolled his eyes and lightly shoved Megan. "Whatever."

"Oh, don't be jealous, Chris, you know I prefer you in the sack."

"Ew," another girl with a jagged haircut said, obviously feeling like I did, that we were venturing into the realm of too much information. I didn't want to know who was screwing who here.

I turned my focus to a table where all the occupants were males. One of them was incredibly big, almost as big as David.

"Who's that guy?" I asked, letting my eyes point the way. "The big one?"

"Oh," Megan's voice fell into a conspiratorial whisper. "That's Jason Fox." For whatever reason, the name seemed oddly familiar. "Total druggie."

That was all I needed to know. I tucked my water bottle back into my bag and stood up, looking around to see if the librarian was about to tell me to sit down again. "Where are you going, Sophie?" Chris asked, his voice anxious.

"Um…" I couldn't find anything to say, so I just shrugged and took off, making a quick line to Jason Fox. I could feel everyone's eyes on me as I did.

"Hey," I said, drawing upon all of my confidence. What did I care what these people thought? None of them knew me.

Jason looked up at me, his deep blue eyes narrowing as he studied my face. Damn, he was kind of intimidating, even if he was wearing a dirty hippie Bob Marley shirt. "Hey," was all he said. His dusty blond hair wasn't long, but I couldn't exactly call it short either, and man, people said my eyes were piercing blue, but this kid might have me beat.

He *had* to know that I was Sophie, the "new girl." That he didn't seem as happy or shocked to be speaking with me as everyone else in the school had, made me a little nervous. I shifted on my feet, shoving my bag back up on my shoulder. "Can I talk to you?"

He continued to study me. "About what?"

Ass. I knew he was holding. I could just tell. "About your shirt," I said, using the snottiest voice I could as I narrowed my eyes back at him.

Finally, ever so slightly, the edges of his mouth curled up. "So talk."

"Somewhere else."

When he sighed and stood up, his friends snickered and made a few crude comments. "Shut up," he said and smacked the back of one of his friend's head as he moved past.

He guided me out of the library and didn't stop walking until we were outside, with small pellets of rain dripping into my hair. "So?" he said, his long legs stopping as he allowed me to catch up to him.

"So I heard that you might know where I can get some ganja."

Jason's face was calm. "I don't know what you're talking about."

Shaking my head, I clicked my tongue at him. "Yes, you do."

"Tom Young's your dad and you're asking me on your first day of school if I can get you some pot?" I nodded. "You're insane. He goes around to third-grade classes and tells kids the horrors of drugs. Well, mainly the horrors of meth, but still."

"Sometimes, but not right now. What does it matter who my father is?"

"How stupid do you think I am?"

I rolled my eyes, leaning back against the moist bricks of the school. "Well, you don't look stupid, but since I don't know you, I have no real way of knowing."

"You do know me." I quirked my brow. "I know you. You're Sophie Young, Tom Young's daughter who used to come up every summer. We ran around in the forests together. You used to shove me off of rocks." Again I intentionally formed a confused expression. "Jesus, you can't remember our dads dragging us all over the damn state while they hiked? Well, back when my dad could still go outside," he finished in a mumble.

A few vague memories came back to me. I looked up at Jason's face. There was a boy I remembered shoving into the mud every once in a while, and then crying when he pulled my hair. "Smile." I could tell by his expression he thought this was dumb, but he plastered a smile on his face. "Yeah, now I remember you."

He folded his arms over his massive chest and cocked his head. "You stopped visiting." As his eyes wandered over my body, his smile shifted into something meant to be seductive. "You got all grown up, didn't you?"

He was not subtle. "So can I get some weed or not?"

"How do I know that you haven't turned into a narc? Your dad's tight with the sheriff, you know."

"Did I tell him about the time you stole his beer when we were twelve?"

He appraised me again and seemed to come to the conclusion that I wasn't a narc. "So, about that pot…"

Jason grabbed my hand and pulled me away from the bricks, and away from the school. I wasn't really afraid, even though it seemed like a natural response would have been fear, especially since he was so much bigger than I was. We stopped just inside the woods that surrounded the park by the school.

"I don't have any for you to buy here. One more 'infraction' and I'll be expelled, and your dad will stop pulling strings for me." He dug into his pocket, pulling out a hard pack of Camel Lights. Flipping open the box top, he plucked out a perfectly-rolled joint. "But we can get high before going back into hell." He nodded toward the school.

"Thank God!" I exclaimed, finding a relatively dry fallen tree to sit down on. "I haven't had any since leaving Tampa." He lit it and took his time taking several long pulls; some to get it going, and others to take into his lungs. Finally, he passed it to me and I felt almost giddy at the feel of it between my fingers as I took a big hit.

"So after school," he said during his long exhale, "you can come back to my house and I'll get you some of your own."

"Thanks." We passed the joint back and forth a few times, and I started feeling fucking great. I ran my hands through my hair and let my eyes slip closed.

"So, you already with Anderson or what?"

I nearly choked. "What? No. He's just…a puppy." Jason's smile widened and I could tell he was pretty fried too.

"Well, then," he said, leaning toward me. I felt a little confused, but did nothing to stop what I knew was coming. "Let me stake my claim." Before I could even process his possessive words, he'd crushed his mouth against mine. It was a great kiss. Then he pulled away and said, "Bet you haven't had any of that since Tampa either."

I smiled, letting a chuckle bubble out of me. Feeling warm and relaxed, I sized Jason up. He was tall and muscular. I should've at least been a little afraid of him, like I was when I saw Big Dalton, but something about having known him when we were kids made him seem safe. I licked my lips, tasting the remains of Jason and marijuana. Then I stood up and pushed him until he was sitting where I had been and quickly moved to straddle him.

I *hadn't* had any of that since Tampa. Taking the smoldering, almost-too-small roach out of his hands, I gave it one last puff before flicking it behind him, listening as it sizzled in the damp foliage. Jason's hands moved immediately to my ass, cupping it, his fingers digging in. I kissed him again, my hands moving to tangle wildly in his hair. Damn, I could get laid before Horticulture. I wondered if little Miss Megan could say that.

He pulled back, still rubbing my ass. "No panties on the first day of school? Jesus, Sophie, you've really turned into a naughty girl, haven't you?"

"You have no idea."

A wicked smile played on his face, but Jason carefully stood me up, letting his hands linger on my hips a moment before brushing one of them in between my legs. "As much as I'd love to explore how much you've grown up, I can't be late to class.

Jerry would have a fit if I got expelled." I assumed Jerry was his father.

I backed up and grabbed my bag, watching as he rose to his full height. Dude must have been at least six-foot-six. "How is your dad?" I asked, trying to remember my manners, but not really giving a shit. I could barely remember the guy anyway.

"Needy as ever," was his reply as he led me out of the woods. "You know he has OCD, right?"

No, I didn't know that and I wasn't sure how to respond, so I stayed silent. When we reached the edge of the campus, he turned to me. "So, after school, meet me out front." Guess I'd scored on my top two priorities.

I nodded in agreement before moving down the path that I thought would take me to the greenhouse. The bell rang just as I entered. Lazily, I walked over to the teacher, holding out my class slip. Chris Anderson was glaring at me. I gave him a little smirk and then shrugged my shoulders before the teacher introduced himself as Mr. Reese and pointed to my seat.

It was then I realized that my table partner was none other than the skilled hands- talented mouth, Rusty Dalton. He looked way too nervous as I approached and was breathing hard, like he'd just been having some rough sex. His eyes flicked toward me for just a moment before moving to the front of the class and then out the window. Okay, so the dude was strange. I supposed if he didn't try grabbing my shit during class, I could deal with strange Rusty Dalton.

"Hey," I said, giving him a tentative smile. I didn't want him to think I was a prick like Anderson and was somehow still pissed at him for running into me. He looked sick as he glanced up and merely gave me a little nod in greeting. "I'm Sophie," I continued quietly as Mr. Reese began talking, bringing the class to order. Rusty Dalton gave me a small half-smile before moving his eyes to the front of the room. I guessed that it was all I was going to get. It was customary to give your name in return when someone introduced themselves to you, but whatever; I already knew it anyway.

I pretty much zoned out until Mr. Reese called on Rusty Dalton. When he hesitated before answering, I tried to remember the question so I could whisper the answer to him. That was a nice thing to do, right? But suddenly he took a very deep breath, his hands clenching together on the desk before his head rose just slightly. "A-A-A-Act-t-tinomycccccetes," he finally said and blew out a breath of relief as Mr. Reese indicated that he was correct.

Chris Anderson turned around and narrowed his eyes at my table partner. "V-v-very g-g-good, D-D-Dalton," he said and broke out in quiet laughter.

Rusty Dalton sighed and lowered his head, looking at his clenched hands. So, what? He had a stutter, which made sense now after hearing Chris and Megan's comments. Jesus, high school sucked.

I narrowed my eyes at Chris and when he turned to me, I said, "Don't be a dick." He glared at me, but thankfully turned back around.

The rest of class was boring. When the bell rang, Rusty Dalton packed up his books and left without saying a word. P.E. went by without incident, except for when I "accidently" slammed my elbow into Chris Anderson's head when we were playing basketball. He was a dick, and while I never really had violent tendencies before, I wanted him to hurt for being an asshole. I wasn't really clumsy, but it never ceased to amaze me how much the other gender would let me get away with. All I had to do was give him big doe-eyes and bat my eyelashes and he was over his momentary anger and sending me puppy eyes back.

Just as promised, Jason was waiting for me out front and gave me a ride to his house in his old beat-up Cavalier. His house felt familiar, but I didn't get much of a chance to remark on that since Jason took me directly into his room where he proceeded to show me his extensive collection of buds and paraphernalia. Before I could get him to reveal his pricing, he swept me into his arms and proceeded to resume where we'd left off this afternoon.

Mere moments was all it took for me to be spread out on his rickety old desktop, my shirt pulled up, bra cups down, pants hanging off of one leg, my head thumping against the wall. Jason was really good. It seemed such a waste for one teenage boy to be so *good* at this, especially in Damascus, Maryland, where it wouldn't be appreciated.

He looked so cool too. Most boys had some kind of epileptic fit, but not Jason. There were a few grunts and "oh, yeahs" thrown in for good measure, but he maintained his cool even through his orgasm. His eyes were on me the entire time, even as he withdrew and peeled off the condom, tossing it into the trashcan.

As I tugged my shirt back down and watched him pull up his pants, zipping them, but leaving the top button unbuttoned, I felt the need to let him know the deal. "Just FYI, Jason, don't go all romantic on me or any shit like that, okay?"

A smile played on his face. "I don't know what you're talking about."

"I'm not the girlfriend type, so don't think that what we just did means anything more than what it was."

He looked unimpressed.

"What?"

"In case no one told you, Sophie Young," he began in a light voice "I'm not the boyfriend type, so we should get along just fine." Then he sat back down on the edge of his bed as I pulled up my pants, shoving my feet back into my shoes. "So about this weed you want…"

ᔕ • ᔓ

Jason had cut me a fantastic deal on the quarter I took home, basically just charging me for an eighth. It wasn't ditch weed either. Little to no shake in that bag. He loaned me a bowl, but it would rarely get used, and gave me a dugout and a one-hitter too. Before dropping me off at home, he took me to the store so I'd actually have food to cook for dinner, and he offered to pick me up for school the next day. I happily accepted, after reiterating that despite the great orgasms we'd given each other, we were not romantically involved. He agreed, saying his life was complicated enough without a girlfriend hanging on him.

After dinner, and a nice soothing walk with the one-hitter, I barricaded myself in my room and waited for the morning to come when I had to go to another, boring day at Damascus High.

Chapter 2

New Girl, Same Dalton

Elliott

I woke up with the worst headache I'd had in a while, which wasn't helped by David's voice booming in the hallway, loud enough to cause the window panes to rattle. He was yelling at Jane to get out of the bathroom while pounding on the door with what sounded like his fist. I would never understand why he didn't just make the short trip to use the bathroom downstairs.

"And don't think I can't tell that you're listening, Elliott. Get your ass up. We've got less than an hour before first period and I'm not going to be late because of you again."

I swore he was like the glue that held everything together around here. To the outsider at school, he probably looked like the one sane guy in the house of the loonies, but Jane and I knew different. Even our adopted father Stephen knew.

David's coping mechanism was being perfect at everything. He got straight A's in every subject, on every paper, and on every test and quiz, and was Captain of every major sport at Damascus High. He was going out with Rebecca, the best-looking girl at school, and managed to be Vice-President of the student government. He'd probably be asked to be valedictorian when he graduated too. Everyone loved him, which was exactly what he was going for.

Jane was a bit different. She wasn't really popular like David. She was friends with Rebecca, but wasn't a cheerleader like she was and most of those girls thought she was weird. Jane molded herself to be as likable as possible, to as many people as possible, so she made a lot of "friends."

But Jane had a harder time with keeping up the prefect façade than David. She had "dissociative episodes". At least, that's what Stephen and Robin called them. Robin was a licensed therapist as well as being Becca's mother, and a friend of Stephen's. Basically, the episodes were just periods of time Jane "zoned out." Unfortunately, even with medication, they still occurred.

As far I as I knew, there wasn't a definitive trigger for Jane's "episodes" and no real way to stop them. She would never tell me what went through her mind during that time, but I didn't blame her for keeping it to herself. If it was something bad and the adults found out, she could go back to the institution and I knew how much she hated that place.

"Elliott, I'm serious! Tick tock, I'm a clock and that means get your ass out here!"

I sighed, knowing that if I didn't move, David would attempt to open the door. That would *not* help my headache, so I swung my feet over the side of the bed, rubbed my hands down my face, pulled a shirt over my head, and stood up. Then I opened the door as I scratched my neck and cocked an eyebrow. "Don't give me that look, Elliott."

I shook my head. "I h-h-have a heada-a-ache."

"Suck it up, dude. Take a hot shower. That'll help." He turned back to the closed bathroom door and started banging on it again. "That is, if we can get Jane out."

"I'll g-go d-d-downstairs," I mumbled, pulling my door closed. I always closed my door. My room was the only place that was mine, only mine, and no one else was allowed in unless I was dying. Stephen promised me that.

The shower, toast, and coffee ended up relieving some of my headache, but the two Tylenol helped even more. As usual, David was behind the wheel of his old International Harvester Scout while Jane sat in the passenger seat, complaining that we never took her car. I sat quietly in the back as usual. There wasn't much I ever really needed to say.

Stephen would have bought David any new car he'd wanted, but David insisted on this old 4x4. He found it on an online auction site and went all the way to western Ohio to rescue it from some old man's barn. Although he was nearly always occupied with school or Rebecca, David spends every spare moment and dollar working on it. He liked to stay busy.

"Jane, next year you and Elliott can fight it out over which car you drive to school, but until I graduate, *I'm* driving. Dad said so." David always called Stephen "Dad." He'd only been adopted two years before the two of us, but he always seemed much closer to Stephen than Jane or me. "And do you know *why* he said so?"

"Shut up, David," Jane whined. I was sure she didn't want to hear it again.

"Because you've already gotten two tickets and backed into that car and you've only had your license for a year!" Jane could never produce an excuse for her lead foot, but it had been one of her episodes that made her zone out and back into that car. To be honest, Stephen would probably want me to drive us to school next year anyway.

"Oh! The new girl starts today," she reminded us.

I groaned and immediately wished I hadn't.

"Dude, don't start. You already had the conversation with Robin and Dad."

It took place the night before.

"It will be good for you, Elliott," Robin said, smiling her shrink smile at me. "At some point you're going to need to build relationships with people who aren't in your family circle."

I shook my head, my eyes darting to Stephen for help. He knew what I was and wasn't capable of, and he would defend me against this highly ridiculous course of action.

"She's right, Elliott," was his soft reply, and my face fell.

"From what I've heard, Sophie Young has had some similar experiences to yours. You could help her. She could help you."

"You want *to get better, don't you?"*

I hated when Robin did that; when she indicated that she thought I was not right to begin with. "B-b-but I'll have to t-t-talk to h-her and wh-wh-what if I..."

"You won't get any better at communicating if you don't try, Elliott. I realize that David and Jane have a tendency to enable you by finishing your sentences, but they won't be around forever, so it's best for you to begin standing on your own two feet now."

My jaw tightened as I remembered. I hated her insinuation that I leaned on Jane and David. I never asked them to take up for me or help me in any way. It wasn't my fault that it was easier for them to finish my sentences than to wait the five minutes it took me to get out a five-word question.

But now I would have to be "paired up" with the Young girl and I had no choice. Of course, neither did she. I didn't even know if she'd been informed yet of the arrangement. As far as "similar experiences," I didn't know why that would be important in the least. If it was true, then she wouldn't want to talk about it either.

The Scout stopped and I realized that we were already in the school parking lot, next to Rebecca. David and Jane opened their doors, but before getting out, David turned around and looked straight into my eyes, like he did every morning before school.

"Don't take crap today, Elliott. If Anderson says anything to you, pop him in the mouth. Dad won't be mad. He knows that little prick deserves it."

David very rarely said anything bad about anyone, but he really disliked Chris Anderson, even though they were both on all of the sports teams together. Every day, David would tell me to stand up to Anderson, to hit him or something, but the thought of actually getting into a fight terrified me more than Chris's verbal abuse. I wasn't necessarily afraid of him because honestly, I could probably take him if my thick mind didn't paralyze me first. All I could do was nod. I knew David didn't want me to "take crap," as he so eloquently put it, but we both knew that today would be no different than any other day.

As I exited the Scout, Jane moved quickly to join her boyfriend Trent who was practically jogging to meet up with her, as Rebecca made her way to David. Both Trent and Rebecca said good morning to me, and I nodded my good morning to them as well.

I didn't know Trent that well, but Jane loved him, so I accepted him. We never spoke much and although he constantly got in trouble for fighting, he was always nice to me.

I walked behind them, not really wanting to be a part of the conversation.

As usual, I went straight to my locker after splitting off from the others. Most of my days repeated in the same fashion, not much deviating from the day before. But today wasn't like that. Usually I could avoid the attention of Anderson by walking far enough away that he didn't notice me, but today he was walking with Connor Hamill and the new girl. Of course, I didn't even realize she was there until I ran right into her. My head was down as usual, and for whatever reason I failed to see their feet as they came toward me.

I ended up knocking into her, sending paper flying and her bag to the ground. Hamill didn't seem to pay me any attention. He was typically decent like that, but Anderson had a field day with it. He never missed an opportunity to make me feel like dirt, especially when there was someone else around he could impress by putting me down. Today it just happened to be Sophie Young.

She was beautiful. I couldn't help but stare a little. Her light eyes were incredible juxtaposed with her dark hair. I'd never seen anything like it.

She appeared to accept my simple apology for running into her and didn't seem to appreciate Anderson's attempts at pointing out my stuttering issue. When David came around the corner, she instantly backed away from Anderson. I didn't know if it was to indicate that she wasn't "with" him or because she was frightened of David, who could look intimidating. Usually he was friendly and everyone liked him, but he had expressions in his arsenal that could make people nervous. He was big, and just imagining the raw force he could use to hit something was scary. Still, I hoped Sophie backed away because she didn't want to be associated with a moron like Chris, and not because of David's intensity.

Even before the confrontation was over, she grabbed her things and walked off. I was thankful because nothing was more embarrassing than having your big brother force someone to apologize to you, except your big brother force someone to apologize to you in front of the pretty new girl.

I wished, as always, that David would see that no matter how much he thought he was helping me, he really wasn't. He couldn't be with me all of the time. If I was just allowed to ignore Anderson, he would have at least gotten bored with it all by now and found a new person to humiliate. But since David kept sticking up for me and forcing Anderson to apologize, I was sure he thought I sat around and cried about it.

All morning, my mind wandered to Sophie Young. Now that I had seen her, Stephen and Robin's little plan seemed to be even less plausible than before. How in the world would I, stupid and stuttering Elliott Dalton, be able to communicate and have actual conversations with *her*? It seemed impossible. Even if I didn't usually stutter, I doubted that I'd be able to get through a conversation with someone so pretty without stammering.

That wasn't even mentioning my social anxiety disorder. Robin thought the medications were effective, and maybe they were, but they didn't do enough. The only difference between now and before I started taking those pills, was that I no longer had violent breakdowns before, and during school. Those had been fun. The only thing that used to calm me down was Jane's voice.

We'd been adopted at the same time and for whatever reason, she was the only one who'd ever been able to talk sense into me when my mind closed down. She was an angel like that.

Now I would be forced to not only associate with Sophie Young, but talk to her too. I tried to calm myself down from the rising panic I felt by reminding myself that I had until tomorrow to figure out how to talk to Sophie Young.

I watched her during study hall. She'd been sitting by herself, but then Anderson's group joined her and she hadn't looked pleased. When she looked over at our table I looked away, and then suddenly she was up and crossing the library, looking more confident than I would have ever felt in a new school.

Then she left with Jason Fox. *Jason Fox* of all people. I didn't have anything against him. Well, except for the drugs he used and sold.

Sophie and Jason didn't return, and when she came into the greenhouse after lunch, I nearly fainted. The only open seat was next to me and Mr. Reese had *promised* it would stay that way, but apparently just like everyone else, his promises meant next to nothing, because Sophie came and sat down next to me.

I tried to calm down by telling myself this would get me used to being around her. After all, tomorrow I was going to have to spend even more time with her. As she sat down, I could smell that she'd been smoking marijuana.

It made me think of my mother; not Stephen's ex-wife, but my real mother. I did my best to push that back, instead trying to concentrate on breathing.

Mr. Reese betrayed me a second time as he called on me with a question about soil microbes and I had to answer. Of course, my slow mouth and mind couldn't figure out a way for me to not sound like a stammering idiot. I could always hear myself think without the stutter, but the moment I pushed air through my voice box, it got stuck.

I was used to the snickering when I had to speak in front of people, and for the most part, all of these kids were used to it and no longer found it funny. But Chris Anderson wasn't one of them. He had to turn around and say "V-v-very g-g-good, D-D-Dalton." Truthfully though, I wouldn't have minded as much if I hadn't been sitting next to Sophie.

Then as Chris laughed in my face, Sophie told him to stop being a dick. It actually made me a little happy that she would do that for me, even though she didn't know me. But when I thought about it some more, the happiness faded. I was such a loser that the new girl had to stick up for me. It was embarrassing. I had no idea what someone like Sophie Young thought of me, but she had to know by now that I was an incredible loser.

As soon as the bell rang, I didn't linger after class, not wanting a typical run-in with Anderson to show Sophie how truly inept I was; at least any more than I had already.

I went to the administration office and sat down, relieved to see only a few other people. I was here for my appointment with the speech pathologist. Every Tuesday and Thursday, I had to finish out my school day with a session with Ms. Rice. She was nice, and typically our sessions consisted of either talking or reading. Even after all the years of coming to Ms. Rice or people like her, my stuttering never got any better. I was sure Robin and Stephen were convinced that I wasn't trying hard enough, but no one wanted me to speak normally more than I did.

As usual, Ms. Rice came out and got me after about five minutes. Once we were situated in the small office, her chair next to mine, she gave me a quick smile. She never sat behind her desk. I supposed it was to make her seem friendly. Perhaps I was supposed to see her as someone equal to me and trustworthy, but she had no speech impediment and probably never knew a day of ridicule in her life.

"So, Elliott, how's the day going for you?"

I shrugged my answer, but knew immediately that she wouldn't approve. She tilted her head and just waited, so I took a deep breath and said, "F-f-fine." I could tell she still wasn't pleased with my response, so I sighed and continued. "P-p-p-p-pretty normal."

Smiling, she handed me a book. It was orange and small, and I knew exactly which one it was.

"Have you been practicing?"

"Yes."

"Would you like to start?"

"N-no."

Again she smiled, taking the book back, flipping it open to the page she wanted me to read, and then handing it back. "Just relax, okay? It's only the two of us and no one else is listening. And look," she said, holding up her hands, "no notebook."

She had stopped taking notes while I read when I told her it made me nervous. "F-fine," I said with a sigh.

"Relax. Let your mind tell your voice box what sounds to produce, and let your mouth do what it needs to in order to let them come out naturally."

Taking a deep breath, I looked down at the book in my lap, feeling frustrated. I hated this page. I wondered if a normal person could get through it without issues.

I tried.

I failed.

Stupid fox. Stupid kid's book. Stupid Dr. Seuss with his impossible words and rhythm! It had taken an insane amount of time for me to get those twenty-five words out.

I looked up at Ms. Rice and I knew anguish was written all over my face because that's what I felt. "Don't look so down, Elliott. You improved there at the end. You stopped the prolongation of the word 'fleas' and there were little to no blocks in the entire paragraph. Your repetitions are what we need to tackle."

I sighed, moving my eyes to stare out the window. It was just beginning to drizzle again.

"Elliott," she said, drawing my attention back to her, "you need to work on relaxing. Being nervous before a sentence or a word makes it difficult for your brain to control your mouth."

"I'm nnnnot nnnnervous," I said.

"The prolongations in that sentence give you away. You need to remember that you have nothing to be anxious about. We're just talking. Your entire body tenses up the minute you have to read."

My hand moved up to my mouth and without really realizing it, I began to chew on my fingernails. I wasn't supposed to do that, so as soon as I noticed, I threw my hand down to my lap. Ms. Rice was right about the nervousness, but I've never been able to tame it. Not even the anti-anxiety pills changed it.

Ms. Rice sighed and held out her hand for the book and I gave it to her, but all she did was hand me another one. It was green with a turtle on the cover. As much as I didn't want to read aloud anymore, I knew that I could at least handle this book better. Before I could open it, she asked, "So what's the one thing in the world that can make you relax?"

I didn't have to think about it, but even as my mind clearly shouted the answer, my mouth botched it up. For some reason, I couldn't get it to form the word. My cheeks ballooned as I tried to force it. My right hand clenched into a fist and I brought it down onto my thigh, hoping to kick-start my brain into working.

This was what Ms. Rice would call a "block." It was possibly more frustrating than the actual stuttering itself. Most people had no idea how difficult it was to be able to think of a word or a sentence in your head, but have your body refuse to let it out. It was trapped in the thick cage of my mind. I sighed, my head hanging low.

"Relax. If you can't get it out, stop trying so hard. Breathe and slowly release it."

I did as she asked, but the word still wouldn't come. We spent five minutes just trying to get it out. Finally, I again looked out the window and focused on the rain that slid noiselessly down the pane of glass. "M-m-m-uuuusic."

Slumping down into my chair, I let my head fall back, my eyes tightly closed, thanking God for at least letting me get the one little word out, no matter how horrible it sounded when I did.

"Very good." Ms. Rice's voice annoyed me. It wasn't very good. It was barely even mediocre. If it was very good, then I would be speaking in complete sentences in front of the entire school with my head held high. "So music relaxes you?"

I nodded and was thankful when she allowed me to get away with it. "Then what you need to do before reading or speaking is to think about the most relaxing music you know. Let that saturate your mind for a moment before trying to talk." She nodded at the book.

"Pick a page. Listen to the music in your head. Relax, and then read."

I sighed and flipped through the pages until I found the passage I could read the best. Taking in a deep breath, I let the sound of Tchaikovsky's Romance Opus 5 fill my mind and I tried to get lost in it. The office disappeared, Ms. Rice disappeared, and the book within my hands disappeared. Halfway through, I felt as relaxed as I was going to be, so I opened my eyes and looked at the words. I tried not to force it. I tried to just let my brain speak to my vocal chords and the muscles in my mouth without pressure.

Three words into the first sentence, my calm broke as I stammered over one tiny little word and after that, it was a disaster.

A hand ran through my hair and I lazily opened my eyes to see Jane sitting in the backseat of David's Scout with me. I normally disliked being touched, but Jane's was soothing. It always took David ten minutes or more to extract himself from all of his admirers, so we usually found ourselves waiting on him. Today, she had slipped into the backseat.

I could tell by the look on her face that her day hadn't been much better than mine. "Can I borrow your English notes?" I nodded and looked at her quizzically. "All I remember is talking about Anglo-Saxon Beowulf something, and then the next thing I know Trent's poking me in the side, telling me that class is over."

"I-I-I'm s-sorry."

"Did your day suck too?" I gave her a pointed look. "Yeah, it's Thursday, isn't it? So I guess you won't be talking for the next two days?" she asked, giving me a little smile. I never felt like talking after sessions with Ms. Rice. "David told me what happened this morning with Chris." I sighed and Jane nudged me with her shoulder until I looked at her again.

"If you won't hit him, then I will. And he said Sophie was there! Oh my goodness Elliott, she's cute, isn't she?"

I scowled. Jane was overly excited at the prospect of a new friend, but I was annoyed she had to remind me that I had nearly knocked Sophie over this morning and then just sat around like a lump while a jerk like Anderson made fun of me in front of her. "Don't worry. She won't go out with him."

I couldn't help it. As much as I didn't want to speak, I had to. "I d-d-don't c-care…" a block formed as I tried to get out my next word and I hated how long it was taking me to get out one simple sentence, "…who she g-g-g-goes out w-w-w-with, J-J-JJJJane." I sighed, annoyed with the time it took to say it, or that I'd actually even bothered to speak in the first place.

My annoying sister just smiled at me and ruffled my hair again. I ducked my head so that she would be forced to stop touching me. "But she's pretty, though, isn't she?"

I gave her a look that told her I obviously thought she was pretty.

"She's in my Photography class. I wonder when her birthday is. I want to buy her a new camera, and some new clothes. I think she would look cute with shorter hair, don't you?"

"S-she looks g-g-good now," I said and then immediately hated myself for it. Jane's smile brightened even more. I was so happy I could lighten her mood. I narrowed my eyes and clenched my jaw.

"Stop, Elliott."

"St-st-stop what? You-you're the one thaaaat n-n-needs to st-st-stop. Don't b-be a…" I halted as I tried to think of a Chopin song that relaxed me before continuing, "mmmatch mmaker. It n-n-never works."

"But you think she's preeeeetty," Jane sang.

"Who's pretty?" David asked as he hopped into the driver's seat.

"Sophie Young," Jane answered.

David's smile grew as he turned around, eyebrows raised, his eyes fixed on me. "You think she's pretty," he said with a nod. I sighed and rolled my eyes in response, fairly certain my face was turning an embarrassing shade of red right about then. "Well, hell yeah, she's pretty," he said, obviously taking my silence as an acknowledgment. He grew serious as he added, "She should stay away from Fox though." He shrugged, turning forward and starting the Scout. "I guess she's like that. We'll find out soon enough."

Thankfully everyone was quiet until we reached home. As we walked up the front steps, David unlocked the door and said, "Dr. Cannatella called out sick, so Dad's staying late." I sighed and pinched the bridge of my nose, knowing what was coming next. "Robin's bringing dinner tonight."

I had no idea why Stephen and Robin insisted on treating us like we were all eight-year-olds, unable to stay in the house for more than a few hours on our own. David, Jane, and I were no culinary wizards, but we certainly could survive cooking spaghetti.

With Robin came Rebecca. Since David's girlfriend was coming over, Jane would invite Trent, leaving me alone with Robin. I shook my head, taking off my shoes carefully and placing them neatly next to the front door. I was mentally preparing for an evening with Robin and her amazing and unending bag of psychological tricks.

Dinner was exactly what I'd been expecting; an elaborate show of how much public affection Rebecca and David could get away with in front of Robin, and how much of a conversation Trent and Jane could have without saying a word. It was truly sickening. Robin tried to spark up a few conversations to include everyone, but as usual, no one was interested. Each time, I shoved some more take-out Italian food into my mouth to save myself the embarrassment of trying to have an actual conversation.

As usual, the two couples disappeared as soon as they finished eating, leaving me with Robin to clear the table. It just wasn't fair. I was fine with cleaning up. It was almost soothing to continue the chores from my past, but being alone with Robin left me vulnerable to an impromptu session with her.

I knew she thought I needed the most help. I was the one who was socially inept and couldn't even hold a proper conversation with anyone in the house, let alone peers or members of the opposite sex I wasn't related to.

I had just finished loading the dishwasher and was turning to make a hasty retreat. "Elliott," Robin said. I sighed and turned around, finding her deep blue eyes studying me. "What are you going to do?"

My brain raced to find the simplest word in my vocabulary to answer her.

"M-m-music."

"Are you going to play piano?" she asked with a smile. Of course she knew that the piano was my preferred instrument, but she asked this question every time.

I swallowed and sucked in a large breath of air. I just wanted to retreat to my room. I pointed to the ceiling as I answered, "Yes."

She cocked her head and brushed her blonde hair over her shoulder, keeping the smile frozen on her face. "The piano's down here."

I could barely contain my annoyance. Of course the piano was down here. It was *my* house; I knew where the piano was. Stephen kept it hostage down on the first floor in an attempt to lure me out of my bedroom. I had a keyboard in my room, along with my other instruments, but he thought if he kept the Grand Piano downstairs I would be tempted to spend more time out in the open. Usually it didn't work, though every time I passed it, I longed to play it.

I took another breath and tried to push out my word, hoping that it would be enough for her to let me be, at least for one night. It was Thursday after all. I'd have to endure sessions with therapist Wallace tomorrow. The block in my head kept me from saying anything. It didn't help that her eyes were fixed on me as she waited in that annoyingly patient way of hers.

Finally, I pushed it from my mind and out of my mouth, stumbling the entire way. "K-k-k-keyyyb-board."

Her smile stayed on her face as she extended a hand and laid it gently on my shoulder. It was times like these that I wished she wasn't a mother; that she could truly just be a clinical, detached professional. It would have been easier to shut her down; shut her out. But she was in my house after she'd just fed me dinner, smiling at me with that motherly grin. "Play the piano for me and keep me company."

Since I'd been taught from a young age that requests were just thinly-disguised commands, I relented. Instead of answering, since I knew I couldn't say no and I didn't want to hear my loser of a voice concede, I just walked out of the kitchen and into the sitting room. She followed me and took a seat on the chaise lounge as I went to the piano bench.

Truthfully, I was excited, since I rarely allowed myself to play the piano. But my excitement only annoyed me since it meant Robin got what she wanted and she could chalk it up to "helping" me. I raised the cover and let my fingers glide across the keys. I had hundreds of songs memorized, so I rarely needed sheet music. Some were from the great composers that everyone knew, and some were obscure little melodies that only true connoisseurs of classics would know, and still others were my own compositions.

I knew which ones Robin liked the best and decided to start with one of her favorites. When I played new songs for her, she always wanted to interpret them and start labeling my emotions as if I picked the song because it reflected my current mood. Heaven forbid I play Moonlight Sonata. She would instantly think I was depressed and wanted to start writing my suicide note. It would take too many words for me to express that Beethoven's piece didn't make me depressed, and it held no connotation of sadness for me.

Robin wasn't an aficionado of music. She heard what she wanted and analyzed it with a shrink's mind. Music wasn't the same for everyone and just because she got depressed by a certain song, didn't mean that everyone did. Moonlight Sonata was peaceful to me. It was what I thought about on the nights I couldn't sleep. I could imagine myself in a moonlit garden, surrounded by night-blooming plants and the sounds of trickling water. I could imagine the moon shining down, illuminating all of the most beautiful things in the garden as the stars twinkled like tiny diamonds reflecting a beam of light.

But all Robin would connect it with was morbidity and death.

"How was your session with Ms. Rice today, Elliott?"

"F-fine," I answered casually. There was no need to go into the depth of my failure.

"David mentioned that you ran into Sophie Young." I stopped playing the lighthearted Mozart piece and I swung around to look at Robin and shrugged.

"Did you speak with her?" she asked in a hopeful voice. I shook my head. I didn't think one poorly-executed word of apology constituted the type of "speaking" Robin was talking about. I turned back around and changed songs. I began the very first song of my own that I'd ever played for her. "Do you have any classes with her?"

She was going to continue to ask me about Sophie Young until she was satisfied. I nodded. "H-H-HHHortic-c-culture."

"That's great!" I sighed, trying to conceal it. "She'll have a friendly face in at least one of her classes. It'll be good for her to have a friend like you."

I wanted to slam my hands down on the keys and yell at her. Sophie Young wasn't my friend, and even if Robin had some weird ideas about how we could help each other through therapy, she *still* wouldn't be my friend. Sophie was too good, too pretty, and too smart to be my friend. There wasn't one person in that school besides my siblings and their significant others who was willing to be a friend to a retard like me.

"She w-won't have m-much trouble finding f-friends, R-R-Robin. She's nnnot liiike me."

I ignored her breathy sigh and continued to play. "You know, Elliott, you're able to speak more fluently when you play. Have you noticed that?" I ignored her, instead directing my attention to the song, hoping to just get through it and be able to go upstairs, away from her; away from everyone.

But Robin wasn't having that. "Stephen says you had a panic attack on Monday." My eyes closed. Now I knew what this whole thing was about. She'd gotten me to play the piano, talk about something else, and now she was going in for the therapist's kill. Although my breathing sped up slightly, I kept my fingers moving along the keys, producing the same perfect sounds as always. "What happened at the mall, Elliott?"

"I d-di-didn't want to gggo." Jane had asked me to and of course, Stephen said she couldn't go alone. Even though I needed nothing from the mall, Jane had guilted me into going.

"But you did and what happened?" she coached.

I exhaled, completing the song before I turned to her, knowing that she would make me look at her at some point. My eyes were still closed. "I c-c-c-cccouldn't breathe."

"Why?"

"T-t-t-too maaaany p-people." Slowly, I let my eyes drift open. "The mmmmedicine d-doesn't w-w-work."

"Even though you don't like the medication, you're able to go to school now, usually without incident, but I guess it's because that's a closed community, so to speak. You know everybody there. Perhaps the mall triggered it because the only person you knew was Jane."

It didn't matter why; it only mattered that I couldn't do it without my body tensing up like it was in a vise while my brain shut down. But Robin wouldn't give up…ever. So it came as no surprise when she said, "You should try it again."

I gritted my teeth.

Yes, trying it again was such a logical thing for me to do. I definitely wanted to go and freak out amongst strangers and have the mall security come pick me up like a rag doll and be ushered to the hospital in an ambulance while the EMTs tried to ascertain whether I was having a heart attack or a seizure. Yes. That made perfect sense.

I stood up. “Where are you going?” Robin asked.

What business was it of hers? I forced myself to ignore my need to obey an authority figure. This was *my* house, not hers. “T-t-tired.”

I started walking toward the steps, but stopped when I heard her voice.

“Elliott, I know it’s hard, but you have to push past it.”

Great advice. That’s like telling a depressed person to just smile, it’s not that bad. It should be a rule that all therapeutic professionals must have some kind of firsthand knowledge of the disorders they sought to treat so that they wouldn’t say brainless things like that. Why didn’t I think of that? *Just push past it*. Great idea. I would have to give it a try. I forced my feet to move and finally I was in the sanctuary of my room.

The rest of the night passed without incident. Robin, Trent, and Rebecca all went home and no one bothered me until I woke to the sounds of David beating on the bathroom door again. I wished Stephen would’ve had enough sense years ago to give Jane the bedroom with the private bathroom, but I understood why he didn’t. Jane had a tendency to cut herself, and having her own bathroom seemed like a bad idea. She could cut herself too deep and bleed out without anyone knowing about it.

But she hadn’t been doing that much anymore, at least not that I knew of. Trent was good for her like that; however, the fear and threat were still there, so I would continue to be awakened by David's fists on the bathroom door while he'd shout at her to hurry up.

I tried to ignore it when David turned his fists loose on my door, yelling at me to get out of bed. "It's Friday, Elliott. Just think; it's almost the weekend and that's two whole days that you can spend alone in your room doing whatever it is that you do!" I was successfully ignoring him up until the point when the doorknob twisted.

I jumped out of bed and grabbed at the doorknob. I tried yanking it open, but I realized that I had locked it last night, like I did every night. I let out a shaky breath, trying to control my body's response. I wasn't going to have an attack. I wasn't going to freak out. This was my house. This was my room. It was only David, and the door was locked.

When I had mastered my emotions and bodily reactions enough, I unlocked the door and pulled it open. David was standing there with a smug look.

"D-d-don't d-d-do thaaat again." His smirk widened. I was sure I didn't sound the least bit intimidating, especially since I couldn't even get out four words without sounding like a loser.

He gave me a mischievous look. "Got you out of bed, didn't it?"

I huffed, moving out into the hall and closing the door behind me. I sulked down to the free bathroom, listening to David resume his pounding.

When we got to school, just like every other day, David told me not to let Anderson bother me, but of course I did. I was happy to see that this time he wasn't accompanied by Sophie Young, but the rest of his followers were tagging along and thought his stuttering jokes were just the funniest thing they'd ever heard. When Chris knocked the books out of my hands, in what he said was "payback" for accidentally knocking into Sophie yesterday, they just roared with laughter. Then he did his signature move of shoving me into the locker with his shoulder as he pushed past me.

I bent down to retrieve my books before David could come around the corner and see his loser of a brother picking up his things.

"Hey," I heard above me. I looked up and there was Sophie Young, giving me a smile that clearly said she was high. I could feel my face contort as I tried to force a greeting from my mouth, but I couldn't say hello for anything. My mind and body refused to work in unison, making me feel like a complete idiot in front of her…again.

To my horror, she crouched down next to me and started pulling papers and books toward her and stacking them on her knee. "I'll kick his ass," she said with a smile. My eyes closed as I felt like the wind had been knocked out of me again. She had seen the entire thing.

When I opened my eyes she was staring at me. I needed to say something. I needed to prove to her that I wasn't a complete idiot-freak-loser, but my tongue seemed to stick to the roof of my mouth. She smiled at me again, pushing the papers into my arms before standing up.

My body finally did something my mind told it to, which was to stand up. She looked up at me with her big, intensely blue eyes and I realized she was much shorter than I was. She should've been taller with all that confidence. "See you in the greenhouse," she said before brushing past me, her shoulder making contact with my bicep.

Letting out an unconsciously-held breath, I looked up at the ceiling. I was an idiot!

I didn't see her again until study hall. She did very little studying while Anderson and his friends gathered around her as if she were the second coming. The bored look on her face made me entirely too happy. Then, when there was fifteen minutes left until lunch, she got up and walked out. It wasn't hard to notice that Jason Fox had left just five minutes before she did.

She was ten minutes late to Horticulture when she smiled at Mr. Reese and said "I got a little lost."

The school wasn't that big. It would have been hard to get lost, but when she sat down next to me, I could smell that she'd been smoking again. As she stared glassily up to where the soil samples were, I could see a small red-purplish bruise forming on the side of her neck.

Why it bothered me so much that Sophie had a hickey, I didn't know, but it did.

Mr. Reese passed out a stack of papers, samples of dirty earth in small circular glass containers, and a microscope, completing my negative mood by reinforcing that today was in fact the day I would *have* to work with Sophie. I was hoping I'd be given at least a couple of hours of reprieve, but Mr. Reese had other ideas. After making one pass with the scientific portion of our assignment, Reese dropped off flowers and other supplies, telling us we had to make an arrangement when we were finished identifying soil types. I tried to let the music play in my head in anticipation of speaking to her, hoping that Ms. Rice was right and all I needed to do was relax and I would be able to have a conversation like a normal person.

When Sophie slid a sheet of paper between us, I glanced at her. She was looking right at me and she was unbelievably perfect. Too pretty. Why couldn't my lab partner be ugly with buck teeth and a lazy eye? Then she wouldn't have been so intimidating. The music fled my mind and in fact, so did everything else, when she smiled at me.

"So now you're forced to talk to me," she said, her tone low and conspiratorial. "Man, this guy's all kinds of random, isn't he? How do you go from soil samples to arranging flowers?"

My mouth suddenly went dry. She was expecting me to speak. She had expectations already and I was going to fail, and then there would be no hope of salvaging her opinion of me. My heart raced and my breathing sped up as I tried to get my brain to work beyond the bare minimum of necessary function. Finally I just busied myself with the soil, sliding the containers under the microscope and identifying them easily myself. I was happy that the samples were contained. I didn't have to touch the dirt; just the glass slides. I didn't even give her the chance to help and by the time I looked back up, she was basically just staring at me. I felt sick. I wrung my hands together as I desperately told my mouth and mind to work together and produce a sound that at least mimicked a word.

My breath caught when she touched my hands and they immediately stilled. "I was just kidding, Elliott. You don't have to talk if you don't want to."

Elliott. She said my name. She *knew* my name. She hadn't made it a joke, imitating my stammer. Then she withdrew her hand and I immediately moved both of mine under the table to my lap, where they balled into fists.

She spoke again, her voice light and casual as if she was talking to a normal person. "So I imagine that you're all sorts of smart because quiet types are always smart," she said, clipping the ends of the stems one by one, "but don't think you're going to carry me through this class. I'm all kinds of knowledgeable and I have a wicked eye for aesthetics." Her expression was as sarcastic as her voice. "I was taking this in Tampa, but I'm not going to carry you either." She pushed the utility knife and foam closer to me. "It's not all arranging flowers and looking at little jars of soil is it? Because in Tampa, the syllabus said we were going to get to play in dirt and actually grow things."

I ignored the way my skin nearly crawled just thinking about "playing in dirt," and instead focused on all the information she'd just shared. She was from Tampa and she thought I was smart. That was a good thing, I hoped. She smiled at me again and then I couldn't help it; I gave her a half-smile back. I glanced at the flowers and began carving the foam to fit in the wide orange vase. When I looked back up, Sophie was staring at me, this time with raised eyebrows. Right. She'd asked me a question. My mouth opened to speak before I even realized I wanted to say something, but all that came out was "Ah-ah-ah," and I sighed in defeat.

"Duh-duh-duh." I looked up to see Chris Anderson, turned around in his seat, giving me a cross-eyed look as he verbally humiliated me. Something launched itself from my table, hitting Chris in the chest. He narrowed his eyes at Sophie.

"Hey, that could have hit me in the eye!"

I realized that the item was a pencil, and that Sophie had thrown it at him. "You're lucky it wasn't the knife. Now turn around and stop making your poor partner do all the work. I know it'll be difficult, but I have faith that even *you* can create something beautiful." Chris huffed, and turned around, and Sophie spun back to me and said, "I told you I'd kick his ass."

I just looked at her. If Robin and Stephen thought we had similar backgrounds, how in the world had she turned out so completely different?

We finished the work before the bell rang and sat there in silence. It was fine by me, because it was hardly fair for Sophie to have to fill the void alone. Since it was Friday and I didn't have to see Ms. Rice, I went to the library to help return books and grade papers. Stephen had arranged it as a way to give me credit for being a student aide. I didn't have to be around anyone other than the librarian, Ms. Peters and I rarely had to speak at all. For the rest of the school day I thought about everything Sophie had said to me.

I had to chuckle from time to time, thinking about what happened before the bell rang. She'd leaned in close and said, "Hey, if everything goes right," I got nervous at that point, "Chris should have a big knot on his head or maybe a swollen nose in about an hour." I wondered what she meant. Was she actually going to punch him? "I plan to 'be clumsy,'" she explained, complete with air-quotes.

It hadn't been the worst day ever, but I was ready to go home. However, as I sat in David's car, I realized that today was therapy day with Robin, and I would find no peace there either.

I wondered if Sophie even knew what was in store for her.

Chapter 3

Friday Night Club

Sophie

My second day at Damascus High started off boringly enough. I avoided Chris and Connor like the plague, even as they followed me around like puppies that thought I had a Milkbone in my pants. The first part of my day was fine. Photography was a waste, seeing as everyone else was developing their film from last week's assignment. Study hall and lunch were again filled with annoying people sitting with me even though I hadn't asked them to.

I did have a conversation with a girl named Andrea Tuttle about what kids did for fun around here. She was as cool as someone like her could be. She was nice and that was…nice, but I bored of it all quickly.

Just as I thought I was about to go insane, I watched as Jason made a point to stand up from his group of friends and walk past my table, his hand tapping his pocket. It amazed me how easy it was just to leave the library. The librarian must not care *at all*.

I waited for just a minute or two before I left and walked to the woods, where I found him waiting. "Thank the Flying Spaghetti Monster!" I said as I sat down next to him on the fallen tree.

"The what?" he asked with a soft laugh.

"Google it." I could've gone into the whole thing with him, but I didn't feel the need. The whole concept of "God" was a sore subject with me. My mother wasn't religious or anything, but she loved to take advantage of people, so she appealed to them any way she could. My freshman year, she made me go to church with her. I didn't really know why, but I thought she just wanted to feel important sometimes. New converts seemed to be exciting stuff at church.

I had to sit through youth group meetings too. They were horrible. People were always talking about "God's goodness" and how he punished the wicked and rewarded the righteous. They went on and on about things like an apple and snakes, and for some reason, because two people wanted to know and understand their world, the rest of us got screwed.

Or something like that.

What did they call it? Original sin?

It was a bullshit concept and the whole idea of some being that loved me when I was good and hated me when I was bad was too close to the concept of shitty parenting. It didn't make sense to me. God should love everyone, no matter who they were or what they did. I already had my mother who hated me for arbitrary reasons. Why did I need some invisible, all-powerful being hating me too? In a child's world, parents *are* gods.

So this youth group leader would assign essays. Yeah, *essays.* One time I didn't capitalize the "g" in god and he made a point to correct it in front of the rest of the flock. I told him to fuck off and that anyone who would get that upset about a letter being capitalized was just messed up. I proceeded to let everyone know *why* there was no "God," and then I invoked the name of Satan just for shits and giggles.

Helen and I were asked to leave the congregation. I paid for it, but for the most part, it was worth the pain.

To this day, I wrote it with a lower case "g." Hell, I even *thought* about it in lower case.

Any deity had to be better than their "God." The same "God" that gave me to Helen and let me suffer because some chick and her man ate an apple.

When I learned about the Flying Spaghetti Monster, the atheist response to divine creation, he became my deity of choice. The FSM didn't say he loved everyone and then punish them just because he didn't like what they did. He didn't say he loved a person, only to abandon them to a life filled with hate.

I didn't want to think about that anymore, and forced my mind away from it all. I watched excitedly as Jason plucked a pre-rolled joint from his pack of cigarettes and lit it. He didn't take long passing it to me and I inhaled deeply, feeling my facial muscles relax just from the first hit.

We were quiet while we passed the joint back and forth, but when he crushed it against the tree, he turned and said, "How was your night with Tom?"

"Boring as hell."

I turned quickly, lifting my leg over his lap to straddle him. His hands immediately moved to my waist, holding me to him as we kissed. He tasted like sour apple candy and chronic. It was only moments until his mouth was at my neck, lapping and sucking. I hated hickeys, but his hands were doing the most intriguing things to my body, so I let him continue on his bruise-producing quest.

He was pressing against me, his hands gripping my hips.

"We can do it later. We have class," I reminded him as I straightened up and pulled away, grabbing my backpack and walking back to school.

I was only a few minutes late to class and came up with some lame excuse as I ducked past the teacher. Taking my seat next to Rusty Dalton, I let my mind wander until the teacher started passing out all the materials we'd need for our assignment. I was in a good mood, so I started to tease Rusty Dalton about how he'd have to talk to me now. Then he proceeded to do the entire soil exercise himself. I didn't mean what I said in a bad or insulting way, but he looked like he was going to throw up or cry, or have some kind of a breakdown, so I let him know that he didn't have talk to me unless he wanted to.

Being high, I was chatty, so I started talking to him about how good I was with flowers and making things pretty or whatever. At one point he opened his mouth like he was going to say something, but before he could really get anything out, Chris Anderson turned around and made fun of him, again. Chris was a prick, so I flung my sharpened pencil at him.

In P.E., I slammed another basketball in his face and then batted my eyelashes until he couldn't stay pissed at me. I wondered how long it would take until I had to do more than flirt to cover up my violent tendencies toward him.

Again, Jason was waiting for me out front and I had expected him to make good on my promise of banging him after school, but we didn't go to his house. He went to mine instead. "I thought…"

He shook his head dismissively. "I have a thing tonight, so maybe tomorrow."

"A thing?" I asked.

"Yeah, it's stupid, but tomorrow I could pick you up early for a little wake-n-bake and then we could go for a hike in the woods." Jason licked his lips and leaned in close to me. "Ever do it in a forest?"

Swampy wetlands, yes. Sandy beaches, yes. Forest, no. I smiled wickedly at him. "Don't come over too early. It's Saturday after all. And don't think that it's a date or anything." Jason sighed and I shrugged. "Just felt like I needed to remind you."

"I won't be over before Tom leaves." At my silent question, he answered, "Your dad would flip if he knew I was banging his precious little girl. He hates me."

"You're his best friend's son."

"Who sells dope and corrupts the youth of Damascus."

I shrugged. "Socrates did the same thing, except for the dope-selling, and now he's studied by everyone." Jason gave me a quizzical look, obviously not knowing or caring about Socrates. "What does Jerry think of your dope-selling ways?"

He sighed. "He doesn't approve, but he doesn't ask questions or make a big thing about it. He can't work and I can't make the kind of money we need by flipping burgers, so he realizes either I sell the shit or we don't eat and he can't go to the doctor or get his meds." His eyes flicked to the clock on the dash. "I have to go. See you tomorrow." As I found the door handle, he added, "Don't bother wearing panties, unless you want them ripped off."

I bit back a laugh and exited the car without saying another word.

I'd just gotten out a few ingredients for dinner when Tom came through the front door. "Hey, kid," he said as he walked into the kitchen.

"It's your off day, where have you been?" I looked down at the fast-food bag in his hands. "You brought food?"

"Yeah," he said, his eyes nervously darting around the kitchen. "I forgot to tell you, but we have an appointment." He held out the bag. "So here, I went out for food."

"What appointment?" I asked, frowning. "I typically stay away from fast food."

"I got you a salad, 'cause I know you have to eat healthy and all that." Again, he was nervous, and his voice told me that he was hiding something, but before I could ask, he said, "Come on, we have to go."

~ • ~

Tom was quiet and nervous during the entire car ride and he carefully avoided answering any question about where we were going. I didn't like it. I hated surprises and I hated being trapped in a car without the slightest idea of where I was going to end up. I hadn't been caught doing anything bad so far, so I didn't think he was taking me to jail or a group home, but then we stopped at a large house.

I turned to him, already feeling betrayed. "What's this? Where are we?"

"Calm down there, Sophie, it's all a part of the agreement."

I breathed out angrily. "What agreement?"

"The agreement with the people in Tampa. In order for you to avoid any kind of severe discipline, I had to take you." I couldn't help but hear an emphasis on the word "had." "You have to go to therapy. This is Dr. Dalton's place. He and Robin Wallace have set up—"

"EXCUSE ME?" I yelled. "I don't *need* therapy!"

Tom sighed and shook his head. "You stole a *car*, Sophia. You didn't think you could just get away with that did you?"

The whole thing pissed me off, ruining my relatively good mood. The word “therapy” snapped the very thin thread within me. I’d been polite and nice so far, but it ended here.

“Of course not, *Tom*.” I spat out his name, unimpressed by his parental authority. “But I thought moving to Podunk, Maryland with *you* was punishment enough.” He sighed again and turned away from me as if I was just going to let him be all cool and calm with this shit. “Don’t you think it’s torture enough to have to live in your shitty little house and pretend like you’re actually my father?”

I watched his jaw clench. His voice was tight when he spoke. “Listen to me, Sophie. I wish like hell I’d been there for you more when you were growing up, but there wasn’t a choice.”

What the hell ever. He was deluded if he thought he didn’t have a choice. Everyone *always* had a choice. He just couldn’t admit that his choice didn’t include me.

“But I am your father, and I will not have you disrespecting me like this.”

I cruelly laughed in his face. “Tom, you’re not my father. You’re not a parent. You’re just the witless sperm donor Helen duped seventeen years ago.”

I ignored his hurt look and realized that it didn’t matter what I thought; I’d be forced to do something I didn’t want to do.

“Let’s get this over with, shall we?” I said as I opened the car door, incredibly ready to be away from him.

I walked quickly up the front steps and banged on the door. Internally, I was in a rage, but there wasn’t anything I could do in this situation. Therapy it was. Just like all of the other things I'd been forced to do throughout my life I would just close my eyes, be a good girl, and wait until it was over.

The door opened and I couldn't help but mutter, "Shit." It was the goddamned Pinny Dalton who was in my Photography class. I knew her name was Jane or something boring like that, but the chick had lots of piercings, so in my mind, I dubbed her "Pinny," as in "pincushion." It wasn't exactly nice, but I wasn't a nice person, and I'd learned long ago it was better to objectify a person by giving them meaningless nicknames based on their random physical traits, than it was to call them by name.

So, great. I couldn't have been more thrilled that not only was there some kind of therapy going on inside this house, but now at least this girl was going to know I "needed" it.

"Hi, Sophie!" she said, entirely too chipper for my taste.

I wouldn't have thought it possible, but my spirits fell even more when I heard voices coming from behind her. Too many voices. So now it was therapy with lots of kids, presumably from my school. That was just great. I could feel Tom coming up behind me, so I pointed inside. "I'm supposed to be in there."

Pinny Dalton smiled and nodded, opening up the door wider. "Hello, Mr. Young. Robin and Stephen are upstairs in the study. They want to talk to you." Pinny snuck her arm through mine and dragged me farther into the house. "I'll keep Sophie company."

Tom moved to the steps as if he knew where he was going and I scanned the chaotic scene before me. Holy shit. It looked like all of the perfect Daltons were here, along with their significant others too. I only recognized two other kids. Andrea, sitting on the couch with her hands folded in her lap, and this girl who looked like someone just shit on her birthday cake. There were other kids as well. Some looked young, like freshmen, and others were closer to my age, but I hadn't seen them before. Maybe they were from other schools, but this was a really small town, so it seemed unlikely.

"What the hell, Sophie?"

I turned to my left and saw Jason coming closer. Pinny Dalton's grip tightened as he approached, but I pulled myself free. "Jason, watch your language, please." She shot him an annoyed look.

I rolled my eyes at Pinny Dalton and went over to Jason. "This was your *thing*?"

He shrugged. "Every Friday night. Just enough shit to totally fuck up the weekend." He leaned in close, the smile evident on his face as he lowered his voice. "But don't forget about me banging you in the forest tomorrow. Just keep that in mind while you're enduring the pain that is group therapy."

"G*roup* therapy?" Therapy was one thing. Sharing things, *private* and embarrassing things, with other kids was something else completely. "You could've warned me, Jason. If I'd known this was what my Friday was going to look like, I would have smoked a bowl before coming…or, you know, slit my wrists."

He grabbed my arm and pulled me away from Pinny Dalton and the others. "Don't say shit like that here, Sophie.

That bitch Robin will commit you and you won't be able to do anything about it."

"I was joking."

"She won't be."

I cocked my head. "Do we have time to get high?" I whispered.

"No. And how was I supposed to know that you were as screwed-up as the rest of us? I had no idea Tom would drag your ass to something like this. You used to be all sweet and goody-goody."

"I stole a car."

I watched with amusement as Jason's face brightened. "No shit? The Daltons all have sweet rides, so if you ever get the hankering to steal another one," he whispered into my ear as I checked out all of the faces, many of them turned toward us, curious, "I bet we could make a run for Mexico."

"So what the hell is this shit?" I jerked my head back toward the group of kids.

"Just what it looks like. The dumbass doctor and the therapist have put together this little group to make the parents of Damascus and the surrounding area feel like their kids won't always be screw-ups. First, it's all about the individual counseling with Robin, then we have group, and then we have to pair off with one of our 'peers.'"

"Oh! I'll be your peer!"

He gave me a look and said, "I already got one," as he jabbed a finger to the corner where the angry girl sat messing with her phone. "I got stuck with Olivia. Bitch is whiney as shit." He pointed to a boy who looked like her. He was laughing at another boy. "That's her brother Jamie."

"So this is what I have to look forward to on Friday nights now?"

"We don't usually have one-on-ones because we're a big group and it's just her and one other guy who comes every other week. But since you're new, you'll probably have to do them every week for a while. Plus, stealing cars is a pretty big thing, you know. Very sexy," he finished, flashing me a smirk.

I heard footsteps on the stairs and Jason glanced up. My eyes followed his as we both watched Tom making his descent. Jason quickly went to mingle with the other Damascus Screw-Ups. I folded my arms around my torso and scowled as Tom approached me.

"Robin's waiting for you. Make the best of it, Sophie. I'll be back to pick you up."

He was trying to be encouraging, but just my being here made me want to hit him. I brushed past him and moved up the stairs. I had no idea where to go, so I just walked down the hallway until I found an open door.

"Sophie." I turned, entering the room. Dr. Dalton smiled at me and motioned to an overstuffed leather chair. "This is Robin Wallace. You may know her daughter Rebecca from school." I shrugged. "Well, I need to get back downstairs, but make yourself comfortable. There's water or soda in the refrigerator." He pointed to the small dorm fridge underneath the elaborate bookcase, but then looked like he remembered something. "Well on second thought, with your diabetes, you should probably just have water."

Nice. Like I needed reminding that I wasn't supposed to have soda. His saying that only made me crave a Pepsi even more. Great job, Dr. Dalton. Tempt the diabetic car thief. Next, why don't you dangle the keys to your BMW in my face? Idiot.

He left and my eyes had nowhere else to settle but on this Wallace woman.

"Hi, Sophie."

I took a deep breath. "Hello."

"Your father told me it was quite a shock for you to learn that you'd be spending time with me this evening. I'm sorry you had to find out like that." I said nothing as I rubbed my hands over my forehead. "I'm not a doctor. I'm a counselor, so we're just going to talk. There's no real diagnosis of disorders, just--"

"I don't have a disorder." I glared at her. Two seconds with me and she already thought she knew everything. Idiot Counselor Bitch.

Her voice was friendly enough, but I still didn't like her.

"This is our first session, so I'll explain some things to you. I'll be taking a few notes. Don't let that intimidate you. After we talk, we'll spend some time in a group setting. I'm sure you noticed everyone downstairs. After that, we usually end the night in peer-to-peer sessions. That is a time when you're not supervised; you're simply being a kid with another kid. It will help the two of you create a bond so that if you ever need anything and don't feel comfortable speaking with me or another adult, you will always have a friend who can help you."

"So who am I going to be with?"

"Elliott Dalton."

"Are you serious?" Robin's face tightened as she wrote something down in her notepad. "Dude can barely speak and I'm supposed to have some kind of meaningful, therapeutic relationship with him?"

She took a deep breath, licking her lips before locking her eyes on me. "Don't count Elliott out, Sophie. He's a very complicated person, and his speech impediment—"

"I don't care about his stuttering. We're in a class together and we work just fine, but I don't understand the point of—"

"Perhaps if you just let down your guard and allow the process to work, you may begin to understand the point of all of this." I sat fuming in silence, willing myself to just get through it. It was still better than a group home or jail. "Tell me about the car you stole."

I looked up at her, shocked by her boldness. "It was blue." I sneered and the bitch just smiled.

"Why did you steal it?"

I sighed and shook my head. This chick wouldn't understand the real reason, and if she did, all she'd do was ask more and more pointless questions. "Because it was shiny and fast and I liked it."

Bitch Wallace flipped open a folder, her eyes scanning the pages within.

"What's all that?"

Again, she smiled at me. "This is basically your life on paper. Medical records, school counselor notes, transcripts, court summaries." My eyes narrowed as she picked up a paper and studied it. Stupid bitch. "You're a smart girl, Sophie. You've always received good grades." She paused. "Except in sixth grade. What happened to make you go from all A's to nearly flunking every subject?" My teeth clenched together and I closed my eyes. I felt sick, just like I did every time I thought about it. "You were able to pull your grades back up though."

She paused and read something else. "How does a girl who's clearly not interested in athletics acquire so many injuries?"

My heart began to race and my breathing sped up as my eyes fixed on a spot on the wall next to her. "When I look at these disciplinary records from your old schools, do you know what I see?" I didn't answer. "I see someone who almost intentionally got in trouble. Detentions, Saturday school; all those are punishments that would take you away from home, but you never received a suspension. Whatever behavior got you into trouble mysteriously disappeared before the offense was elevated to that level. What a good way to escape spending time at home."

"Shut up," I said quietly, though clenched teeth.

Despite my harsh words, her voice was even gentler when she said, "Why did you steal the car?"

Slowly, I answered. "Because I liked it."

Again she smiled almost condescendingly, letting me know she saw through me, and leaned in. "I'm much more perceptive than a high school guidance counselor. Please don't try to pull the wool over my eyes. If you're honest with me, I can be honest with you when I say that I can help." I didn't need help. She glanced at her watch. "We can be done for this week. It's nearly time for group."

"Goody." I stood up and crossed the room.

"Sophie?" I paused, my hand on the doorknob. "Thanks for coming today."

Chapter 4

Dark and Tortured

Sophie

I descended the stairs after finishing with Bitch Wallace and ignored the way everyone looked at me as I entered the large living room. There was a little bit of room next to Andrea on the long sofa and a wide-open spot in-between Rusty Dalton and one of the little freshmen guys. I moved over to the sofa and flopped down. “This blows,” I said under my breath.

“Just breathe.” I looked at Andrea, but her eyes were fixed ahead. “Let your mind go somewhere else and before you know it, it’ll be time to go home.” I wanted to ask her why she had to be here. She seemed perfectly normal to me, but before I could, Wallace came in and sat down. This was the most ridiculous thing I could imagine doing on my first Friday in Damascus.

I did what Andrea suggested and let my mind wander after Robin introduced me to the Damascus Screw-Up Club. I thought about getting high a lot. I thought about the shiny, fast, blue car. I thought about having sex with Jason in the morning.

Luckily, I didn't have to talk. Only about half of the kids did, but I didn't listen because I didn't care about their ridiculous stories.

Half an hour into it, I felt my eyelids droop. I wondered if I could get away with sleeping through it all. I was just about to test it when Andrea said something. Apparently she hadn't been paying attention either, so she had Wallace repeat the question. "Oh, um, I'm doing fine. I ate lunch today and had a taco for dinner."

Okay, I obviously missed something important. Was this group about our eating habits? It wasn't until Wallace asked her about throwing up that I realized Andrea was here because she had a couple of high-profile eating disorders. It seemed anorexia was her disorder of choice, but she'd been opting toward bulimia since everyone kept track of what she ate now. When asked about the emotions she had after admitting to tossing her taco only moments after eating it, Andrea took a deep breath and answered, "I was relieved."

"What made you feel relieved?"

"The taco was easily ninety to a hundred calories by itself, and as soon as I get home tonight, my mother's going force me to eat some fatty baked good with her and she won't let me leave until it's been down for an hour. So at least I know that the hundred-calorie taco isn't going to combine with the five-hundred-plus calories she's going to push on me."

Andrea was clearly nuts. She was like a size two or four or something, and nowhere near fat. Most of all the girls in Tampa had eating disorders too, and not one of them was fat before acquiring the starving or puking habit. She was decently pretty, although being in the same room as Rebecca Wallace would make every girl want to toss their lunch. That girl was like a life-sized Barbie doll.

I let my mind wander again until the whole group-sharing experience was over. Everyone got up and instantly found their designated peer and moved off to various locations throughout the downstairs. I just sat still on the couch. Obviously I was supposed to be paired with Elliott, but I had no intention of running over and being all buddy-buddy with him.

This afternoon in the greenhouse, I'd been stoned. I was always friendly and chatty when I was stoned, but this was an entirely different situation. I was being forced to interact with him now and the rebel in me, well, she rebelled against it. It wasn't anything personal against him.

From my peripheral vision, I could see him sitting over there, his hands fisted in his lap. It wasn't until Bitch Wallace stood up and called his name that he moved. He tensed as he lifted his head to look at her. "Elliott, why don't you show Sophie your house? I'm sure she'd like to see the game room." He nodded and looked at me nervously, standing up.

Sighing deeply, I stood and went over to Elliott. He looked absolutely gorgeous. Pitiful, but pitiful in a gorgeous way. Who would have thought such a hottie like him would have such a hard time talking?

That couldn't be the only reason he was in the Damascus Screw-Up Club with the rest of us. When he didn't speak, I felt horrible for him, so I made the decision not to give him a hard time. It wasn't his fault we were stuck together like this. "So you have a room of games, or what?"

His mouth kept opening and closing. At one point I could see his tongue pressing against his lower teeth, trying to form a word, but then his mouth snapped closed again. In the end, he simply decided to nod and then walked out of the large room and down the hall. Having no other choice but to follow, I walked behind him, taking in the expensive décor, wondering what it would be like to live in a house like this.

He stopped in front of a door and nodded toward it. I moved around him and peered into the room. Just about everyone from the living room was in there, excluding the Daltons, Pinny's boyfriend, and Barbie Wallace. I looked back to Rusty Dalton and asked, "Are you going in?"

He shook his head quickly. "T-t-t-too maaaany p-peeeeople."

It was a little packed. Jason was in there and I wanted to go hang out with him, but I was supposed to be hanging out with Elliott. I shrugged, taking a deep breath. "So show me the rest of your house."

He gave me a small smile and a nod. When he started walking, I walked with him. He didn't really point out anything, or say anything, but only a complete moron would need the kitchen or the bathroom pointed out to them.

He took me upstairs and I huffed as we passed the study where Bitch Wallace and I had our first little "chat." Most of the doors in the hallway were closed, and he opened them for me, letting me look into each room. It was the strangest home tour I'd ever been on, but this was definitely the strangest Friday night I'd had in a long time. The last one had been six months ago and it involved copious amounts of acid and freaky talking tree people.

Finally he stopped at a door he seemed hesitant to open, so I just waited, feigning disinterest. When he finally opened it, a concentrated look upon his face, I realized this must be his room. I peered in and asked for confirmation. "This your room?"

He nodded, but made no sound or gesture to invite me inside, so I decided to be obtuse and just walk in. As I did, I heard a shaky little breath come from him. The room was very nice. It was large and very clean and organized; the opposite of my tiny little space in Tom's small house. One entire wall was taken up by a built-in bookshelf that he'd filled with books, CDs, and even old vinyl albums.

Along another wall, the one I was closest to, there was a door to what I assumed was his closet, and there were musical instruments hanging up: three guitars, two violins, and a banjo too. Below them was the most expensive keyboard I had ever seen sitting on a simple black base next to a desk with a very expensive-looking laptop. On the opposite wall there was a soft, comfy-looking couch and nothing else. To my left was his bed. I found myself idly wondering if that was where the great Megan Simons/Rusty Dalton Bang had occurred.

His stuttering drew my thoughts back and I turned around and smiled. He looked like he needed an invitation into his own room. I had no idea what it was that he was trying to say, so I pointed at the guitars. "Obviously, you're into music."

He stepped inside, turning to take a cursory glance at his instruments. "Y-y-yes."

I moved farther into the room, sparing a sideway glimpse at him to ensure he was cool with it. "So do you take any of the music classes at school?"

"N-n-no."

I was sure he was good enough to make the band or whatever they had at Damascus High. It seemed strange that someone who seemed to love music wouldn't get involved in the school's music program. "Why?"

After a deep breath, his brows creased, and his eyes dropped to examine the tan carpet. "T-t-too m-many p-p-peeeeople." He halted for a moment before continuing. "Y-you have t-to d-do r-r-rec…h-have t-to p-play in front of p-peeople."

Yes, that would obviously be a problem for Rusty Dalton. "Can I look at your books?" He nodded before perching himself on the edge of the bed, looking up at me.

I perused his selection, utterly fascinated. "D-d-do you liiike…" I turned and watched as his face grew red trying to get a word out, his cheeks ballooning out. It made me uncomfortable for him. It must suck having to struggle so hard just to say a simple word.

"Books?" He nodded, blowing out a breath and giving me a crooked smile. He should smile more. "Yes. I like books."

"D-do you h-have m-m-m…a lot?"

"Um, no. Usually I just get them from the library." Helen hated spending money on me and most of mine needed to go for necessary things. I had yet to see what the high school or the Montgomery County Public Library held. I hoped it was stocked full of good ones, but if not, I saw now that I could just borrow one from Rusty Dalton. "A fan of Seuss?"

He looked to where my finger pointed and his face turned red again. "N-n-no. It-it-it's fffor m-my…"

He was obviously anxious again. "Seuss is cool." I ran my hand over the binding of some of the more academic-looking spines. The dude had Russian literature. "Have you read this?" I asked, pulling out Tolstoy's *War and Peace*. He nodded emphatically, like he really enjoyed it. I couldn't help but give him a genuine smile. Most people at school probably figured he was stupid or retarded in some way, but Jesus, the guy read some of the most complex literature out there. I was certain that Chris Anderson and that blonde bitch Cierra hadn't even heard of Tolstoy. My hand stopped again and I pulled out another familiar book, *Crime and Punishment.* "I like Dostoyevsky better."

I went and sat down on the couch, idly flipping through the pages of the book. He nodded, his hazel eyes bright, as if to say he enjoyed Dostoyevsky better too. "He's much more existential, isn't he?"

He smiled. "D-dark and t-tortured."

I looked at him then, *really* looked at him, while my fingers ran lightly over a page. No one I'd ever met knew anything about Tolstoy or Dostoyevsky. His eyes immediately dropped to his lap, watching as his hands clutched each other and released continually. He didn't like being around a lot of people. He was clearly musical and liked to read, particularly authors who were dark and tortured. I wondered if he was dark and tortured. Just seeing how he was treated in school would be enough to validate that.

"Elliott?" He lifted his head and looked at me. "Why do you let Chris treat you like that?"

His eyes widened, his mouth opened, and his jaw jutted out. Then his breathing sped up, causing his chest to rise and fall rapidly. He looked like he was going to get sick as he tried to form words.

"Sophia!"

I turned toward the open door and stood up. "That's Tom. I guess it's time to go home." I returned the book to the shelf and walked to the door. "I like your room. See you Monday."

Very quickly, I found myself back downstairs and rolled my eyes as I saw Tom talking to Jason. "And you're staying out of trouble?"

"Yes, sir."

I couldn't help but smile behind Tom's back, earning a pointed look from Jason. "Tom? You ready or are you here for therapy too?" I got out of there quickly and waited in the car until he joined me.

"You survived, huh?" I folded my arms over my chest and stared out the window. I might have to live with him, but I didn't have to talk to him. "Look, Sophie, I'm—"

"Whatever, Tom. Can we just go now?"

࿐ • ࿐

I barricaded myself in my room for the rest of the night while Tom sat in his recliner watching some sporting event and drinking beer after beer. Around midnight I snuck downstairs for something to eat and found him passed out. Just perfect. I'd be happy when he had to sleep at the station.

Morning came quickly and I found myself waiting for Tom to leave. Finally, at a quarter to eight, he stumbled out to his car and took off. I wasted no time getting ready: Showering, brushing my teeth, dressing, checking my blood sugar, getting my insulin ready, eating, and packing a few things to eat just in case. By the time Jason arrived, I was bored out of my mind.

"It's about time," I said as I slipped into the passenger seat.

"Not my fault. Jerry wanted to have some kind of heart-to-heart talk with me this morning."

"About what?"

He smiled widely. "He knows you and I are…doing whatever it is we're doing."

"And?"

He licked his lips. "I'm not to get you pregnant and under no circumstances am I to sell you drugs."

I laughed. "Well, I agree about the pregnant thing, but I think the last part needs to be amended. How about we go with 'under no circumstances are you to sell me drugs and get caught?'"

"I like it. Oh, and he wants to know how many times you wash your hands a day."

"What?" I asked with a laugh.

"Yeah, it's his messed up OCD way of figuring out if you're worthy of his only son."

"Jeez. How do you stand that? Does he count how many times *you* wash *your* hands?"

"Yeah, he has a chart. He also stands next to me half the time, reminding me how long to wash, how to properly get under my nails, and how even if I washed, I still need to sanitize right after just to be sure. Oh! And he goes nuts if I touch the handles of the faucet without using towel."

"Damn."

"Yeah. You get used to it after a while. The color-coded towels and washcloths are annoying though. I always forget which is which and it puts his whole day into a tailspin."

"How can he go hiking or rock climbing with all those phobias?"

"He can't anymore. He hasn't been outside of the house in years. The doctor visits him at home along with a social worker who asks me a bunch of idiotic questions about how my dad's OCD makes me 'feel.' If his friends want to see him, they come over. As long as he's on his meds, he's okay, but we still have to clean and disinfect for hours after someone's visited."

"So the other day when I was over, he was hiding in his room because he was afraid I'd infect him. Did you have to clean after I left?"

"Yep," he answered, his face conveying how tedious he found it all. "But since you were mainly in my bedroom, it wasn't that bad. He never goes in my room."

I was uncomfortable with learning anymore about Jason and his dad, so I remained silent. It only took a few minutes to drive to where we'd be hiking. I didn't care how long it took because I was with Jason, and being with him held the promise of certain things that I really, really wanted right now.

We'd only been walking a few minutes before he asked, "So what did you think of the thing last night?"

"What? The Damascus Friday Night Screw-Up Club?" I rolled my eyes. "It was super awesome."

"How was your alone-time with Robin?"

"Who?" I pretended I didn't understand. "Oh, you mean 'Bitch Wallace?'"

"Guess that sums it up, doesn't it?" He looked around and then copped a squat next to a tree. I mirrored his actions and watched as he pulled out his little sack of green and plucked a paper from the pack. "Just a word of advice; the more you tell her, lies or not, the less likely she'll out you in front of everyone."

I sighed heavily, but felt marginally better when he passed me the joint. "The whole thing's so dumb."

"Yeah, but you have to do it."

I quirked an eyebrow and tried to keep the hit in for as long as I possibly could. "So why are you there?" I exhaled slowly.

"Tom," he said quickly. "He knows how dependent Jerry is on me, so he makes nice with the police on my behalf. Jesus, what the hell would my old man do if I wasn't there to wash his clothes, cook him dinner, or keep his house clean? Just because he's OCD doesn't mean he can do all of the cleaning he has to do to feel comfortable. That would mean touching the toilet and dirty silverware. I could just imagine Jerry lying on the floor after one of his benders and not being able to pick his sorry ass up, freaking out about the creepy-crawly flesh-eating germs covering his body from our obviously-infected linoleum."

So Jerry was a drinker too. I wondered how alcohol affected his already heavily-medicated body. Perhaps he and Tom have old-guy keg parties. Then I realized that together they were "Tom and Jerry." I stifled a laugh.

Jason said nothing, so we sat in silence, finishing the joint. It wasn't until he'd sprawled out on the dirty, leaf-covered ground that he asked, "So how was your time with Dalton?" His voice was light, as if he thought it was funny that Rusty Dalton was my partner.

"He's all right." Jason snickered. "What?" He opened his eyes and gave me a disbelieving look. Despite my numbing high, my body tensed in preparation for him to say some negative shit about the boy with the stutter. I actually kind of liked him. He was unassuming and it was obvious that the cards he'd been dealt sucked beyond the telling.

"It's just that…Never mind."

"What?"

"He's fucking weird, Sophie."

"So are you, but I still hang out with your dirty ass."

"My ass is *not* dirty. Elliott's all socially stupid and shit. I mean, the kid never talks and when he does, it's all da-da-da and ma-ma-ma and I-I-I-I c-c-c-c-can't taaaaaalk l-l-l-like a n-n-n-n-normal human being."

Okay, so I totally wasn't impressed with Jason's capacity for compassion. "Wow. I didn't know you were such a prick, Jace."

He sat up and shot me a dirty look. "I'm not being a prick; I'm simply stating the facts. When they first got here, you should have seen him. One time, I swear to God, the teacher found him hiding under his desk."

I had no idea about the hiding thing, but it was ridiculous for Jason to be so mean because he had a stutter. "Maybe he has a hard time talking because he knows dickheads like you judge him for something he can't help. Who cares about any of that anyway? He's still a person. He has a mind and soul, and deserves to be treated like a human instead of some—"

Jason laughed. "Oh my God! Sophie, you're in love with the retarded Dalton kid, aren't you?"

I shot him a glare. Of course I wasn't in love with him, but it pissed me off that Jason would call him retarded just because he stuttered. "Fuck you."

I stood up, but he grabbed my wrist and roughly yanked me back down. Just as I hit the ground, he ensnared me in his arms, pulling me down and pressing me against him. I tensed for a moment, but worked to relax. I straddled him, his hold on me unrelenting.

"Don't be mad, Sophie. Feel free to make fun of me about having to spend time with Olivia. If you want to get to know a true Damascus Screw-Up, spend some time with her. She can't even kill herself properly. Like she didn't know in order to bleed out quickly, you have to hit an artery." He looked disgusted, but stopped talking.

"Don't be mean, Jason."

"Don't be bossy, Sophie." Then his mouth was on my neck. "Don't I owe you some good forest sex?"

Chapter 5

Lab Rat

Elliott

She had been in my room. She'd touched my books and we had what could have been considered an actual conversation, especially for me. I'd been proud of myself for not being a complete freak about it, but then she just looked at me and, much to my horror, asked me why I let Anderson treat me like he did. As if I had a choice.

I agonized over that question for the rest of the night. After everyone left, Robin thought it would be a good time for us to have our official session. We were in Stephen's study just like every Friday night. It was incredibly unfair that I had to have a session every week when nobody else did. She and Stephen must have thought I was pretty far gone.

"So, Sophie's nice, isn't she?" Of course she'd want to talk about Sophie. I nodded. "I noticed that you two didn't stay downstairs." I shook my head. I supposed she got those keen observational skills from her many years in college. "Did you show her your bedroom?"

I narrowed my eyes. "Th-th-the door wwwas o-open th-the entire t-t-time." I had done that intentionally, even though a closed door would have made me much more comfortable.

She smiled. "Thank you, but I'm not really worried about that. It's your house and you're allowed to have guests in your room if you wish. I'm just surprised. From what Stephen tells me, you don't allow people in your room."

"S-sh-she likes b-b-books," I said, by way of explanation.

"That's wonderful. Did you two have a nice conversation?" I blatantly rolled my eyes and motioned to my mouth and throat. Obviously I didn't have a good conversation with her, due to my inability to actually talk like a normal person.

"Elliott," Robin said, "there will come a point in your life when you can't blame your speech impediment for everything." She used that soft motherly tone that reminded me why I probably never got anywhere in therapy. We were too close and too comfortable with one another.

Usually my emotions were held very squarely in check to avoid my blowing up and subsequently sounding like a moron when I couldn't manage to have a proper tirade. However, right now I was about to explode. How could this woman sit here and tell me I couldn't blame my stuttering for not being able to communicate effectively? She had *no idea* what it was like to have a million thoughts you wanted to share, but couldn't because of some physiological or mental glitch. My hands balled into fists and I pressed them into my thighs.

I tried to let Tchaikovsky's *Song Without Words* run through my mind to soothe me, but how could she think that I wouldn't want to have a normal conversation with a pretty girl my age? How could she imply that I didn't even make an attempt? She knew I sat up every night reading children's books aloud, trying to harness my voice and get rid of my impediment. Why did she have to keep pulling and tugging at me so much? David and Rebecca were most likely having sex right now, Trent was probably in the midst of doing something far more reproachable to Jane than I could even think about, and yet here she was telling me that I use my stuttering as a crutch to avoid people.

"I-I-I d-d-d-doooon't b-b-bl-bl-blame…" I couldn't manage to get the rest of my words out. They were blocked.

She cocked her head and looked at me like I was a four-year-old. "Elliott, I'm sorry if I upset you. That wasn't my intention. I know and understand your stuttering is something that's not your fault and you can't control it. However, please understand that I also know your history and I'm aware that with or without your stuttering, you would still avoid building relationships with people."

I kept my hands clenched. I would not be talking about all of this again tonight. Wasn't it enough that I'd let Sophie into my room and at least *tried* to talk with her?

"It took you a *very* long time to form a bond with David and Stephen."

"Th-they're d-dif-different. W-w-with J-J-JJane, I—"

"Yes. I understand the difference, but even though you've finally accepted them as family, you still don't allow them to touch your things or enter your room. You still keep them at a distance."

I was feeling defiant, so I shrugged. "M-m-maybe I just dddon't l-l-like them."

Much to my dismay, Robin smiled at me. "I know you like them, but you refuse to allow yourself to grow any closer to them because you have a fear that everyone you love will either leave you or hurt you."

"Th-that's n-not t-t-t-t…" I stopped and sighed. I usually didn't argue with adults. I was raised to respect authority figures and not talk back, but in my sessions, I realized the rules had changed. Robin *wanted* me to express myself.

"If it's not true, Elliott, let's talk about your mother."

"N-no!" Now I was sorry I opened my mouth at all.

"What about your father? Would you care to talk about him?" My whole body felt so tight, I thought it would snap at any moment and break. I tried to keep the emotions down, but the tears burned my eyes, though I refused to let them fall. I shook my head. "So you still don't want to talk about your mom and you don't want to talk about your father. Should we talk about Joseph?"

My chest tightened and my lungs seized. "D-d-don't," I begged, unable to keep my tears back now. I didn't understand why she was being so cruel. Instinctively, I drew my legs up to my chest and wrapped my arms around them. I couldn't breathe and fought hard against the instinct to crawl under a table. My heart felt like it was going to thump right out of my chest. "P-p-please, d-d-dddon't."

"I know this is difficult, Elliott. I can see that it causes you an extreme amount of stress and anxiety, but you cannot let this rule your life. You keep so much of yourself hidden that it will only fester inside and break you. You've never said anything about him in all our…" I started to feel lightheaded and my body began to tingle. She was still speaking, but I was only vaguely aware of her coming over and putting one hand on my arm, and the other on my forehead. "You need to relax, Elliott. No one is going to hurt you here."

At some point, Stephen came into the room. I could barely focus on anything, but somehow through the haze of panic, I recognized his gray-speckled dark hair. Being around men when I was in this state never really helped anything. My panic attacks always seemed less intense when men weren't around. Then I felt something sharp jab into my arm and slowly began to realize, as my body relaxed, that he'd given me a sedative. Finally, I was able to breathe and the tears drained from my eyes.

There was no way to measure how long it had been from the onset of the attack to the point where I was finally able to stand up by myself, but I had a feeling it had been a good chunk of time. I licked my lips and moved to the door. "I-I'm gggggoooing to sssleeeep now."

My legs shook and I wobbled. Stephen offered me assistance, holding out his arm to steady me, but instead I placed my hand on the wall and waited until I felt sturdier.

Very, very slowly, I went into the hallway, too sedated to care much that David, Rebecca, Jane, and Trent were there too. I hadn't realized I'd made enough noise to alert them. Using the wall as a guide, I kept my eyes on the floor as I walked to my room. Once inside, I locked the door and grabbed my iPod. I flopped down onto my bed, put the ear buds in, and found my Classical playlist as I closed my eyes and concentrated on my breathing. In and out. In and out.

But as I lay there, my body nearly helplessly sedated, my mind moved back to Sophie's question about Anderson. The answer was inextricably linked to what just happened in Stephen's study.

I was unbelievably thankful when sleep finally overtook me, rescuing me from my wandering mind.

~ • ~

On Saturday, I was awakened by soft knocks on my door. My head hurt and my body felt heavy as I rolled out of bed and stumbled to the door. Jane waited on the other side, giving me a small smile. "It's noon and Stephen said you need to eat something."

"I-I'm not h-hungry." I sounded tired, even to myself.

Jane nodded. "I told him you'd say that, but you have to come out sometime. He's going to leave for the hospital soon, so make an appearance, eat something, and then you'll be free to lie around until Monday morning. If you don't, he'll just call Robin." I sighed as I came out and closed the door. Her smile faltered and she reached up to run a hand through my hair. "It'll be okay, Elliott."

That was what she said all the time. But we both knew that wasn't true, because "okay" wasn't something people like us ever got to be.

Reluctantly, I went downstairs and had lunch with my family, but not before Stephen looked me over. There were times when it was really useful to have a doctor in the house. Like the time Jane "accidentally" cut herself while attempting to recreate a Bobby Flay dish, or when David dislocated his shoulder playing football with his jock friends in the backyard, or when I was sick with the flu, even though I *hated* the medicine he made me take.

Today, though, I was annoyed that Jane and David were watching me as I sat at the island on a kitchen stool while Stephen took my temperature, examined my ears and eyes, and tested my reflexes. While he checked my blood pressure, he asked all of the normal doctor questions like how I'd slept, how I felt, and if anything was bothering me. As usual, I kept my answers short. Afterward, he held my face between his hands and looked directly into my eyes, as though he was *searching* for something, and they would somehow give him the secrets of deconstructing Elliott.

After a long moment, it became really uncomfortable, so I averted my eyes and grabbed his wrists to pull his hands away. Nothing like being a lab rat first thing in the morning.

I ate my sandwich and listened as Stephen and David discussed whatever sport interested them at the moment. I thought it was basketball, but I could never keep track. David had practice this afternoon and then was taking Rebecca shopping. I could tell Jane desperately wanted to be included. It was moderately amusing to see David casually ignore Jane's pleading eyes.

It wasn't until Stephen stood and glanced at his watch that David finally asked her if she'd like to go to Gaithersburg with them. Jane let out a squeal of delight she'd been containing, and clapped her hands like a three-year-old about to take a trip to the ice cream parlor. After Stephen gave her the speech about the importance of thrift and knowing the credit card limit, all eyes turned to me.

"Please go with us," Jane begged.

I just shook my head, my eyes squarely on Stephen, hoping he wouldn't make me. I could see the dilemma working itself out inside his brain. If he made me go, I would most likely have another attack and since I'd had one on Monday, and then another one last night, he had to figure it would be too much stress for my body to handle. Then again, he also hated leaving me alone.

Just thinking about that made me upset. I'd been with Stephen for five years and I had never done anything to harm myself or others, or his property. All I wanted was a moment's peace in my own house, and I didn't understand why he always had to make such a big deal out of leaving me alone.

"All right, Elliott," he said with a sigh. "But keep your phone on, and if you need anything, page me."

He turned to David. "How long do you expect to be gone?"

David gave me one of his signature pitying looks, and then addressed Stephen. "Maybe eight or nine? He'll be fine, Dad." He turned to Jane. "Be ready by four. Becca can't stand to be kept waiting."

Jane sighed. "As if we don't already know that."

Finally, Stephen and David left. I rinsed my plate and put it in the dishwasher, marginally happier now that I would have at least three or four hours to myself. I could play the Grand Piano or even sing if I wanted to. Not that I ever had, but Ms. Rice had told me once that people who stutter could usually sing without impediment. Well, at least most of them could. I was interested in hearing my voice stutter-free.

"Want to watch TV?" I turned to find Jane behind me, and shook my head. "Please? Don't spend the rest of the weekend in your room. If you're not going shopping with us, then at least spend a little time with me." I sighed and she smiled, knowing that she was the one person I couldn't say no to, especially when she started pouting. "Yay! We can listen to music instead."

So I found myself lying on the floor with Jane, no lights on, as the sounds of her favorite New-Age musician filled the room. The weather was overcast so without lights, the living room was dim enough to be comfortable and relaxing. Typically, I found some of this music a little "out there," but this CD was nice and soothing. It was peaceful to lie on the floor and stare up at the ceiling, not feeling pressured to think about anything in particular.

"Elliott," Jane broke the silence, her voice very soft and soothing like the music, "what happened last night?"

I sighed. Jane wasn't really being nosey just to be nosey; she was just a curious person and I couldn't fault her for it either. We met when we were eleven, and even though we'd only known each other less than six years, she was the closest thing I had to family. From the moment I met her in our foster home, she was my best friend. If there was anyone in the world I could talk to, it was Jane.

"S-she asked a-a-bout mmmy p-parents and J-J-J-Joseph."

She rolled onto her side, facing me, and ran her hand through my hair. Almost instantly, I closed my eyes, bracing for the tears. I didn't want to cry, but Jane had a way of making me feel safe enough to do it.

"So did you tell her anything?"

I shook my head. I'd been too busy freaking out and failing to get adequate air into my lungs. "S-she already kn-knows. Sh-she haaaas th-the files."

"Maybe, but Robin likes it when she can get you to have a breakthrough. She's supposed to push."

"Y-y-you t-t-t-tell hhhher things?" I turned to look at her.

She shrugged. "It's easier that way."

"Sh-she asks a-a-about your p-p-past?"

"Yeah, but I can't help her with that so much, you know? If I can't remember it, I can't talk about it. We talk about things like shopping or movies, and when I zone out, she asks me questions." I narrowed my eyes and she shrugged again. "I guess I talk because when I come back, she's got pages of notes and she brings it up in our next session."

"D-do you liiiike th-that?" I asked, because I knew I wouldn't like having someone talk to me when I was basically not there mentally.

"Not really. There are some things that are meant to stay in the past. I don't need to know about them." Her hand stopped its movement in my hair and she lay back down again. "One of my old therapists said once that old wounds are the hardest to heal and the scars they leave are the most painful," Jane sighed and let her eyes slowly close, "so I'm not really in a rush to remember my old wounds."

We continued to lie on the plush carpet, not really speaking, and more just enjoying each other's quiet company. Finally she had to get ready and I sat down at the Grand Piano and played for nearly two hours, nodding to Jane as she ran for the front door, as fast as she could go. David's constant honking distracted me, causing me to shift from one of my most soothing compositions, to something rather aggressive and violent.

The phone rang. It was Stephen checking up on me. I hated talking on the phone. My stuttering never seemed to improve, even though it wasn't face-to-face contact. It took me nearly three minutes to spit out that I was fine. I wondered what he thought could happen to me in a few short hours.

It didn't take me long to migrate back up to where I was most comfortable; my room. I'd been strumming my guitar mindlessly, letting my fingers find a melody while I let my mind go blank. It was pleasant, listening to the music I was producing without really thinking about anything. This was why I liked music. Depending on my mood, it could either have a lot of meaning, or none at all. I'd been at it for a while before any coherent thought passed through my mind and when it did, I was surprised that it was about Sophie Young.

I wondered what she was doing with her weekend and why it was that Robin and Stephen seemed to think her past was similar to mine. I hoped it wasn't. I didn't think it could be. She didn't seem to have any problems engaging people socially, and exuded confidence in all of her actions. The only negative trait I could find was her association with Jason Fox and her obvious use of the "product" he sold.

I couldn't deny that I would have preferred she not hang out with him, but I couldn't very well expect her to spend time with me when she didn't have to. I mean, my company left a lot to be desired.

If I was normal, we could talk about books, and I could…

I needed to stop. This was a waste of time. I thought I'd killed the part of me which dreamt of magically being different, but every once in a while, it popped back up and I was shoved back into reality once more. Of course, part of me wished that Sophie and I could be like David and Rebecca, or Trent and Jane, but Sophie liked boys who could talk and converse - who were normal.

Setting down my guitar, I lied back down on my bed again and let myself wish that I was someone else. It was unfair that not only had God given me the inability to speak fluently, but also saddled me with one of the worst childhoods anyone could imagine. I was happy to have Stephen take me in, that was for sure, but there was no erasing the past.

Jane's old therapist was right. Old wounds were hard to heal and what's left behind hurts. It wasn't like I didn't want to heal, because I did. I knew that I would stutter with or without the emotional baggage that came along with a childhood like mine, but it would help if I didn't have so many things nagging inside my head all the time.

I could live with the stutter if I could give back the past, but I couldn't help thinking that if I didn't stutter, I could better deal with my past. My stutter kept me isolated. I knew most of the students at school thought I was mentally challenged as opposed to just verbally challenged. My stuttering brought forth my social ineptitude, and they interpreted it as a mental deficiency. There were occasions when I'd been able to do something close to socializing with someone outside of my family, but it hadn't lasted long. Usually I found out they did it on a bet.

That's why Robin and Stephen's expectations concerning Sophie had me worried. What was her motivation for getting to know me? Why would anyone want to put that much work into getting to know someone like me? I mean, I actually felt bad for people who had to sit and wait for my mouth to catch up with my mind.

I fell asleep before anyone came home, but was woken up by David banging on the door. I responded with "Wh-wh-what?"

"Nothing," he said, and then "No, Dad, he was just sleeping. He's fine." Obviously Stephen called him to ensure I was okay. I seriously didn't understand why he was always so worried.

Chapter 6

Down

Elliott

I spent Sunday in my room, only emerging to eat. Stephen tried to engage me in conversation, but I just wasn't up for it. I shrugged, nodded, and shook my head in answer to all his questions.

This morning, just like every weekday morning, I awoke to David pounding on the bathroom door. Remembering his trick of wiggling the doorknob, I got out of bed and flung open my door. "Morning, Sunshine," David beamed.

The ride was no different than any other day. To be completely honest, I'd really wanted to stay home, but that would never happen. The highlight of my morning, however, was when I passed Sophie in the hall, this time without having some kind of incident with Anderson, and she smiled at me. It was just a second or two, but it was a real smile. The only bad thing was that I didn't get to smile back.

For the remainder of the morning, I wondered how her weekend had gone and what she had done. But by the end of lunch, when I saw her leaving the cafeteria just moments after Jason Fox, I realized that her weekend had probably included him. It disturbed me and then I felt ridiculous for feeling that way just because Sophie had most likely hung out with her friend. I didn't *own* her. She wasn't mine, she wasn't going to me mine, and she wasn't even my friend. She was being forced to spend time with me.

I just wished she was my friend.

When Horticulture rolled around, I was feeling incredibly down. She was late again, giving an obviously fake apologetic glance at Mr. Reese before slipping into her seat next to me. For whatever reason, my mood had turned angry. I wasn't really upset with *her*, but more with my inadequacies as a human being. She turned to me and shot me a small smile. "Hey."

I sighed and gave her a nod, thinking that if I attempted a verbal greeting, it would sound stupid or hostile, or not come out all. She leaned a little closer, taking a peek at my notes, and that annoyed me. It wasn't fair for her to use me simply because she was too busy doing whatever it was she did with Jason. "Did I miss much?"

My jaw clenched. "N-n-no," was all I managed to get out, but then I grudgingly slid my notebook closer to her so she could copy my notes, because honestly, it wasn't her fault I was so incredibly socially defunct and undesirable.

I tried to pay attention to what Reese was saying, but since I'd given my notebook to Sophie, and couldn't take notes, there was little point in it. After a few minutes, she slid the notebook back and I readjusted it and looked down. She'd written "Thanks!" in the margin and drew a little smiley-face. As

I looked out the window, I wondered if Jason Fox got smiley faces. She didn't seem like a smiley-face kind of girl.

The rest of the class went by in a blur. All I did was stare out of the window. I wondered if people like Chris Anderson, Megan Simons, Aiden Montgomery, or even Connor Hamill realized how appealing their lives were. I wondered if they had a clue as to how much people like me coveted the ordinary, boring life they probably thought they were living.

I had to stop. If I didn't snap out of this mood soon, Stephen would notice and then he'd make me talk to Robin before Friday. Tomorrow was another session with Ms. Rice. I might implode if I had to have sessions with both Ms. Rice *and* Robin.

The bell rang, startling me. I looked down at my notes with the smiley face and realized I hadn't written anything else. I would have to get them from Jane tonight. I slammed it closed and shoved it into my bag, along with the textbook. "You okay?"

Turning to my right, I found Sophie looking at me, her mouth twisted up and her eyebrows knitted together as if she were trying to figure out a puzzle. She was incredibly pretty. Too pretty for me to look at, too pretty for me to talk to, and definitely too pretty to even imagine her wanting to know me. "F-f-fine."

"Fine? Fine, like, you're fine or fine like, you're agreeing that you're okay, or fine like…"

I sighed as I stood, swinging my bag up onto my shoulder. "I-I-I'm f-ffffine, S-S-S-SSSS…"

At that point, Chris Anderson noticed I hadn't left the room and was talking with Sophie, so of course, he came over, shoved me, and said, "*So-phie*. It's not that fucking difficult, you 'tard."

He'd shoved me into the table behind me, forcing me to sit down on it. The table squeaked and the feet scraped against the floor loudly, which only drew more attention to the scene. My thigh hit the edge of the table and while I hadn't thought Anderson shoved me that hard, I could feel the heat of the impact down my leg.

"Why do you have to be such a dick?"

For a quick moment, I closed my eyes and took a deep breath. What a perfect situation. Yet again Sophie was defending me, so not only was I not a normal person, I was also an emasculated, non-normal person. Opening my eyes, I stood up straight and pulled my bag back up my shoulder as I tried to slip out behind her.

"For Christ's sake, while I think having pity on the less fortunate is admirable, he can't even say your fucking name."

"So that makes it okay to physically assault him?"

I had extracted myself from behind Sophie, but as I was walking away, leaving them to continue their argument, I felt fingers encircle my wrist. Immediately I looked down to where Sophie had a hold of me. "He's a *person*."

"Not much of one."

I barely looked at her as I pulled my arm free. With a deadly glare, she looked at Anderson, her face flushed. As soon as she turned to me, though, her face softened and she got the same look of pity that I'd seen a thousand times before. "S-st-st-stop."

Anderson laughed as I hurriedly left the classroom. "Yeah, S-S-Sophie, just s-s-s-st-st-stop!"

Ms. Peters saw my face and didn't make me do anything for my final period. I just sat in her tiny little office, sinking further and further down into the old armchair in the corner. The final bell rang, but I continued to sit there a few more minutes. As usual, David would make us wait, and I didn't look forward to sitting in the Scout with Jane. She would try to talk to me and I was in no mood for talking.

Most of the students were gone by the time I walked through the parking lot. My whole body tensed even more when I saw David's Scout. Jane sat on the bumper with Trent standing between her legs, while David was sprawled atop Rebecca on the hood of her car. There were times when I didn't mind their very public displays of affection, and then there were times like now when I wished I could just burn my eyes out to avoid having to witness it. As I moved closer, I realized that I would have to burst my ear drums as well, since they weren't the quietest bunch.

None of them even realized I was there until I opened the door, slid into the back seat, and slammed it loudly. It was another five minutes of "ohs" and "uhs" and "damn babies" before David and Jane extracted themselves from their respective partners and decided it was time to leave. I sat perfectly still, my eyes fixed on the clock in the dashboard as they hopped in, both rubbing their mouths and straightening their clothing out. It was disgusting.

"Hey, Elliott," Jane said happily, but I didn't respond or even react. I was upset and angry. I knew they didn't deserve to be on the receiving end of my anger, but I had no other outlet. I didn't want to talk to them and they couldn't make me.

"What's up, bro?"

I continued to stare at the clock as the time changed and wondered how long it would take my two genius siblings to figure out I wasn't talking. "What happened today?" For a moment, my eyes flicked to Jane, but I recovered quickly, moving them back to the clock. I hated how transparent I seemed to be.

"Elliott, don't be an ass."

I didn't respond. David had no choice but to start the car and drive home.

~ • ~

Tuesday was even worse. Sophie smiled at me in the hall again. Unfortunately, today Anderson made it a point to be waiting for me and gave me another signature shoulder shove. Typically, they didn't hurt all that much, but this time he didn't just connect with my side, but with my ribs. I spent most of the day pretending that it didn't hurt, and trying to convince myself of that fact.

In Study Hall, David asked me about it. Obviously one of his friends ran and told him. Even though I didn't confirm what happened, he spent the next fifteen minutes coming up with plans to make Anderson bleed without getting himself expelled. He said all of this in front of Trent and Rebecca. I didn't need to see the pity in their eyes to know they were thinking about how utterly useless I was.

I allowed myself a quick glance up at Sophie's table and followed her eyes over to Jason Fox. He would be getting up soon and she would be following him again. I didn't want to see it, so I left the library early, not bothering to look behind me when Jane called my name. I spent the remainder of the period and all of lunch in Mr. Reese's empty greenhouse, separating and categorizing seeds for him.

Sophie didn't even bother coming to class.

Ms. Rice was as determined as ever, even after I told her that I didn't want to practice. I had my whole silent thing going and hadn't spoken in about twenty-four hours. It worked for me, but she made me speak anyway, and simple sentences left my mouth that sounded like Dr. Seuss on a carnival ride.

Four-year-old kids everywhere could say that sentence just fine, but it stuck in my mouth, instantly making it abundantly clear that I couldn't speak; I couldn't be normal; I couldn't do anything right.

My ribs hurt as I shifted in my chair.

Wednesday proceeded in much in the same fashion as the day before, except that I didn't look up from the tiled floor to see if Sophie smiled at me in the hall, and I walked faster than I usually did, trying to outrun Anderson. But he was persistent, so I couldn't really avoid him. This time it was the "send Elliott's books and bag flying and laugh" game. It was just as humiliating, yet I didn't have to acquire another bruise for it.

David had been stalking Anderson all day and was around the corner when it happened, making me feel like even less of a man than when I woke up. I skipped Study Hall and lunch and spent the hour in the greenhouse again, my head pillowed on my arms as I stared out the window.

Sophie was on time today. Before she could say anything, I pushed yesterday's notes toward her and turned away to stare out of the window again. When the bell rang, I grabbed my notebook and flew out of the classroom, anxious not to be harassed again by Anderson because I was speaking to Sophie.

Wednesday night, Stephen again tried to engage me in conversation and after failing, he gave a few pointed looks at Jane and David. They disappeared upstairs and within a half an hour, Robin was at our house, looking at me like I was a lab rat again. Instead of making me go upstairs into Stephen's study to have a session, Robin spoke to me downstairs, while Stephen remained in the room.

"So how are you, Elliott?" I shrugged. "Not talking again, I see. I thought we'd pushed through all that." No, *she* had. I'd merely been in the room when she'd her own little "breakthrough" she was calling mine. I didn't want to talk. I didn't have to and I wouldn't.

After a sideways glance at Stephen, Robin smiled at me. "You have your entire family worried." I sighed, not knowing how I was supposed to respond to that. Of course I knew they were worried, and as much as I cared for each of them, it didn't bother me. I was allowed to have my own feelings, wasn't I? I wasn't supposed to put on the act of the good son, was I? That was David's role. "Would you like to play the piano, Elliott?" I shook my head.

"Son, please." At his soft plea, I closed my eyes. I wished that I could be like David for him. I wished he could truly help me the way he wanted to. I wished that I could be close to him and I wished that I was normal for him. It was heartbreaking enough to know I would never truly be comfortable around him simply because of his role as a father and authority figure, and also his gender, but it tore at me that I couldn't even engage him in simple conversation.

I scratched idly at Stephen's expensive dining room table, keeping my head down. I was suddenly very tired and although I heard their voices, nothing really registered in my brain. The skin on my forehead stretched as I held my head, the gravity pulling it toward the table. I breathed deeply, trying to calm and center myself. "I-I w-w-would liiiiike t-t-t-o go, go t-t-to bed now." As Ms. Rice would say, at least I finished strong.

On Thursday morning, I was fully prepared to stay in bed and ignore David's booming voice, but again he pulled the jiggle-the-doorknob-trick, which instantly caused my body to produce an excessive amount of fear-induced adrenaline.

I wasn't surprised when David silently accompanied me to my locker before first period, and then walked me to class. He was protective like that, even if it meant making me feel like a bigger baby for letting him play my personal bodyguard for the day. I hadn't slept much the night before, so I didn't have much fight left in me. Besides, it seemed like a better option to have David hawk me than to be shoved into the lockers again.

"Sophie," he whispered. I looked up at him, wondering why he would say her name, but he just nodded in front of him. "I'll see you in Study Hall."

When he left, I looked up and there was Sophie, standing outside of my first period class, her eyes directly fixed upon me. I felt trapped. I didn't think I could walk into class without acknowledging her, and I didn't necessarily want to, but I was still feeling irrational resentment toward her. What if I accidentally spewed that resentment and she saw how truly vile I was?

Then I remembered my inability to speak like a normal person. She came over and my feet stopped. "Hi."

I nodded to her. "H-hhhi."

Taking a deep breath, she cocked her head as she looked up at me. "So, there's this foreign film festival in D.C. this weekend…" she paused for a moment. "…Well, all next week too, but this Saturday is Russian movies and they're going to play *Prisoner of the Mountains*, which is based on Tolstoy's *Prisoner of the Caucasus* and also *Anna Karenina* from like the early 1900's, and I know it's not all dark and tortured, but I was wondering if you wanted to go."

My brain attempted to process the information. I was still stuck on Russian movies before I noticed her looking around nervously. Maybe she didn't want to be seen with me and I was supposed to answer quickly. I was pretty sure she was asking me to go to Washington D.C. with her on Saturday and for a moment, my heart quickened as I thought about spending time with her. She wasn't even being forced into doing it.

I opened my mouth to answer, but the block formed and I closed it again. My fists clenched at my sides and I hoped that Anderson wasn't around to watch this, because if he was, I would pay for my inability to get out a simple "yes." I opened my mouth again, meaning to respond, but all that came out was something that sounded like "da-da-da, na-na", which wasn't even close to the three simple letters I needed. I knew that I looked like an idiot, my face twitching as I tried to force the word.

She put her hand on my arm and I stopped trying to speak and simply looked at her. "Elliott," she said with a smile, "just shake your head for no, or nod for yes."

I wondered if she thought I was an idiot. I felt like one, but I pushed all of the negative thoughts away and nodded, frantically. Then finally, my mouth cooperated, and I was able to mutter, "Y-y-yeessss."

Her smile seemed to grow bigger and I felt my heart pound in my chest. "Good. I hope you have a car, because I don't, but I can totally chip in for gas."

I shook my head and wanted to tell her that she didn't have to because I would be more than happy to drive her anywhere she wanted to go. For once, I was thankful for my mouth not being able to comply. I would have sounded so dumb.

"You don't have a car?"

"N-n-no, I-I-I ddddo. I-I-I just d-d-d-don't neeeeed g-g-gas money."

She smiled again, gave me a little nod, and went to move past me, but then stopped. When she turned back, her forehead was creased and she was chewing on her bottom lip. "Not that you think it is, but I just want you to know this isn't, like, a date or anything. I don't..." Her voice trailed off and she sucked on her bottom lip again as she tucked her hair behind her ears. "I don't really date and I don't do the whole girlfriend thing, so don't…I mean, like I said, not that you are, but don't expect like…romantic anything. We're just two people who like Russian novels, watching Russian movies, okay?"

I nodded and I couldn't help but smile a little. She gave me a parting nod before turning and walking away.

I was fine with it because the pressure of a date would have been crushing. There was no way that I could expect her to want something romantic from someone like me. Just two people who like Russian stuff. I could handle that, although I hoped the theater wasn't packed. I didn't want to have a panic attack in front of her. She didn't ask Anderson to go to D.C. with her. This brightened my mood.

The day flew by and I was surprisingly happy. It seemed that my inability to be a normal human hadn't stopped Sophie from wanting to go to the movies with me. Even at lunch, when Sophie followed Jason Fox out of the cafeteria, my mood stayed positive because she hadn't invited Jason either. She'd asked *me*.

When she arrived twenty minutes late to Biology, I put my notebook in the middle of the desk and took notes on another sheet of paper. She, Sophie Young, the talk of the high school, had asked *me*, Elliott Dalton, the outcast, to go to D.C. with her on Saturday.

Even my inadequacies with reading children's books with Ms. Rice didn't spoil my good mood. Of course, Jane and David were extremely interested in what Sophie wanted and since I gave them no information during the day, they were waiting to accost me on the ride home. David had practice, so he wanted information as quickly as possible so he could get back.

I wasn't purposely keeping information to myself, but it would be easier to not stutter and stammer my way through it more than once. I still needed to get Stephen to give me the okay, which meant asking him tonight when he got home. David and Jane would get the story then.

Before I could even taste the enchiladas Stephen brought home for dinner, Jane bounced in her chair and said, "Sophie talked to Elliott this morning and he won't tell us what it was about. Make him."

I tried to ignore her while shoving in a small bite of the food. David looked highly amused as his eyes danced around the table, taking us all in one-by-one. I looked at Stephen and while his expression was one of curiosity, he addressed Jane. "Perhaps it's not our business to know. Elliott doesn't make you tell him what you and Trent talk about, does he?"

Jane could barely contain herself as she obviously wanted to know what was going on. It was oddly satisfying to be able to keep something from her. "But Sophie's not Trent, and Elliott's not me. Elliott barely talks to anyone and now…"

I sighed. I hadn't wanted this conversation to be dictated by someone else. I looked at Stephen and set down my fork, but the moment I opened my mouth, it was apparent that I wasn't going to be able to push the words out. I thought about music and heard the composition I'd been working on in my head. When I looked back up, I saw that Stephen was patiently waiting, Jane was quivering with excitement, and David looked more amused than he should. "S-sh-she w-w-wants tttto go ttto a f-f-f-fo-fo-fo…a couple of m-m-movies w-with mme on SSSaturday."

I was relieved to finally have it out and did my best to ignore Jane's childlike clapping and David's not-so-subtle grin. "That's great. Which movie?"

This was going to be the part Stephen didn't like. He thought we were going to Frederick or Germantown to watch a regular movie. "T-th-there's a f-f-film f-f-fest…"

Stephen's eyes widened and he set down his fork, giving me the look I hated. "The foreign film festival in D.C.?" I swallowed hard, the tone of his voice scaring me. Nodding, I tried to stay positive, even though fear was clutching me tightly. He looked at me in silence for a moment longer before twining his hands together in front of him. "No. Absolutely not."

I was about ready to protest when Jane huffed, "That's not fair, Stephen. Why can't he go?"

He turned his cool gaze to her. "It's over an hour away, Jane. It would be an all-day trip and…"

"Dad, Elliott's a safe driver and he never gets in trouble *ever*, and it seems a little unfair to tell him he can't go simply because it's far away. We live in B.F.E.; *nothing's* close."

Stephen sighed and rubbed his temples. "He'll be away from anyone who can help if he has a panic attack." He paused, thinking. "D.C. is such a large city and the crime rate's… Perhaps you can go with him, David." My jaw dropped. He was actually suggesting I needed a chaperone?

David laughed. "I can't cramp his style like that, old man. Don't you remember what it was like to be seventeen and on a date?"

"I-i-it's n-n-n-not a…ddddate." Stephen turned his focus back to me. "I-I-I w-w-won't p-p-p-p," the word "panic" stuck in my throat and I realized with all my stammering, I would never be convincing. I tried again anyway, "P-p-panic." I locked eyes with him as I took deep breaths, hoping that he could see that this was important to me. I never asked for anything and I never caused trouble. "P-p-p-please?"

He was silent and then he let out an elongated sigh. As soon as he opened his mouth, I could tell what was coming and excitement filled every part of my body. I almost bounced like Jane. "You will have your cell phone on you at all times. You will let Sophie know that my number is on speed dial. You will tell her about your attacks and indicate that should the situation arise, she's to call 9-1-1 and then call me, understand?" I nodded. "And you will call in every hour to let me know you're okay."

"B-b-but we'll b-b-be wwwwwatching a m-movie," I complained, pushing my luck.

"Fine. Every two hours." Stephen picked up his fork and pointed at my dinner. "Now eat."

David clapped his hands once and made me jump. "Look, he's smiling! Dad, when was the last time you saw him smile?"

Chapter 7

Take Two

Sophie

My weekend consisted of Jason and boredom. While sex in the woods on Saturday was fantastic, on Sunday, Tom never left the house, so I had to come up with an excuse for going outside just to smoke a little pot.

The week started out just fine: class, Study Hall, smoking pot, and sex with Jace during lunch. But Rusty Dalton was acting strange. Not that I really knew what strange was for him, having known him all of a couple of days or whatever. Prick Anderson had shoved him, laughed at him and generally treated him like dirt. Perhaps it wasn't really my place to stand up to Chris like I did, but I couldn't help it.

Tuesday and Wednesday were the same. Rusty Dalton seemed…depressed. Of course, it could have stemmed from the full-on body-check Anderson had given him on Tuesday. I didn't see the whole thing, but it looked like it hurt.

I felt bad about not going to the greenhouse on Tuesday, but Jason and I had really gone at it and there was no way I could go to class looking the way I did. Wednesday, Rusty Dalton let me copy his notes, but he wouldn't look at me.

It was Wednesday night when I found the advertisement about the Russian foreign film festival. I really wanted to go, but I couldn't very well walk to D.C. Jason would never go for something like that, and he'd think the movie was just another excuse for a make-out session, so I decided I'd ask Rusty Dalton. Even though we'd been forced together last Friday, it was actually okay, and it looked like he didn't have a bad time either. With all of those Russian novels he'd read, I figured he'd want to go.

I had thought for a moment that he'd say no. Hell, as he came closer with Big Dalton next to him, I thought that I wouldn't even be able to ask. But he agreed and so Thursday night at dinner, I told Tom about it. Of course, my sperm donor of a father was actually a little pissed that I didn't *ask* him, but I didn't care. He didn't own me and if he said that I couldn't go, I'd steal *his* stupid SUV and go anyway.

He asked who I planned to go with and I told him about Rusty Dalton; of course, I called him Elliott for Tom's sake. After dinner, Tom made a phone call while I cleaned up. By the time the dishes were washed, rinsed, dried, and put away, he was leaning against the counter, his hands crossed over his chest. He was actually kind of close to me; closer than I was comfortable with, so I hung up the towel and moved a foot or two back. "So this Elliott kid's record is clean."

I gaped at him. He'd actually called the police station and got one of his friends to run a report on him. "Tom, seriously?"

"He had a parking ticket last year, but paid it in full the next day."

I shrugged, my arms crossing over my chest, mimicking his stance. "So does that mean I can go?"

"Yes. But I'm warning you, Sophie, if you betray my trust in you, you'll have an awfully hard time earning it back."

I managed not to smirk at him. *He* was warning *me* about breaking trust? How fatherly. "Fine."

School was all right on Friday. I smiled at Rusty Dalton in the hall and he actually smiled back. As far as I knew, Anderson didn't mess with him. Probably because Big Dalton was stalking his little brother's every move. I was suddenly very happy that I had no siblings. Photography was fun for the first time. The teacher let us pair up and we got to go outside and snap away. Pinny Dalton grabbed my arm and told me that I was going to be her partner. She was kind of a cool chick; a little on the weird side, but cool enough for me not to hate her instantly.

She talked a lot, but not like Megan Simons. She wasn't just telling me about her conquests, or what or who so-and-so did last Friday night. Mostly, she talked about things she liked, asking me what I liked in turn. We decided to take pictures of the silent park and the even quieter woods, which suited me just fine, because I could get high a little earlier than planned. Thank the Flying Spaghetti Monster for my one-hitter.

Although I could tell that Pinny didn't like me getting high, she didn't say anything either. She just milled around, taking pictures of bugs and leaves and rotting foliage. Two deep-ass hits were all I needed. It was early and I was still toasty from the wake-and-bake this morning.

Afterward, when we were tromping through the woods, Pinny asked me about Tampa and how I liked Damascus. She asked me all kinds of random questions. If I liked movies. If I saw *Avatar*. If I thought the school was too small. If I had a dog. If I was allergic to pets. I just laughed. There was something strange about her and the way her mind worked. I liked her.

"So Pin...um, Jane, what's up with your dad and that Wallace chick?"

A wry smile formed on her face. "Do-gooders with no social life beyond each other."

I raised my eyebrows, and then took a quick shot of a mushroom growing from the side of a tree. "So are they like, you know, knocking boots?"

Again, Pinny laughed. "Wow, that was so totally nineties, Sophie." She twirled around for some reason and then continued, "But if by 'knocking boots' you mean 'having steamy sex,' I think so. I mean, I have no idea how steamy it is, but I would imagine there's more to their relationship. She's always at our house, but they never act like a couple around us, so I don't know."

"How can you stand it?"

"Obviously you're not a fan of Robin?" I shrugged in reply. "Elliott's the one who gets stuck with her the most."

I bit my lower lip. "So what's *his* deal anyway? I mean, beyond the stuttering thing."

Pinny stopped walking and regarded me carefully, her eyes narrowing. She made me uncomfortable and I was about to tell her to forget it, but then she said, "Elliott's got anxiety issues."

"He doesn't like people?"

She took a deep breath and then started walking again. "People don't like Elliott; at least that's what he thinks."

I thought he was okay. I mean, I realized that high school kids might not be mature enough to get over a slight communication problem, but it seemed strange that "people" in general would have an aversion to him. "Why would he think that?"

Pinny didn't answer, instead quickly aiming her fancy-ass camera at me and snapping a picture before I could bat it away. "So are you coming tonight?"

"I didn't think I had a choice."

I looked at her as she looked at her watch. "We should head back." The walk was silent until we hit the edge of the woods, the school clearly in sight now. "So what do *you* think of Elliott?"

I didn't know how to answer. It was an odd question. I didn't know if I had an actual opinion about him yet. "He's all right."

"You guys are going to D.C. tomorrow, right?"

Obviously he'd told his family, which was…okay, I supposed. He probably had to ask permission or something. "Yeah."

"That'll be awesome. Elliott rarely ever does anything fun. He lives too much in his head. Way too intellectual. Plus he, like, never leaves the house. When I do manage to drag him somewhere other than school," she sighed, "well, it's not pretty."

My conversation with Pinny about Rusty Dalton haunted me after Photography. I had no clue as to why I should be interested in any of it. But it *was* interesting getting the sister point-of-view on him. Still, she must have realized why he lived in his head. No one seemed to care enough or have the patience to have an actual conversation with him. He probably pushed the rest away to avoid all the verbal stumbles.

But maybe there was more to it.

~ • ~

I called Tom and let him know I had a ride to the Screw-Up Club, but refused tell him from whom. He was at work, so I wouldn't see him until Saturday morning anyway. It wasn't like he went out of his way to find a suitable ride for me. Obviously, since we were going to the same place anyway, Jason drove me to the Daltons. Dusted and sexed we walked in together, ready to get the shit over with.

Unfortunately, the moment I stepped through the door, I had to go upstairs to see Bitch Wallace. She sat there staring at me for a long time and I felt like I was in a bad movie. Didn't we do this little dance last week? I had no intention of giving in. I could sit here all night, entertaining myself with my thoughts.

She broke first and I had to smile, but what came out of her mouth had me beyond pissed. "So, Sophie, are you sexually active?"

What the hell! Was that her business? I mean, really? I opened my mouth and asked the first thing that came to my mind. "Do you suck Dr. Dalton's cock?"

The bitch in me cheered as she blushed, all wide-eyed and shocked, but she didn't respond. In fact, she did absolutely nothing but look at me. I folded my arms over my chest, scowling at her. "What does it matter if I'm having sex?"

"Are you?"

Fine. Play the fucking game. Right. "Yes."

"When did you become sexually active?"

It took everything I had not to throw something at her. My hands fisted. I was supposed to trust this bitch? "What do you want to know, specifically? The first time I fucked, the first time I gave head, or the first time I was finger-banged?" I asked, purposely using the most offensive language I could think of.

I watched as she managed to keep her cool. "Any."

I didn't want to tell her anything, but I could tell that she wasn't the type to back down. "Consensually?"

"Any," she said again. Damn. I'd hoped to shock her just a little.

"The first time I had a sexual experience was when I was eleven, but the first time I *chose* to have a sexual experience was when I was fourteen." My jaw clenched as I glared at her, suddenly very angry. "Do you need details for your sick little notebook there?"

Wallace had stopped the nearly constant scratching of her pen against the yellow legal pad. "Is that something you'd like to talk about?"

"No."

"Who was it that…"

"I said I didn't want to talk about it." I sunk lower in my chair.

"Could we talk about your mother?"

"No."

She sighed and I felt a small bit of satisfaction denying her any more insight into the mind of Sophie. It served her right, and I was sure it would nag at her. "Okay, so how is school going?"

"It's going how school usually goes."

"Is there a reason you're so confrontational?"

"I don't like you." She wrote something on her little notepad. "I don't like that you feel you have the right to know things about people. I don't like how you assume that I'm fucked up. I don't like how you just made me sit here for a half an hour for no reason. I don't like your face. I can't fucking stand your voice, and I'd rather be anywhere but here right now."

Then the bitch smiled at me and I wanted to kick her teeth out. "Well, we can call our session over for the week. I would like you to think about what has you so angry. I usually bear the brunt of it, but very seldom is it about me." She leaned toward me, her hands clasping together as her elbows rested on her thighs. "Everything you say in here stays with me, unless you tell me you're going to hurt yourself or others." She paused and licked her lips, her eyes softening. "The bad things that happen in children's lives are not their fault. I'm not here to punish you, Sophie. I'm here to help."

Standing up, I couldn't help but shake my head. "I'm not seven. Stop talking to me like I'm a child. It's awesome that you and Dalton have put together this little Screw-Up Club, but you don't have anything I want and you can't help me with shit."

"Sophie…"

"You think because you have a degree or whatever, that automatically you're qualified to help me with shit you have no clue about?" I made my way to the door, but then stopped and turned back around. "Don't ask me about my sex life again. Go watch some internet porn or get spanked by the good doctor, but don't think I'm going to give you *any* information about what I do and who I do it with."

I stomped downstairs and ignored everybody. Even when Jason came and stood next to me, I didn't look at him. "For shit's sake, what the hell happened? You're radiating hate."

I didn't say anything, but just gave him a pointed look instead. It was great that he was an excellent sex partner and could give me the mad hook-up and all, but I wasn't about to get all touchy-feely with my emotions with Jace. Leaving him standing there, I moved across the room and sat down on the couch. Instinctively, my legs came up to my chest and I wrapped my arms around them.

Stupid bitch. Was I sexually active? What the hell? She was twisted, and now she'd gotten me mixed up in her twisted shit. Why did it make a difference if I have sex, or when I have sex, if I'm here because I stole a car? And I didn't steal it. I was going to give it back. I just needed it to…

My thoughts were interrupted when Andrea sat down next to me. Then I looked around and noticed everyone was grabbing a seat. Pinny Dalton threw me a little wave, but I was too pissed to acknowledge it. Then Bitch Wallace came in and it took all my effort to remain seated. I caught her eyes on me more than once, and I bit the inside of my cheek to stop myself from having what I was sure would be considered an "emotional outburst." I didn't pay attention. Jason's partner, Olivia, spoke for a little bit, her voice sounding just as angry as I felt, and then her twin brother spoke. I had no idea what it was that they were droning on about.

I was so furious that I would be subjected to this every Friday night until I graduated. Suddenly, a detention center didn't sound so bad. At least there they wouldn't care when I'd had my first sexual experience. Stupid Wallace. Stupid me. I shouldn't have said a damn thing.

Stupid, stupid, fucked-up Sophie. Now the thoughts were there, stuck in my head again. Even if I barricaded my door, I doubted I would be able to sleep tonight. I *hated* this feeling and wanted to get high again.

I had no real way of qualifying if my life would be different had Helen left me here when she took off, but it was the biggest "what if" in my life and I had nothing else to dwell on sometimes. When I was a kid and hurting from one of Helen's fly-off-the-handle reactions to something small, or when one of her boyfriends decided to look at me a little *too* closely, I would dream about the life I could have had with Tom. I would have been overly-protected. When I was in Junior High, he could have brandished a shotgun every time a boy came around. He could have threatened me with military school if I misbehaved or got a shitty grade.

But that fantasy always faded fast in the harsh light of the reality. Now, at seventeen, I was stuck with what the past gave me; with what *other* people had decided *for* me. I was here with the Screw-Up Club, desperately trying not to listen to their shit because I had enough of my own.

"Sophie?"

I tore my eyes off of the carpet and looked up at Bitch Wallace. "What?" My voice was hard and I wanted her to hear every ounce of the hate I felt for her and her little games.

"I just asked if there was anything you'd like to share tonight."

I licked my lips, pasted on the nastiest smile I could, and cocked my head. "Yes. I want to share how *stupid* I think this whole thing is. Do you honestly think that this is meaningful in any way to me?"

Oh, how I wanted to punch the shit out of her when she gave me that smile again. "Thank you for sharing your thoughts."

I rolled my eyes, but Bitch Wallace turned to look at the others, not even acknowledging my anger. “So now we can pair off.”

Chapter 8

Art and Music

Sophie

After we were told to pair off, I didn't waste any time. I jumped off the couch and found Rusty Dalton sitting on a love seat next to Pinny Dalton and her boyfriend. Rusty's eyes seemed to widen as I stomped over to him. Ignoring everyone else, I grabbed his wrist, pulling him up with all of the strength I had and dragging him along with me. I didn't stop until we were outside of his bedroom, where I dropped his wrist and looked at him expectantly.

His eyes moved from me, to the door, and then back to me. He really couldn't be confused, could he? Wasn't it obvious that I wanted to go into his room? Wasn't it obvious, I was not happy with being here tonight and wanted a little time away from the prying eyes of Bitch Wallace?

I sighed and my lips settled into a line. Finally, he opened the door and I moved inside quickly. Immediately I went to the leather couch and flopped down on it. I had no idea how long I lay there in silence, and I had no idea what Rusty Dalton was doing.

I was trying just to push past the lingering thoughts and memories in my mind, when he said, "D-d-d-do you w-w-wa-want to llllisten to m-m-music?" I sat up and looked at him. Just like last week, he sat carefully on the edge of his bed, looking like he'd run laps at the gym.

He seemed incredibly uncomfortable and suddenly I was struck by the feeling that I had to do something to help him. It seemed fairly evident that I was the one making him uncomfortable, so I took in a deep breath and nodded. "Sure. Music is fine." In all honesty, it would be a good distraction from what was going on in my head.

"W-wh-what d-d-do you l-l-like?"

I stood up and went over to the bookcase. "Whatever you want to listen to is fine. I don't really listen to music all that much."

As I trailed my hands over the spines of his books, I heard him fiddle with the equipment. I pulled a large book from the shelf and smiled to myself as Classical music filled the room. I should have known that Rusty Dalton was cultured enough to listen to this kind of music by choice, instead of only when someone forced him to, like most kids our age.

I sat back down on the couch with the book on my lap and looked up at him. He seemed a little more laid-back as he sat on the bed, eyeing the book. "Classical?"

He smiled. He really should do that more. "It-it-it's r-r-relaxing." He swallowed as he looked down at the book, and then back up. "D-do you l-l-liiike ar-art?"

I shrugged. "Don't know. I like photography though."

When I opened the book I saw it was a compilation of famous pieces of art throughout history. Some of them I recognized, and some I didn't. Looking back up at Rusty Dalton, I asked, "Do you like art?"

"I'm…I'm n-not g-g-good at it, b-b-but I l-l-like llllooking at it."

"Which ones do you like?"

"I-in th-that book?" I shrugged, and then held it out to him. He came closer to take it. I felt oddly happy that he was close to me. Even though we sat less than a foot from each other in the greenhouse, it seemed like all other times, he kept his distance. I watched as he flipped through the book quickly and then held it back to me.

Flaming June by Lord Frederic Leighton. It was painted back in 1895.

"You like this one?" He nodded. "It's very pretty." It was of a lady in a chair or something, sleeping. She had on this vibrant orange dress. I wondered why he liked it. I mean, it was pretty, but I had no clue why he would pick it out from the thousands of pretty pictures in the book. Figuring it would take him a lot of words to explain, I didn't ask.

"What else?" I gave him the book again.

He flipped to another page and he must have really liked the painting, because he smiled at it. “Th-this one.” *A Sunday Afternoon on the Island of La Grande Jatte* by Georges Seurat. It looked stiff and formal and like something my dead Grandma Catherine would’ve liked. I quirked an eyebrow. His smiled held. “It-it’s in Ch-Chi-Chicago. I t-t-took a fffield trip to s-s-see it.”

Interesting. That was quite possibly the longest sentence I’d heard from Rusty Dalton, and it was about a piece of boring art. So not only did he read difficult literature, Russian no less, he also liked music and art that most people our age wouldn’t even care about. “Are you from Chicago?”

The smiled faded, but he nodded. So he was from the Midwest. It was amazing they made Greek gods in Middle America. I knew he was adopted by Dr. Dalton, so obviously he moved here with him, but I wondered what circumstances led him to the adoption. It was totally not my business and I’d just gotten done telling Bitch Wallace that I didn’t care about any of the other kids and their stories, but with Rusty Dalton, I found myself interested in how he came to be the person before me.

He was absolutely gorgeous and should have been the most popular guy in school, but instead, he got picked on by a miniature poodle named Chris Anderson.

“Where are your real parents?”

Jesus, he looked like I’d punched him in the gut. Obviously this was a sore subject and I felt like shit for asking, so I did my best to remove the tortured look on his face.

"Do you like Dr. Dalton?" He shrugged while nodding his head at the same time. I supposed that meant, "kinda, sorta."

"I hate Wallace," I offered.

The smile returned. "S-sh-she's hard to liiiike." He rolled his eyes. "Sh-she's an-annoying."

I laughed as I began to flip through the book again.

"No, sand in your bathing suit is annoying. The neighbor's yipping dog is annoying. Wallace is…she's evil."

"Sh-she's just d-doing her j-job."

"I didn't hire her." I closed the book, and set it down next to me. "Is she over here all the time?"

"A lot."

"That's gotta suck for you." Rusty Dalton's smile widened and he nodded. "So, your sister Jane is in my Photography class." He nodded. "She's pretty cool." He nodded again.

"Why is she involved in all this?" I hoped he understood that "all this" meant "The Damascus Friday Night Screw-Up Club."

Rusty Dalton seemed to think for a moment. I had no idea if he'd tell me, since it was clearly not my business. But after a few moments, he opened his mouth and looked straight at me.

"J-J-JJJJJaaane's m-mind w-works d-differently th-th-than m-m-most people's." He stopped, running a hand through his hair. "Sh-she's fr-from Ch-Chicago too."

"Did you know her before you both were adopted by Dalton?"

He nodded and smiled. It was more of a tight-lipped smile than he'd given me before. "I-I-I w-w-wouldn't g-g-go wwwithout her."

I wanted more information in spite of myself, but wondered how long it would take to get it. It wasn't like Rusty Dalton could just tell me quickly what the deal was. I hated that I felt like I didn't have the patience to sit around and listen to him fumble for words and that made me just as bad as Jason or Chris. I didn't want to be frustrated. It wasn't fair to him.

"So, Dr. Dalton adopted you and Jane at the same time? Were you both at the same…I mean, he found you both at the same place?" I felt naive. I didn't know how the whole adoption thing worked.

He looked away. "Y-yeah, we-we were with the s-s-saaame f-f-foster fa-fa-family."

Glancing at his wall of music, I asked, "Do you only listen to Classical?"

He shook his head emphatically. "N-no, b-bu-but my sp-speech…," at this point he started using his hands, motioning to his mouth and throat, "therapist…" He sighed after finally getting the word out, taking a deep breath and closing his eyes. "It h-helps me relax."

"So what else do you have up there?"

He looked at his music collection, and then went to his bedside table, and tossed me an object. "Look." When I caught it, I realized it was his iPod. I'd never had one, which I didn't mind, since I'd never had much use for music. I must have been looking at it weirdly because Rusty Dalton said, "P-push tttthe bottom bu-button." I did as instructed and it lit up, showing me various pictures and words. "N-now sc-scroll."

I messed around with it for a while before looking back up at him with an amused expression. "I wouldn't have pegged you for a country fan." He looked at me like he had no idea what I was talking about. "Johnny Cash?"

Again, he shook his head and gave me a smile. "C-Cash isn't c-c-country, S-S-SSSSophie. C-Cash transcends genre."

"Oh, I see."

"Y-you d-d-don't llllisten to Johnny Cash?"

"Not one song."

"Y-you've never h-heard *RRRRing of F-Fire*? Never h-heard *A Boy N-Named SSSue*?"

I smiled. I could tell how much the idea of my Johnny Cash ignorance offended him. "Sorry. You'll have to educate me in the car tomorrow. Speaking of which, do you know where I live?"

He shook his head, so I gave him directions. "The first movie starts at ten."

"It-it's at lllleast an hour drive."

"So you'll pick me up at like eight-thirty?"

"I-if th-that's what you waaant." Then he seemed to be thinking real hard. I went back to flipping through the art book until he said, "S-Sophie." When I looked up, I could tell that something was really bothering him, like more than usual.

"S-S-SSStephen ssssaid I h-have to tell y-you ab-about m-m-my at-at-at…" He stopped, looking even more frustrated. It was painful to watch, but I tried to keep my face neutral as I waited patiently. I didn't know if me looking at him helped or hindered his speaking process. "I-I sometimes," he began again, "h-hhhave p-p-p-panic at-at-at-at…" his eyes closed as he tried to say the word.

I had no idea if I should or not, but I went ahead and finished for him. "Attacks?"

He opened eyes and swallowed hard while nodding. "If-if it ha-happens to-to-tomorrow, y-y-you sh-sh-should c-c-call…"

I thought that the music was supposed to help his stuttering, but perhaps it was the subject matter that was making it worse. I'd already figured out what he was going to say, so I waved my hand dismissively. If I stuttered or had anxiety attacks, I wouldn't want anyone to dwell on it much. "Yeah, I'll call the EMTs or whatever, and Dr. Dalton. But you're not going to have an attack of any kind tomorrow." He narrowed his eyes. "You'll be with me. I'm super non-threatening and if anything makes you anxious, I'll punch it for you."

That earned me a little crooked smile. "You sure you don't want any money for gas?" He shook his head. I got up to put the art book back on the shelf when glanced at his clock. "It's time to go." I crossed the room and looked over my shoulder before leaving. "I'll see you tomorrow."

I went downstairs and found Jason sitting on the couch, next to Olivia. I plopped down beside them, not caring if I was interrupting their conversation. "What's up?"

"Waiting to be released from hell," he scowled.

"Don't you have your own car? Can't you just leave?"

He nodded to the large clock on the wall. "There's five minutes left, Sophie. God knows I don't need Jerry getting a call about how I failed to stay the entire fucking time." He turned to me now, completely ignoring Olivia. "So do you want to do something tomorrow?"

"I'm going to D.C."

"Really?" He seemed overly interested. I nodded. "It'd be a good trip for smoking out, if you want--"

"Yeah, actually, I'm going with Elliott to see a couple of foreign films and I don't think he smokes."

It was strange the way his face fell. "Elliott Dalton?"

"Do you know any other Elliott's?"

"It's going to take the entire trip for him to even say good morning."

I sighed. "I don't like it when you're a prick, Jace. Stop it. We can do something on Sunday, okay?"

He held up his hands. "Oh no, I'm not down for Elliott's sloppy seconds." I punched him in the shoulder and finally his smile was back. "Ouch, jackass, it was just a joke. I've got a book by the Dalai Lama that might help you with your violent tendencies."

"Shut the hell up, dick. Do you want to do something on Sunday or not?"

"What will you tell your dad? He won't want you going out with me."

"It's not going to be a date. I'll just tell him that I'm going out to explore the great town of Damascus. Besides, he'll be at the station all day."

"There's this cave near the Monocacy River where I'm just dying to have my way you."

I turned to him and whispered, "You could always come over tonight and climb the tree to my window. Tell me it wouldn't be a rush to do me in Tom's house."

"Sophie, your dad's here!" I looked up at Pinny Dalton and smiled before looking back at Jason. I figured I'd be seeing him later tonight. I'd have to remember to leave my window open. Typically, I made sure everything was locked up tight.

Tom was waiting in the driver's seat. He gave me a tentative smile when I slid in. "How'd it go, kiddo?"

"Like therapy, Tom. You know, you didn't have to leave the firehouse. There are plenty of people who could've given me a ride."

"Do you think you might be able to call me 'dad' again sometime?"

Had I ever called him dad? I kept my eyes forward, refusing to look at him. I didn't want to see any Daddy puppy eyes. I wasn't required by any legal agreement to call him dad.

"I've seen you for a total of maybe five hundred days in the past fifteen years, Tom."

"Soph, you know if I could've changed things, I would have. If I'd have known what was going on in Tampa…" I turned to glare at him. Obviously he was still working through the conversation he'd had with Dr. Dalton after my physical.

"What? What would you have done, Tom? If you wanted me so bad, you could've…you could've fucking fought for me."

"There was no judge in the U.S. that would have given you to me when you were a baby, Sophie. A single father raising a daughter on a fireman's salary? They would've said that my line of work was too dangerous and would have taken me away from you too much and…"

"But you didn't even try. Did you have any idea what type of person Helen…" I was getting tired and my heart was pounding. It was hot in the car, so I rolled down the window, hoping the air would stop the mental fuzz in my brain. "Shit," I whispered as I remembered.

"What? Sophie?"

Reaching down, I fumbled with my bag until I found my glucose meter. "Calm down, Tom, I just forgot to check my blood sugar and I didn't eat dinner."

"Sophie! It's nearly nine thirty!" Thomas Young, firefighter and paramedic, was speaking now.

Thank you, Mr. Clock. Even through my haze I rolled my eyes. Quickly, I pricked my finger with the lancet and got a decent-sized drop of blood onto the strip. My head was hurting now and the five seconds it took for the meter to analyze the blood seemed incredibly long.

Shit.

Shit, shit, shit. It was fifty. Pretty damn low.

At this point, I realized that Tom had pulled the car over and was speaking to me, but I couldn't really understand what he was saying.

"Could you get into the front pouch of my bag and get me one of those sugar packets?" They weren't as convenient as the diabetic glucose tabs, but they were more efficient and tasted better. Plus, Helen never bought the tabs for me. I could steal the sugar packets off of any restaurant table. Tom placed it in my hand and I ripped it open, wasting no time pouring the sugar into my mouth.

He said something again.

"Quiet." I wasn't trying to be rude and I knew as a trained paramedic, he probably had something valuable to say, but I just needed him to leave me alone. "One more?"

He handed me another one and I poured it into my mouth, starting to feel just a little better. It was another few minutes before I felt somewhat normal. "We can go home now."

Tom just sat there, and then pointed out of the window.

Oh.

We were home. Slowly, I opened the door and got out of the car, holding onto my book bag, still a little shaky. Tom rounded the car quickly, grasping my upper arm. Although it was a gentle offer of help, I flinched, yanking my arm away. "I'm fine. I just need dinner."

He was silent until we got inside and watched as I grabbed food so I could make myself something to eat. "What?"

"What exactly just happened, Sophie?"

"I told you; my blood sugar dropped too low, so I got it back up."

"I *know* it was too low. You *have* to eat. Do you have any idea what could've happened?"

I wanted to tell him to shut up because *of course* I knew what happened and what it could have lead to, but my energy level forced me into silence. My hands still shook a little, but I started giving my regurgitated answers. "My brain would suck up all of my energy and start shutting down some non-essential functions. I know that. I injected too much insulin, that's all. I keep the sugar packets around because it goes directly into the bloodstream, counteracting the insulin."

"And what happens when you don't get sugar?" He sounded so amazingly condescending when I didn't fully answer his original question of what could've happened, like I hadn't been dealing with this stuff on my own since I was four or five years old.

I sighed and shrugged, trying to spread the mayo on the bread with my shaky hands. I'd been living with this bullshit for years. I already knew this and so did he. I resented having to say it. "I go into shock, and possibly a coma."

After I ate, I felt a hell of a lot better, but it still took another hour before Tom got off of my ass and went back to work.

I barricaded the door after brushing my teeth and had just gotten into my pajamas, when there was a soft knock on my window. I jumped and my heart rate accelerated. Shit. Breathing deeply, I calmed myself. It was only Jason.

I went to the window and slid it open. "I can't believe you actually came. Why didn't you just use the door? He's not home."

He hopped from the tree and into my room with ease. "Banging Tom Young's daughter in his house is too good to pass up. He's such a hard-ass. This is the shit I'll remember for the rest of my life; how could I *not* climb up the fucking tree? It wouldn't be as epic."

Immediately his hands were on me and I found myself stumbling back until I was pressed against my low dresser. The force of my body pushed it against the wall with a thump.

"Be good, Jason."

"Be good?" he whispered. "Be good when you're wearing what I can only describe as the worst pajamas I've ever seen in my entire life? Those clothes deserve to be ripped to shreds and you need to be punished for even putting them on. They do nothing to show off your tight, little rockin' body."

Perv.

I smirked. I had my reasons for wearing sweat pants and an old shirt. It would hardly be appropriate to wear a thong and half-shirt to bed when I lived alone with my father, would it? I mean, what if I had to get up in the middle of the night to pee? What if I physically bumped into him? A shudder ran through me. "Sorry, Jason," I said, all sweet and nonchalant, "but I forgot that you were even coming over tonight."

He actually growled as he went for the stretched collar of my shirt. I grabbed his hands. "Don't actually rip it. It's my favorite shirt, asshole."

Chapter 9

Freak King

Elliott

Sophie had just left my bedroom and I was left alone to reflect. It was the most talking we'd ever done. Whatever she and Robin discussed in her session this afternoon had left her extremely agitated. I had to shut my eyes when she spoke during group because it was too painful to watch. Most everyone in the room had gone through those emotions at one time or another, and many of them had expressed it in the same way. Still, it was painful. She'd been so angry.

Then she'd grabbed my wrist and yanked me out of the living room. I didn't know what to do when she stopped at my bedroom; even though it was obvious she wanted to go inside. My heart started racing, and although she'd been in it the week before, I still panicked just a little.

We'd talked about art and music, which were fairly safe topics and ones I enjoyed talking about. When she asked about my parents I couldn't say anything, so I kept quiet and she quickly changed the subject.

I was thinking about what songs to play for her in the car tomorrow when there was a knock on my door. It had to be Robin, reminding me of my session. I went into the hallway, making sure to close my door behind me.

Once situated in Stephen's study, Robin gave me her warm smile. "Elliott," I begrudgingly looked at her, but in reality I was fearful of a repeat of last week, "I want to apologize for what happened last time. I didn't mean to upset you like that, but walking around with those secrets buried inside does you no good."

I closed my eyes. "B-b-but y-y-you already kn-kn-know."

"I'm only aware of what's in the file, and we both know not everything is in there."

She sighed and I opened my eyes. "I don't have to be the one you tell. I'm not oblivious to the fact that you're not entirely comfortable around me, but you should tell someone. You should let *someone* help you."

I was about to protest. I wanted to tell her I didn't need help and these things inside of me were going to stay there until I died. It didn't matter how many people I told, or how many people wanted to help. Robin continued, "I understand you not wanting to confide in Stephen and David, but you always have Jane."

"Sh-she's g-got her own th-things to-to-to deal with." It was true. Jane had guessed some of it, since she'd been with me when I was fresh out of my father's house, but she had enough to worry about with her own memories, lost or not.

"Okay."

I looked back at her in surprise. That was it? She was letting it go? "Stephen tells me you're going to D.C. tomorrow?"

I nodded, happy with the change of topic.

"Foreign films with Sophie?"

Again, I nodded.

"That should be fun. I take it you've hit it off then?"

Shrugging, I answered, "I d-don't know." There was something I had to ask her, even though I knew I wouldn't get an answer. "W-why's sh-she here?"

"You know I can't tell you that, but I hope she'll tell you herself."

I wanted something more eloquent to say, but the way it came out was, "She's lllllliiiiike me?"

Robin leaned forward. "I think you two have a lot in common." She sighed and cocked her head, studying me the way Stephen sometimes did. "D.C. is a bit of a drive. What do you think you two will talk about?"

I shrugged. I actually had no idea, but I wanted to talk to her about something, even if my stuttering would make it painful. "S-sh-she likes aaaart. Sh-she d-doesn't kn-know Johnny C-Cash."

She leaned back. "So you'll share your musical expertise with her?" I shrugged and her smile faded. "Elliott," she began, her voice oddly careful and even, "as I said, you and Sophie have a lot in common. I don't know her complete history, but there's… I want you to be careful. I don't think it's a good idea for you to be *involved* with her."

This woman baffled me. She was the one who paired me with Sophie in the first place. She was the one who said interacting with her would be good for me; now suddenly she was warning me against being involved with her. This made no sense. "W-w-w-what d-d-ddddo you m-m-mean?"

"David and Jane have someone, and it's perfectly normal for you to want something similar, but your situation is quite different. *You* need to be careful."

I struggled, trying to figure out what she was talking about. Jane and Trent. David and Rebecca. They were together, as in *together*. Robin was saying that I shouldn't be…*together* with Sophie?

"I-I-I d-d-don't un-un-underssssstand." My frustration was definitely affecting my speech.

Robin was quiet for a moment as she inhaled deeply; probably trying to figure out how best to make an idiot like me understand what she was trying to say. "Your…life experiences are unique to you, Elliott. The others don't have those same experiences." I wanted to act like a regular teenager and say "well, duh," but I held it in. "What's happened to you can haunt you more than what they have experienced. Sophie's past can haunt her in ways that the others would have no idea about." She licked her lips. "I'm just suggesting that if you find yourself…attracted to Sophie, you need to think before you act upon it."

I shook my head as I let out a frustrated breath. I knew my unique history made me different from the others. I thought that went without saying, but if I was hearing her correctly, Robin was telling me that I shouldn't have a romantic relationship with Sophie, which was laughable. First, I doubted that Sophie would want to be romantically involved with someone like me. Second, she seemed to be involved with Jason Fox and third, we weren't even friends, really. At least I didn't know if we were. Besides, she'd made a point to say it wasn't a date.

"Th-th-that sssseeeeems unf-f-fair, Robin."

She folded her hands in her lap and gave me a pointed look. "You remember a few years ago, don't you, Elliott?" My breathing sped up. "That was with someone who *didn't* have issues of her own."

Oh. I wished it hadn't taken me so long, but now I knew what she was getting at. She wasn't talking about a *romantic* relationship with Sophie. She was talking about a *sexual* relationship. I hung my head as I ran both hands through my hair. Leave it to Robin to dig up memories I had tried desperately to bury.

I didn't know how long I'd sat there looking at her feet, but when I looked up, she was simply studying me. Elliott Dalton, Lab Rat. "I h-h-hadn't p-p-p-p…" the word wouldn't come out, so I went another way, "…Th-th-that w-w-wasn't m-my in-in-intention w-w-with, S-S-SSSophie."

Now Robin was full of sympathy. It oozed from her; from her motherly voice to her creased brow and downturned mouth. "Elliott, it wasn't your intention back then either, but it happened. It's okay that it happened, but I don't want you to go through that again. There's so much more you need to deal with before you get involved like that."

I buried my head in my hands. She was basically telling me that of all the freaks in the world, I was the king. Being the "Freak King" meant I would need years and years of intensive therapy just to form a normal, healthy relationship with someone of the opposite sex without some doctor prescribing a multitude of pills and helping me to "work through my past."

By the time I looked up, I felt tired and annoyed. "W-w-well, y-y-you d-d-d-don't nnnnneed t-t-to worry. Sh-she d-d-d-doesn't liiiiike m-m-me liiiiike th-th-that."

"Elliott, please don't be upset."

"I-I'm t-tired. C-c-can I g-gooo now?"

❧ • ❧

Since it was Saturday, I was not awakened by David yelling at Jane, but by my alarm clock. I groaned as I looked at the time, wondering for a brief moment why I was getting up so early. Then I remembered. I was going to D.C. with Sophie today.

It wasn't a date. I knew it wasn't a date, but I was excited nonetheless. I practically shot out of bed and flew out of my room and into the bathroom. I showered and dressed quickly, happy that I'd picked out my clothes the night before. My iPod had finished syncing, and I hoped Sophie would like the music I'd chosen. It had taken me quite some time to pick out the best songs from my library.

I was nervous and my discussion with Robin last night hadn't helped. Stephen was downstairs as I went to get some quick food for breakfast. I let him say his piece and remind me that I was to check in every two hours before confirming that I'd told Sophie about my attacks.

I poured two cups of coffee into travel mugs, said goodbye, got into my Jetta, and headed over to Sophie's house. I made good time and was actually a few minutes early.

As I was climbing up the stairs, Mr. Young stepped out of the house. I forced myself to speak. "H-h-hhhhello, ssssir."

With narrowed eyes, he looked me up and down. Sophie's father was tall and muscular; an incredibly intimidating man. "Elliott," he said, stopping in front of me, "bring her back in one piece and if you put your hands on her in any inappropriate way, I'll find out. Got it?"

I gulped, surprised by the automatic assumption I'd do anything to hurt his daughter. "Y-y-y-y-yes, ssssssssir."

Finally, he smiled. "Have fun and drive safe."

I stood frozen until he was in his SUV, pulling slowly out of the driveway. Before I could make it the rest of the way up, Sophie was in front of me, closing and locking the door.

"Hey, Elliott."

"H-h-hi."

"Did Tom threaten you with his shotgun?"

I could hear the sarcasm dripping from her voice and I felt myself relax. "H-he m-made sssure I kn-knew to t-t-take care of y-you."

She shook her head and started off the steps. I followed. "It's humorous that Tom wants to go all overprotective-Daddy on me now." She stopped at the car and looked back at me. "Just a few years too late."

I watched as she got in before I rounded the car and did the same. "I b-b-brought y-you c-c-c-coffee." I shrugged as she looked at the travel mug. "I-I d-d-didn't kn-know if you d-dr-drank it or not."

"Thanks." She grabbed it and took a sip. "So, are you going to school me or what?"

I glanced at her and she nodded at my iPod. I turned it on, pushing it down into the dock. "I-I-I d-d-didn't know w-what you l-liiiiked, so I j-just l-l-loaded a b-b-bunch of ssssongs on here." She looked at me expectantly. "Y-you c-can f-flip th-through it and f-find something you liiiike."

Sophie smiled at me, but sighed. "The point isn't for me to find something *I* like; it's for you to expose me to new music to see *if* I like it, right?"

"Th-then just p-p-push play." She did and Camille Saint-Saëns came through the speakers. I'd made it the first song because it was a sort of lighthearted piece and typically put me at ease. Not only that, but I thought she'd enjoy the story behind it.

From out of the corner of my eye, I saw her eyes narrow. She took a sip of her coffee and then turned to me. "It's not *all* going to be Classical, is it?"

"N-no."

"Okay, so spill it, Elliott. What's the song and why should I like it?"

The way she said it made me smile. "I-it's *D-danse M-m-macabre* and y-you'll liiiike it when y-you know w-what it's a-about." I paused, trying to gauge her reaction. She seemed eager for me to continue. "I-it's th-the d-dance of d-death." She laughed softly and instantly the tightness in my chest lessened. "B-basically, D-death p-plays the f-f-fiddle ev-every Halloween in a gr-graveyard and th-the skeletons r-rise up and d-dance w-with him. Th-there is a k-k-king and a p-peasant and a p-p-p-pretty girl. D-d-death basically t-tells them that n-no m-matter wh-who you were in l-life, e-e-everyone ends up the ssssame in the end."

The road was quite empty this early in the morning, so I risked another look at her, wondering if she was thinking I was an idiot. She said nothing, facing forward as she listened, and then I saw the dawning realization in her eyes. "So, right now, there're skeletons dancing with Death?" I nodded and looked back to the road. "I like it."

I was relieved. I'd been incredibly nervous about the whole trip, and the music I'd chosen had caused me a bit of grief. I wanted her to like it because if she did it, then by extension she liked at least a piece of me.

"Most people don't understand that, you know?" She'd returned to looking at the road. "People get so caught up with the pseudo-reality of right now that they forget death comes to us all, one way or another."

The song ended and I felt the need to prepare her for the shift. "N-now it'll be a f-few C-C-Cash songs sssssince y-you obviously n-need s-some education in the f-fundamentals of music." *Ring of Fire* came on. "Th-this is p-p-probably one of his m-most well kn-known ssssongs…but n-n-not my f-f-favorite." After that *Long Black Veil* played and I told her that the Dave Matthews Band did a live version of it. Finally, there was *The Man Comes Around.* While I loved the song, one of Johnny Cash's best in my opinion, the Bible passages always put me on edge.

There was some small-talk about each song that came after, ranging from Neil Young to JayZ, and from Tool to the Mamas and the Papas. Some songs she knew, and some she didn't. We were about halfway to D.C. when Sophie wanted to stop at a gas station to use the restroom. While she got out, I filled up the car and called Stephen, letting him know I was still breathing and cognitive.

When she got back, it wasn't hard to tell that she'd gotten high. We took off again and I tried not to focus on the funky smell or the way her blue eyes were glassy and bloodshot. We drove silently for a while as she leaned her head back, eyes closed, listening to the music. I tried to figure out whether she got high to tolerate being with me, or if she just usually got high in the mornings.

As Tom Petty started singing about wildflowers, I was trying to decide if I should just say something or let it go. It wasn't like she was shy about asking me questions, so I took a deep breath and tried to relax. "S-Sophie?" She turned to me, a slight smile on her face. "Y-y-you d-d-don't have to hide th-that you're h-h-high."

She was silent for a moment before shrugging. "I didn't know if you'd care or not." Suddenly, she sat up a little straighter. "Did you want to smoke? I wasn't trying to be rude." I shook my head. "Are you sure? I would think a little pot might help with some of that anxiety."

Again I shook my head, hating that she knew I even *had* anxiety. "I j-just d-d-didn't want you to th-think I w-w-would j-judge y-you for th-that." Well, it wasn't entirely true. I didn't like that she got high and wished she didn't, but it was less about her, and more about my mother.

"I'm sorry, Elliott. I wasn't trying to be…I mean, I just figured with your dad being a doctor and all that you wouldn't be okay with me…"

I had to laugh. "Y-you-your d-d-dad's a ffffff-ffffire fffffffighter, S-Sophie." Her smile widened as she nodded. "W-why d-do y-you liiiike d-d-d…g-getting high?"

While her smile remained, it slipped into a lazy grin as she laid her head back again. "Everything's much fuzzier and I can focus on my thoughts instead of just getting lost in them." She paused for a moment. "I mean, it's like this music. If I wasn't high, I'd hear it and maybe I would like it or maybe I wouldn't, but being high, it's totally clear. I can really *listen* and absorb the music and find the meaning in it."

Again, we were silent for a while before she asked, "Do you like Damascus?" I shrugged. It was okay. I had people here who cared about me, but I probably wouldn't have chosen it as a place to live. "You know the worst thing about Damascus? The pot. It's not as good as what I could find in Tampa."

"D-do you miss an-anything else a-a-about Florida?"

She took a breath. "I miss all the people. Not everyone knew everyone. It was a lot easier to blend in and…disappear."

I thought about it. It was strange for Sophie to move here to live with her father. It seemed like an odd fit; a teen-aged girl living with her father instead of her mother. Stephen was still married to Kate when he adopted us. When they got divorced, she didn't want any of us, so the court had no other choice but to leave us with him.

"D-do you liiiike l-living with your d-dad?"

Her face fell just a little. "Tom's okay. He drinks, but he's not much for interaction, so it's not like I'm subjected to any kind of strict parenting. He's far better than Helen." She sighed. "I just wish he'd realize that it's a little too late for him to play the father figure. I mean, I barely know the dude."

The song changed and I was about to tell her who it was when she smiled widely. "This is Otis Redding." I returned her smile, happy that she knew Otis. "My grandmother used to listen to him. Dude's awesome."

"I-I kn-know." Another Sophie-approved musical choice. It was amazing how happy it made me that she not only knew who this was, but also liked him. I wanted to ask her a million questions, but since I'd never really been good at having conversations, I didn't know how many questions would be appropriate. Luckily, Sophie saved me.

"Why do you like music so much?"

I licked my lips involuntary, hoping that I could get the words out and not sound like a moron. "I-I'm-I'm g-g-good at it." I shrugged. "L-listening t-t-t-to it m-m-mmmmakes me feel n-normal." I'd gotten it out, but I was pretty sure I sounded like an idiot.

After a moment of silence, Sophie ran her hands through her hair and pulled it across to one side. She looked absolutely excellent doing that. "Have you always stuttered?"

Her question took me off-guard. I swallowed hard and shook my head. "N-no. M-my m-m-m-m," I sighed in frustration. I wished I could close my eyes, but since I was driving, I figured that wasn't a good idea. Taking a deep breath and thinking of one of the compositions I'd written years ago, I tried again. "M-my m-m-m-mom s-s-said tttthhhat it st-started w-when I was f-f-five."

"Wow. Do they know why?"

"N-n-nobody kn-knows w-w-why p-people start st-stuttering. N-neurological, physiological dis-disruption, m-maybe?"

Again, she was quiet and I thought she was just listening as Otis Redding gave way to Blues Traveler. Honestly, I was happy for the break in the conversation. It would've been fine if we were talking about her, but she was asking about me now and that was difficult. "Where's your mom now, Elliott?"

My heart raced and my breathing quickened. My hands tightened on the steering wheel involuntarily and I could feel the onset of the panic. I desperately willed it away. If I panicked, Stephen would be right. Robin would be right. They *couldn't* be right about me. So I took deep breaths.

"Elliott? Are you okay? You don't have to…"

I blew out a steady stream of air, hesitating at first, but then I figured I should just tell her. This was what I wanted with Sophie Young, wasn't it? For her to know me the same way I wanted to know her. "Sh-sh-she's d-d-dead."

"Oh. I'm sorry."

The pity in her voice made my body tense even more. Everyone always pitied me. She didn't even know the whole story. But I plunged forward, hoping that by giving her some kind of detail, perhaps she'd think of me as something other than a freak, like the rest of the school did. "Sh-she k-k-killed herself."

"Oh."

I risked a glance and then turned hastily back. I'd gone this far, so I might as well tell her the rest. It wasn't how I wanted the drive to go, but it was too late to change that now. I felt nervous energy replacing the panic, making my knees bounce. "Sh-she w-w-was a heroin ad-ad-addict. One d-day sh-she c-came into m-my room and st-started t-t-to ssssay a-all this w-w-w-weird stuff and sh-sh-she had a g-g-g-gun in her hand and…" I shook my head, wishing that I could bang it against something. The story was horrible and came with visuals. Plus, it took so long for me to get it out, which just made everything much more painful. "Sh-she j-j-just p-put it to her h-head and p-p-p-p…sh-shot herself."

"What the *fuck*?" She sounded so angry and was staring at me with such a strange expression. "Why the hell would she do that in front of you? How fucking old were you?"

I shouldn't have told her. That was a mistake. Of course she'd have more questions. Now I felt like a bigger freak. "I-I w-w-w-was seven."

"Jesus Christ!"

"I-I think it w-w-was ssssupposed t-to be m-m-me and h-her."

"What?"

I didn't want to say it again, but I knew I had to. "I-I think sh-she w-w-was going t-to t-t-take m-me w-w-with her."

"Are you fucking serious?"

Her volume made me flinch. "D-don't y-yell, S-S-Sophie. I'm-I'm-I'm ssssorry." How was I supposed to correct this now? I was such an idiot.

"What the hell are you sorry for, Elliott? What your mom did was messed up. I'm sorry for getting loud, but Jesus!"

"M-m-my m-mom loved me, S-Sophie," I said quietly. I knew my mother loved me. I never questioned that, ever. "B-b-but sh-she loved hhhhhheroin m-m-more." Even that wasn't the full story, but I'd shared enough and no longer wanted to talk about my family. My mother hadn't *wanted* to kill me. In the end, that's why she didn't, although there had been many, *many* nights that I wished she had.

"I'm sorry, Elliott, I didn't mean to…" Sophie's voice was softer than I'd ever heard it before.

It took me a while before I was able to force air through my voice box, but when I finally did, my voice was nearly as quiet as hers. "It's o-okay, S-Sophie."

I wasn't upset with her, but I felt tired after telling her all that; having it replayed in my head for what had to have been the millionth time. I scrolled through the music on the iPod until I came to Billie Holiday. Then it moved into Nina Simone.

It was during the quieter tones of Nina's slower songs that I felt myself relax again.

We were silent for nearly the rest of the ride to D.C., and I felt imprudent for having said anything at all. It was ridiculous for me to think that Sophie would want to know something like that. It wasn't until we entered the city that Sophie spoke to me again. "I'm sorry I asked about your mom. I know I don't want anyone asking about mine, so…"

"It's o-okay."

She turned away from me to look out the window. "Do you know where you're going? The movie should be starting soon."

I had to smile. She obviously didn't know what an over-thinker I was. I had Googled the film festival and the theater, and had it programmed into my GPS.

Chapter 10

Human Bondage

Elliott

The theater was almost empty. We watched the first movie, *Prisoner of the Mountains*, which I had no real feelings about. I was sure it was a perfectly fine movie, but I was preoccupied because I was sitting next to Sophie, and I was much more interested in her. I'd read the story before, but she was entirely new to me.

I tried to pay attention. I really, really did, but since we were sharing an armrest, at times we'd go to put our arms there at the same time. I'd never believed it before when I read it in books, but I swore there was some kind of chemical exchange between us. It wasn't like the sedatives from Stephen's syringe; a sharp whip of pain followed by heavy lethargy. It was more like a constant flow of oxymoronic calming excitement traveling through my veins.

When the movie was over, we had about two hours until the next one started. "Do you mind if we go get something to eat?" Sophie asked. It was lunchtime and I was hungry too. I was about to tell her that it was fine and ask her what kind of food she liked when she continued. "It's just that I can't…I have to eat on a semi-regular schedule or my blood sugar goes all wonky. I must have too much insulin or something. I'm sorry."

She looked almost nervous when she said it. "T-th-that's f-f-f-fine, S-Sophie. Ther-there's f-f-food all u-up and d-down this r-r-road." She smiled at me and to my complete and utter amazement, grabbed my hand and started pulling me toward the exit.

I barely had time to rid myself of the shock when I found myself out on the sidewalk, still being yanked behind her. She pulled me into a small pizzeria. "I hope you don't mind. Pizza's quick, cheap, and easy."

She let go of my hand as she slid into a booth near the front window and I sat across from her. There were a million things I wanted to say, but stutter or not, I wasn't sure if I would be able to say any of them.

I wanted to know why she looked nervous when she told me she had to eat. I wanted to know if she felt the chemical surge between us too. I wanted to ask how she got the little scar on the top of her forehead that was mostly disguised by her hairline. I wanted to ask why, out of everyone, she asked me to go to the movies with her.

But I didn't ask any of those things. Instead, I just watched as she pulled a small black pouch out of her bag and unzipped it, then sanitized her hands and looked up, giving me a little shrug. "Sorry, I have to." I had no clue what she was apologizing for, or what she had to do, so I just sat, watching her.

The pouch held a little plastic container, a digital monitor, and some flat thing with a button. Finally, I realized she was going to test her blood sugar. She put the lancet in the little stabbing device and pushed a test strip into the monitor. I winced with her as she depressed the button on the device and pricked her finger.

A small drop of blood formed and she held it to the testing strip. It beeped five times as she took her napkin and pressed it to her bleeding finger. A number appeared and she shrugged. "Good thing pizza's full of carbs."

"I-i-is it o-okay?"

Again, she shrugged as she removed the lancet from the device, closing up the pouch and sanitizing her hands again. "It's okay. A little low, but…"

"D-do you h-haaaave t-to take in-insulin?"

She nodded. "Yeah, I just took too much or didn't eat enough...I should've had popcorn at the theater, but it seemed too early."

The waitress arrived and Sophie and I decided on a pizza. When she left, I continued asking questions, but not the ones I really wanted to know the answers to. "S-ssssso, w-w-w-what's the w-w-worst thing a-about h-h-having di-di-diabetes?"

She took a sip of water and thought for a moment. "Knowing that it won't just go away. Not being able to eat everything I want. Making myself bleed at least four times a day. Jabbing myself with needles. Knowing my life will probably be shorter than everyone else's because of it. Yeah, basically everything." She was quiet for a moment before adding, "I hate needles and blood."

I just nodded. I wouldn't like any of that either. I didn't have a blood phobia or anything, but I'd seen enough of it gushing from various parts of my body that I wouldn't want to stab my finger every day.

"So what's the worst part about having a stutter?"

My breath caught. I hadn't been prepared for that. I should have expected some kind of reciprocal question, but for whatever reason, I hadn't given it a thought. She was looking at me now, her eyes questioning as she stirred the ice around her glass with a straw. I took several deep breaths. I wasn't going to freak out. If I wanted to be normal, I would have to talk to people, even beautiful people like Sophie.

"Uh..." I began smoothly. There were so many things that I hated about having a stutter, it was hard to know where to begin. "I-I-I c-can't ssssay everyth-thing I w-w-want to say. N-n-no matter h-how h-h-hard I t-try, I c-c-c-can't c-control it." I shrugged. "B-b-basically everything." I'd looked away from her, but then forced myself to turn back. "P-p-people think I-I'm s-s-stupid."

I mentally kicked myself for saying all that, even if I was proud that I'd gotten through it. Sophie was looking at me with what had to be pity in her eyes. I hated pity. I looked down at my hands as I fiddled with the edge of my napkin.

"I don't think you're stupid, Elliott."

I looked up at her and I was sure my expression reflected my shock. While I knew she didn't think of me the way Chris

Anderson and the other kids did, I still operated under the assumption she thought I was somehow mentally deficient. She gave me a small smile and I returned it. "Th-thank you."

She shrugged. "I've seen your room. I don't think stupid people read the books you read, or know anything about art, and I'm sure some stupid people play music, but they're probably not all that good."

I allowed myself a chuckle over that. "Y-you h-haven't heard me p-play."

"Doesn't matter; I already know you're awesome at it."

Wow. That was such a nice compliment.

"I'm sorry about earlier." I gave her a questioning look. "When I asked about your mom. It wasn't…"

Sighing, I dropped my head and looked at my hands again. "I-it w-was a long t-time ago, S-Sophie." While it was true that it was a long time ago, I could still see the scene before me when I closed my eyes. There weren't any words to describe the lifeless body of your heroin-addicted mother slumped on the floor in front of you, while her blood and brains slid down your door.

I could still remember the smell.

She had done it in front of my door, so I couldn't get out without stepping over her. The doorknob was red with blood. The only thing I could do was back away. No one else had been home at the time. I had no idea how long it took for my father to come back, but I remember shivering as I sat in the dark corner of my closet. I had never been so happy to see him in all my life. That feeling was short-lived.

"So ask me something."

I looked up, blinking, willing myself to come back to the present. "W-what?"

"It's only fair, right?"

"W-why did y-you m-move to D-D-Damascus?"

She shrugged. "I stole a car. The judge said I had to come here."

My eyes widened. "W-w-why d-did you steal a c-c-car?"

Her smirk faded quickly. "Um, I had to go someplace."

"W-was it y-your m-m-mom's c-c-car?"

"No. Helen's piece of shit wasn't worth stealing. It was our neighbor's." She rubbed her hand over her face like she was tired. "But it wasn't like I was out joyriding, you know."

"W-where d-did you h-have t-to go?"

She took a deep breath and shifted her eyes away. When a bell dinged behind her, she turned toward the sound, and then turned back. "Look, it's our pizza."

We ate very quietly and I was amazed that I'd thought asking her a few questions would clear things up, because in reality, all it did was add more questions to the list.

I tried to pay for the pizza, but Sophie took out her own money. I didn't want it. I even tried to give it back to her but she wouldn't take it, telling me once again that it wasn't a date and so she could and should pay for half the pizza. I felt bad. It was fine that it wasn't a date, but Stephen had been giving me money since he first took me in and I rarely ever spent any of it. Sophie's dad was a civil servant and I knew he couldn't be making that much. Not wanting to offend her, I folded up the bills and stuck them back in my pocket.

When we got outside, I turned to head back to the theater since it was nearing the time for the next movie, but Sophie stopped me by putting her hand on my arm. "Do you want to skip *Anna Karenina*?" She tilted her head as she looked up at me, and her big blue eyes locked with mine. "I mean, we both already know the story or whatever and there's a cool-ass bookstore over there," she said, jabbing her thumb up the road.

"S-sure."

She looked happy and I was glad that my agreeing with her made her smile. "Great." Then it faded as her brow creased. "So, um, would you mind if I smoked?"

It took me a moment to process her question. It's not like I was asked every day if I cared if someone used an illegal substance. "Uh…n-n-no."

She let out a relieved breath before smiling again. Once more she took my wrist and tugged me toward the bookstore. Before we got there, she ducked into a small alleyway. It was filthy-looking and made me feel quite uncomfortable. "You stay here," she said as she let go of me. "I'll only be a second. Just…just cough really loud if you see someone coming."

Now I was Sophie's lookout. That made me uncomfortable, but to be perfectly honest, she probably could've talked me into robbing a bank. So there I stood, facing the street, watching for any signs of someone headed our way.

It wasn't long before she emerged. The odor clung to her, faint, but definitely there, and probably just like Jason, she didn't think anyone could smell it. Her eyes were a bit glassier than at lunch and she had a certain kind of lazy look on her face.

I wished she didn't get high.

"Ready for the bookstore?"

I just nodded and she turned, taking off up the street. Of course, I followed, my long legs making it too easy to catch up with her. The bookstore was old and dusty, and nothing like the new chain bookstores. There was a small café attached to it and plush armchairs scattered throughout. It was easy to see how much Sophie liked it from the moment she stepped in. She even turned around to look at the tinkling bells on the door as it closed behind us.

Personally, I didn't care what kind of books were in this little shop, as long as they made her happy. I followed her through the weaving stacks until she found a section that interested her and ran her hand lightly over the spines of the hardback books.

I couldn't help but smile. She was lost inside her head and from the look on her face, she was enjoying it. "I love this place. They should get one just like it in Damascus." I silently agreed; then I could take her every day and see her happy like this all the time.

I watched Sophie closely as she pulled books halfway off the shelf and studied the covers, and I suddenly wished I owned more books that interested her.

"I couldn't bring all my books from Tampa." She turned to me, her cheeks reddening for some reason. "Not that I had that many, but I could only bring a few paperbacks." She grabbed a couple and then went over to an armchair before stopping and looking back at me. "I promise I'm not going to make you stay here until I read all of these. I'm just going to skim through them and remember the best parts."

I smiled at her again. "I-it's okay, S-Sophie. W-we can ssstay as l-long as you w-w-want."

My body felt weak when she smiled at me again, excitement shining in her eyes. I followed her, thinking she was going to sit down, but instead she went to a different section. After moments of scanning, she reached out and grabbed a book, shoving it at me. "You don't have this, but you'd like it."

I read the title: *Of Human Bondage* by W. Somerset Maugham. I must have looked shocked, because she laughed. "It's not crazy-kinky or anything like that. It's kinda dark and tortured."

With that, she turned and I followed her to the armchairs. We sat in adjacent chairs and I couldn't help but steal glances at her out of the corner of my eye. She was so enthralled by the books she'd chosen. It was interesting the way her face shifted expressions as she read different excerpts and how her lips moved as she read each word. I wondered how many times she'd read each one.

I read the introduction to the book she'd handed me and I knew I'd probably enjoy it. Of course, the minute she said I'd like it my mind was made up. I was going to buy it. I was also going to buy those books for her. I was sure that she would refuse or try to keep me from doing it, but I was going to find a way.

After awhile, my cell phone rang, startling me out of my plotting. I dug it hastily out of my pocket and checked the caller ID. It was Stephen. I'd forgotten to check in with him.

Without even saying hello, I said, "I-I'm s-sssorry. I-I f-f-forgot. I-I'm f-f-fine."

"How are the movies? Are you in one now?"

"Uh..." I didn't know how to respond. Did I tell him the truth? Was that okay? I was a horrible liar, even over the phone, so I just went for it. "We-we're in a b-b-bookstore n-now."

"Oh. Did you get something to eat?"

"Y-yes."

"Do you know when you'll be heading back?"

"N-no, b-but p-p-probably sssssometime ssoon."

"And you're having fun?"

"Y-yes, S-SSSStephen." Sophie smiled down at the open book

"Then I won't keep you. Just make sure you call me."

After I told him that I would call him again soon, I looked at Sophie. She was still engrossed in one of her books. It wasn't until I snapped the phone closed that she looked up at me.

"He always keep such close tabs on you?" I nodded, not feeling the need to tell her that typically I never did anything but go to school and come home, so there wasn't much of a need to keep tabs. "That's gotta suck."

I just shrugged and we went back to reading. After awhile, I knew we had to leave because I feared her father would send out a search party for us. Stephen would be his second-in-command. "W-w-we should p-probably go now."

She looked at her wrist, even though she wasn't wearing a watch, and sighed. "Wouldn't want Tom to think I ran off." She stood and I did the same, taking the books from her hands and walking toward the front of the shop until I felt her hand on my arm. "Those books go back there."

I turned to find her pointing toward the stacks. "I-I-I know. I'm b-buying them."

She looked suspicious. "Not for me, I hope." I shrugged. "You can't buy them for me, Elliott."

"W-why not?"

"I'm not a charity case, that's why. If I really wanted them, I could buy them myself."

I frowned. It was just as I had anticipated, but I shook my head. "N-no. I-I'm buying them f-for you. Ch-Ch-Christmas p-presents."

She rolled her eyes, but smiled. “Christmas is months away and I’m not getting you anything, so I can’t accept the presents.”

At least she was being honest. I sighed. “F-fine. I’m b-buying them f-f-for mmmmme, a-and you can b-b-borrow them an-an-any…w-whenever you’d like.”

She glared at me and I could tell she was trying to figure out a way to talk me out of buying the books again, but how could she do that when I’d made it clear I was buying them for myself? She exhaled loudly. “Has anyone ever told you that you can be quite annoying?”

I smiled, hoping that I wasn’t really annoying her, and then I proceeded to the register.

Chapter 11

Stupid School Girl

Sophie

The ride back to Damascus was pretty chill. I'd smoked a little before we left and Elliott's choice of music amused me. I'd liked just about everything I'd heard on the ride to D.C., but for the ride home, the music was just so perfectly suited for a nice toasty buzz. If I didn't know any better, I would have thought he planned it that way.

Elliott was an incredibly nice guy. Not just a nice guy, but a real gentleman or whatever. He hadn't looked at my tits once. He didn't smack my ass or make raunchy comments. That was a new thing for me.

Basically it meant he made me really nervous. I mean, he'd even brought me coffee this morning. I knew it wasn't a big deal or anything, but it was thoughtful and considerate, and who in my world did that?

He called me out about smoking pot. I loved that. He didn't make me feel bad about it, and just said that I didn't have to hide it from him. Now that was a notion that made me nearly piss in my pants with fear. Not hide? Jesus. What would that be like?

I realized that smoking pot in front of him wasn't exactly sensitive. Even if he said it was fine, I knew he probably hated it. But weed wasn't smack and I wasn't his mother. If he really wasn't okay with it, he should say so instead of waiting for me to read between the lines.

I'd truly enjoyed my time with him. He didn't pressure me and things felt natural between us. Plus, his stutter kept him from saying all the unnecessary shit that people felt compelled to say.

The shit we did talk about was intense, but crazy-cool too. I'd never met anyone who could talk about Johnny Cash and then tell me some screwed-up story about his mother all in the same day. And he didn't freak out about it; I did. If his mother wasn't dead already, I'd kick her in her teeth for doing that to him.

The movie was okay. Movies made from books were almost always like that. He seemed to be fine with skipping the last one.

As we pulled up to Tom's little house, I felt the urge to kiss him. It was strange because I didn't want to kiss and grope him…although he was totally grope-worthy. The closeness of his body made me tingle, which made me want to be all sweet with him, and possibly even have a real end-of-first-date kiss or some shit.

That was when I kicked myself.

I was not that girl and he was not my *boyfriend*. This wasn't a date and I wasn't sweet. Kissing Rusty Dalton? What was next, holding his hand and stroking his cheek? I felt like such a moron, but when he'd asked me which book I wanted to borrow first with that sexy, unassuming smile of his, I couldn't help myself.

This was messed up.

I felt messed up as I leaned over the console and pressed my lips against his. My heart started beating faster. What was I doing? My head told me this was wrong. These were fifth-grade antics, so I brought my hand to his thigh. It rested there for only a moment before I moved it up, closer to where the bulge in his pants was growing.

He was hard and that made me happy, because it meant that I didn't make as big a fool of myself as I had thought with that stupid-school-girl-kissing shit. He wanted me too.

Then his chest heaved as he pushed my shoulders back. Our lips lost contact and I withdrew my hand. I was about to get pissed until I saw his face. His eyes were steadfastly glued to the ceiling of the car and he was panting.

He wanted me. I could tell that he wanted me, so what the hell was going on? I thought for a moment that maybe he was a virgin, but that couldn't be, since Megan Simons had clearly said they'd had sex. She could've lied, but why? Maybe he just liked taking things slowly, or perhaps he was playing hard-to-get. Either way, he didn't shove me back because he didn't want me. I licked my lips and breathed out. "Sorry."

I shouldn't have touched him. While I was normally impulsive, I should have controlled this better. I should've known that a small, innocent kiss was something I could never do. I should have seen that I would screw it up in some way, and I shouldn't have even tried it in the first place. Now I'd probably emotionally scarred him for life because here he was just dropping off some effed-up girl and minding his own business and then I…

Shit! Why couldn't I just be a normal girl?

Shaking my head, I whispered, "Sorry," again.

Elliott turned to me, eyes wide, lips pressed together. He shook his head almost violently as if needing me to know something important. Finally he spoke, or rather, tried to speak. "N-n-n-nooooo, S-S-S-So-Soph-Sophie." That was the worst I'd ever heard him butcher my two-syllable name. "P-p-p-p…"

Without thinking, I ran a hand through his hair and he closed his eyes for a minute. I had no idea where that action came from, but suddenly I was comforting him. I'd never comforted another living soul in my life, but somehow I knew it was the right thing to do. I removed my hand and looked away. "I didn't mean to make you uncomfortable," I whispered.

I dug around in the bag in the backseat and pulled out a book. "I'll take this one first." He nodded, his lips pressed tightly together again. "Thanks, Elliott," I said casually as I popped the door open. Once I was standing outside, I leaned down and said, "I'll see you, Monday."

He looked at me and his mouth opened as if to speak, but I quickly looked away.

Shit. I felt like an idiot as I shoved the door closed and walked up to Tom's house. The porch light was on and I didn't even have to unlock the door, because he pulled it open himself.

"Spying?"

Although his eyes narrowed, he gave me a smirk. "Just making sure the delinquent didn't manhandle you."

As Tom shut the door behind me, I said, "Manhandle? Elliott Dalton? Obviously you don't know him."

"He's an adopted kid in therapy, Soph, how well do I need to know him?"

I shook my head. "You're an ass, just like everyone else in this ignorant town." Before I could get reprimanded for my use of "unladylike language," I held up my book. "He tried to buy me some books, and when I wouldn't let him, he bought them for himself and said I could borrow them. Not much worry about manhandling from a dude that buys classic literature, Tom."

He gave me a weak, apologetic smile. "I'm not trying to be overprotective, I just-"

"Good, because you're a little late for that." I watched as his expression changed. "I'm going to bed."

"Did you eat?"

I sighed at my pointlessly concerned parental figure. "Like I said, Tom, a little late."

~ • ~

"What's that smile for?"

I looked over at Jason as he buttoned up his jeans, his smirk telling me that he already knew what my smile was about. "I was just thinking if there is a god, it's definitely a chick. *That* was awesome."

"Glad to be of service," he said with laugh.

I stood up, tugging down my top and looking around the narrow cave. It was damp and fairly cold, but for some reason, it seemed like a natural place to be. "So how many girls have you deflowered here?"

"Deflowered?" he asked, the laugh still present in his voice. "I've never deflowered anyone, Sophie."

"What?" I was honestly shocked. A dude like Jason would be a great first time. "You're full of shit. Come on, I'm not your girlfriend. I swear I won't be offended if you tell me the truth."

He lit a cigarette and then sat down on a jutted-out rock. "I've never had sex with a virgin, Sophie. That's the truth."

I smiled as I moved to sit down next to him. "Well let me go out and find you one, 'cause, Jesus, it'll be that girl's lucky day. You know what you're doing."

He shook his head. "No, thanks." I quirked my brow. "Too much responsibility. There'll have to be hearts and flowers and lots of foreplay."

"You're good at foreplay." That was the truth.

He shrugged. “Doesn’t really interest me. I don’t really think it’s a turn-on having to do all the work, while the girl just lies there.” He gave me a look. It was the first time since we’d started the conversation that he actually looked at me. It made me slightly uncomfortable. I didn’t know why, I just knew that it did.

“A girl like you is perfect for me. Experienced.”

I wrinkled my nose.

He saw my expression and quickly said, “Not, like, slutty experienced. You get what I’m saying. You know what you like and you don’t wait around for me to give it to you; you make it happen. I don’t need some sappy virgin that’s going to want me to meet her parents afterward.”

A girl like you is perfect for me. I cringed. I totally didn’t want to get into being perfect for Jason. I stood up quickly, running my hands through my hair. “So can you score acid? I haven’t tripped in a long time.”

I was perfect for no one.

“The last time I tripped, no one was guiding me and there were Tree People and they started out like the Ents in *The Lord of the Rings* but ended up like the tree from one of the Poltergeist movies, trying to eat me and all that shit. So, it’d be nice to—”

“What the fuck are Ents?”

I sighed. Jason was not cultured and I wondered if he even owned a book. “Haven’t you seen *Lord of the Rings*?”

"That's gay, Sophie. Fucking hairy-footed little people and elves and shit?"

I decided to let it go, otherwise I might geek-out on him. I guess if the movie didn't have a car chase or something exploding, a guy like Jason wouldn't be interested. "So, acid. Can you get any?"

"I sell weed, Sophie."

"So that's a 'no' to the acid? What about painkillers? Does Jerry have a script? Bet he's on Methylin for his shit, right?"

"Yeah, but he uses those pills." He rolled his eyes. "He counts out three a day and would probably throw knives at me if there were any missing."

❧ • ❧

I woke up on Monday feeling foolishly excited to see Elliott. It made no sense for me to feel that way about a boy. I mean, yeah, he was incredibly good-looking and I could completely see myself banging the living shit out of him, but he was *too* nice. What the hell would I seriously do with a nice guy like him? Why the hell was I excited?

We watched one movie together, ate pizza, and listened to music, and now I was ready to…to what? It totally wasn't me to be all puppy-dog with boys.

And when the hell had he become "Elliott" and not "Rusty Dalton?" I totally didn't need to crush on Elliott Dalton of all people. I would just hurt him.

Jason was early as usual, and we clam-baked on the way to school. Smoking a joint with the windows rolled up tight got me really high. I was incredibly thankful to smoke his free pot.

I saw Elliott in the hallway before first period. His hair was shorter. I wasn't sure if I liked it. For some reason, that small half-inch of hair being gone made me a little sad. It wasn't long enough anymore to fall over his eyes when he looked down.

I watched him like I normally did, but as usual, he never looked up. It was better that way. If I saw his hazel eyes, I was sure that I would swoon like a silly little girl. I hated myself for having these feelings.

I needed something to numb them; to snuff them out. I didn't want to feel this shit. I didn't deserve to feel this shit.

Jason had told me that if I wanted something other than pot, Aiden Montgomery was the person to see. I knew of him. He was nice-looking; not a dirty hippie like Jason, and not quite a jock like Anderson. Apparently Aiden had been out on the Chesapeake Bay in the summer and was involved in a boating accident. He now had a plethora of pain pills at his disposal. Apart from that, he was Damascus' resident hard drug dealer.

I hoped that by the weekend I'd be trippin' balls. That would be all it took to get back to my regularly-scheduled life and forget about my "feelings" for Elliott.

The day sucked. The only class before lunch that was remotely interesting was Photography. Pinny Dalton and I developed our film in the darkroom together. She talked almost constantly about her boyfriend and how much she loved him, and then switched into how one day she wanted to be a professional photographer or a history teacher. She couldn't decide. It was mind-numbing, but nice. I liked Pinny, despite her non-stop talking. She wasn't too deep and she smiled at me like we were already old friends. Plus, she took my mind off all the stuff I didn't want think about.

The post-lunch pot helped me not turn into a gooey mess in Horticulture. I was confronted by Elliott's amazing eyes, but managed just give him a small nod instead of throwing myself at him.

He looked tired. I wanted to talk to him, but it was incredibly awkward. There was no privacy at school and what the hell would I have said anyway? Most of the class I just daydreamed about being somewhere else. I did my best to ignore that somehow I had managed to let Rusty Dalton get under my skin.

It was so messed up. I was so messed up. Sophie's number one rule was to not let anyone in; especially idiotic high school boys.

But he wasn't an idiot.

Damn. I needed to pull my head out of my ass.

Thank the Flying Spaghetti Monster the bell rang and I could leave this den of torture and go to…well, to another den of torture – P.E. But at least there I could take out my aggression by being blatantly clumsy.

It was on Wednesday that I found the opportunity to talk with Aiden. I skipped Photography when I saw him in the hallway. All he did was smirk at me when I asked to talk to him privately.

We went out to his brand-new Escalade. The windows were tinted and I suspected that they were too dark to be legal. "So, what's up, Sophie Young?"

I smiled at him, leaning back against the door. His olive skin offset the brightness of his eyes. "Jason doesn't sell acid and I want some." There was no need to dance around the topic. He had something I wanted.

His smile grew. "Are you a narc, Sophie?"

I huffed. "Of course not. Would Jason sell to me if I was?" He shrugged and I sighed again. "No, I'm not a narc."

"Jason says you're cool."

"Then sell me some acid already." He gave me another smirk. It was beginning to annoy me. This whole thing should've been pretty simple, just like going to Walmart. But there he was smirking at me like he couldn't care less about the whole thing. "What?" I asked.

"Are you Fox's girlfriend or what?"

I couldn't help but laugh. I was no one's girlfriend; that was for sure. "No. Why? Do you have something against selling to girlfriends of Jason Fox?"

He shook his head. "Like he has enough game to get a girlfriend."

Boys were morons. "He bones like a porn star, Aiden, but I'm not his girlfriend."

"If he's so great, why aren't you?"

Taking a deep breath, I moved closer to him. “Why buy the cow when I can get the milk for free?” I’d heard a million people say that about my mother and her boyfriends. I paused for only a moment before continuing, “I don’t want a boyfriend.”

“But you have sex with him, right?”

I gave no other response than a quick roll of my eyes. Wasn’t that what we were already talking about?

“Do you want to have sex with me?”

It was nearly time for lunch when I walked back into the school, still feeling empty as usual, with a hit of acid wrapped in plastic hidden inside the pocket of my jeans.

I looked at no one, especially Elli…no…Rusty Dalton, as I waited for Jason to finish his lunch so we could go smoke.

Chapter 12

Challenging the Realities

Sophie

Thursday morning was the start of an annoying day. Boneheaded Jason Fox never picked me up for school, so I had to take the public bus, which made me late and resulted in a lunchtime detention.

It wasn't like Jason didn't go to school. He wasn't sick or anything. No, the asshole was there and accounted for, he just hadn't bothered coming to get me. Due to my detention, I didn't get the chance to talk to him because I had to report to the office halfway through Study Hall. Instead, I found myself in the last few moments between lunch and Horticulture listening to Andrea Tuttle puke up her lunch.

She came out of the bathroom stall, pulling her hair back and looking at herself in the mirror. She turned sideways, studying her profile. I could tell she wasn't happy with what she saw. She looked fine to me, maybe a little too skinny, but I wouldn't tell her that. She wouldn't believe me anyway. I'd known enough girls in Tampa with eating issues, and telling a bulimic girl she was too thin would just send her into hysterics.

She bent down and turned on the tap, scooping water into her mouth before swishing and spitting it out. Standing up straight again, she turned it off and looked at me through the mirror. "Don't tell anyone, okay, Sophie?"

I shrugged. "Who am I going to tell?" I didn't think Megan or Chris would really give a damn if Andrea puked herself into an early grave. Her friends didn't seem the type to be overly-compassionate. Hell, a bitch like Cierra probably knew and shoved her thousand-calorie slice of pizza under Andrea's nose every day.

"You'd be surprised."

"By what?"

Andrea studied herself again, sighing and tugging her shirt down like she was covering up some non-existent roll of fat. "By how many people here would rat on me if they figured it out. If Robin Wallace or my mother found out…"

"Screw Wallace," I huffed, "and screw your mom too." I was in a horrible mood. Usually by this time I was nice and high, but thanks to Mr. No-Show Fox, I was sober and there were still hours left in my day. "I would never say shit to Wallace."

She turned and gave me a smile. "Thanks, Sophie."

As we headed out of the bathroom, I decided I didn't care if she went into hysterics, I had to ask. "Why do you do it? Do you really think you're too fat? I mean, I know you're smart and shit, I just don't understand."

"It's a control thing," she admitted quietly. I turned to her. She looked incredibly nervous, as if she was completely exposing herself. "It's the only thing I have."

I wanted to ask her more, but it would have been incredibly inappropriate and totally not my business. Plus, the more I pried into her life, the more she'd start to pry into mine and I already had too many people interested in the life and times of Sophie Young.

I entered the greenhouse and immediately my eyes were drawn to my work partner, Rusty Dalton. I'd done my best over the course of the week to keep a good and healthy distance from him, only really talking to him when absolutely necessary. He seemed to be doing the same. I was sure he was mortified that I'd practically jumped him in his car last Saturday.

Hell, *I* was mortified. I felt pathetic. What was I supposed to say?

Before I could get to my desk, Chris Anderson jumped up and blocked my path. "Sophie!"

I sighed. "Chris," I answered, sounding unenthused.

"So, you know, there's a dance coming up in two weeks."

I just stood there waiting for the asshole to ask. He kept looking at me as if I was supposed to throw myself at him at the mere mention of a school dance. "And?"

"Do you want to go with me?"

"Seriously?"

"Yeah, seriously," he replied, his tone turning a bit indignant.

"No, I don't."

His eyes darkened. I'd seen that look before on other boys; other men. As much as I disliked Chris and didn't really care about his feelings, I certainly didn't want to make an enemy. Up until this point, I'd been able to peg him with basketballs and then manipulate him into thinking it was purely accidental. I didn't want to piss him off. I barely knew him, or what he was capable of.

"I don't really dance, Chris, and my father is…"

"Are you going with Jason Fox?"

I smiled as I pictured Jason and me, stoned at a high school dance. "No. I doubt he's the semi-formal-in-the-gym kind of guy."

"Are you dating him?"

What the hell was it with these stupid-ass Damascus boys? "He's a friend, Chris." I turned around quickly to see that Mr. Reese had taken his place at the front of the class. "Class is starting." His glare didn't let up. "Ask Megan. She'll want to go with you." Megan was constantly talking about boys, but about Chris most of all.

He let out a heated breath. "Of course she wants to go with me, Sophie, I'm not brainless." He could have fooled me. I nearly said that to him, but I stopped myself. "I've already tapped that."

Chris Anderson was an ass. Megan wasn't my favorite person in the world, but he didn't have to be so crass about it. She really liked him. "Then don't ask her, but I'm not going with you."

I pushed past him, annoyed that I actually had to shove him out of the way in order to get to my seat. Elliott's eyes were fixed on his notebook, but I knew he'd seen and heard the entire exchange. I hoped he got a little bit of joy out of watching me shut Anderson down. If I was the type to go to school dances, I would take Rusty Dalton and ask him in front of Chris.

Then again, who knew if Rusty Dalton would accept and why was I thinking about that anyway? Thinking about stupid high school dances with stupid high school boys was stupid.

❧ • ❧

"What the hell?"

Jason shook his head as he lit the joint, not looking at me. "What's your deal, Sophie?" He sounded bored.

"Why'd you ditch me yesterday? Why're you acting like you're avoiding me today?"

"Jesus," he sighed. "We're smoking together, right? How is that avoiding?"

I grabbed the joint and inhaled. Thank the FSM for this at least. Jason had yet again failed to pick me up for school this morning. Yesterday I had to get a ride home with Andrea. "What the hell?" I repeated as I held in the smoke.

His face was so tense. He looked absolutely pissed and I had no idea why. Everything was cool on Wednesday, although now that I thought about it, he was very quiet on the ride home. I wished he would just tell me what the hell was wrong with him and stop acting like such a needy girl.

"Jason," I said loudly as I exhaled.

"You didn't have to fuck him."

"What?" What the hell was he talking about?

"Aiden. He would have sold you that tab without you letting him hump you in his SUV."

Jesus Christ. *That* was what this was about? Because he thought I had sex with Aiden? I'd just *barely* made out with him. "I didn't do him. Wait. You think I did him for the acid?" What an ass. "I'm not a whore." I paused for emphasis. "And just in case you're wondering, I don't do you for pot either, you ass. I give you money, the same as the rest of your customers."

He rolled his eyes and I wanted to smack him. "Whatever."

"First off, I can have sex with whomever I want. Second, I *didn't* have sex with him, but if I did, it would be because I *wanted* to, not because I wanted acid. Third, what the hell's your problem? I told you from the beginning that I'm not your girlfriend, which means I can do whatever I want with other people."

I grabbed the joint from him with one hand and smacked him in the chest with the other. "You don't *own* me." I inhaled deeply, hoping that the pot would wash away what was transpiring.

"Thank God for that," he mumbled.

"Don't be a douche, Jason." I hated possession. I hated boys thinking that the minute you touched their penis, you were theirs.

I shoved the joint back at him and he took it, shrugging his shoulders.

"Aiden Montgomery is a dick. You didn't have to bang him." He took a hit and as he held it in, he continued, his voice sounding distorted. "Don't you even want to know *how* I know about your Escalade-rocking?" He paused for the briefest moment. "Because he *told* anyone who would listen, Sophie." I sighed, wishing he was lying, but knowing he probably wasn't. *That* was annoying considering I *didn't* have sex with him. Obviously Jason thought I was lying.

Finally sitting down next to him, I exhaled before plucking the weed from his fingers. "So this outburst of yours is less about anger over me having sex with someone, and more about who that someone might've been?"

For a moment, Jace was silent as he lit a cigarette, apparently finished with the smoldering roach between my fingers. He ran a hand though his hair and for the first time locked his eyes with mine. "He's a douche, Sophie, and you'll be lucky if he doesn't have the whole thing on YouTube by the weekend."

I blew out the hit, flicked the joint down, and listened to the satisfying sizzle as it went out. "I didn't have sex with him," I repeated.

"Yeah, right. He's done just about every girl in Damascus above the age of fourteen, so I'm not surprised he went after you too." He wrinkled his nose and shook his head. "Seriously, Sophie, you should get tested now."

"Whatever." I could tell by his voice he wasn't seriously concerned for the health of my vagina.

"Well, if your naughty parts start itchin', don't say I didn't warn you."

ல • ல

"Where are you going?" I asked Jason, as he headed toward the Dalton's stairs. I wasn't happy to be here again.

He shrugged. "My turn with Robin."

I made a face, indicating my disgust. "Yuck." He turned and ascended the stairs. I'd be left alone with the rest of the Screw-Up Club until he returned, and then I'd probably have to be subjected to Bitch Wallace too.

Everyone was sort of milling around, except the Daltons and their entourage. They all sat together on the couch. Well, Elliott was sort of sitting with them. It was obvious that he was a part of their group, but equally obvious that he was a fifth wheel. I turned around quickly, not wanting to engage Pinny Dalton or her brother before it was absolutely necessary.

Moving through the hall, I found Andrea Tuttle next to a table filled with food. She looked absolutely miserable and probably wanted to gorge herself sick. "This is probably the least comfortable place for an anorexic-bulimic girl, you know."

She looked up at me. "Yeah, but Dr. Dalton's watching. I have to at least *look* like I'm contemplating eating something."

I turned, finding the handsome doctor easily. He was in casual clothes, leaning against the archway that led to the kitchen. He wasn't only looking at Andrea. Dr. Dalton's perfect cinnamon-brown eyes took in each of the kids in the room.

So, he was the spy. The *sexy* spy. "Damn, he's fine." Andrea just snorted. "What? You don't think he's sexy as hell?"

She turned to regard him, her eyes traveling from his feet up to the perfectly-groomed hair on his head. Damn, his hair looked good. "No, he's sexy, but every soccer mom in Damascus has tried to get with him."

"Well, I'm not a soccer mom."

"Ew, Sophie. *Please* do not throw yourself at Dr. Dalton."

Sighing, I tore my gaze from him and turned to her. "Who says I'd *throw* myself at him? Perhaps I would seduce him until he threw himself at me."

Andrea laughed. "Did your dad put you in therapy because you live in a delusional fantasy world, or what?"

I cracked a smile. Andrea was pretty damn funny. I guess I liked her. "Shut up."

"I'll make you a deal. The day you get Dalton, and by that I mean *Doctor* Dalton, to beg you to sleep with him, I'll eat an entire meal, with dessert, without tossing it five minutes afterward."

"Well, now you've ruined it. How could I call myself your friend if my happiness cost you those calories?" Andrea rolled her eyes and looked like she was going to say something else, but didn't get the chance.

Dr. Dalton made his way over to us and gave me a winning smile. Part of me swooned and the other part was annoyed by my newfound ability to swoon over all things Dalton. "Sophie," he said smoothly, "your father is concerned that perhaps you're not eating enough."

Andrea's eyes widened and I said, "What?"

"He's concerned that…"

Then I remembered last Friday night and my hypoglycemic episode. "I missed *one* meal."

Thankfully, at that very moment Jason found me and let me know it was my turn with Wallace. While I hated my time with her, I was grateful to be spared a lecture on the importance of monitoring my diabetes.

I found her waiting for me, her worthless little notebook on her lap. "Hello, Sophie."

I wondered if they taught all shrinks how to speak like that in school. All calming and soothing and shit. "Hi," I said as I plopped down in the chair. Our eyes locked, and I wondered if we were going to play the staring game today.

I didn't have to wait long for the answer. "How was your trip to D.C.?"

"Good." Did she ask Elliott that question? What was his answer? Did he tell her that I practically assaulted him before getting out of the car?

She smiled. "That's great. I think Elliott enjoyed it too." After a moment of silence, she said, "Let's talk about our goals." She paused to gauge my reaction. "First, I would like to preface this conversation by telling you that it doesn't take a lot of effort to recognize some of the traumas you've undergone as you've grown up." My whole body tensed. "It is also very clear to me that you are reluctant to talk about it. Just so you know, I'm not asking you to talk to me because I'm a therapist Sophie, but because in the long run, it would be far better for you to work these issues out with a trained professional."

I shook my head. She didn't know shit. What she had were assumptions. "What *things* are you talking about?"

I was tired and I really wasn't in the mood. I didn't care what goals she had for me. I didn't really care what she knew about me or my past, and I certainly didn't want to hash out issues that were nothing more than history now.

"I'd like to talk about some of the broken bones and contusions that are very clearly visible on some of your x-rays. Your father released them for me to review with Dr. Dalton."

"I'm clumsy."

Wallace shook her head. "I don't believe you."

"I don't care if you do."

"Why are you protecting your mother? Your father has custody now. She can't hurt you anymore."

I had to hand it to her. She was ballsy and straightforward. I looked down at my hands as they picked at the worn fabric covering my knee. "I don't know what you're talking about."

"Sophie."

I looked up. I just wanted her to drop it. I didn't understand why she wanted me to talk about my mother. If she and Dr. Dalton had figured out where my broken bones came from, then why the hell did I need to talk about it?

She just sat there looking at me. "Can't you at least start with an easy topic? Maybe just *pretend* that trust is something that needs to be built?"

"Do you have a hard time trusting people?"

Narrowing my eyes at her, I shook my head. "What do you think?"

Her lips pursed together and she acted like she was truly studying me. "I think you only trust yourself and your trust is very hard to win but once someone has it, you give it to them freely."

She was so damn wordy. "I don't know about all that, but if you think I'm just going to trust you because you've got some degree or something, you're an idiot."

She gave me a smile that was probably supposed to make me feel like she was my friend, but it didn't work. She still just seemed like some woman trying to weasel things out of me; things she wasn't supposed to know.

"You're right, Sophie." Of course I was right. I didn't need her to validate it. "If you're uncomfortable about jumping right into the hard stuff, let's talk about a lighter subject."

I shrugged, letting her know she could try.

"How are you enjoying Damascus High? I know you have a class with Elliott, and Photography with Jane, but how are you transitioning?"

That was what she wanted to talk about? I was beginning to wonder if Wallace was trained at all. "School's fine."

"I think it's great that you're a photographer. I've always thought that having a creative outlet is vital. Perhaps someday you'll show me your work."

The rest of the session went the same way. Wallace kept asking me small questions, unrelated to my past, my mother, or what she perceived as my "issues". Group was boring as hell. Jason's partner, Olivia, talked about something. I didn't know what exactly. Maybe something about being picked last for dodge ball as a kid or something ridiculously simple like that.

Honestly, I didn't want group to end. It meant that I would be alone with Elliott, and I didn't want that. I was already entirely too wrapped up in him. He should've just stayed "Rusty Dalton" and not "Elliott", who liked Russian novels and music, and had lived in Chicago with a heroin-addicted mother who shot herself in the head.

I sighed deeply. It was no use. I was already attached to the good-looking social outcast who stuttered and didn't smile enough. There wasn't any stopping how I felt about him. The only thing I could do was stop myself from *acting* like a fucking fool.

So when group was over, I looked over at Elliott and saw him sitting there as usual, as everyone else got up and headed to various parts of the house. I waited. Finally he looked at me. Still, I didn't move; even my face was frozen in place. I didn't know what I was doing or *why* I was testing him, but it felt vital that I force him to make the first move.

His brow creased and his tongue flicked out over his lower lip quickly, his hands rubbing up and down on his thighs. I was making him nervous. He opened his mouth in an attempt to say something, but then gave up and closed it. He let out a breath. Still, I waited.

It wasn't until he tilted his head toward the stairs that I let myself move, my lips curled up in a satisfied smile. I didn't break first. I caught sight of his uneven smile as he stood.

Wordlessly, I followed him up the stairs and down the hall to the only place I felt comfortable in the Dalton house. It wasn't until we were in Elliott's room that I spoke. My eyes were fixed on the wall, but I knew he was looking at me. With a short nod to the instruments, my voice all soft and girly, I said, "Play something for me."

Chapter 13

Normal

Elliott

My brain didn't start working again until Sophie disappeared into her house. I was such an idiot! She'd kissed me and I hadn't been prepared for it. Her roaming hand on my leg was also shocking, because her initiating something like that with *me* had never crossed my mind.

After I dropped her off, I sat at the curb outside her house far longer than was appropriate, and had to force myself to leave before her father came out to scare me away. Even when I got to my house, I sat in the car for nearly a half-hour.

It would have been extremely embarrassing to answer questions about how my day in D.C. went while sporting a relatively painful erection.

Even after all that time, it didn't subside, so I had no other choice but to go inside and hope no one noticed. I had the bag from the bookstore to keep in front of me, but thankfully I didn't need it, since the house was quiet when I walked in. I had expected Stephen to be waiting at the door, checking me for any outward signs of anxiety or stress. If not Stephen, then perhaps Jane would be waiting to interrogate me about how pretty Sophie was. The evidence would have spoken for itself.

I didn't know where Stephen or David was, but Jane must've been in her darkroom. Sometimes she lost herself in there, spending hours and hours developing film the way I spent countless hours with my instruments.

Thankful that I wasn't ambushed, I rushed up to my room, letting the bag drop to the floor as I locked my door.

I was such a freak. A normal teenager could have thought about baseball, grandmothers, dead puppies, or some other clichéd thing to get his penis under control. Not me. As usual, once it was sprung, it had no intention of leaving willingly.

This had happened before, most notably after the thing with Megan Simons my freshman year.

It wouldn't go away, no matter what I did. There were no real words in the English language to describe how painful something like an erection could be after a couple of hours. I did what I could to relieve the situation, but it had never been natural for me to masturbate.

I was feeling so desperate after a hot shower and multiple attempts at making it go away, that I was beginning to consider asking for help.

I hated even *thinking* about talking to Stephen about the depth of my dysfunction, but he was a doctor and no matter how scared I was of exposing my situation, he probably had some kind of drug that could help me.

I wanted it to go away. I thought of Sophie in every inappropriate way while attempting the act that so many people felt was natural, but as the hours drifted by it became too painful to even touch, and I felt dirty with guilt and shame.

I *had* to go talk to Stephen and hope that he had something to alleviate the situation. It took everything I had to force myself to stand up and walk to his room. It was late and Stephen had been working so many hours at the hospital. I didn't want to disturb him.

My jaw tightened as I knocked and then waited. I heard a thump and a rustle. My heart started to accelerate. This was a horrible idea. I heard a murmur and I wondered if Stephen was talking to himself. Had I not been preoccupied with the pain I was experiencing, I would have realized sooner that Stephen might not have been alone.

I should have just dealt with the situation on my own. How asinine could I be? I turned and practically ran back to my room.

With the door shut and locked behind me, I realized that I was back to where I started.

I very carefully sank down onto my bed and thought about everything I possibly could that wasn't related to sex. It took a while before my mind settled on something that could possibly work. It was already on my mind and now was the perfect time to relive it.

As I thought about my blood-and-brain-splattered door back in Chicago, the physical pain lessened.

~ • ~

I awoke on Sunday to the sound of knocking. The clock read twelve-thirty. It had been a long day yesterday, and an even longer night. It wasn't until the wee hours of the morning that I fell asleep.

"Elliott, I'm not going to stand out here forever, you know. I don't care what Dad says, I'll open this door and drag you out."

I sighed deeply, shoving the covers off of my legs as I rolled out of bed, tugging on my shirt. I had to put up with David waking me up five days a week, but now on Sunday too? Before I went to the door, I looked down, double-checking that the erection hadn't returned in my sleep.

Thankful that it hadn't, I finally unlocked and opened the door. "W-w-what?"

David was wearing his large, dopey smile and pointed to his head. "Rebecca's over giving haircuts today and if you don't hurry, she'll give you a bowl cut."

I rolled my eyes, but nodded. "R-R-Rebec-c-c-ca d-d-did that?" I nodded to his hair. Rebecca was fairly vocal about her enjoyment of David's slightly longer hair. I didn't want to know this, but apparently it felt good when she ran her fingers through it.

He shrugged. "It's for the Homecoming court."

Knowing I needed to leave my room before Stephen became worried and called Robin for another session, I said, "I-I-I'll be d-d-d-down in a m-m-m-mmmm…"

"Minute, got it. I'll tell Becca to choose something other than a mullet or a bowl cut."

He winked good-naturedly before turning and retreating down the hall. I shut the door and locked it. Looking down, I saw that the bag of books was still by the door where I had dropped it last night. I bent down to retrieve it and as I created a spot for them in my bookcase, I very carefully trained my thoughts on something other than Sophie. There was no need to accidentally excite myself again.

Not after last night.

⁂

Monday was the beginning of a strange and confusing week at school. Sophie didn't speak to me at all on Monday, nor did she look at me more than once. The smile she gave me wasn't real.

I didn't understand it. I thought our trip had gone well, and *she* had kissed *me* at the end of it, not the other way around.

Then on Tuesday we had to complete another task together, and again she barely acknowledged my presence. Maybe my inability to be normal had cost me her respect. Maybe she realized after Saturday that I had absolutely nothing to offer. Maybe she regretted even asking me to go with her.

It could have been any number of things. Maybe it was my failure to return her kiss or my inept speaking ability. Perhaps it was because I foolishly told her all that stuff about my mother. Maybe it was that I didn't get high like she did.

I was a social leper and Sophie Young had figured it out.

When I entered Ms. Rice's office that day, I was in no mood to read children's books. The word "depressed" didn't even begin to cover the depths of my current emotion. I hated my stuttering. I hated my family history. I hated Stephen and Robin for forcing me to talk to Sophie. I hated just about everything.

So when Ms. Rice asked me if I'd like to pick the book today, I crossed my arms and refused to speak. She tried, but couldn't get me to budge. I hated that she took my silence as her failure, but I had nothing to say.

I didn't speak to anyone that day. The worried looks on everyone's faces didn't escape me, but there was nothing to talk about. I didn't want to hear my own stuttering, stammering voice. I didn't want to hear or acknowledge the verbal ineptitude that I was sure had pushed Sophie away.

Wednesday, Stephen decided that he was concerned enough to call Robin. Once again, I found myself in his study, pinned to the overstuffed chair by the weight of Robin's stare. "Elliott, what has you silent again?"

Everything, I mentally answered her.

"Did something happen last weekend on your trip to D.C.? Was Sophie…?"

I fought against my urge to speak, but I lost the battle. If I didn't speak up, Robin would come up with her own scenario. She would decide that something horrible happened and that Sophie had somehow caused me to regress. She would tell Stephen and then I'd never be allowed to go anywhere or be alone in the house again.

"N-n-no. I-I'm ffffffine, R-Robin."

Clasping her hands in her lap, she leaned forward, piercing me with her shrink stare.

I sighed exaggeratedly. "I-I'm ffffine," I said again. One day, she'd believe me when I said that.

That day wasn't today.

"No, you're not." For a moment, she was silent and then her expression changed. It was as if she was deciding something. Finally, she shifted her expression back to neutral. "Why did you go to Stephen's room last Saturday night?"

My eyes widened. He told her about that? I was back in my room before he even opened the door. How could he have known it was me? Had she been in the room with him? Were they a couple now? Were they…

"Elliott?"

I was tired of being different. Even if I had a horrible childhood, why couldn't I at least pass as normal, like David? Why did I have to be the one with no friends? Why did I have to be the person Chris Anderson made fun of? "I-I w-w-want t-t-to be n-normal." I grimaced as the words came involuntarily from my mouth.

It was out there now, and Robin was all too ready to pounce on it. "Define 'normal.'"

I shook my head and lifted my eyes toward the ceiling. She knew what normal was. Everything I wasn't. I wished that I could have taken my bumbled words back, but I couldn't. I had to sit there while Robin scrutinized me, probably making mental notes about my posture or how I picked absently at the skin on my left hand.

"Elliott, this notion you have about what is 'normal' is keeping you from seeing that it isn't the same for everyone. It's a very subjective concept."

Again I shook my head. I'd already said too much. I couldn't do much more harm. "N-n-n-no. I-I-I…"

I took a moment to compose myself. Her appearance radiated nothing but patience, so I tried to articulate what I truly wanted out of life. "I-I w-w-want t-t-to ttttalk liiiiike n-normal p-p-people." Running both hands down my face, I let them fall to my lap as I closed my eyes. "I-I w-want to have f-f-friends."

I heard her sigh but I couldn't bring myself to look at her again as she processed what I said. I didn't want to talk to her. Why I had said anything at all was beyond me.

"You have friends, Elliott." I shook my head in response. "I know for a fact David and Jane consider you a friend. And what about Trent and Rebecca?"

"Th-they h-ha-have to p-p-p-put up w-w-with me. Th-they h-have to liiiike me." I opened my eyes and fixed them on a picture behind Robin's head, enabling me to look past her, but still see her.

She smiled as a mother would. If she had been sitting closer, perhaps she would have ruffled my hair. "People don't do what they don't *want* to do on some level. We all like you because we want to like you. What about Sophie?"

I shook my head, lowering my eyes once more. I didn't want to talk about Sophie. She wasn't my friend and I couldn't expect her to be. She'd given it a shot on Saturday and I had failed to give her reason to like me.

⁂

Thursday, I looked on as Chris Anderson asked Sophie to the Homecoming dance in front of me. It would be a complete and total lie if I said that I wasn't extremely happy that she'd turned him down flat, but when she finally made it to our table, I kept my eyes down.

It wasn't until Friday when I finally felt some hope. She was confusing and I had no clue what went on inside her head, but as the group session ended, Sophie didn't move. It took forever for her to finally look at me and when she did, she remained frozen.

I had no idea what she was doing and why. I nearly panicked. Was she trying to tell me that she had no intentions of keeping up the pretense of being interested? Was she just being defiant? She was making me insanely nervous. I already felt like a complete idiot around her.

Then in a last-ditch effort, I nodded toward the stairs and she finally smiled. I felt like I could breathe again. My nerves were still getting the better of me as she followed me to my room.

We were always good in my room and as I entered, I hoped with everything I had that we could just be like we were before, and forget the strangeness of the week.

It took her a minute, but finally she said. “Play something for me.”

Her voice wasn’t confident like usual. It sounded sad, or maybe resigned. It was soft and it seemed as if she actually thought I might say no to her request.

I followed her eyes to my guitars and for some reason, my nerves settled down immediately. She took her usual seat on the couch, and studied me as I pulled down my favorite Gibson and sat down at the desk chair.

Although I kept my eyes cast down, I took a few glances up as I played. She just sat there watching me, her knees pulled up to her chest, arms wrapped around her legs. I couldn’t read her face, so I had no real indication if she thought I was good, or if she even liked what I was playing.

I played someone else’s song. It was too soon to expose any more of myself by playing something I had written.

After I finished, I set the guitar down. “That was nice,” she said before turning to my bookcase.

I fixated on her hands. Her fingers were constantly moving. She rubbed the pads of her thumbs over her nails before balling her hands into fists and then uncurling them.

She was just…odd. Maybe she was high again.

It wasn't as if I had lots of experience with her, but she seemed different, and not as relaxed as she usually was. "A-are you o-okay?" I asked before I thought better of it.

Finally she looked up and smiled. "Yeah," she answered, her voice airy, "why?"

I shook my head, but watched her closely.

"I'm just…you know, its Friday…and I'm here."

Oh. I could see why that wouldn't be enjoyable for her. She was vibrant and fun and here she was, stuck with me. I looked down, feeling that once more there was no hope for me, but when she spoke again, I forced myself to look at her and noticed her whole demeanor had changed.

"Not that I'm upset about being here, you know, with *you*. That's not what I meant at all. It's just this fucking therapy shit. I mean, really. Between Olivia's anger and Andrea's vomit, I don't know what I'm supposed to do." She gave me a tentative smile that widened when I returned it.

"I know this can't be fun for you either, right?" I shook my head in response and she continued. "I mean, you've got to be around all this shit constantly."

She shifted, and then sat cross-legged. I tried to ignore that her shoes were on the couch. She leaned toward me. "So give me the scoop. I'm sure it was all covered in group before I got here, so there's no harm in telling me. Besides, I'd find out anyway."

I didn't follow what she was asking me about. "Th-the sc-scoop?"

Looking like I should know what she was talking about, she said, “Yeah, the scoop about the other Screw-Ups. What’s up with them? Why are they here?” When I didn’t respond, she continued. “Like your brother, or his girlfriend.”

While I didn’t exactly feel comfortable telling other people’s stories, she was right. Nothing I would tell her hadn’t been covered openly before. There would really be no harm in it. “D-D-David w-w-was c-c-conceived t-to b-be a mmmmatch ffffor his b-brother...”

“What?” she asked, her expression indicating she didn’t believe me. “A match?”

“A d-donor.” I watched as Sophie wrapped her mind around the concept. “His b-brother w-was sick. H-he n-needed all sssssorts of t-t-transplants and s-s-so they m-m-made D-David.” She looked stunned. “B-but w-when the t-transplants f-f-f-faaaa, were unsuccessful, h-his p-parents d-didn’t wwwwant him.”

“You can’t be serious.” Her shock was obvious. I nodded. “They *harvested* organs from him?”

“W-well that w-was the p-plan. Th-they took p-part of his liver and sssssome marrow, but w-when it d-didn’t w-work…” There was no need to finish the sentence. I was sure she got the idea and I really didn’t want to talk about what his parents put him through after that.

Typically, no one saw his pain, but every once in a while, when it got too much, he couldn’t reel it in. Stephen invested in a punching bag for the basement when he came home to a demolished wall and five broken bones in David’s right hand.

David's name meant "well-beloved" and "dear." That was exactly what he was now. It was why he tried so hard to be perfect for everyone.

"B-B-Becca's d-d-dad llllleft when sssshe w-w-was little. Hhhhe w-was m-mean."

"Well, if I was married to someone like Wallace, I'd leave too."

It wasn't a nice comment to make, especially since she didn't have all the information, but I ignored it. I thought about what I wanted to ask her all week. "S-Sophie?"

"Hmm?"

"Ar-are w-we f-f-fr-friends?"

She just stared at me and blinked. For a moment, I felt a flash of panic. Maybe I shouldn't have asked. Maybe she was going to say no. Maybe she was going to laugh at me. I didn't want either of those things to happen. I wanted her to say that we were absolutely friends, but either way, I felt relieved that I'd asked.

Chapter 14

Friends

Elliott

The panic I felt waiting for her answer finally subsided as she gave me a reassuring look and said, "Of course we're friends."

I studied her closely to see if she actually meant what she said or if she was just trying to sugarcoat the situation. Her smile seemed natural and she was looking right at me, so I felt relatively comfortable believing her.

While her words gave me some comfort, it also stirred up a plethora of follow-up questions. "W-w-why d-d-don't y-y-you t-t-t-t…" I sighed deeply. I probably wouldn't be able to get anything out, but I had to keep trying.

"Why don't I what?"

"T-t-talk t-to me at sc-school?"

The look of confusion faded as she ran her hands through her hair and let out a low breath before biting her lip. "This week was just… It wasn't you. I wasn't trying to be rude."

That wasn't a reason or an explanation. It was avoidance and it was clear to me what the problem was. She thought we could be friends outside of school, but while we were there... I really couldn't blame her. I knew she wouldn't want to be tied to a social pariah like me.

"I-is it b-because of hhhhhow I t-t-t-taaaaalk?"

She sighed and looked extremely annoyed. I felt really small and wished for the millionth time that I could be like David and Jane and just be comfortable and fit in, or at least act like it.

She leveled me with those intensely blue eyes. "You're not listening, Elliott. It's not *you*, okay?" She shook her head and pointed to herself. "I'm not…Look, we're friends, okay? And I don't care about your stutter. I'd much rather listen to you talk than that idiot Anderson, but I'm not like all the other kids. I don't…" She huffed. "I don't *talk* to friends at school. I mean, really, have you seen me really have a conversation with anybody? Chris? I think you've already figured out he's not even close to being my friend. And everyone else is just…filler."

While it was true that typically I only really saw her talk to Anderson, and it was never in a *friendly* way, there was a piece missing. "W-what about J-J-Jason?"

She ran her hands through her hair again and pulled it to the side, leaving her neck exposed. I tried not to look. I tried not to focus on how smooth her skin was. I tried not to see that I could pick up the rhythm of her heart by watching the pulsing vein in her neck. I tried not to see the four small raised marks that looked like the tines of a fork.

"You want to come out to the woods with us during Study Hall and smoke pot? If so, you're invited. Jason's...well, he's a family friend. I used to go hiking with him when I was a kid."

She stood up, turning her back to me as she began looking at my books again, her slender fingers gliding along the spines. Her fingernails were short, unlike Jane or Rebecca's, and she had little nicks and scars on her fingers and hands. "I never took you for someone who *wanted* to talk at school. Every time you do and a dick like Anderson says something, you go all quiet and look like you can't breathe. If you really want to have public conversations, we can..."

"N-no." That was *not* what I wanted. She was right about Anderson, and about me. "I-I-I just w-w-wanted to know if w-w-we were f-friends."

Sophie turned around. Again, she leveled a look at me. "Well, why wouldn't we be?"

Because she was so much better than I was. Because she was normal and I wasn't. Because she could be friends with anyone and I pretty much had nothing to offer.

I shrugged. If I was going to take her at face-value, then I could assume we were, in fact, friends, so asking her to do something with me in that capacity should be no big deal. After all, she asked me to go to the movies with her last weekend.

So why did my chest feel like it was about to explode? If she already confirmed we were friends, why was I dreading her rejection?

"S-So-Sophie?" She looked up. "D-d-do y-y-you w-w-w-want t-t-to g-go…"

"Elliott, don't." She cringed. "Please don't."

Any and all hope I had that I could just be a normal person and have a normal friendship fell apart. I hadn't even been able to properly ask her.

"Please don't ask me to that ridiculous dance. I don't… they really aren't my thing."

My hope swelled again. "I-I w-w-wasn't g-g-going to ask a-a-ab-b-bout the d-dance," I finished quickly.

"Good," she said, sounding relieved. "Because they're kind of lame, don't you think?"

I just gave her a hesitant smile. What I had in mind didn't require any dancing or streamers in the high school gym. I'd never gone to a dance. They might very well be lame, but I highly doubted going anywhere with Sophie would be lame at all.

"What were you going to ask then?"

"W-w-would y-you g-g-go sssssomewhere w-with me?"

Sophie chuckled and before I could misinterpret, she answered, "Somewhere? That's a little vague, Elliott. 'Somewhere' could be Mexico or 'somewhere' could be the library. Both of which I'd say yes to."

That made me happy. I felt triumphant, as if I had actually asked her to cross the border with me. "I-I-I d-don't know w-where. Just ssssomewhere. Just to h-hhhhhang out." I took a few deep breaths. The word "hang" was nearly blocked and I thanked God that I was able to get it out.

"Yeah, sure."

"D-do you w-w-want to g-g-go t-tomorrow?"

She frowned. "Oh, shit, I can't."

I must have made a face because she said, "I'm not just blowing you off, Elliott, but unless you want to drop some acid with me tomorrow, I'm going solo."

That wasn't the response I'd anticipated. I was expecting the normal girl letdown responses. "W-w-w-why a-ar-are you g-g-g-going to d-dr…"

"Because Damascus is a boring-ass town and I haven't tripped in a while."

"Do y-y-you lllllllike i-it?" I sighed. Obviously she liked it. I was such an idiot. "I-I m-mean, *w-w-why* d-d-do y-you llllllike it?"

Her expression changed and she got defensive. "Why don't *you* tell Anderson to fuck off?"

"I-I-I w-w-wasn't j-j-judging you, S-SSSophie. J-just asking."

She flopped down on the couch and raised a hand up into the air, watching as she made her fingers dance. "You obviously don't like that I enjoy drugs."

I wanted to protest and let her know I wasn't judging her even though I *hated* that she did drugs, but she kept going, answering my question.

"I partake in pharmaceutical and psychotropic drugs because I like that version of reality better. Have you ever done any drugs?"

"Wa-wa-wa," was all I could say, so instead I shook my head.

"No painkillers or nitrous oxide at the dentist?"

"W-w-well, yeah, I-I've h-had p-painkillers b-befffffore." Sedatives more times than I could count.

"Didn't you feel numb, I mean, not just that it took away whatever was aching or in pain, but like, mentally numb?" I nodded. "I like that. It makes everything a little fuzzy around the edges. Acid's awesome because reality shifts for a little while and the impossible happens. This reality," she said, waving her hand around, indicating my room, my house, this town, this world, "is just an illusion, Elliott. Even something as simple as smoking a little weed taps you into something…more, something better."

I shook my head, not wanting to judge her, but needing to let her know I completely disagreed. "M-m-my mmm-mm-m-mom…"

Sophie sat up and stared pointedly at me. "Your mom was a heroin addict. It's not the same thing. I don't do anything that's addictive or could permanently distort reality."

I failed to see the difference, but I kept my mouth shut.

"Look, I've done coke, but I wouldn't touch smack for anything. You wouldn't know, but rolling on ecstasy changes everything. I've never felt so loved and…loving." Her face shifted into an expression of longing before she looked down. "I…I don't expect you to understand it and if it's not your thing, that's cool, but *I* like it."

She looked back up, seeming perfectly normal again. "So tomorrow I'm dropping acid and going on a little spirit walk in the woods."

My heart raced. My breathing changed and all of a sudden I felt panicky. "In th-th-the w-w-w-woods? S-S-SSSSophie, y-y-y-y…wwwwwhat if y-y-you g-g-g-get l-l-l…"

"Calm down, Elliott," she said, her voice soft, but full of concern. She was worried about me. "Seriously, slow your breathing down. You're going to pass out."

I did my best to focus on my breathing, slowly dragging air in and letting it out even slower, but I still felt shaky. My lungs were tight. Sophie was going into the woods alone while hallucinating. People got lost in the woods all the time without acid to disorient them. She couldn't do that. I didn't want to hear about her going missing, and I didn't want to watch as people searched for her.

Why would she do that? Why was she so casual about drugs, as if every kid our age was into it?

"S-S-SSSSophie."

She stood and crossed the room. Before I realized what was happening, I felt her hand in my hair. Instantly, that chemical thing between us happened and I closed my eyes, my body relaxing just a little. My breathing slowed, as did my heart rate. How did she know how to do that?

"Elliott, I'll be fine. I promise. The woods near my house. I swear I won't go far."

❧ • ❧

Once again, I sat in front of Robin, waiting for her to get to the point of what she really wanted to talk about. We'd been dancing around the topic for the past twenty minutes. Finally, she said, "It was a difficult week."

Even though she didn't phrase it as a question, I knew she was asking me to validate what she'd said. "Y-y-yes."

"Because you don't feel normal? You feel different than the other kids?"

I looked down, but nodded.

"Do you only feel different because of your speech issue?"

I shook my head. I didn't want to tell Robin anything. I wanted to be in my room; however, it didn't matter what I *wanted* because my mouth opened, as if on its own, and I heard myself say, "I t-t-told S-S-Sophie a-a-ab-b-b-b," I paused, but I couldn't take it back. Robin would make me finish the sentence, so I continued. "A-a-about m-my mmmmmm-mm-mom."

Looking up, I saw the surprise on Robin's face. "Oh?"

I nodded.

"How do you feel about that?" she asked.

I shrugged, not really knowing how I felt.

"Sophie is obviously someone you feel you can trust. That was a big topic for you to discuss with her."

"Y-yeah." I shouldn't have told Robin. Now I'd be forced to talk about it.

"How did she react?"

I thought about her loud voice and the scowl on her face. "Sh-she w-w-was m-mad."

"At you?"

"A-at my mm-mm-mom."

"And how did that make you feel?"

I closed my eyes. It was always easier to answer Robin's incessant questions when I wasn't looking at her. "She d-doesn't kn-know."

"What doesn't she know?"

"M-my mmm-mm-mom. Sh-she th-thinks my mmmmmom w-was b-bad."

"Did she tell you that?"

I opened my eyes and shook my head. "B-but m-my mmm-mm-mmom w-w-wasn't b-bad."

"No. Your mother wasn't bad. She was sick."

"I-I d-don't think S-S-Sophie understands th-that."

"Addiction and depression are illnesses. Your mother didn't make the choice to be sick."

I suddenly became conscious that my breathing had sped up and my fingers ached. I looked down at my right hand and saw that they were digging into the arm of the chair. My knuckles were white and I had the urge to do something else with them. "I-I kn-know."

"Breathe deeply, Elliott." I closed my eyes again and tried to do as she asked. "Did you talk to Sophie about your father?"

Every muscle in my body seemed to tighten. My lungs seized and I gasped for breath. "N-n-n-no. P-p-p-pleeeeease d-d-don't, Robin."

"Okay." Her voice was soft and soothing, the way a mother's voice would be. I forced my thoughts away from my parents and wondered if this was what Robin sounded like when Rebecca was young and had a bad dream, and she tried to comfort her.

"Focus on breathing, Elliott. Relax and try to calm down."

She was silent for awhile as I did my best to regulate my breathing. It wasn't until I opened my eyes again that she spoke. "Have you written anything new?"

I knew she was asking about music compositions. I shook my head. "D-D-David ssssays B-B-Becca's p-p-planning a t-t-t-trip t-to SSSSSSp-SSSSpain."

Robin smiled. "She's got enough money saved, and so does David from what I've heard. Of course I'll be worried about them, but they're eighteen, and are entitled to go off on their own. Does Sophie mention her mother?"

I sighed and then shook my head. "N-no." Besides drugs, Sophie didn't really mention a lot about anything.

❧ • ❧

Most of Saturday was spent lying on my bed, worrying about Sophie doing drugs and being alone in the woods. I had never dropped acid before, but I didn't think it was necessary in order to know that it was an incredibly senseless idea when you could get lost so easily.

When I wasn't actively worrying about Sophie, I was thinking about how she ran her hands through my hair. No one but Jane knew how just that simple act could calm me down. How had she known?

Sophie and Jane shared Photography class, but there was no way Jane would tell her something like that, and it's not like Sophie would ask her about it.

It didn't matter. Her fingers sliding through my hair felt utterly fantastic. I wondered how I could get her to do it again.

I felt like a creep. Like a creepy creep planning out various ways to get a girl to touch him.

Then I felt worthless. Thinking about `Sophie and touching wasn't going to lead to anything productive, and I knew from past experience that it would just prove painful and send me into a fit of depression. I didn't need to spend another night hoping to all that was holy that my erection would fade.

On Sunday I waited until eleven to call Sophie. Stephen had Mr. Young's number written down in the address book in his study. I thought eleven was enough time for someone to recover from tripping on acid. I dialed, going over what I -planned to say.

Although I thought about music in an attempt to calm myself, when I heard Sophie's father answer the phone, I froze.

"Hello?" There was pause and I tried to force words out of my mouth, but I only seemed to be able to make a clicking sound. "Hello?" he said again, this time in a more irritated voice. He sighed heavily before hanging up.

I couldn't even use the phone like a normal human being. I hated being me.

Trying again, I redialed the number. "Hello?" His voice was booming and more than just a little scary.

"H-h-hhhhhh…"

"Who is this?" he demanded.

Taking a deep breath, I closed my eyes and let Schubert's Opus 90 Number 3 fill my head before I opened my mouth to speak. "MMMMMister Y-Y-YYYoung? Th-th-this is E-E-Elli-Elli-Elliott D-D-Dalton." I hated my own name coming from my mouth. “C-c-c-c-can I t-t-talk t-t-to S-S-SSSSS-SSSS…” I choked on her name.

“You want to talk to Sophie?”

“Y-y-yes, sir.”

“Hold on.”

There was a rustling sound and footsteps, and then a few knocks. I could hear Sophie’s father saying something about sleeping all day and then nothing for nearly a minute. “Mmmm?”

“S-S-Sophie?”

There was a deep intake of air. “Elliott?” Her voice was rough and slightly scratchy. “‘Sup?”

“I-I-I j-just w-w-wanted to make sure y-y-you w-were okay.”

A breathy chuckle answered me. “Of course I’m okay. I told you I would be.”

There wasn’t much more for me to say. If I had any courage, I’d ask her to do something with me today. If I was really forward, I would ask her to run her hands through my hair again. If I could speak like a normal person, I would say *any*thing just to keep her on the line.

Since I wasn’t courageous, or forward, or normal, I settled for, “O-o-okay. Sssssee y-you t-t-tomorrow.”

I hung up without waiting for her to say goodbye. I was just as awkward on the phone as I was in person, and she shouldn't have to be subjected to that.

The rest of my day was spent listening to music and thinking of Sophie. She was my friend. Finally I had someone besides Jane who *wanted* to be friends me. Despite all of the differences, between us with her drug-use and my inability to fully communicate, we were friends. That thought would carry me through until I could see her again

Chapter 15

Hi Good

Sophie

I opened the door to put the phone back after Elliott hung up and found Tom standing right outside. He hadn't been home at all last night and must've come home early this morning.

"What?" My voice was rough and raw, even to my own ears. It had been cold and damp in the woods, and after tripping all day yesterday, I'd probably come down with a cold. That, or I'd been yelling and screaming the whole day, but I had no recollection. "Your boyfriend has a pretty awful case of stuttering."

I sighed and pushed the phone at him. "Way to state the obvious, Tom." I shivered when his hand brushed against mine as he took the phone. "And he's not my boyfriend."

"You've been here a few weeks now and you haven't had one phone call. Then all of a sudden, out of the blue, this delinquent of yours calls. The same delinquent you went to D.C.

with, mind you, and you're going to tell me he's not your boyfriend?"

"Whatever, Tom." I'd almost closed the door in his face, but then opened it again. "He's my partner in Horticulture, okay? He's the one your wonderful, extraordinary Wallace paired me with for therapy, got it?"

"So he's not your boyfriend?"

I just stared at him for a moment, giving him my best "duh" look. "Yep, you can keep your shotgun on its rack for a little while longer."

"It's okay if you do have a boyfriend though, Sophie." He looked flustered and shifted uncomfortably. "I mean, it's okay if you have friends."

"Whatever," I said again. Usually the best thing about Tom was how little he spoke to me, and now it seemed like he wanted to be my best friend and have a heart-to-heart.

"Do you?" he asked quickly.

"Do I what?"

"Have friends, Sophie." I was too worn-out to express my annoyance. "I mean, you don't bring anyone over and you never talk about—"

"We," I said, pointing to him and then back to myself, "don't talk. It's not our thing, and it doesn't matter if I have friends. I don't need them and if I had any, you'd just call them delinquents."

"Sophie, you know I don't—"

I cut him off, already tired of his voice. He had about as much right to know shit about me as Wallace did. "I'm going back to bed." I stepped back and pushed the door closed, making sure to barricade it once more.

I couldn't really get back to sleep. I kept thinking about Elliott. I'd been trying to call him Rusty Dalton again in my head, but to no avail. I'd been doing just fine ignoring him, and my growing feelings for him, until the end of group therapy on Friday. I'd made him work for it that time. I didn't make the first move.

And he did it. He'd met my challenge.

With just a light nod of his head toward the stairs, he'd managed to make me come undone. Then he played guitar for me and it was exactly what I thought it would be – Perfect.

I'd never been one to go all mushy over musicians or, hell, anyone for that matter, but when he played guitar for me, looking all nervous and shy, I melted. I, Sophie Young, melted like a twelve-year-old girl at a Jonas Brothers concert.

It was… disgusting. And embarrassing. And fucking wrong, but intimate and special too.

If that wasn't bad enough, he asked me if we were friends. What was I supposed to say? "No, we're not friends because I'd like to see your naughty bits?" The worst part of it all was that I didn't *just* want to do him. I wanted to hold his hand and shit. I wanted to touch his face just to feel it.

I was so silly about this boy.

So when he asked me if we were friends, of course I said yes. Elliott walked around every day with this look on his face like he'd just had to put his puppy to sleep, or someone just insulted his dead grandmother. I didn't want to be the cause of that look. I wanted him to be happy.

I felt so silly. I couldn't believe I was having *urges* to hold someone's hand. It wasn't right. It wasn't natural and I hated it all.

Monday came ridiculously fast and I did my best to muddle through. I smiled at Elliott in the hall and tried to keep my thoughts platonic. When that didn't work, I tried just thinking him as a purely sexual being, but that seemed off too. Why couldn't I see him as just another high school boy? Why the hell did I have these impulses to be sweet and *romantic* with him?

It was wrong; so fucking wrong.

Despite my conflicting emotions, I promised myself that I would talk to him more than I had last week. He seemed to want it. Maybe he *needed* that. Thankfully I wouldn't have to worry about talking to him until Horticulture.

During Study Hall, I met Jason in the woods as usual. He was sitting on our fallen tree, puffing on a blunt. I was surprised. It was the first blunt I'd seen him use.

"What's up with that?" I asked as I sat down next to him. "No papers?"

He shrugged. "Someone owed me. Paid me with this." He took a hit and I laughed when his face twisted up. "Shut up," he said, his voice strained as he held in the hit.

I took it from his outstretched hand. I hadn't hit a blunt in a long-ass time. They were usually party favors and not my everyday smokes. "How was your weekend?"

"Shitty."

"Why?"

He shook his head. "My dad."

I passed the blunt back. "What happened?"

"Got tanked on Saturday and carried it through to Sunday."

"Didn't you say he drinks a lot?"

"Yeah, but…"

When he trailed off, I looked up at him. He looked sad. "But what?"

He let out a harsh breath, his eyes fixed on the glowing end of the blunt. "Nothing."

I sighed. Was I supposed to pry? Could I just let it go without being a shitty person? Was I Jason's friend now too? If I was, wasn't it my duty to pull all the shit out that was bothering him? Before I could even think about answering my own questions, he continued. "Sometimes he drinks *too much*, like even *more* than too much, and now he's off his meds. He's nuts without them."

"Doesn't he just pass out? I mean, after drinking? That's what Tom does." I wanted to tell him to hurry up and take a hit so I could take another one, but I thought it'd be rude.

Shaking his head, he finally pulled another drag and passed it to me. "No. Usually he passes out, but when he drinks like *that* and he's off his medication, he gets mean."

I nearly choked on my hit. Why the hell was Jason confiding in me? What? Did I have the words "trusted confidante" tattooed across my forehead? Did I radiate friendship? "Mean? Like what? He hits you?"

"No. I'm about twice his size. It'd be hilarious if he tried. Come on, Sophie."

"Well, don't get snarky, I just asked." I couldn't even remember how big his dad was and I didn't see him when I was over at his house, so how was I supposed to know?

"No, he gets... He starts calling my mom a whore and…"

"Your mom's dead."

"No shit, Captain Obvious."

"Again with the snark. You don't have to be an ass about it." When I saw his head hanging low, I mumbled, "Aw, shit, Jace," I nudged him with my shoulder, "fuck him."

He looked up, this time with a small smile. "Can I fuck you instead?"

I beamed at him, happy that his mood had turned around. "Hell yeah, but you'll have to be quick. I have to be in the greenhouse soon."

He made no move to make with the sexing, so I took another hit.

"Sophie?"

"Hmm?"

"Do you want to go to Homecoming with me?"

I couldn't help but laugh, coughing on the smoke as it released from my lungs. "Hell no, I won't go to the dance with you." His face fell and I realized he hadn't been joking. "Seriously? You're asking me to that lame-ass dance? Why?"

He shrugged. "I'm a guy. You're a girl. Guys and girls go to dances."

He had to be kidding. "*I* don't."

"Are you going with *Dalton*?"

Holy Shit. Anderson thought I was going with Jason, and Jason thought I was going with Elliott. Could it be any more like a romantic teen comedy? "Jesus, you don't listen, do you? I just said that I don't go to dances, all right?"

"Fine," he sulked.

"What's your deal?"

He shook his head. "Never mind. It was dumb. Forget it." He paused. "You gonna pass that blunt or what?"

~ • ~

I made sure to look encouragingly at Elliott when I got to our lab table. I didn't want him to think that we weren't friends. It wasn't his fault that my whole system of beliefs was being challenged. Again, I did my best to think of him as a purely platonic friend, but I'd never had many of those, so it was easier to imagine myself slowly working him over.

Still, by the end of the hour, I just wanted to hold his hand and run my fingers through his hair again. I'd done it twice now and both times it seemed to calm him down or give him some kind of comfort or something.

I wanted to see him lit up with happiness.

I told myself my thoughts were ridiculous when the bell rang, and I stood up and gathered my books. I remembered that friends usually parted ways with some form of verbal goodbye, so I turned around to find that he was standing too.

Shit, he looked nervous again. The dude clearly needed to relax. It was no wonder he had panic attacks.

His eyes were fixed on Anderson's retreating form, but when he finally looked at me, he flashed me that sexy little smile.

I had to stop myself from keeling over. He had a tiny little scar above his top lip and I wanted to know how it might feel under my fingertip. Wait, did friends trace each other's scars? Before I could drool or attack him again, I smiled and quickly said, "See you."

"S-S-So-Sophie?" he called before I could do more than turn around.

I faced him again. "Yeah?"

"D-d-do you w-w-waaaant t-to d-do sssssomething th-this w-w-w-w-w, on Saturday?"

I realized that last Friday I'd never given him the chance to ask me to hang out again. We'd gotten too deep into a conversation about drugs. "Um, yeah, sure." Relief seemed to flood his features and the rise and fall of his chest slowed to a normal pace. "What do you want to do?"

My positive response caused him to brighten. "I-I w-w-want to-to take you sssssomewhere."

I looked around as the classroom started to fill up with kids from Mr. Reese's next class. "Where?"

He was noticing their arrival as well. "I-it's a p-place I-I-I f-f-found."

"Hi, Sophie!" I turned around and found myself face-to-face with Megan.

I nodded in greeting and watched as her eyes slid over to take Elliott in. She was looking at him in such a weird way that I turned to see his expression, but he was too busy studying his shoes. At some point, I was going to ask him about the great Simons/Dalton Bang, but this was not the time.

"I have to go. I need to be physically educated." I wondered if Elliott needed any physical education, and if he'd let me play teacher. I sighed. I needed to get over this shit quick. "Later."

Elliott left and I tried to leave too, but Megan grabbed my arm. "Andrea, Cierra, and I are going to Baltimore tomorrow to shop for dresses. You want to come?"

I really, really didn't, but when Andrea asked me the next day to go with her, I couldn't say no. I was going soft. She begged and pleaded. She said that if she had to be in a car alone with Megan and Cierra for an hour each way, her brain would melt.

I joked and told her that it would at least make her a few pounds lighter. She shook her head and kept begging.

That was how I found myself in the back of Megan's crappy car, listening to Cierra brag about how she gave John Wozniak a blow job at some party last weekend. I mean, really, was that really necessary to share? I didn't walk around telling strangers my sexual business. We weren't even friends.

"I now have a new mental picture to use when I want to make myself throw up," Andrea whispered to me as we walked behind Megan and Cierra into the dress shop. I smiled. Andrea was kind of awesome.

"Um, why aren't you going to the dance again, Sophie?" Megan asked as she pushed up the strap on the orange dress for the third time and flipped her dirty-blonde hair over her shoulder. It was for a much bustier girl with a different skin tone, but Megan seemed to think that a simple padded bra and a spray tan would fix it.

"Because it sounds fucking lame."

"Aw," Cierra said as she turned away from the mirror for the first time in ten minutes, "did no one ask you?"

I gave her a smirk. "Dances just aren't my thing."

She frowned, her eyes narrowing. "Exactly what *is* your thing, Sophia?"

I shook my head. "You couldn't handle it if I told you."

Before Cierra could say anything else, Megan turned to Andrea and said, "That dress is so cute."

Andrea looked at herself in the mirror. She'd been avoiding it since putting on the tight black garment. Then she sighed and turned toward me, but kept looking at the mirror. "Sophie?"

"It's nice." I could tell by her face that she wasn't happy with her body, her thin fingers picking at the fabric covering her abdomen. "I think you should get it."

She finally looked at me, her eyes silently pleaded for something. "But…"

I shook my head. "You look really good in it."

I stood up quickly, somewhat annoyed at myself for even caring about Andrea and her ridiculous body image. "I'm going to look around the square. I'll meet you guys in an hour."

Not waiting for their response, I left the boutique and wandered around the small shopping square. I could have gone to the bookstore, but once the cool fresh air hit my face, I changed my mind and decided to take advantage of the opportunity to be alone.

There was a park nearby, overlooking the water, so I found a nice secluded wooded area and packed up my one-hitter. I wouldn't have lasted another second with Megan or Cierra unless I caught a buzz. They talked constantly and the topics of conversation were less than appealing.

I was all about getting your sexual freak on or whatever, but I surely didn't need to hear about Cierra and John, and I would've died a moderately happy woman if I hadn't gotten the scoop about Chris Anderson's curved cock and his nipple rot.

Still, I was happy not to be stuck at home. My new fascination with Elliott had taken over most of my moments of mental freedom. Sitting at home thinking about the line of Elliott Dalton's lips certainly wouldn't help me with anything.

I was nice and high by the time I slipped the dugout back into my pocket and went for a walk in the square. I probably could have stopped with just two small hits, but I'd done six or so, which left me more than just slightly buzzed. I was having trouble focusing my eyes as I stumbled along. Usually pot didn't mess me up this badly. The sidewalk seemed uneven and for being a cooler evening, there was a surprising amount of people I had to dodge. Maybe my sugar was whacked.

"You okay there?"

I looked up to find green eyes staring directly into mine. I stumbled back and took in the man before me as his hand shot out to steady me. He was clearly older, but not too old, with shaggy blond hair. Both ears were pierced with hoops running through them and he had his labret pierced too. His arms looked strong and were covered in a full sleeve of tattoos. I bet Pinny Dalton would've thought he was sexy, even though her own boyfriend was about as cookie-cutter as they came.

"I'm good," I finally said, my voice much softer than usual.

"Hi Good, I'm Ian. Damn, your eyes are…"

With a smirk, I batted my eyes exaggeratedly. “Yeah, I know. Genetic freak.”

I knew it was wrong. I knew I should’ve just walked away, and gone back to the dress shop, but this guy was cute and it wasn’t hard to understand what he wanted with the way he was looking at me. If I wanted to get over my immature crush on Elliott, this was my chance.

Chapter 16

Brown and Gray

Sophie

It was getting late and I knew that I had to meet the girls soon, but I was enjoying the time I was getting to spend with my new "friend." Ian and I had found a bench to sit down on and we fell into easy conversation.

His hands were clean, but the fingernails were black underneath. When I asked him why, he confirmed my suspicion. He was an auto mechanic. Looking at his hands gave me another insight into who this man was; Ian wore a gold band on his left ring finger. It figured.

As much as it should have, the fact that he was married didn't deter me in the slightest from making subtle sexual innuendos, and it sure as hell didn't stop him from returning them, or putting his hand on my leg.

When he asked, I said that I was from Gaithersburg and that I was nineteen. He didn't ask much else, and it wasn't difficult for me to recognize that he wasn't exactly interested in discerning the truth. Nor was he interested in anything much beyond what most men were.

In all honesty, I didn't mind. I was pretty high and enjoying it all.

It wasn't long before I was pressed up against the side of a building with his hands moving all over my body. I was still clothed and there was no flesh-on-flesh action except for his mouth attacking my neck. I wasn't going to have sex with him, but his attention felt wonderful.

We were like that for a good long while until his cell phone rang. He muttered, "Shit," before easing me down so I could stand. While he lied to his wife on the phone, I straightened out my clothing and wiped my mouth with the back of my hand.

"What time is it?" I asked when he hung up.

"A quarter to eight."

"Damn. I have to go."

He pressed me up against the wall again and whispered against my neck, "Me too." His hands moved to my tits as he ground his pelvis into my stomach. "Give me your phone number."

I shook my head. "Give me yours." A sound came from his throat before he nibbled on my earlobe. "I'll call you, I promise, but I have to go."

It was only after another couple of minutes of dry humping that he finally let me go, writing his number down on an old receipt. After saying goodbye to him, I hauled-ass back to the dress boutique. When I got there, Megan and Cierra looked annoyed, while Andrea seemed genuinely relieved.

"What the hell, Sophie?" Cierra snapped.

"Sorry." I shrugged. "I lost track of time."

"We were worried," Megan added. "I mean, it's a safe area and all, but then we couldn't find you at the bookstore and--"

"Sorry," I said again, making sure they knew I was annoyed right back.

"Whatever," Cierra sighed. "Let's just go."

❧ • ❧

The rest of my week quickly fell into the same vicious cycle: School, home, sleep. At school, I got high, smiled at Elliott while trying to talk to him as casually as possible, and only paid enough attention in class to not fail. Once I got home, it was all cleaning and cooking to stave off boredom, and talking to Tom on his off-days just enough to keep him moderately satisfied and off my back.

Sleep consisted of me barricading my bedroom door and letting myself get so exhausted that I finally couldn't keep myself from slipping into unconsciousness.

Friday was the only exception. I had to do the Screw-Up Club thing again. I couldn't wait until I didn't have to sit down with Bitch Wallace every week, but just like last time, I found myself facing her.

After asking me again about school, she hit me with, “Did you have fun in Baltimore?”

I sighed. “Why do you have to keep talking to Tom? Isn’t that, like, against the rules?”

She smiled and I cringed. “It’s against the rules for me to tell him what you say, but he’s free to tell me about anything that’s troubling him. He’s concerned that you don’t have friends, but he was happy that you went out with those girls on Tuesday.”

“They’re not really friends. I just went for something to do.” I didn’t want to have another conversation with anyone about who was or wasn’t my friend, so I tried to change the subject. “I’m concerned that Tom doesn’t have a girlfriend. Why don’t you talk to him about that?”

“What concerns you about it?”

I had just been bluffing, but now I tried to come up with something. “Don’t you think it’s strange for a man to live his life without, you know, a woman, or women, around?”

“How do you know he doesn’t have a girlfriend?”

I shrugged. “He hasn’t introduced me to anyone and there’s no evidence anywhere in his house. I mean, tube socks on the living room floor doesn’t impress the ladies, so clearly he has no--”

“Did your mother have boyfriends?”

Instantly, I felt tense and angry. “I don’t want to talk about my mother, or her boyfriends.”

"Why? You seemed okay to talk about your father and his lack of girlfriends. What's the difference?"

"The difference is that I don't want to talk about my mother and her boyfriends," I repeated, this time louder.

"I heard you." Bitch Wallace took in a deep breath. "I just didn't know if there was some reason *why* you didn't want to."

I looked down and lied. "No."

"Have you spoken to your mother since you've been here?"

"No."

"How does that make you feel?"

I sighed, hating these questions and how I felt like I had to answer them. "I'm happy not to talk to her. I have nothing to say and I don't think she'd have much to say either. I'm sure her life is a whole lot better now that I'm not there."

"What makes you say that?"

"Because she doesn't like me," I answered quickly. "Can we talk about something else, please?" Why couldn't she understand that I had no interest in talking about my mother?

She paused for a moment and then asked, "There's a dance at school coming up, are you planning on going?"

Damn, what was with these Damascus people and this pointless dance? "No."

"Don't like to dance?"

I gave her a tight-lipped smile. "Don't like stupid shit."

She just looked at me for a moment, a seemingly genuine smile gracing her features. "What's your earliest memory, Sophie?"

"What?"

"The first thing you can remember."

"Why?"

"I find memories interesting," she answered. Sitting back, she folded her hands over the notebook that sat in her lap. "My first memory is of my father opening the front door. I couldn't have been very old because I remember how big he was, silhouetted against the setting sun. I remember running to him and hugging his leg."

I let myself relax just a little, resting back against the overstuffed chair. "I don't remember anything like that."

"But you do have a memory of something. What is it?"

I cracked my neck before dragging a hand down my face. "If I tell you, will you not call on me during group?"

"It's a deal."

"I don't know how old I was, but I can remember a very long car ride. I was crying and I remember my mother was in the front seat."

"Was it day or night?"

I shrugged. "I don't know. It was dark inside the car, but lighter outside."

"Do you remember anything else?"

I let the memory play in my head again. It was hazy and warped as I watched my mother's hair billow in the wind. "Helen's hair was long." Taking a deep breath, I shook my head. "Why's this important? Why do you give a shit about some stupid car ride?"

"I don't know if I give a shit about it, Sophie." My eyes widened at her use of the word "shit." "I just wanted to hear about it." She leaned forward. "What's your best memory?"

I swallowed. Even if I didn't want to comply, my mind was already scanning the past. There were very few good memories and of those, it was difficult to discern the best. "I don't have one."

"Do you have a worst memory?"

"There are too many to choose just one."

~ • ~

As my finger ran along the ridge of the now-worn spine, I smiled when I saw Elliott's copy of *Of Human Bondage*. Obviously, he'd read it. "Did you like it?" I asked, turning to him.

He eyed the book. "Y-y-yes."

"I thought you would." I turned and then flopped down onto his couch, staring up at his ceiling. "I like your room." I had told him that once before, but it was worth repeating. His room was calm and peaceful. There was nothing soothing in Tom's whole house, much less my room.

I glanced up at Elliott. Like most Friday nights, he sat on the edge of his bed, looking incredibly uncomfortable. I didn't quite understand why he didn't just sit on it like he owned it. I fought the urge to push him back so he'd look like a normal guy hanging out in his room. As tempting as it was, it'd be hard not to straddle him and run my hands over his chest. Everything about his posture screamed that he was anything but relaxed.

I wondered if I was the one who made him like that. Perhaps he typically sat on his bed cross-legged and looked all kinds of comfy. I didn't know, and had no way of ever finding out. I couldn't just *ask* him if I made him uneasy.

Turning my eyes back up to the ceiling, I figured I might as well talk about something. "Dr. Wallace asked me about my earliest memory. Does she ask you about your memories too?"

"Y-y-yes."

"Do you tell her about them?" I turned back.

He shook his head.

"She wanted to know my best memory and my worst memory. Why would she want to know that shit?"

Elliott shrugged. "Sh-she p-p-p-probably w-w-wants to get to kn-know y-you."

"Maybe she should start just by asking what my favorite color is."

"B-b-brown." He looked at me. "Y-y-you w-w-wear b-brown a lot."

What the hell? I sat up and studied him more closely. He wasn't looking at me anymore; he was busy looking at his fingers which were fiddling with the bottom of his shirt. My stomach fluttered when I realized he'd been paying attention to what I wore every day. It worried me that I was so excited about this, but I pushed the worry back. Elliott had figured out my favorite color by simple observation.

"You wear gray a lot." Nearly every day. It probably helped him to blend in; to not be noticed as much. Maybe that was why I liked brown so much. Brown and gray tended to blend in easily.

Looking at me again, Elliott nodded, his lopsided smile returning. "I l-liiiiiike g-gray."

"But it's not your favorite." I looked around his room again and confirmed my suspicions. "Your favorite color is blue." He had a blue book bag, a blue iPod, a blue computer, and a blue bedspread. His car was blue too.

He nodded. "I-It's sssssoothing."

I wanted to sit with him on the bed. I wanted to position us so that our legs were crossed. I wanted to hold this boy's hands. Even though I fought against it, I wanted to soothe him like his favorite color did.

~ • ~

Elliott picked me up on Saturday at nine in the morning. Tom had already left for his day of rock climbing near the Potomac with some of his firehouse friends, so thankfully, Elliott and I didn't have to put up with his fatherly antics. Apparently my father and his friends were *hardcore* climbers and didn't care about the cold weather. Elliott didn't tell me where we were going, but he did tell me to wear boots.

He brought me coffee again.

We drove south on Burnt Hill Road for a bit, but still said nothing. "Are you taking me to Sugar Loaf Mountain?"

"N-n-no," he said, his eyes conveying his panic. "D-d-d-d-do you w-w-w-want to gggggo there?"

I smiled and shook my head, hoping it was enough to squelch his fears of doing the wrong thing. "I want to go wherever you were taking me. This just felt like it was the way to Sugar Loaf."

"I-i-it is, b-b-b-but w-we're nnnnot gggoing that ffffar. I-i-is that o-o-okay?"

"It's fine, really, I just…it's one of the places I actually remember Tom taking me when I was little, that's all."

"W-w-we c-c-can g-go, S-SSSophie."

"No, really, wherever you're taking me is fine."

Soon he parked the car and I realized that we were in what looked to be a park or natural wildlife preserve.

I hadn't figured we'd be going hiking, but at least I had on my boots. It was fairly chilly out, so there weren't many people around.

We had been walking for at least fifteen minutes before I finally asked. "So, we're hiking?" It was dumb. Obviously we were hiking. Duh.

Elliott turned and looked at me. I could've gone faster and I think he could've too, but we seemed to both be intentionally staying side by side. "J-j-just for a l-l-little b-bit."

"Tom used to take me hiking and rock climbing every summer. I didn't take you for a nature kind of a guy. Do you like hiking?"

"S-S-SSStephen and D-David l-like c-camping."

While that was interesting, I hadn't asked about Dr. Sexy or Big Dalton. "Do you?"

He shrugged.

"But you go anyway?"

Elliott nodded and stepped over a fallen branch. Then he looked back to watch me do the same. "W-we all g-go. JJJaane, R-Rebecca, and Trent t-too w-when he's allowed. I t-t-try t-to mmmmake the b-best of it. S-S-Stephen d-doesn't lllike w-when I'm home alone."

He was seventeen. It made no sense that Dr. Dalton would treat him like such a baby, but I chose not to comment on it. "Sounds…crowded. Does Rebecca's mom go too?" I really wanted to call her "Bitch," but I left it at "Rebecca's mom" in case Elliott had some kind of fuzzy feelings for her.

"S-s-s-ssssometimes."

"Do you all sing *Kumbaya,* eat s'mores and do a little group therapy session?"

He smiled at me and I swear my heart stopped beating for just a moment. "S-s-sometimes, ex-except n-no sssinging. R-R-Rebecca h-has a terrible v-voice."

I was thankful that he wasn't offended I'd made fun of his family and friends. "So are they cool?"

Elliott gave me a look and I answered his silent question. "Rebecca and Trent."

"Th-they're o-okay."

I kicked some damp leaves out of my way. "She's a cheerleader."

"Y-yes."

"Does she act like one?"

"Sh-she's o-okay."

"Stop thrilling me with your use of adjectives. You make me want to run out and be their friends too. What with them being so 'okay' and all."

"S-s-sorry."

"It was a joke, Elliott."

"I-I know."

I looked up and saw an amused expression on his face. "So give me something else. They both can't just be 'okay.' You have to know more about them and have an opinion."

"B-B-Becca p-p-pretty much h-has one e-e-emotion th-that she l-lets an-anyone sssssee."

I smiled. "Does that correlate with the stink-face she's always wearing?"

"Sh-she's nnnot l-like that w-w-w-with p-p-people she t-trusts."

"And Trent?"

He shook his head. "I-I-I l-llllike T-Trent, he j-just c-c-c-can't c-c-c-c...H-he's g-good with JJJaaane. H-he c-can b-br-bring her b-back w-when her mind is sssssomewhere else."

Okay, that made no sense. "What? Where does she go?"

Elliott sighed as his shoulders slumped forward. "J-JJJaane d-doesn't remember an-anything b-before sh-she w-was t-ten, a-and s-sometimes s-she zones out."

I remembered him telling me that her mind worked differently, but what the hell was this "going somewhere" and "zoning out" shit? "What? She's like 'not there' or something?"

He nodded, facing forward, his eyes fixed ahead of him. I saw a clearing up ahead and figured that was our destination. "Did you find this place on a camping trip?"

"Y-yes. N-no one else sssssaw it, sssso it's j-just m-mine. I t-t-try nnnnot to think of o-other p-p-people c-coming here."

It would be mine too. There was something exciting about going someplace with Elliott that no one else knew about. There was something absolutely mind-blowing about him sharing something like this with me.

I caught sight of a stream. It was truly a gorgeous day. The woods thinned a bit by the water and I could see clouds, but not many, and the sunlight made the colorful fall leaves bright.

"I can't believe there are still flowers blooming!" I couldn't stop my feet as they moved me quickly into the sunlight and the flowers. Sitting down, I brushed a few fallen leaves away and touched the delicate petals of one flower, careful not to pull or press too hard.

"Y-you like f-fl-flowers?"

"Apparently." In truth, I'd never cared much for flowers. Sure, they were pretty to look at, but all the ones my mother ever planted withered and died.

I liked this place. It felt peaceful.

"I think I'm just amazed that they're still blooming. And these leaves! I mean, Tampa isn't *anything* like this." When I was by the stream and the sunlight hit my body, I tilted my head up to the sky, as my eyes slowly closed. "And I *love* the sun."

Chapter 17

Faramir's Wildflower

Elliott

I knew that I wanted to bring Sophie to this little spot by the stream. The fall day made the scene even more beautiful than ever. The oranges, reds, and yellows of the leaves looked so brilliant against the blue sky. I thought that she would like it, but I never dreamed that she would like it this much. Her eyes lit up and her face brightened, and it wasn't from the sun, but from excitement over something as small as little purple and pink wildflowers peeking out over top of the layer of fallen leaves.

I hadn't known her for long at all, but already I wanted nothing but good things for her. She deserved good things.

Despite her drug use, and her seemingly careless behavior, she seemed like a good person. Other than a few people who had to be nice to me, she was the only person at school who didn't look at me like I was a complete waste of space. I hadn't wanted her to, but she had defended me several times and I couldn't fault her for some of her less attractive qualities. She was no more in control of her drug use than my mother was, and she held no more peace about whatever past haunted her than I did.

I'd heard about her and Aiden. No one told me directly, but I'd have to be deaf not to have heard the guys in class talking about it. I didn't know if it was true. I hadn't wanted to believe it and I still didn't want to. I didn't want her to be like that. I didn't want her to be with Jason or Aiden, or anyone else for that matter, but she wasn't mine. I couldn't tell her what to do or who to be. Or who to be with.

Even though the gossip at school was that she was loose with her affections, I couldn't help but think that she wasn't *really* like that. People at school exaggerated and lied all the time, and I had no proof that she was anything but who she was with me.

With me, she was a nice person who treated me as if I was normal.

I looked down and saw she still had her face tilted up. I loved the way the sunlight illuminated her smooth skin. Her eyes were still closed and I could only imagine what she was thinking of in that moment.

I wished it was summertime, so that she didn't have to wear her coat. I wondered if the rest of her skin would shine in the sun too.

I had to stop myself from thinking about the rest of her skin because that led my mind to thoughts it didn't need to have. It was well-documented that I had very little control over my body, and I didn't think I could even go on breathing if I embarrassed myself in front of her like that.

Sitting down on the leaf-covered bank of the stream, I continued to watch her until her eyes opened and she looked at me. She was still touching the flower.

"This is nice," she said, her voice nearly too soft for me to hear. "I should've brought my camera. We're supposed to be taking pictures of nature for class."

"Ssssorry. I-I-I sh-should have t-t-told you—"

She cut me off, as she waved a dismissive hand. "Cut it out, Elliott. It would have ruined the surprise and besides, we can always come back another time."

She'd just said she'd willingly come back here with me. I felt overjoyed.

She brushed a stray lock of hair off of her forehead, and then laid back, pillowing her head on her folded arms. "When you were little, did you ever look up at the clouds and make pictures out of them?"

I tilted my head to look up at the large puffy clouds, and wondered how long it would be until one of them opened up and pelted us with large drops of rain. I thought back to when I had first met Jane. She'd always made a game out of everything. I could remember lying on our backs in the yard of our foster parents' house, looking up at the sky. The grass had tickled my ears and I busied my hands by pulling up clumps of it.

"I-I-I never sssssee an-anything other than c-c-clouds."

Sophie shifted, turning toward me. "That's bullshit." She wrapped her fingers around my wrist and tugged me down. There wasn't much I could do but lie down next to her. I liked the sound of the leaves crunching under the weight of my body. I'd never been allowed to go outside and play in the fall leaves like other children.

She let go and then pointed up. "See that one? Tell me what it looks like."

"A c-c-cloud."

She rolled onto her side to face me, propping her head up with her hand. "You're a musician, Elliott. Music is creative, which means you have a creative mind. How can you like art if you don't let your mind make something out of nothing?" She lay back down again and pointed. "*That* is abstract art. So what do you see?"

I sighed. "I-I-I don't kn-know." That was a lie. I could see pictures in the clouds, but I had learned while playing the game with Jane that I didn't see what everyone else saw. Jane saw bunnies, dragons, boats, and trees. I didn't see any of those things. Every cloud was interpreted in my mind as something painful.

I felt inadequate, but that was normal for me. I would have given anything to be able to tell Sophie that I saw a horse or cat, but I couldn't. I heard her take in a deep breath and I hoped it wasn't in preparation for telling me how truly defunct I was. I already knew.

"See that cloud?" She pointed again. "That's a guitar. And that one? That's Chris Anderson's head getting smacked by a volleyball."

I squinted. "I don't see either of those."

She chuckled and I looked over at her. “That’s because I’m fucking with you.” She paused. “They’re just clouds.”

I shook my head. I didn’t want her not to see pictures in the clouds. I *wanted* her to see horses and bunnies and guitars.

We were silent for a while and although I wanted to keep looking at her, I forced myself to stare up at the sky.

“Soooo,” she began, “we established yesterday that you like gray, but your favorite color is blue and mine is brown.” The leaves rustled next to my ear. She was on her side now, looking at me. “What’s your favorite fruit?”

I couldn’t help but smile. “A-apple. Y-yours?”

“Red grapes. Favorite beverage?”

“I-I lllike c-coffee, b-but S-S-SSStephen w-won’t let me drink it a-all d-day.”

“I like Pom Juice, but it’s expensive.” She reached out with her finger and touched the purple flower again. “Favorite *Lord of the Rings* character.”

“Th-that’s e-easy. B-Boromir.”

Sophie’s smile widened and she was all sparkly skin and twinkling eyes. “Boromir’s pretty bad-assed. I like Gollum and Faramir.”

As I chuckled, I realized I felt comfortable with her. “Th-that’s llliiiike good and e-evil, S-S-SSSophie. H-h-how c-can you lllliiiike b-both?”

She laughed and I was taken in by the sound. "Because everyone's a little bit of both, don't you think?"

I didn't think I agreed with her. I knew from experience that some people were nothing more than pure evil, but maybe it wasn't right for me to have such extreme thoughts. If I took Sophie, for example, I thought she was nothing but goodness, but to hear other people talk, one would decide that she wasn't.

Since we were asking questions, I had some I needed answered. I wanted to know if she'd ever think about giving up drugs. I wanted to ask her why she did all the things she did. If she truly was the person she was with me, why did she have the impulses that drove her to do drugs and have so much sex?

It bothered me that I didn't know these things about her. It bothered me that even *she* might not know these things about herself.

She shivered, and I asked, "A-a-are you c-cold? W-w-we c-can ggggo, if you w-want."

She studied me like Stephen always did, and then shook her head. "I'm good. What's your middle name?"

For a moment, I wondered why she would want to know my middle name or anything that I liked, but I supposed that friends knew those things about each other. Perhaps she was just being nice and asking so that I felt like we truly were friends. Or maybe, she *was* my friend like she said she was, and really did want to know.

"A-Al-Alexander."

"Are you named after somebody?" When I shrugged, she offered, "My middle name is Catherine, after my grandmother."

She was silent and then I realized that it was my turn to ask a question. There was so much I wanted to know about her, but I didn't think it was appropriate to ask everything I wanted to know. I could ask her about Tampa, but we'd talked about it before. She missed the pot. We'd already talked about diabetes.

I wanted to ask something deep and meaningful, but I settled for, "W-w-what's y-your ffffavorite class?"

"Photography," she answered immediately. "You?"

"H-H-HHHHortic-culture."

She grimaced. "Yuck. Why?"

"I-it's in-interesting and I d-don't hhhhave t-to t-talk." I didn't mention how I seemed to have adopted Kate's love of plants or that now that I was sitting next to her, it was rapidly becoming the best part of my day.

"What do you want to do after high school?"

"C-college." I didn't tell her about the opportunity I had to leave high school a year early.

"And after that?"

"I w-w-wanted t-to be a doctor, lllliiiiike S-Stephen, b-but I c-c-c-can't t-talk r-right, sssso that w-wouldn't in-inspire much c-c-c-confidence from the p-p-p-p…" I had to close my eyes to block out Sophie's face as she waited for me to spit out such a simple word like "patients." It wouldn't come. My hands curled into fists and pressed against my body as they usually did when I tried to force out a word.

I probably looked so ridiculous and I hated myself even more than usual. Our conversation had been going so well.

Something warm and small slipped over my hands. My eyes popped open as my face relaxed. I looked down at my hands, which were now covered by hers, and then back up at her.

"Just relax, Elliott." She smiled at me. It was like a sedative. All the tension melted away at the sound of my name.

"Patients." Her eyes were drilling into mine and although it felt like I should've been nervous, I wasn't. "Sssso I'll p-probably j-just be ssomeone who w-works in a l-lab."

Sophie sighed, but her expression was unchanged. "You should be a doctor. Not all doctors have to talk all that much, right? Oh! You could be like Wallace and listen to people all day long and say nothing but 'Hmmmm,' and 'I see.'"

I could never be a therapist and there were other reasons why I'd never be a doctor. She was rubbing her thumbs lightly over my knuckles, drawing my attention back to my hands. When I glanced up, she was looking at me and nibbling her lip. It was just a fraction of a second later that she quickly moved her hands away.

She was on her feet before I could even register my own sadness about no longer feeling her energizing, yet calming touch. I watched as she did a cartwheel and then back flip. She baffled me.

When she was finished, she sat down again, but much farther away than before. "Pretty good, huh?"

I nodded as I sat up.

"Helen put me in gymnastics when I was little." Her voice was sad and her eyes seemed distant and dark. "She told everyone that I was clumsy, but I was really good." She paused. "She took me out of the class when everyone began to realize she was lying."

"W-w-why would she l-lie about y-y-you being c-c-clumsy?"

Sophie didn't answer; she just fiddled with something inside of her coat pocket. I thought about what she'd just told me and married it to what Robin and Stephen had alluded to. If a parent was mean to their child and left bruises and broken bones, it would make sense to stick the kid in a physical activity and blame all the marks on that.

In that instant, I went from having no feelings at all about her mother, to hating the woman I didn't even know.

"I'm going to smoke." She held up a little box. "Sure you don't want to get high, Elliott?" Before I could answer, she shook her head and looked away, mumbling, "No, of course you don't."

I had made the connection now. Sophie used drugs because her mother was mean to her. I understood her reluctance to come right out and say it, but I wanted her to. Maybe if she talked about it with someone like me, someone who would understand, she could stop doing all of these self-destructive things.

Maybe if she *did*, I'd feel comfortable enough to tell her the quiet secrets that plagued me.

❧ • ❧

We sat next to the stream for as long as the weather would let us. She was high, her eyes bloodshot and glassy, but she was no less of a good companion. When the sky finally did open up and drop rain on us, she didn't get mad, like Rebecca would have, and she didn't dance around in it like Jane; she simply looked up, wearing a soft smile that was just barely detectable.

We were incredibly muddy by the time we got back to the car, but I had towels in the trunk, so very little of it got on the upholstery or carpet.

Sophie hadn't wanted to go home yet, so we drove around in the rain listening to music. We didn't really talk much beyond my telling her what song was playing and her telling me if she liked it or not.

When I finally did drop her off at her house, she asked for my e-mail address and if I had an instant messaging account. I gave her my e-mail, and told her that I could easily get an IM account. When I asked why she wanted my e-mail, she laughed and gave me a look. "So I can e-mail you, Elliott."

At home, I realized how brilliant she was. I could "talk" to her without stuttering. I quickly went to my computer and turned it on, excited to find I had an e-mail waiting for me that wasn't from a Nigerian Prince or some online college. I opened the email from "YoSoph."

So thanks for the day. I loved that stream! And the leaves! And the flowers! And the…okay, I pretty much loved it all. I have questions for you. Send them back and then I'll send you my answers. Don't forget that Reese wants the name of the plant we're going to grow on Monday. I vote for marigolds since no one can mess up growing marigolds.

So here are the questions:

1) Favorite food

2) Favorite cartoon

3) Favorite article of clothing

4) What 4 things can you not live without?

5) Absolute all-time favorite movie?

Bonus: What are you listening to and why should I like it?

It seemed completely wrong that I was this nervous to respond to a simple e-mail. I realized at this moment I was incredibly caught up in Sophie. It felt destined. It felt right to want to be close to her, but it was also new and strange. I didn't have much faith that I could keep her interested.

There was a part of me that desperately wanted her to be more than just my friend. David had friends, but they weren't as important to him as Rebecca was. Jane depended on Trent in a way that she would never depend on anyone else. I wanted that. I wanted Sophie to be there for me when no one else would. I wanted Sophie to be the most important part of my life.

As always, there was a dominate part of me that felt I would never be good enough for her to even be my friend, never mind my *girl*friend. It wasn't just her. I didn't feel worthy of Stephen adopting me either. I didn't feel worthy of Jane's love, and I didn't feel that I deserved the automatic respect that David gave me just for being his adopted sibling.

There was a reason I didn't have any friends. There was a reason no one at school beyond my siblings and their partners wanted anything to do with me. Unfortunately, that reason would probably keep Sophie from me too.

As I re-read her questions, the importance of how I would answer them weighed on me. If we were starting up a correspondence through written word, I could answer completely, and not leave anything out the way I would have if we were speaking.

Taking a deep breath, I began.

Sophie,

Thank you for a great day too. I thought you would like the little spot by the stream and I would be more than happy to take you there again when you have your camera.

As for Reese's project, we can do marigolds if you want, but I think those are too simple. We'd get a better grade if we did some kind of organic vegetable. I know it's going into winter, but Stephen has a greenhouse and I'm pretty good with plants. It would be easy to do, maybe not as easy as marigolds, but worth it.

I'll answer your questions and send you some of my own.

1) *Favorite food: Stephen's ex-wife, Kate, used to make some kind of curry dish with chicken, rice, potatoes, and onions. It wasn't Indian curry though, it was Thai, and I have no idea how she made it. I haven't had it in a really long time.*

2) *Favorite cartoon: I don't have one. I was never allowed to watch them when I was a kid, and I don't watch much TV now. When I do, it isn't cartoons.*

3) *Favorite article of clothing: This is an odd question, but I suppose I have an affinity for my green button-down shirt. Rebecca bought it for David, but it was too small for him. I almost never wear it (it's too nice for school), but I still like it.*

4) *Four things I can't live without: 1) My Gibson 2) My iPod 3) Coffee 4) Jane. I assume that food and water are provided, since no one can live without those things.*

5) *Favorite movie: This is too hard. I can't choose one. I might be able to give you one per genre if given enough time. Sorry. One movie I can watch over and over and over again without getting bored is Eternal Sunshine of a Spotless Mind, but I don't know if it's my all-time absolute favorite.*

Bonus: I'm listening to Matisyahu, Time of Your Song. You should like it for its pure style alone, but also because he's a Hassidic Jew who blends rap and reggae into something unique and while he's religious, his music is more spiritual than preachy. I'll send you the link.

Now my questions.

1) *What do you want to do for the rest of your life?*

2) *Are you a cat person or a dog person?*

3) *Do you believe in paranormal activity?*

4) *Sunrise or Sunset?*

5) *If you could go anywhere in the world, where would it be?*

Bonus: What did you think of Matisyahu?

Oh, and why "YoSoph?"

I hope you have a nice Sunday. See you Monday.

Elliott

Chapter 18

Peppers and Sprouts

Elliott

I had wanted to use my five questions to ask her all of the deeper things I wondered about. Like why she got high all the time, what she liked to do first thing in the morning, what she thought of the war, why she stole that car, what she thought of me, if she could ever imagine *not* getting high, and what made her want to be high all the time. Just like when we were in the woods, I stopped myself because all those questions might upset her.

I didn't want to upset her. I wanted her to smile like she had when she saw the flowers among all the leaves. If the rest of the weekend went south, I'd at least have that.

She didn't respond Saturday night, but I went to sleep excited about our new form of communication. I'd always hoped that I would be able to express myself better where Sophie was concerned, without having to fumble over every syllable, and now I would be able to.

I woke up on Sunday with a terrible headache, but a few cups of coffee alleviated it. I tried not to feel anxious, and forced myself not to turn on the computer right away even though I desperately wanted to. Stephen was already at work, giving me the opportunity to drink more caffeine than I usually did. I knew it wasn't a smart idea to drink so much coffee when I already had anxiety, but it gave me something to do other than constantly check my e-mail.

I tried to have a conversation with Jane, but her questions about what I had done with Sophie yesterday made me nervous, on top of being anxious and jittery from the coffee. While I loved Jane in a way that I would never love anyone else, she could pressure me just as much as anyone when she wanted to. She understood without my ever having to explain things to her, but there were times when she'd be deliberately obtuse.

This was one of those times.

She didn't even know Sophie, but ever since Robin announced that she and I would be paired up, Jane was going crazy with wild scenarios of Sophie and me going to Homecoming together, or the two of us being soul-mates. But she was ignoring the simple fact that apart from her, I wasn't able to be close to anyone. She was ignoring how clearly dysfunctional I was.

Jane wanted me to be healthy, in part because she loved me and wanted the best for me, but also, if I was healthy, it meant that she was too. We were both fairly messed up. She just hid her wounds better. Under her bubbly personality was someone deeply in pain. She hated to acknowledge it, just like we all did. She pierced her body for the same reason she cut herself. The pain helped her deal with the mess on the inside.

Trent helped her feel normal and it seemed she felt that if I had someone like him, it would make her feel better. It would validate her if I shared the experience of being "healed" by another person. I didn't think it worked like that though and I was pretty sure she was faking it most of the time.

I didn't listen as Jane chatted with herself. I thought about Sophie. She knew about my mother and she still liked me. She didn't call me a freak, at least to my face, and wasn't running in the other direction. Yesterday she'd even talked a little about *her* mother. It wasn't much, but I didn't need to be a rocket scientist to read between the lines. It was a start.

I hated Sophie's mother.

As much as I wanted to go back upstairs and power up my computer after my fifth cup of coffee, I couldn't. I got roped into playing the Wii with Jane and David. He had come home after practice, still smelling like sweat and grass. Although I said no at first, Jane pouted me into playing, so I spent an hour and a half indulging her before nervously climbing the stairs to my room.

Perhaps Sophie hadn't written back. Maybe she came to her senses and decided I wasn't worth all the time she devoted to me. Maybe she wrote back and let me know that all my questions were obtuse and she wouldn't answer them.

As I opened my door, I listened to my heart pound. Maybe five cups of coffee was a little too much in one sitting. I deliberately slowed my breathing and turned on my computer. A minute later I was reading an e-mail from her.

Elliott,

Organic veggies it is, but I have to warn you that despite my passing grade, I possess no green appendages, and that includes thumbs. They're not even slightly green-tinted, but we'll give it a try.

Here are the answers to my questions:

1. *Favorite food – Brussels sprouts. I know, I know; who in their right mind loves Brussels sprouts, and the follow up to that question is why would they admit to it?*

2. *Favorite cartoon – I could watch Sponge Bob for hours. Patrick kills me.*

3. *Favorite article of clothing - Vintage Red Hot Chili Peppers t-shirt, circa 1991*

4. *What 4 things can you not live without?- RHCP t-shirt, one of any number of Classic novels, Brussels sprouts, and weed*

5. *Absolute all-time favorite movie? – Hands down* Sliding Doors. *Alternate universes based on choices you make…completely intriguing.*

And now your questions:

1) *What do you want to do for the rest of your life?- Party like a rock star.*

2) *Are you a cat person or a dog person? – Neither. I have enough to take care of.*

3) *Do you believe in paranormal activity? – Like ghosts and stuff? Maybe, but I hope that there are*

no ghosts. When I die I don't want to be hanging around watching stupid living people living stupidly.

4) *Sunrise or Sunset? – Sunset.*

5) *If you could go anywhere in the world, where would it be? – I hate this question, Elliott. I'm never going anywhere, so why think about it? But if that's a cop-out answer and you need an actual destination, I would pick Amsterdam for obvious reasons.*

Bonus: What did you think of Matisyahu? - I liked the song. Where do you find all this music?

"YoSoph" is for Sophia Young, only backwards and shortened. Not super-original I know, but it's a bit more interesting than "EDalton123," don't you think? (That was a joke. I'm not really making fun of your e-mail address, okay?)

I'd send more questions but Tom's taking me to some kind of gathering. He says it's going to be "fun." Apparently there will be fried fish and football. Oh, and a crab-boil, which just sounds very Maryland-y. I'm super-excited to have my whole day commandeered by his day off.

So I'll see you tomorrow. Here's food for thought until the next time…If you could turn Chris Anderson into any inanimate object, what would he be?

Later,

Sophie.

I wished that I understood her better. Although I was happy with this new form of communication, she didn't give me much to work with. What she did give me was a very bleak picture. Not that the picture I painted was much better, but from her e-mail I got that she can't live without marijuana, her goal is to party, she doesn't want to hang around after she dies, and she doesn't like to think about all the places she'll never go.

Turning away from my computer, I slid over to my keyboard, plugging in my headphones and letting my fingers fly over the keys. There were times when I composed and it was a very cognitive thing. I had to think about the notes and how to arrange them. Then there were times when the music simply poured out of me, the composition already complete in my head and I didn't know where it came from. This was one of the times when I didn't have to work for it. The music just flowed, leaving my brain to pick up whatever subject was floating through my mind at the moment.

At first I thought about her blue eyes contrasting against her light brown hair, but then I wondered if Sophie truly felt as empty as her responses sounded. Perhaps they were all she would allow herself. I understood what it felt like to dream about things that I was sure were impossible to achieve.

Even though there were a million things that I never really thought I could have, I still tried for them. Maybe Sophie gave up. Maybe she had given up all hope and settled for the small contentment she had now.

I wondered what had made her give up. I wondered what her mom had done to her to make her simply not care anymore.

ﻌ • ﻌ

Everyone was gathered around the large dining room table. By "everyone" I mean my adopted family, Trent, and the Wallaces. It was like most evenings when both Robin and Stephen were not working. The more I thought about it, the more I was convinced they were in some kind of relationship. While I picked at the Chinese take-out and thought about Kate's home-cooked meals, I watched them.

Robin looked at him a total of two times, and he looked at her five times. Even when they were talking to each other, they were looking at something else. She was obviously much better at pretending than he was, but I wondered how I had failed to notice this before. How long had they been together and why wouldn't they just tell us?

This was the problem. It wasn't that I didn't like, or didn't trust Stephen, and Robin was as enjoyable as a therapist could be, but they both seemed to act like we were all fragile and would break at any moment.

Even with all of our collective pasts, I thought we could handle the news that they were dating or sleeping together, or whatever it was that they were doing. It would actually be a good thing; a positive thing. Couldn't they figure out that perhaps it might be good for us to have this knowledge? Maybe putting a label on something could help us. Maybe we needed to know that she was a mother figure, and not just some professional shrink trying to analyze our every move.

"Elliott?"

I looked up at Stephen. He had apparently been speaking. "Y-y-yes?"

"Robin asked you a question."

I turned to her, becoming aware that Robin had always worn two hats in this house. Right now she looked like a mother.

"I just asked if you had sent in your college applications yet."

Even though I was only a junior and it was much too early to be submitting applications, my guidance counselor, Stephen, and I all agreed I could skip my senior year. I had no desire to prolong my time in high school and although the prospect of college scared me, being away from my tormentors always seemed like a good idea.

The problem was that although I'd filled out the paperwork, I'd done nothing else. I sighed, knowing that both she and Stephen wouldn't like the answer. "N-no."

I heard Stephen sigh and I turned to see his disappointed face.

"He still has tons of time," Jane said in my defense.

"But you've had the applications completed for months, Elliott. You wanted to go a year early." It wasn't hard to hear the displeasure in my adopted father's voice. "Why don't you just send them off?"

"Do you need to fine-tune them?" Robin asked.

I looked at her and saw that her therapist hat was back on. She studied me, trying to figure out what my motive was for dragging my feet. When I glanced over at Stephen, he was studying me with his doctor's eyes, most likely running down any kind of physical or medical reason I hadn't done it yet.

"N-n-no," I answered.

"He probably wants to make sure he's only applying to the schools he *really* wants to go to, right, Elliott?"

I had no response for David. I hadn't sent in my applications yet because the thought of doing it caused my lungs to seize and my heart to race. The thought of putting everything about me down on paper, and having someone decide if I was good enough to get into their school, tore at me.

Even if I was accepted to every school where I applied, at worst I would have to leave this house and the comfort of my room and the small cocoon of safety I had woven here. At the least I would have to travel to Frederick Community College thirty minutes away. In either case, I would still have to be around all new people.

Chris Anderson was mean, but at least I knew it.

I was aware that college was expected, and to be honest, I wanted to go, but knowing that unless I went to the same school as the others, I wouldn't know anybody, scared me. Rebecca, David, and Trent were planning on going to Stanford. If I was accepted early, I would still have to leave Jane, and now Sophie.

If Trent went to Stanford, Jane would go next year. How could I go somewhere without her? I didn't even know if Stanford was where I wanted to go.

"If you need some help with--" Robin began, but was cut off.

Rebecca sighed dramatically, causing all eyes to fall on her. "Leave him alone, Mom. He just said that he didn't need any help."

I never actually said that, or anything like it, because no one usually allowed me much more than a single syllable answer.

"I-I'll send them i-i-in on M-Monday," I said to placate everyone.

Trent caught my eye and gave me a small pitying smile as he scratched his scuffy chin. It meant he was going to divert the attention away from me. He did it a lot and he was good at it. "Stephen, did I tell you about my new motorcycle?"

Stephen cocked his eyebrow, "It came with a helmet, I hope."

~ • ~

Sleep didn't come easily. Sunday nights were the worst. Even though I had successfully navigated through another week of small-town high school just a few days before, Sunday nights were when I was prone to small panic attacks.

Sure, I knew what to expect when I got there, but that didn't stop me from freaking out about it. I knew my stutter hadn't magically gotten better over the weekend, and that the same small-minded people were going to make fun of me before school even started tomorrow.

The only thing that calmed me somewhat was the knowledge that I would see Sophie Young.

Chapter 19

Deeper

Sophie

After writing a quick e-mail to Elliott that answered his questions, I got dragged out of the house by Tom. The only reason I didn't pitch a fit was because it was going to be at the Fox's place, so Jason would be there.

Apparently Tom went to a lot of get-togethers with the Fox's and the Collins'. Olivia was Jason's partner in the Screw-Up Club and her brother Jamie Collins was also a member.

When I got there, I was surprised by how many people were crammed inside the little house. We couldn't all fit, so there were quite a few people outside, keeping toasty around a fire pit, and holding beers. I wondered how much work this little gathering would end up being for Jace. Having an OCD parent who threw get-togethers had to be exhausting. He probably had to clean for hours just to get the house ready and then after we all infected the place, would have *days* worth of cleaning. As much as I would've hated it, Tom should have held this gathering at his house.

Wait. Didn't Jace say that his dad hadn't left the house in years? What was that called? Agoraphobia in addition to OCD? So if he wanted to see friends, it *always* had to be at his house and then they had to clean for days afterward, I supposed. Damn. Jace's life sucked.

A football game kept most of the adults blind and in the living room, so everyone under the age of nineteen was out back, sitting around a second fire pit. I was sitting between Jason and Olivia, watching as he packed a bowl.

I had to give him props. Dude was packing up a huge glass piece while all the adults sat inside his house watching the Redskins get spanked. No wonder he was one step away from juvie - not that I could talk.

"Pass that shit over here." I turned to see one of his friends holding out his hand. He had a lighter in the other. I think his name was Jesse. Megan liked to talk about him. Apparently he's got some kind of massive penis that scared her, you know, in a good way.

"Whatever, Jesse. This is my gathering and I say thaaaaat..." he drew out the word as he let his dark eyes travel over everyone and then stopped when they landed on me, "Sophie gets the green hit."

I smiled. Nothing like the green hit when smoking out of a glass pipe, and his shit looked good today, all green and sticky with some orange fluff to accentuate the sparkly crystals.

The bowl went fast, but I got decently high from the two big-ass hits I took. There was a loud noise from inside, presumably due to a touchdown or a fumble or some such thing.

It reminded us that there were adults, responsible people, in our midst and the bowl was promptly hidden beneath an upturned flower pot.

Everyone kind of drifted away, here and there, leaving me to sit with Olivia and Jason. I was content to enjoy a silent high, but apparently they weren't. Olivia mumbled something I didn't quite catch.

"Oh, shut the fuck up, will you?" I looked over and saw him giving Olivia an exasperated expression. "Just because my dad invited your mother, doesn't mean I need to listen to any more of that shit."

"Screw you," was Olivia's witty retort.

"Nah, pretty sure I'm not your type, and I heard somewhere that you think you're too good to suck cock." With that, Jason got up and walked off toward the house.

"Wow," I said.

"He's a prick. I can't believe you let him stick his dick in you."

I turned to Olivia now, studying her face. She was scowling, of course. Every time I looked at Olivia, she was scowling. "What?"

"Oh, you heard me."

"How do you know we—?"

Olivia gave me a look that said, "Duh," but she said, "He gave you the green hit, didn't he? In front of all his friends? I've known him since we were in diapers and that's code for marking territory. I'm surprised he didn't pee on you too."

I hated possession. He wasn't *dating* me. I was just having sex with him. I thought about responding, and setting her straight about what was going on between Jason and me, but decided against it. Saying anything at all would give the impression that I cared.

Silence loomed and it was uncomfortable.

"So…"

"So," she repeated, "we're practically sisters, did you know that?"

"What?" It made no sense. We weren't friends, so how could we be sisters? Was it just the pot clouding my mind and making it impossible to understand her meaning?

"Your dad's boning my mom."

My eyes bulged. "What?" I blinked, looking back at the house. "Since when?"

"Since before my dad died, and he died five years ago."

My mind raced, the pot helping it produce more scenarios than necessary. "What? Wait. Tom's doing your mom?" She nodded. "He was sleeping with her while she was still married?"

Olivia let out a low chuckle and nodded. "Your dad and my dad were friends from high school. I wonder if my dad ever humped your mom. Maybe it was some kind of…"

I stopped listening when she mentioned my mother. My whole body tensed and it wasn't from the cold. Standing up, I took a deep breath, closing my eyes and trying to regain the high I'd just been experiencing. "I'm going to find Jason."

"Shit, Sophie." I felt Olivia grab my arm and I fought against the urge to hit her. I didn't like people grabbing me. "I'm sorry if I…"

"It's cool, Olivia. I don't care that he's doing your mom. I just don't want to talk about it." I sighed. "I'm cold. Jason can warm me up."

Once I found him, he tried to take my hand, but I pulled it away and tucked it in the front pocket of my hoodie. I followed him into the house and through the kitchen, pausing to watch Tom for a quick minute. He was next to a dark-haired lady. They didn't touch until something happened on the TV and they both jumped out of their seats and cheered. During the commotion, before everyone settled back down, their hips touched and he pressed his hand against the small of her back. She looked up at him with a smile and he gave her a soft smile in return.

"You suddenly interested in the 'Skins'?"

I nearly jumped. I didn't answer, but instead let Jace grab me around the waist and drag me through the hallway.

"You know, we don't just have to have sex all the time," Jason said as he watched me pull my hoodie back over my head.

We were in the bathroom and I could hear Tom cheering and laughing from the living room that was only about five feet away. I drew my attention back to Jason's face as his tongue swept out to lick his bottom lip.

"What?"

"We could go do something together sometime that *doesn't* involve condoms and sticky messes."

Sick. Boys were disgusting and - hold up - what boy didn't want to do things that involved sticky messes and condoms? "What are you talking about?"

Jason gave me a shaky smile and then stood up, bringing his pants up with him. "You know, we could do what normal…" he paused, looked down at the floor and then back up at me, "people do."

"Normal people? What the hell are you talking about, Jace?"

His smile disappeared as he took a deep breath. "Do you want to go to a movie sometime or something?"

Shit, this was not happening. Jason was just a hook-up and a "hook-up." I had been clear about that and now he wanted to go to the movies with me? I could feel my anger building. "What? Do you want to hold my hand and give me sweet kisses on the cheek while I wear your jacket or some dumb shit like that now?"

It was mean and harsh, and I hated the look on his face when I said it, but it had to be done.

"Jesus, Sophie," he hissed quietly, his gaze moving to the floor.

"I told you that I don't date. I don't want to be someone's girlfriend. I don't want the hearts and flowers, and I don't want a sappy love poem you stayed up all night writing, okay?" I ran my hands through my hair. "And last I knew, neither did you."

"I just asked about a movie, okay? I didn't propose."

"Fine. No, Jason, I don't want to go to a movie with you. I'd rather let you bend me over your dirty bathroom sink and fuck me so hard that I scream and lose my voice. Okay? Is that acceptable for you, or do you have to buy me dinner first?"

Jason shook his head and then turned to face the mirror. He stared at himself for almost thirty seconds until he turned around to look at me again. When he spoke, his voice was quiet. "I didn't say that I wanted to be your boyfriend."

He was calm and I did my best to quell the rising panic. "Good. Because I told you from the beginning that I'm not the girlfriend type."

"Yeah, I remember."

"I don't hold hands," I said while smoothing down my hoodie, trying not to think about how desperately I had wanted to hold Elliott's hand.

"I get it."

My jaw clenched just as my hands balled up at my sides. After a deep breath, I said, "I don't want sweet kisses and whispers about love and bullshit."

"All right, Sophie," he exhaled.

I put my hand on the doorknob and twisted. “I’m not your fucking girlfriend, Jason. Don’t think that I am.”

“Why are you so messed up?”

I ignored his question and left the bathroom.

It was another two hours after that before Tom thought it was time to go home. I could tell by the lazy smile on his face that he was over the legal limit.

“Give me your keys, Tom.”

“You can’t drive, Soph.”

I sighed and held out my hand. “I’m sure the court would make an exception if it meant no one gets killed by a drunken fireman today.”

He got this look on his face. It was all sad and disappointed. “Sophie, I…”

“Just give me your keys.” My voice held no anger, no harshness. I was tired and I wanted to go home.

He extended his hand and dropped the keys into my palm. “I didn’t mean to drink so much. I’m sorry,” he said as he slipped into the passenger seat.

“It’s cool.”

“No, it’s not cool. I’m your father and I’m setting a bad example.”

I revved the engine as I turned to him, horrified to find that he was a sappy, sad drunk. “Forget about it. We’re cool.”

He was silent for a moment. "Did you get something to eat? I should've made sure that you…"

I shook my head and put the SUV in gear. His fixation on my eating was starting to annoy me. "I had food, Tom."

"Dad," he whispered as I pulled away from the curb.

I ignored him for the rest of the ride home, but thought about his secret, or not-so-secret, relationship with Linda Collins. Tom drank too much and messed with another man's wife. I wondered if everybody in Damascus was a screw-up.

"Are you hungry?" I asked as I followed him into the kitchen.

"I am."

I nodded and he sat down at the table while I gathered food. I wasn't high anymore, and I hated it. As my hands went to work cleaning the lettuce and carrots, trimming the fat off the steak, and prepping the oven to broil, my thoughts were on all the subjects I didn't want to think about.

Today made it twice that Jason had asked me on what sounded like dates, even though I'd been clear with him that I didn't do that shit. It made me uncomfortable to think that Jason somehow wanted something more than I did. I had no interest in him beyond his ability to make me feel good through sex and weed.

Now he wanted more.

I had no more to give.

I'd just stood up after grabbing the large ceramic bowl for the salad when Tom asked, "Why are you so sad, Sophie?"

I stopped moving and stood perfectly still, panic and fear rising as I watched him get up out of his seat and come toward me. What the hell? "What are you…?"

Tom extended his hand in my direction and I instantly dropped the bowl, hearing it crash to the floor. As he moved his hand dangerously close to my face, my arm instinctively came up to block it and I smacked it away quickly as I stumbled backwards until my back hit the counter.

"What the hell are you doing?"

Tom looked at me, his drunken face registering his shock. "I was just going to touch your hair, Soph." He paused, his eyes on me as I wrapped my arms around my torso. "When you were little," he began slowly, "you used to let me brush your hair."

I didn't remember that. I felt sick. His hands were slack at his sides as he just looked at me. Swallowing hard, I brought my hand to my mouth. "I'm not little anymore, Tom."

Very, very quickly, I left the kitchen and found the bathroom, just barely making it to the toilet before throwing up.

Shit.

I rose up off the floor and grabbed my toothbrush. I knew that Tom didn't mean to scare me. I knew that he wasn't someone who wanted to hurt me, but I couldn't just let him touch me. I didn't care why he wanted to, whether it was to hurt or comfort, I wouldn't let him.

My head pounded with horrifying thoughts. I felt so sick.

After brushing my teeth and washing my hands, I went to my bedroom, and heard Tom clinking around in the kitchen. Packing up my bat, I stuck my head out of my opened window and took two hits.

I grabbed a piece of gum, dropped some Visine in my eyes, and then headed back downstairs to finish cooking dinner. The pot was working, and I felt much better, but regardless, I tensed again as I entered the kitchen.

Tom was butchering the Romaine and all of the ceramic shards were gone from the floor. I wanted to cut the lettuce myself, but that meant I would have to stand next to him and take the knife. I didn't want him to be that close. The thought of having to stand right next to him made my stomach churn, and I was suddenly struck by how unfair everything was.

It wasn't fair for me to have these reactions to Tom, my own…father. It wasn't fair that all he wanted to do was touch my hair and I had an involuntary, instinctive reaction. It wasn't fair that I hated him so much for something he didn't even do.

This shit wasn't his doing.

But it didn't matter that it wasn't my father who did this to me. It only mattered that he was too close to me. It only mattered that he…

I felt sick again. I tasted bile and my throat burned. My cough alerted Tom that I was there and he turned around, eyeing me. He looked completely sober now as he placed the knife on the counter, and smoothed a hand over his trimmed goatee.

I pointed to the lettuce and managed to say, "Do you want me to do that?"

Although he nodded, I waited until he'd crossed back over to the table before I moved to pick up the knife.

"You okay?"

Breathing in deep, I bit back the nasty words that floated in my mind before they could get to my mouth. After I had filtered through all the snotty, bitchy remarks I could possibly say, I settled on a quiet, "I don't really want to talk, Tom. Can I just make dinner?"

"Yeah, Soph," he responded softly. I was intensely aware of his eyes on me. It was different than when I was in my mother's house. He wasn't looking at me in the same way the constant flow of men that filtered through back in Tampa did. Every once in a while, I'd glance at him and could tell that he was mainly just trying to figure me out.

I wondered if he had yet, or if he ever would.

Chapter 20

The Elliott Effect

Sophie

Once I knew Tom was sleeping, I stuck my head out of the window and took another couple of hits off my bat. I got entirely too fucking high. It was after eleven when I opened the e-mail from Elliott.

Sophie,

I hope you have an excellent time at the football fish fry fun-fest.

Via e-mail, Elliot's whole tone changed. He was witty and I liked to imagine him taking great care to write things like "football fish fry fun-fest" just to make me smile.

I don't think it would be appropriate for me to tell you what I would turn Anderson into. It's not very nice.

Since you didn't have time to ask questions, I'll go.

1) If you could spend a day with anyone, living or dead, who would it be and why?

2) What's your favorite holiday?

3) If you could magically have either unlimited wealth or unlimited health, which would you pick?

4) Why don't you eat anything other than a Pop-Tart or an apple at lunch? Don't you get hungry?

5) Is partying the only thing you want out of life?

Bonus: Did you learn anything new at the gathering today?

I'll see you at school tomorrow. I assume that these questions and overall content of our e-mail correspondence won't be mentioned there.

Elliott.

I smiled. Getting his e-mail was the bright shining spot in an otherwise stupid day. Even though I was insanely tired and incredibly high, I hit reply and wondered if he would check his e-mail before school tomorrow.

Elliott,

You're all about the random questions, aren't you? Here goes:

1) *Is spending the day alone an unacceptable answer? People kind of bug me. But again, if that's a cop-out and you need an actual person, I do enjoy hanging out with you.*

2) *My favorite holiday? I don't know. Maybe Columbus Day?*

3) *I would pick unlimited wealth. While I'd love magically ridding myself of diabetes, being poor sucks, and with money I can buy health.*

4) *I hate eating and not in the Andrea Tuttle kind of way. It's because of my diabetes. It's a pain in the ass to figure it all out, so lunch is the one time I try not to think too much about it.*

5) *I'm sure I could think of other things I'd like to do besides partying, but most of them I'll probably never do, so why think about them?*

Bonus: Did you learn anything new at the gathering today?

I learned entirely too much at the "fun-fest" today (btw, you forgot crab-boil). I will file it all in my "Things I Can't Unlearn" folder.

My five (some of these are specific, so I won't be able to reciprocate an answer, but you can ask me specific in return):

1) *When did you discover music? Like when did you know you could play it?*

2) *Do you cuss? 'Cause I've never heard you.*

3) Do you believe in "God?"

4) Do you write your own music?

5) Why don't you call Dr. Dalton "dad?"

Bonus: Have you ever been to a concert? I heard the Chili Peppers are playing in D.C. sometime close to Christmas. Could you be around that many people?

In regards to school and these questions...I don't want or need other people knowing the answers, Elliott. We're friends, like I said, but I don't need someone like Anderson or Cierra knowing who I am, so I'd appreciate keeping our discussions at school about something other than our e-mails. Sorry, I'm fucking rambling because I'm slightly high and unfocused.

Shit. Should I have deleted that? Was it rude to mention getting high to him when his mother was a dead smack addict? Being friends was hard and to be honest, I didn't want to offend Elliott. If it had been anyone else, I wouldn't have cared.

He told me that he wouldn't judge me.

Screw it. Why was I continuing to put so much thought into this shit? I was going to send it as it was.

Is that cool about the questions being private, especially at school?

See ya.

Sophie.

Jason was quiet on the drive to school Monday morning, even as I rolled a joint out of my stash for the ride. I felt bad about the way we'd left things the day before and thought the joint would be appropriate.

It wasn't that he was giving me the silent treatment, because he *was* talking, but he wasn't talking *much* and he wasn't *saying* anything.

As we pulled up into his usual parking spot, I said a quick goodbye, figuring that he would either get over it or not, but either way it wasn't my problem. I'd been honest with him and I didn't think that there was anything wrong with that.

I caught up with Aiden Montgomery in the hall before Photography and bought two Vicodins off of him.

I hadn't slept much the night before and instead of being sleepy, I found myself wired. I figured that the Vicodin would help my body and mind relax just a little. Rationally, I knew I'd overreacted to Tom, but my irrational mind still made it impossible for me to stop the involuntary shoulder shakes that happened at irregular intervals.

Maybe the pills would stop it. I snapped one of them in half and downed both halves to make it work quicker. And work quick, it did. Pinny Dalton nudged me and my head slipped off of its precarious position, resting on my hands.

"What?" I looked around, my gaze finally falling on her left arm where she'd drawn pictures with her fine-point green Sharpie. She was an odd one to figure out. She seemed pretty pristine, but she was pierced and drew on her skin daily.

"Class is over, Sophie. Are you okay?"

"I'm fucking great. How are you?"

I took another half right before Study Hall, and then took the last half after smoking out with Jason. I was fairly incoherent during Horticulture and I was pretty sure that I nodded a hello to Elliott, but after that it was pretty much a crapshoot as to what else happened.

To be honest, it was nice. Painkillers always left me feeling like I was floating on a cloud, all the rough edges of the day smoothing out into a nice, warm and cozy fluffy pillow.

I should've gotten more from Aiden. I wondered if I would see him again before the end of the day. Maybe Jason could just lift one of Jerry's for me.

"…o-okay?"

I blinked and raised my head off the desk, my lazy eyes easily landing on Elliott's beautiful hazel ones. I couldn't keep myself from smiling. "Hmmm? Okay, what?"

He looked at me in concern. "A-a-are you o-okay?"

I nodded and his glance shifted toward the door. "C-class is d-d-d-d, o-over, S-Sophie."

Looking around, I finally noticed that the room was nearly empty. "Oh." I stood up and collected my notebook, the sheets of paper still blank. "Guess I forgot to take notes."

"Y-you c-can borrow mine."

I shook my head as I shoved the book into my backpack. "It's cool, but thanks. I'm sure it was all soil pH this and microbe that." The intensity of his stare made me glance away again. I didn't understand why he was looking at me like that. "So we should do something on Saturday," I said lazily

I looked back at him as I began to walk away. He was nodding, a small smile on his face. "What do you want to do?" I asked when his feet finally carried him toward me.

"S-S-SSStephen is inviting y-y-y-your d-d-d-dddd…"

Out in the hall, I stopped outside the door, giving the other students a little room to enter. "My what?"

"F-father," he spit out, "and you for d-dinner."

"What? On Saturday?"

"W-well the d-dance is on S-S-Saturday, ssssso it w-would just be mm-mmm-mmme a-and…"

I sighed. It was nice of Tom to tell me about all of the social engagements he'd signed me up for. "Well, what about Friday? The game and parade are on that night, so doesn't that mean the whole Screw-Up Club will be cancelled?" I could hope, couldn't I?

Elliott nodded, which made my day. It was then that my head began to feel like it was floating again, the blood inside of it seemingly swishing this way and that. For a moment, I let my eyelids droop and took in a deep breath.

I had eaten lunch, hadn't I?

Shit.

I opened my eyes and suddenly everything slowed down. People were moving dangerously fast outside of my darkened bubble, but everything on the inside was slowed down and muted. The only thing I could hear was the thudding of my heart. Elliott's lips were moving, but I had to strain to hear him.

I didn't know if it was the low blood sugar or the Vicodin, but I felt like shit.

Involuntarily, my body rocked forward as my mind raced, yelling at it to respond. There were things I had to do when my blood sugar was low, actions I had to take, but my body was slow and sluggish so it wouldn't let me.

Strong hands like vices grabbed onto my upper arms as I came crashing into Elliott's chest. I pulled back and then came face-to-face with him.

It took a moment before my body caught up with my mind, and I took a deep breath, licking my lips. I pushed away from him gently and stood up as straight as I could. "Sorry. Just dizzy."

His eyes narrowed as his chest rose and fell quickly. My body began to move now, and I shrugged off my backpack, sinking down onto the ground to search through the front pouch. I was vaguely aware that Elliott had crouched down next to me, but I couldn't think about him or his eyes right now. I had to get sugar into my bloodstream.

When my sugar was low, my thoughts were slow and scattered; on Vicodin my thoughts were speedy, but this was entirely new and kind of scary. Usually I could do all of this faster, but today I was a river of mud. All my thoughts were shooting me in different directions.

Yes, I should get the sugar packets or the glucose tabs Tom bought for me. Yes, I should get them into my mouth as quickly as possible. Yes, Elliott was standing right next to me and we were in the middle of a crowded hallway. Yes, I wanted to kiss him, but the last time hadn't turned out so great.

Crap. Focus. Blood sugar. Sugar. I needed to focus on the task at hand.

Still my hands fumbled with the zipper. They shook as they tore open the packet and I found myself hoping that I'd either just pass out or feel better already.

Then finally, there was sweetness on my tongue, and the instant placebo effect kicked in, making me feel minutely better. Even if it was psychological, I loved the hope it gave that really, really soon, I'd start to feel better. The world would begin to brighten again, the haze disappearing. I would be able to hear the sounds around me instead of being deafened by the thump of my heart. I could control my body again.

Probably two or three minutes later, I stood up, three empty sugar packets in my hands. I felt hot, but relatively okay. I knew Elliott was still next to me, but I couldn't focus on him yet.

Shit. Had I even eaten breakfast today?

I breathed in slow and deep and finally gave Elliott a small apologetic smile. "Sorry."

He shook his head, looking concerned. "A-are you, o-o-okay?"

"I have to eat." Looking around, I saw that we were alone in the hall. "You're late for your next class."

Elliott shook his head again. "I-I don't h-have one." He brought his hand to my elbow. "D-do you w-w-want to g-gggo to the n-nurse?"

I wasn't sure if it was his question or some kind of instinctive reaction, but something compelled me to say "No," very loudly while jerking my arm away. Nurses never led to good things, so there was no reason to go see one. It also registered that I felt a little sad he was no longer touching me.

I wondered if the day could get any weirder.

"I'm okay, Elliott." I ran my hand through my hair. "I'm just going to go sit outside. The cool air will help."

"D-do you w-want mm-mmme to g-go with you?"

Did I want him to come with me? No. I didn't. Not because I was a bitch and didn't like him or whatever, but because this shit was getting too deep already. I was fucking hanging on this e-mailing thing we'd *just* started. Hell, when we were next to that stream, surrounded by fallen leaves and wildflowers, I'd practically told him about Helen, and that was something I promised myself a long time ago I'd *never* tell anyone.

The feelings I had for him were intense, and I didn't like it.

It was sloppy and I was an idiot for feeling that way. I needed to stop this infatuation. Things were always easier without all this emotion.

But even as I said that in my head, trying to convince myself that I didn't need or want anything like this, my mouth responded, "Yeah, sure."

Outside, the cool, crisp and slightly wet concrete of a low wall helped cool my burning face, while I focused on deep breaths. I was feeling better overall, but felt a little jittery.

"I-I-I'll g-go get you ssssome more food."

"No," I said quietly, craning my neck to look him in the eye. "This is fine." I held up my hand and waved the apple I'd swiped from the cafeteria before coming outside. "Just sit with me."

Struggling, I sat up, my shoulder brushing his. I hadn't realized that he was so close. Even though I knew I'd be sorry to lose the contact again, I automatically slid away a little and busied myself with my glucose monitor.

I wanted to tell him everything about me, but the thought that someone would know me, *really* know me, made me keep my mouth shut.

After getting my blood sugar reading, I took small bites of the apple and thought about how this happened. I'd thrown up last night, barely ate any dinner, skipped breakfast, forgot lunch, and hadn't made any adjustments to my insulin.

We must have been sitting outside for a long time because students began filing out of the building. "S-S-S-SSSo-SSSSophie!"

I looked up quickly at Elliott, but he hadn't been the one calling me. To my left, Anderson was smirking at me. I quickly glanced at Elliott again. He was looking down, his hands clenched in his lap.

"I-I'll sssssee you t-tomorrow, S-S-Sophie."

I sighed, but he got up and walked away quickly, leaving me there with Anderson.

"You are such a humanitarian, spending your time with the friendless." He sat down next to me, the smirk still on his insipid face. Just the sight of his vapid, intentionally-messy hair ticked me off.

He leaned in closer, "What? Does a guy have to be a total loser to get your attention? You're so giving to the less fortunate. I find that *sexy.*"

"Chris," I began slowly, "I feel like shit right now, so could we maybe continue this conversation, oh, like, never?"

He laughed and shook his head. "I know your game, you know."

"My game?" This was going to be good.

"Yeah, your—"

"Need something, Anderson?"

I looked up to see Jason, who was at least a foot taller than Anderson, scowling down at him.

"Just talking to my girl Sophia, Fox. Don't you have some pot to sell to ten-year-olds or something?"

Jason smiled, but crossed his arms over his chest.

I rolled my eyes. Boys and their pissing matches and dick measuring. I shook my head and stood up. "Actually, Chris, Jason's my ride so…"

"I can give you a ride home, Sophia." I wish he'd stop calling me Sophia. He knew I preferred to be called Sophie. He did it just to be a prick. "At some point you'll want something classier than—"

Feeling another insult coming, I leaned in closer and his smile widened. "Chris," I said, saying his name all low and seductive, "not only is he going to give me a ride home, but he's going to *give me a ride.* And that will never be you."

For a moment he was quiet, his eyes flashing something dark, but after a moment, he said, "You say that now, Sophia," before walking away.

•

After dinner, I signed on and found that Elliott had written me back. I loved his e-mails. He was so smart and wordy. I liked it. The feeling was a bit scary, but I tried to push past it. It made me feel good that someone could be so interested in me for some reason.

Sophie,

Your five:

1) *When I was twelve, Stephen bought me a guitar as something to focus on. He would say that I have a "natural talent for music." I'm not sure why. I remember just picking it up for the first time, strumming it and then being able to pick out a simple tune within minutes and play a song that first night.*

2) *I guess in my head I curse, but they're just such throwaway words that I don't waste my time trying to say them. Typically the cursing in my internal dialog is limited to "hell" or "damn," I think. I was brought up not to do it at all, so I just haven't really done it much.*

3) *Yes, I do believe in God.*

4) *I can't help but write music. Sometimes music wakes me up in the middle of the night and I can't sleep until I get it out.*

5) *I don't call Stephen "Dad" like David does, because he's not my father. I'm not like David. I'm not looking for a "dad" to replace anything in my life.*

Bonus: I have not been to a concert and don't see myself being able to go to any time in the future. Although I'd love to say otherwise, I don't think I could be around that many people, no.

Now my five:

1) *Why don't you call your father "dad?"*

2) *Do you believe in God?*

3) *You said that you write. What do you write?*

4) What's the meaning of life?

5) Why were you really high today?

Bonus: When do you want to get started on the project? We'll have to start soon in order to have something in a month. Since we have to produce a plant, I thought of Brussels sprouts since you like them so much, and they're a hardy late fall/early winter harvest vegetable. Then we'll do the written essay.

Elliott.

I wasn't shocked that Elliott had reciprocated my question about fathers, adopted or not, but his fifth question threw me for a loop. How should I answer that? *Should* I even answer that? Did I even know why I got so high today?

Obviously not eating was a mistake, and that aided in how the pills and weed affected me, but I knew that breaking the pills up would make them stronger and work faster. Still, I took all four halves within the span of three hours or so.

It didn't matter why I got high today, because it was the same reason I got high every day. I liked it. I liked the numb buzz, the smooth edges, and the slight hum inside my head. It made it easier to ignore all the things I hated to think about.

I didn't feel bad about it.

I decided I would answer his question and try to be sensitive to his past while not revealing too much about myself. There was only so much that I wanted *any*one to know about me.

There were also things I never wanted anyone to know, but it was becoming more difficult to keep them from the surface. I could feel Elliott slowly wearing my resistance down.

Chapter 21

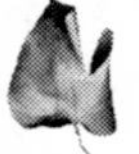

Seeds

Elliott

Sophie was just…*strange* on Monday. She was clearly high, but there was no way for me to know if it had to do with her blood sugar, or if she was using that as a cover for whatever she was on.

I still couldn't help but wonder why she would want to feel like that. I had the overwhelming urge to get her to stop; to force her to figure out why she did the things she did. Like I needed her to tell me explicitly that her mother had abused her and that she used drugs to cope. I wanted her to tell me those things. I wanted *her* to *know* those things about herself. I wanted her to acknowledge them. If she told me, it would be a kind of validation of our friendship.

Although I knew she had agreed to do something with me this weekend, and that most likely she and her father would be here on Saturday, no definite plans had been made.

It would be a lie to say that I didn't lock myself away in my room for the sole purpose of reading my email. It was rapidly becoming the best part of my day. It was like having a little snippet of Sophie's life; a little secret we shared that no one else knew.

It was clichéd, but her last response made my heart skip a beat. While she didn't outright say that she'd rather spend a day with me than anyone else, she alluded to it, and although she called my questions "random," she'd still answered them all.

Elliott,

Sorry about what happened today. Didn't mean to nearly faint on you or anything. Not *how I originally planned my day.*

Here are the answers to your five:

1) *Biologically, I share DNA with Tom. Apart from that, I have no evidence that he's my "father" or my "dad." So he is "Tom." To be fair, Helen is just "Helen," so it's not like I singled the man out or anything.*

2) *Do I believe in "God?" Which one? Honestly, it doesn't matter, because the answer is no. And since you said yes to the question, I'm sure you want to know why, and here it is: god is like a parent, right? We're all "children" of god or whatever? Here's the thing: I think your god is a shitty fucking parent and I want nothing to do with him.*

And yes, I know you're supposed to capitalize the "g" and all, but that's out of respect and clearly I don't have any for "god/God."

Sorry if you're offended. I hope you aren't, but there it is.

3) *As of late, I don't write much of anything. I used to write emo poetry and short stories, but I've learned that if I want to be creative, taking a picture is just better.*

4) *The hell if I know the meaning of life.* Is *there a meaning behind it?*

5) *I was high because yesterday sucked and I like being high. I also forgot to eat and still took my insulin, so I went a little hypoglycemic and it wasn't what I wanted. Thank you for your help and I'm sorry if it made you feel uncomfortable.*

Bonus: We can start the project whenever. If you want, I can come over tomorrow or Wednesday after school, whatever's good for you. Wallace won't be there, will she?

Now my five:

1) *Why don't you have a class after Horticulture?*

2) *When were you adopted by Dalton?*

3) *Why do you believe in god/God?*

4) *Do you have any real brothers or sisters? You know, biological?*

5) I imagine everyone's going to the football game on Friday. Are you going or do you want to do something else? I don't know what yet, but it'll be better than a high school football game.

Bonus: Would you increase your IQ by fifty points if it meant having a huge visible scar on your face?

See you tomorrow,

Sophie.

I quickly wrote her back, not wanting to lose my immediate reactions and responses.

Sophie,

You don't need to thank me for helping you. I was worried about you. Why did yesterday suck? Did getting high help in some way? Because it seemed like it just made today horrible too.

In response to your answers:

Why is taking a picture better than writing? Could I see some of your photographs?

You should come over tomorrow. Can you stay for dinner? As far as I know, Stephen will be home, so Robin will probably not be here.

If you don't mind, I am going to change the format a little. I'll respond to all of your questions as usual, but perhaps out of order.

First, I believe in God, even though God cannot be proven through scientific means. There are certain things in this world that cannot be adequately explained, but it doesn't mean that they are untrue or invalid.

While I wouldn't consider myself "religious" at this stage of my life, I am spiritual in my own way. There was a time when religion dominated my life, but now I feel spirituality has a balanced place within me.

Your assessment is accurate if you truly believe that we are "Children" of God. I can see where He would seem neglectful, cruel, and only capable of conditional love. However, if you shift the paradigm and theorize that we aren't children of God, but a piece of Him/Her/It, then it becomes a different story. In that case, we are creators and not victims forced to suffer through the whims of a fickle God.

This is a new concept for me, since I was taught something vastly different when I was a child. I've thought a lot about this, and there are some days I forget I no longer believe that old dogma, but most of the time I remember that God loves me because I'm a piece of Him.

At least I hope I am.

I grew up with a biological brother and I was adopted by Stephen when I was twelve. We moved to Damascus when I was thirteen and Kate divorced him when I was fourteen. I know you didn't ask about all of that, but in case you're building a timeline of important events in the miserable life of Elliott Dalton, you now have more information.

I don't have class after Reese's because on Tuesdays and Thursdays I have speech therapy. Since I'm apparently the only one in Damascus with a speech impediment, Ms. Rice comes from D.C. Stephen gives her quite a lot of money to drive all that way, but she has to do it during business/school hours. On Mondays, Wednesdays, and Fridays, I'm an aide for Ms. Peters.

I am not going to the football game on Friday. I know David wants me to see him play, but I don't think I could handle that many people in such a small area. I would love to do something with you on Friday. I don't know what though.

As for the bonus question, I would take the points. With a stutter like mine, I don't think a scar on my face would hurt anything.

So now my questions (returning to old format):

1) *When you were very little, what did you want to be when you grew up?*

2) *You indicated that other than DNA, you have no evidence that Tom's your father. Did you get to spend much time with him when you were growing up?*

3) *When did you start getting high?*

4) *Do you have any brothers or sisters?*

5) *Why didn't you make fun of me, or at least treat me like a freak like everyone else does, when you first met me and heard me talk?*

Bonus: If you could undo one thing in the past, what would it be? It could be something personal (something you did or experienced) or not.

Are you staying for dinner tomorrow? If you do, I'll have to let Stephen know. I'm not sure how much you know about Jane, but I'm pretty sure she's going to try to commandeer you at some point. She collects friends like David collects sports paraphernalia. Just be prepared.

Bring your camera, please.

Have a good night, Sophie.

Elliott

I knew my constant questions about drugs were blatant, and if someone else read it, like her father or Stephen, she would get in trouble, but I still wanted to know.

I set about doing my normal after-school routine of homework, music, dinner, and then reading a few children's books out loud. I would have to see Ms. Rice tomorrow and it always seemed to go just a little better when I practiced a lot the night before.

It was hard for me to focus. I kept thinking about Sophie and then about me. Then I just plain thought about "Sophie and Me." I didn't understand it. Despite popular belief, I was a smart person, but I couldn't wrap my mind around whatever was happening between us.

It was confusing. I'd never really had a friend in my life, beyond Jane. I supposed that Trent, Rebecca and David were my friends, but they *had* to be. This was the first time that someone besides Jane was *choosing* to spend time with me.

I knew we were opposites in a lot of different ways, but it didn't seem to matter. There was something instinctual about my wanting to be closer to Sophie. It wasn't because Robin and Stephen forced a connection. Honestly, all that had done was put me on edge and made me dread having to speak with her in the first place.

But now that we had some solid history of spending time with each other, it seemed much more natural and right, which was confusing and it scared me. Not that I thought it would happen, but it was entirely possible that at any moment, Sophie could turn into the female version of Chris. She could realize I wasn't worth her time and not be my friend anymore. There were a number of ways she could destroy me.

I didn't understand it, but it felt right to open up and be vulnerable. *That* is what I could not grasp. Why, at this point in my life did I feel like I *needed* someone like Sophie? No, not *like* Sophie. *Sophie* herself.

I waited until bed to check my e-mail once more, convinced that she had more important things to do than answer my questions, but desperately needing to see if she had.

I was probably more excited than I should've been when I saw her reply waiting in my Inbox.

Elliott,

Tomorrow's fine. I'll stay for dinner. Are you aware that with your first three questions, you actually asked a total of nine? Do you think you're sneaky with that shit? But, like you, I will do my best to answer all of them.

Taking pictures is easier than writing because it's harder to interpret. If someone finds a picture, typically it's just a picture to them. Words get you in trouble. Yes, of course, you can see my portfolio sometime. It's only fair after all; I've heard you play your instruments.

I have no siblings and spent about a month each summer with Tom, but just because I was in Damascus, staying at his house, didn't mean I spent time with *him. The month usually consisted of me at his house while he worked. On his days off he dragged me to climb rocks or hike with his friend (Jason's dad).*

When I was very little, and still thought that I could do anything and be anything, I wanted to be a firefighter like Tom. Pretty stupid kid, huh?

I started drinking when I was eleven, smoked pot for the first time at twelve, ate mushrooms on my thirteenth birthday, dropped acid on Christmas that same year, rolled on E when I was fifteen, did my first line of coke also at fifteen, and banged meth once last year. I know you didn't ask about any of that, but in case you're building a timeline of Sophie Young's history of drugs, you have all the info you need.

If I could undo one thing from the past...I would undo the night Tom and Helen met.

I wasn't an asshole to you because 1) I'm not mean and 2) your stutter doesn't define you, Elliott.

I'll send you my five, but I probably won't read your responses until tomorrow.

1) *You said that smoking pot doesn't help your anxiety, but how do you know that?*

2) *How long have you been in speech therapy? Does it help?*

3) *Do you like chocolate?*

4) *Do you think that people are inherently good or bad? And why?*

5) *Anderson's smaller than you, so why do you let him get away with that shit?*

Bonus: If you were famous, what would you want to be famous for?

See you tomorrow,

Sophie.

❧ • ❧

School went by quickly on Tuesday. I had intended for Sophie to just ride home with us, but she said she'd meet me in a half-hour or so. She left the school property with Jason Fox, as usual, and when she rang the doorbell around four-thirty, I could tell she was high.

I didn't ask her about it as I led her through the yard to the greenhouse out back. I'd gathered all of the supplies and sat down on an overturned bucket, letting her sit on the bench.

"How do you know about organic gardening?" she asked as I pulled the starter plants out of their plastic pots. Like every other time, it took a second to get used to the dirt on my hands. I'd just started taking Horticulture in September, so the practice still wasn't easy for me.

"K-Kate l-liked plants." She bought them all the time and would "rescue" them from other people. Before she divorced Stephen, our house was filled with them. I'd counted one time and we had over fifty plants, each with their own watering schedule and sunlight needs.

"She's Dr. Dalton's ex-wife? So she would be your adopted mother, right?"

Although she was technically correct on both counts, I said nothing.

"She taught you about them?"

I nodded, twisting my body over to the raised bed, digging into the dirt. It took some concentration, as always, but I managed to scoop up the soil. "W-we never t-talked mmmuch, b-but w-when she had to re-pot something, w-we did it t-to-together." I punctuated my words with a shrug.

Her eyes narrowed as she watched me tuck the first plant into the soil. "Should I help? Is there something other than planting I need to do? I told you I wasn't going to let you carry me through the class."

I smiled, remembering how awkward that day was for me. I'd wanted to say a million things to her, but next to nothing came out. The awkwardness of talking with Sophie was still present, but it had changed a bit. Now there was a slightly different tension between us and I recognized that I was having difficulty balancing our e-mail conversations with our face-to-face interaction. It was easy to type words out onto a computer and hit send. It was incredibly hard to speak the same words.

"Y-you can help if y-you want." I pointed to the rest of the plants on the floor. "W-we have t-to p-p-p-p-p-pppp," I stopped trying to push the word out and sighed. I'd said "plant" just moments before, but now it refused to come out. "do all of th-them," I finally finished.

I glanced up at her, feeling embarrassed about the verbal block I'd just had in front of her. "Y-you can t-take p-p-pictures. W-we have to document e-each sssstage."

Sophie nodded and reached into her bag, pulling out her camera. It definitely wasn't up-to-date, and now I understood why Jane had wanted to buy her a new one. "Didn't we need to take pictures of the seeds and sprouts and stuff?"

I nodded. "B-b-but I d-downloaded the p-p-pictures ssssince we d-didn't have enough t-time to grow them from sssseeds."

Sophie nodded and started snapping a few pictures before and after I planted them. It only took a minute or two and then she found herself a white bucket, turned it over, and sat down next to me.

"I love dirt." I looked at her questioningly and she graced me with a smile, like the one she'd given me that day in the bookstore. "Seriously," Sophie said, her voice light and airy, "don't you just love how it smells? How it feels?"

If my mouth worked like a normal human being's, I would have joked about her being some kind of Earth-loving-pagan-hippie or something, but since I knew I would stumble over the words, I just smiled at her even though the concept of *playing* in dirt sort of frightened me. "I used to get into so much trouble for playing in the mud!" She laughed a little as she said it.

Her eyes softened just for a second, but that moment passed quickly and she sighed, the light leaving her eyes as her mouth settled back into a frown. I wished she would smile again. I wondered if she was reacting to the thought of getting into trouble. Trouble meant punishment, and I remembered what that was like.

"I-I-I've never p-played in mm-mmmud." I looked down at my hands in the soil and wondered if that was why I actually enjoyed working with plants. Plants lived in soil and soil was dirt, and dirt was dirty, and I'd never been allowed to be dirty like that.

"Oh, come on," she scoffed, "no child has ever *not* played in mud or dirt, at least once anyway. It's like a…a thing, you know, rite of passage or something."

"I-I c-couldn't."

"Why?" Her voice still held a disbelieving tone, but there was curiosity within it as well. I wished I hadn't said anything. It was like talking to Robin; any small detail I dropped would be picked at until meaning was given and everyone understood it.

Not that Sophie was like Robin. She didn't pry. She wasn't asking in order to press me into saying something about anything. She was just asking, but answering was harder than typing. "A-ask m-me in an e-mail."

It was the first time since we'd begun the e-mail correspondence that one of us had mentioned it. I looked at Sophie out of the corner of my eye to gauge her reaction. While I heard the sigh, her face held no clue as to what she was thinking.

❧ • ❧

"This is seriously what you guys eat for dinner?" Sophie pushed a piece of overcooked broccoli to the side of her plate. Nervously, I watched as she turned to Stephen. "You're a doctor. Aren't you supposed to be peddling good, whole foods?"

Stephen cleared his throat, taking a quick glance at me before regarding Sophie. "We all keep pretty crazy hours. It's just easier to bring home take-out."

"Did you already invite Tom to dinner on Saturday?"

He blinked, looking at me and then back at Sophie. "Yes, will you be able to attend?"

"What were you planning on serving for dinner?"

Stephen looked down. "Take-out."

Jane, who'd been remarkably quiet through most of the meal, said, "You're having Sophie and her father over for dinner on Saturday? The dance is on Saturday."

"Which is precisely the reason why we invited them. The house will be quiet." Stephen smiled.

"Aren't you going to the dance?" Jane asked, running one of her hoops over and over through her ear and turning to Sophie. "It's Homecoming."

Sophie groaned and shook her head, twirling a long noodle on her fork and sighing again. "What time is dinner on Saturday?"

"I figured around six or seven."

Sophie licked her lips, looked at me, and replied, "Then I'll be here at four to start prepping food."

I had no idea that not only would she *want* to come for dinner, but that she would volunteer to cook as well. I wondered if she liked to cook and where she'd learned.

"S-S-Sophie, you d-don't have to…"

She held up her fork, the noodle hanging limply off of it and scrunched up her face. "Seriously? This isn't food. It's mush." She turned to Stephen before continuing. "Not trying to be a bitch or anything, but I'd rather spend a few hours cooking than eat something like this again." She blinked, chewed on her lower lip, and then added, "No offense."

He grinned. He admired people like Sophie. It seemed to me he wanted me to be more like her and say things like that. "None taken. We haven't had a home cooked meal in—"

"Years," David finished, giving her one of his most charming smiles, and then nodded. "You'd be my favorite person in the whole world if you made enough for leftovers."

Everyone was excited about the meal and I could tell it made Sophie uncomfortable, so after dinner we put our dishes in the sink and I took her upstairs where we did what we always did: listened to music and enjoyed each other's company.

Chapter 22

Jane Didn't Mean To

Elliott

Sophie's father arrived at around seven to take her home. We'd made plans to shop either Friday night or Saturday afternoon for the ingredients for whatever it was she'd be cooking. Truth be told, not only was *I* excited, but I could tell that Stephen was just as enthusiastic about the prospect of a home-cooked meal. Of course, Jane and David were disappointed that it would be taking place while they were at Homecoming, but the idea of *leftover* home-cooking was still cause for happiness.

We hadn't had much decent food since Kate left. Stephen worked so much, Jane wasn't to be trusted with the cooking utensils, David burned everything he touched, and I had no creativity when it came to food. If I were responsible for feeding everyone, we'd have peanut butter and jelly sandwiches every other day with grilled cheese and canned soup in-between.

It was hard not to be excited about Saturday. Honestly, just the fact that Sophie would be coming over again was exciting.

Immediately after she left, I sat down to reply to her e-mail from the night before, wanting her to have it when she got home, just in case she felt like reading something from me.

Sophie,

Thank you for coming over tonight to work on our project, and staying for dinner. We're all looking forward to the meal on Saturday. I feel bad that you will be cooking for all of us, but I'll help as much as I can. I don't know much about cooking, but I'd like to learn.

Jane and David actually contemplated staying home from the dance just to get some decent food, but abandoned the idea when they realized that Rebecca would be on the warpath. An upset Rebecca is a sight to behold. I don't think David's room could take another beating.

I'll get into your questions right away.

I have no idea if pot would help with my anxiety, but I don't want to try it to find out either. It's not something that's ever appealed to me.

I didn't have chocolate until I was eleven, so I didn't develop quite the addiction to it as other people seem to. It's okay. I like chocolate, but as far as sweet things go, I could take it or leave it. Though I seem to be smitten with all things gummy: bears, worms, fruits, anything. I love them for reasons I don't quite understand, but when David gave me my first gummy bear, I knew it was meant to be.

I've had speech therapy sessions twice a week since Stephen adopted me. I think it's helped. It takes a lot of effort to try to make a stutter diminish, get better, or go away, and I don't think mine ever will, but I still hope for it. That's why I see Ms. Rice every week; that's why I spend at least an hour or two reading to myself every night. She has a thing for children's books, but I tend to like non-fiction or classic literature.

If I were famous, I would want it to be for doing something important. I don't know. I don't really want to be famous.

I can't say if people are inherently good or bad. I would like to think that people all start out good and may become corrupted over time, versus thinking there are people who are just plain evil out there. If a good person is corrupted, at least they were good at one time. Evil people who are born evil would have no concept of being good. That's fairly scary.

I'm not sure what I think. Like I said, I would like to believe that people are good, but experience tells me that perhaps what I would like to think, and reality, are two different things.

I don't like confrontation. Nothing Chris Anderson has ever done is that *bad. I'm sure that makes me a wimp or something, but I don't need or want a physical altercation, and since I can't do much verbally to set him straight, I let it go. There's only another year and a half of high school and then I'll be free of him.*

What do you think I should do? It's not like anything he says to me is inaccurate.

So here are my five (and I promise to stick to five this time):

1) *When is your birthday?*

2) *Do you have friends back in Tampa?*

3) *Describe yourself in three words.*

4) *What was the best day of your life?*

5) *What are you most afraid of?*

Bonus: If you could be any animal on the planet, what would you be?

Goodnight, Sophie.

Elliott

~ • ~

School on Wednesday started off just fine. I avoided Anderson in the halls and a minute later I received a smile from Sophie. Nothing major was being covered in any of my morning classes, so I didn't need to pay close attention, but when lunch came, the ease of the morning faded quickly.

Jane wasn't at lunch and Trent was silent, but fuming.

Rebecca and David both tried to engage him in conversation, but he wouldn't respond.

After a short while, I felt a presence over my shoulder and when I turned, I was shocked to find it was Sophie standing there, chewing her bottom lip. She looked at Trent and then to me. I couldn't tell if she was worried, upset, or nervous.

"S-S-S…"

I trailed off as she locked eyes with me. "Jane's in the bathroom." Then she glanced at Trent, her eyes narrowing. He looked up, but when I saw his face, he didn't seem worried.

Turning back to me, Sophie motioned to her torso as she said, "She's, um…" She shook her head, her coloring paler than it usually was. "She's bleeding."

I looked at her in surprise and I stood up as my brain processed the information. Jane was bleeding. Sophie wouldn't have come to our table unless it was bad. I looked at Trent and he was doing nothing. It was as if he was frozen. I wanted to hit him until he moved, but there was no time. Jane needed me. Not Trent, but *me*.

She was bleeding.

I probably should have said something to Sophie, perhaps a "thank you," but I could only think of getting to Jane. It wasn't until I hit the hallway that I realized there were at least four girls' bathrooms and I had no idea which one she was in.

"Over there," Sophie said, pointing to one a few yards down.

I quickly looked back at the double doors to the cafeteria. I wondered if Trent was still sitting in his seat, paralyzed with fear. Realizing that every second wasted out here was a second that Jane was alone in there, I made my feet move.

I couldn't have cared less that it was a girls' bathroom. I didn't care who was in there or what I saw and how inappropriate it would be. I pushed open the door and went in.

She was in the very last stall. It felt strange and wrong to be in the girls' bathroom, but it was Jane. *Jane*. I couldn't just leave her there or wait for Rebecca to save the day. I doubted that Rebecca *could* have saved the day. She was good with David, but when talking to Jane, tact was important, and Rebecca didn't really have any when it came to her.

I could see the lower half of her body. She was sitting on the tiled floor, her legs crossed. I wanted to cringe. *Jane* was sitting on a public bathroom floor in front of a toilet. When I saw a small pool of blood on the floor next to her, and that made everything else unimportant.

I could hear her sniffle as I knocked gently.

"I didn't mean to, Elliott."

I pushed the stall door open and looked down. She peered up at me, all crumpled and wilted like a dying flower. Mascara ran from her eyes, leaving two black and gray streaks down her cheeks. "It was an accident."

The white fitted button-down was red near her belly. The fabric clung to her abdomen. "J-JJJaaaane?"

"I swear I didn't…"

It wasn't important what she said after that because I would only nod my head like I believed her, even if I didn't. She was this way every time, and I didn't know what to believe.

Every time she'd done something like this in the past, she swore up and down that she didn't actually mean to cut herself.

I could tell it was deep; much deeper than some of the other times. She'd been doing so well. As far as I knew, it had been seven months since the last time. Stephen letting her get piercings had seemed like it was helping.

I squatted down, and looked closer at her torso until my eyes were drawn to her right hand. "J-Jaaane." She looked up and I glanced back down at the scalpel in her hands. Her hollow gaze followed mine, and she seemed to hear my unasked question as if I'd spoken it aloud.

"I don't know, Elliott." Her voice was barely a whisper now, her other hand coming up to cover her mouth. More tears welled in her eyes as she shook her head. "I don't remember getting it."

I sighed and then carefully removed the instrument from her hand. I knew she'd never intentionally hurt me, but it didn't matter who was wielding a sharp implement, I was going to move as slowly as possible. Being stabbed and sliced was painful.

Taking the scalpel from her, I froze as I felt her hands wrap around my wrists and I looked up into her panicked eyes. "Don't tell Stephen, please. Don't tell him, Elliott."

"C-c-can I-I s-ssssee?" I pointed to her stomach. It looked like blood was still seeping.

"Don't tell Stephen," she said, louder.

"J-JJJaaaane," I began, knowing there was no way to keep him from knowing, "D-D-D-David p-p-p-p-probably already c-c-c-called hhhhhim." It was difficult to get the words out with her hands grasping my wrists so tightly, coupled with that panicked look in her eyes.

"David was dialing the phone when we left the table," I heard behind me. I hadn't known that Rebecca was there.

"No! No, no, no!" She got onto her knees, moving her hands from my wrists to fist my shirt right under my chin. "I don't want to go back, Elliott. Don't let them put me back there."

I took hold of her hands and sighed. I knew she was talking about the hospital, and I knew she never wanted to go back. I also knew that she was being watched like a hawk to see if she would "accidentally" cut herself again. I felt so bad for her. I didn't know how to help her; how to get her to stop cutting.

I knew it wasn't an accident, but I had no idea if she remembered it or not.

The theory was that her episodes made her lose time or black out. Usually when it happened she'd just sit and stare at nothing, but sometimes she would do stuff. Crazy stuff, like taking the ashes of Stephen's dead mother and sprinkling them onto the kitchen floor. Or shredding a piece of clothing she'd just bought. Crazy stuff like taking Biology supplies and cutting herself until she bled.

I dropped the scalpel behind me and uncurled her fingers from my shirt and held her hands. "Y-you w-won't go aw-w-way, J-J-JJJJane." I gave her hands a squeeze and she closed her eyes.

"But this is bad," she whispered.

"I-I-I kn-know."

"They'll take me away again."

I shook my head. "Th-this is jjjjjust a lllliiiiittle sssslip-up. Th-th-th…" I tried, but I couldn't get it out, especially since I didn't know if it was the truth. They might very well ship her back to Baltimore.

Rebecca sighed. "We have to get her cleaned up, Elliott. I'm not sure Sophie can keep the bitches of Damascus out of here for long." I grew a bit more anxious because it was important to Jane that no one but us, Trent, and David know about her cutting.

I turned to face her and she held out a handful of paper towels. "Th-thanks." I asked her again, "C-c-can I sssee?"

She nodded and let go of me, pulling up her soiled shirt just over her stomach. While the cut was still seeping blood, it wasn't as deep as I feared. I held the stack of paper towels over the wound, pressing it gently.

"Trent and I had a fight," she whispered. I looked at her questioningly and she continued, "He kept talking about going to Stanford in the fall, and going on and on about it, like it would be the best thing in the world for him. I reminded him that he'd be leaving me alone and that if he really wanted to be with me, he could go to the community college in Frederick for a year until I graduated."

"Asshole," Rebecca hissed.

"And he said that he wouldn't. And then I said he didn't really love me and he looked me straight in the eye and said that maybe he didn't."

Becca left, muttering, "I'm going to kick him in the balls."

Jane sniffed and brought my attention back to her. "W-we shhhhould go." Taking her hands, I pulled her up, careful to keep the towels against her.

"I know he loves me."

"O-o-of c-course he lllllllloves you, J-Jane."

We walked to the sink. She started crying harder when she looked in the mirror. I turned on the water and grabbed more paper towels. I gave her some dampened ones for her face and then I pulled the stack away to see how the wound looked. The flow of blood had slowed. I pressed the towels back against her.

"H-h-hold this."

She did and I went to clean up the blood from the floor. "Don't let them take me, Elliott. I can't go back there again."

"I-I kn-know." I went to her, quickly tossing the towels in the garbage. "W-we should go."

Jane let me lead her almost to the door before she stopped and refused to go any farther. "I didn't mean to do it, Elliott."

I nodded. "I-I know."

Satisfied, she moved forward again and as we exited the bathroom, and I was thankful that it was still lunch and the halls were empty. "Th-thank you," I said to Sophie as I passed her. She didn't have to stand guard, helping to secure our privacy, but she did.

Sophie took in Jane's abdomen and she swallowed hard. She looked away even as she asked, "Is she okay?"

"Y-yes."

"Jane!" I looked over to see that David had joined us. "Damn, Jane," he sighed. "You were doing so good."

"D-did you c-call S-Stephen?"

He nodded but before Jane could get upset with him, he passed me my bag and then picked her up in his arms.

He started walking toward the front of the school and I turned back to Sophie. "W-we have to t-take her t-to the hospital."

She looked shocked. "Is she going to be okay? What the hell happened?"

"I-I'll e-mail you." I pointed behind me. "I-I have t-to go."

"Yeah," she said, waving her hand at Jane and David's back. "Yeah, go. I'll take notes in Reese's class for you."

I nodded, letting myself smile just a little. "Th-thank you."

• • •

It was just after nine that night when I powered up my computer. The day hadn't been what I expected. Stephen and Robin made the decision to keep Jane in the hospital overnight.

Not because the cut was so bad, but because they wanted to watch her to see if she needed to be taken away again.

I hoped she'd come back home tomorrow.

Despite my concern for Jane, I smiled when I saw Sophie's e-mail in my inbox.

Hey Elliott,

How is Jane and what the hell was up with that? Normally I'm not so demandingly nosy, but that was some crazy shit. I hope she's okay. I'm sorry I couldn't do more. I don't handle blood all that well. Funny coming from a diabetic, right?

So I guess I'll just answer the questions.

My birthday is May 26th. I have no friends back in Tampa. Three words to describe myself? Three separate words or like a three-word sentence? Forget it. I'll do both. Sentence: Pissed Off Bitch. Words: High, Tired, Angry.

I don't know when the best day of my life was. Maybe it's still to come, but if you need my best one so far, I suppose I'd go with the time we spent near that stream. I know all we did was talk or whatever, but it was a good day. I like the days when I don't have to deal with all the shit in my life.

I'm afraid of a lot of things, but don't tell anyone, okay?

If I could be an animal, I would be a house cat. I could lie around all day passing judgment on humans, eat all their food, and then get catnip for being "cute."

Now mine:

1) *Why didn't you ever play in the mud as a child?*

2) *Why did Kate and Dr. Dalton get a divorce?*

3) *When is your birthday?*

4) *What did you want to be when you grew up? Is it different than what you want to be now? (I'm aware that I'm sneaking in an extra question here.)*

5) *Do you hate your mom for what she did?*

Bonus: Should I have done something else for Jane today? I didn't really know what to do.

Anyway, I hope she's okay. She seemed like she was really looking forward to the dance. I hope she still gets to go.

Will you go to school tomorrow? I'll see you, or, you know, maybe not.

Sophie.

I sighed. While I enjoyed being able to communicate with Sophie, sometimes the questions were difficult. I was sure she felt the same way. I'd expected the question about mud and my birthday, and childhood dreams weren't difficult for me, but I hated thinking about Kate leaving and I didn't want to talk or write about my mother.

Still, this was our silent agreement; to ask and answer things we wouldn't be able to talk about otherwise. I couldn't help but think that if I didn't answer fully and honestly, I would be damaging the trust that was building between us.

I was tired. Incredibly tired. It had been an emotionally draining day. Jane didn't want me to leave the hospital, and I would have stayed there all night with her if it was possible, but hospitals had rules, and so did Stephen and Robin. I didn't think they were trying to be mean, but it wasn't hard to see that Jane and I had come to depend on each other. While they didn't want to break that bond, they also wanted to make sure we could stand on our own and not be "co-dependent."

I saw nothing wrong with having at least *someone* to depend on.

Regardless, I couldn't stay with her and had to leave her there alone. She looked very frail in that large bed, an IV in her arm. They weren't giving her anything but saline, but I guessed they wanted to keep their options open.

At least they didn't have to use the restraints this time.

I stayed up only long enough to return Sophie's e-mail and then lay down for another fitful night's sleep.

Chapter 23

Intensity

Sophie

"Oh, fucking *Christ*!"

"Nope, still just fucking me," Jason said into my ear with a chuckle.

Sex outside in Florida was a lot more comfortable than in Maryland on a cold fall day. Coats get in the way. I was sure we looked anything but sexy; Jason with his pants around his ankles, bare ass out in the thirty-degree air, and me with my pants hanging off of my right foot, pressed up against this big old tree.

The intensity with which he nailed me the past couple of days was about to send me into orgasmic overload. He was either working out his anger with me through sex, or the dude was in love with me.

I hoped it was anger.

Anger I could deal with. Anger I could understand.

He'd been strange and distant on Monday, not really speaking when he picked me up for school. I felt bad, but that moon-eyed crap he'd been pulling had to stop. I wasn't his girlfriend, and I never would be.

It was tough love time. I had to snap his ass out of whatever fantasy he was living in where we had more going than a mutual orgasm arrangement. I got my weed from him. I paid him money for that. We had sex and made each other feel good. It was simple. There would never be any movies, or dinner, or goddamn hand-holding.

It wasn't until after school the day the whole "Jane Dalton Freak Out" happened that he decided he would talk to me. And what romantic words they were. "Hey, you want to have sex after you're finished with that joint?" At least it was better than asking me to the dance or to see a movie.

Yesterday, I had gotten home from Elliott's feeling all kinds of weak. First off, why the hell did I volunteer to cook fucking dinner on Saturday? Why couldn't I have kept my mouth shut? I was pretty sure Wallace would be there with Dr. Sexy and Tom, so now instead of being there a few hours, I basically signed myself up for at least five.

At least Elliott would be there.

I felt vulnerable because Elliott and I had slipped into this casual friendship and while I liked it, there were things that made me completely uncomfortable, like sharing pieces of our lives that no else was privy to. I felt ridiculous after saying that I used to get into trouble for playing in the dirt, and I felt horrible when I didn't believe that he'd *never* played in the dirt.

Who would just make that shit up? Then he told me to ask him in an e-mail, and I instantly thought that he probably had shit in his past he didn't want to share either.

We seemed to be using our newly-acquired e-mail conversations for topics we really couldn't, or wouldn't, say out loud. I didn't think that I had admitted too much, but I had this feeling deep-down that it would only be a matter of time before I would. That was scary. I didn't *want* to talk about Helen. I didn't *want* anyone to know about any of it.

I pushed aside all my thoughts and fears about Elliott as Jason grunted his way toward the homestretch and I just concentrated on the waves of sexual bliss coursing through my body.

After he tossed the condom behind him, we cleaned ourselves up a bit before exiting the woods and headed to his car.

❧ • ❧

After dinner, I typed out an e-mail to Elliott and then flopped down on my bed, wishing I was high. It was too risky to do it hanging out the window, especially when Tom was still up, so I only did that on rare occasions. I was stone-cold sober.

That made everything difficult. I just wanted the comfort of the dull buzz. I certainly didn't want all these stupid thoughts going through my head. I was angry. I was pissed at Jane for bleeding on the bathroom floor. What the hell was up with that?

Why the fuck did I have to care? Couldn't she just go back to being Pinny Dalton like before? Why did I have to get suckered into having the warm-fuzzies for her? Why the hell did

I care about any one of them? My plan had been to *not* have friends. I didn't want them.

But now I had them.

Then everything shifted rapidly and I thought about the time I had spent with Elliott talking about the mud. I had no idea why I wanted to figure him out so badly.

I'd never given a shit about any other person. I usually didn't care what someone's name was because it didn't really matter. I just needed to know how they fit into my life. I just needed to know what they had that I needed. Because who gives a shit that Jason was a guy who sold pot to support his father? Why the fuck did I need to care that his mother was dead and his OCD father was a drunk?

The messed-up part was that now that I knew all that, I fucking cared. Now he wasn't just some dude I got my weed from. Now he wasn't just some guy I banged. Now he was Jason and all his problems.

And the mud! Why the hell hadn't Elliott played in mud before? Why did I need to know? I wished I had some answers as to what the hell was going on with me.

He would tell me. He answered every question I asked him. I didn't deserve the trust he gave me. There was no way I deserved it.

Every rule I had for myself was slowly deteriorating. Next thing I knew I'd be shopping at the Gap, and drinking Starbucks mocha-latte-choco-shit in a cup.

I didn't even know who the hell I was anymore.

So I made up my mind.

I went to my window and got incredibly high until my thoughts slowed down into something more manageable.

Yeah, things were definitely better when I was high.

I felt like my thoughts had been smothering me. I no longer gave a shit if Tom caught me because at least my idiot mind could slow down.

Now I could just be chill.

My room was locked up tight, but I still couldn't sleep. It was a little past one in the morning when I read Elliott's reply to my e-mail.

Sophie,

Jane is okay. Stephen kept her at the hospital. I didn't think the cut was that bad, but I'm pretty sure they left her in to "observe" her. He and Robin always do this when she has an episode. I told you that sometimes she just sort of zones out. When she's in that state, there are times when she hurts herself. The real questions are if she remembers it and if it's a planned or premeditated thing.

I don't really get it and it's incredibly scary. She says she doesn't remember even getting the scalpel from the Biology classroom.

I never know why it happens to her. Beyond certain emotional events, there are usually no triggers that anyone's been able to figure out. Unlike this one, they just happen. She told me that she had a fight with Trent. I like Trent, but it's hard to know what to expect from him. I don't think he meant for this to happen.

Jane wants him to stay close to Damascus for his first year of college, but Trent's always been a bit wishy-washy.

Enough about that. I'm tired. On to your questions:

My real father was pretty particular about things like dirt and mud. He had a lot of rules. I wasn't allowed outside when it was raining or snowing. Well, I wasn't allowed outside much at all. I was allowed to walk to and from the school bus, but when I came home, I had to take off my shoes or snow boots outside. We didn't even have any indoor plants like I did with Kate.

Kate left Stephen, as far as I know, because he was never home. He went out and adopted the three of us and then left her alone to raise us. I don't think she really wanted us in the first place. We weren't meant to hear that part when they were fighting, but they were yelling and they probably didn't realize they were loud enough for me to overhear. She kept saying that Stephen spent too much time at the hospital and she couldn't help all three of us by herself, so she left and divorced him.

My birthday is June 29th.

The first thing I ever wanted to be when I grew up was a fireman too, but I think it's because the other boys at school said that's what they wanted to be. I mean, I've given it quite a bit of thought because firemen and paramedics are pretty close to real-life super-heroes. It's not original, I know. The fireman stage didn't last long. We have that in common.

About my mom: I don't hate her for what she did, or who she was. I wasn't in my mom's head, so I don't know why she did it. But she did. It doesn't make her a bad person. My father said that she damned herself to hell by killing herself, but it could have been her salvation instead. How am I to know?

My mother loved me regardless of her addiction and killing herself. I love her regardless of those things too. I wish every day she hadn't done that, but I don't hate her for it.

As for your bonus question, you did fine with Jane. Thank you.

Here are my questions for you:

1) *Do you dream?*

2) *Of the many things that you're afraid of, what's one of them?*

3) *Do you like Damascus?*

4) *How did you get those four marks on your neck?*

5) *You said that you "banged" meth. "Banged" means "injected" right? Like heroin? Why'd you do that? Wasn't it scary?*

Bonus: What's for dinner on Saturday?

Goodnight, Sophie.

Elliott.

Elliott's reply about his mother just hurt. I knew it was e-mail, but I could feel him through his words. I would've hated her if I were him. I would have cussed profusely when talking about her, but he was respectful and loving. I felt horrible for him.

I didn't like to leave Elliott's e-mails sitting unanswered and felt like I needed to answer them right away because I didn't want to leave him hanging. I wanted him to know that whatever he said didn't make me feel any different about him. He was my friend. I had told him that and I believed it, so it was important to make sure he knew that I wasn't judging him.

Elliott,

Your first question confuses me. Are you asking if I dream, as in "someday my prince will come" or as in are my neurons firing rapidly while I sleep? Because no to the first and yes to the second. I dream when I sleep. I remember them because I don't usually sleep straight through the night. Unfortunately, they're never the type of dreams I want to remember.

I like Damascus as much as anyone can like a small town. Life is usually life no matter where you're living it. It's no better or worse than Tampa. Like I told you before, it's just much more difficult to be anonymous here. That sucks.

Three of your five questions are tough, and I don't really want to answer them. Just so you know, it's only because it's you asking that I'm even entertaining the thought of really answering them. I'd tell anyone else to fuck off.

One thing I'm afraid of is the dark. I don't like it; never have. I'm okay outside at night if there's no cloud-cover when the moon is bright and I can see my surroundings, but I don't like going into darkened rooms.

The marks on my neck are from a fork. A fork got stuck in my neck.

Banging does mean injecting. I did it because I was at a party and a guy had it and it was something new. It wasn't a horrible experience, but I don't like blood and I don't like needles. Apart from having to inject myself with insulin and make myself bleed in order to control my diabetes, I'd rather not have anything to do with it recreationally.

> *Bonus: I was thinking about making chicken and noodles on Saturday. Or I could make a stir fry. Any preference and/or suggestions? Nothing spicy though, because I hate spicy food.*
>
> *Now my questions:*
>
> *1) Do you miss Kate?*
>
> *2) Since you asked me, where in the world do you want to visit?*
>
> *3) Do you believe in evolution or divine creation?*
>
> *4) Even though you don't like confrontation, I would imagine that you also don't like it when people make you feel like shit. Don't you want to punch Anderson in the mouth just once?*
>
> *5) What's one thing that scares you?*

Okay, that's it. Have a good night. I hope you get some sleep and if you can't, I hope you have some good coffee. S.

Chapter 24

On Eating and Cooking

Sophie

Elliott wasn't in school on Thursday, but I did get an e-mail from him.

Sophie, I read as I let my book bag fall to the floor. I would worry about fixing dinner later.

Jane got to come home and as far as I know, she won't have to go away. Trent was over today and they seem to have made up. Both of them are acting as if their fight never happened. Stephen is letting her go to the dance, so she couldn't be happier. I'm not sure what the long-term plans are yet.

I think you should make whatever you want on Saturday. You're doing all the work, so it should be what you want. Chicken and noodles sounds fantastic though.

I do miss Kate. Apart from apparently never wanting to adopt us, she was always kind. She made good food and was good for Jane to have around. Jane doesn't remember her mother, or most of her childhood, so she adored Kate as a mother figure.

If I could visit anywhere, it would be Ireland, I think. My mom was born there and she used to talk about it all the time. Well, not all the time. She probably only mentioned it once or twice, but it's one of the few things I remember about her, so it's grown to be something very important to me.

I don't really want to hit Chris. I'm not a fan of violence and I try not to react in a way that would make me be like him. He seems to enjoy hurting people. I don't. Even though he makes my life harder than it has to be, it would do nothing if I hit him back, even just once.

I believe in both evolution and creation. Just because God made the world doesn't mean that the world he created didn't change over time. Who's to say that God's seven days and man's seven days are related at all in terms of time? What was seven days to God could have been a million years for man. Who am I to know the measurement of God's time? Religion and Science can come together. Most people are just too narrow-minded to see that.

By the way, I respect your use of the term "god" instead of "God." I don't believe in pushing religious views on others.

One thing that scares me? There are a lot of things that scare me, but some more than others. One would be college. I want to go but it seems to be giving me quite a bit of anxiety. Everyone thinks I should skip 12th grade and go. It's not that I *don't want to, it's just that every time I start thinking that today's the day I'll mail in my applications, my hands refuse to pick up the envelopes. I don't know what it is exactly, but I'm sure it has to do with all those people that inhabit a college, and how I won't know a single one of them.*

I could apply to Stanford, which is where David and Jane intend to go, along with their significant others, but I'm not sure that's what I want.

So, now for mine:

1) *Why don't you like spicy food?*

2) *How does one get impaled with a fork?*

3) *Why don't you like talking about your mother?*

4) *Why would you just put something like meth into your body simply because someone offered it to you?*

5) *Are you upset with me for asking these questions?*

Bonus: I'm thinking of a number between 1 and 100. Guess what it is.

I'll see you tomorrow. We'll go to the store directly after school. Everyone will be busy with the game, but if you still want to, we can do something after grocery shopping. It'll be too late to go to that little spot by the stream, but we can find something else to do.

Have a good night, Sophie.

Elliott

He certainly wasn't holding back with his blunt questions. I would answer them though, just as he answered all of mine. As much as I didn't want to admit it, I was the one who opened these floodgates and now I couldn't close them.

It was a weird thing to *want* to tell someone shit I'd never even wanted to think about before. I had no idea what it was about him, but Elliott was able to make me feel like it was okay to share.

Not that I wanted to. I wished to the FSM that he hadn't asked me any of these questions, but he did, so I would reciprocate his honesty and trust. I might not tell him everything, but I wouldn't avoid the questions.

No matter how badly I wanted to.

Elliott,

I'm glad Jane is okay and can still go to the dance. I'm sure it wouldn't have helped if she had to miss something that obviously means so much to her. She told me all about her dress during Photography.

No, I'm not upset about you asking those questions; however, to be perfectly honest, I hate every single one (except the bonus. You're thinking of the number 73, aren't you?).

I don't like talking about my mom because I don't really like her. I would rather just banish her from my mind, and not talking about her makes that possible. She's in Tampa and I'm in Damascus, so there's really not that much to say.

Banging meth was dumb. I know it was, but I did it anyway. I don't know why, other than because it was there. I'm kind of a "I'll try anything at least once" kind of girl. I don't know.

I don't like spicy food because it can hurt.

One gets impaled on a fork by falling on it.

I paused my typing for a moment. I wondered if I was being unfair by not elaborating. I wondered if he would pick up on it, and if he'd mind. I wasn't trying to give less than I took with Elliott, but these answers fell into the realm of things people didn't need to know. They were things I didn't want to think about, and I was quite frankly *not* high enough to go in-depth.

I didn't want to think about the fork, or about Helen.

Here are my five for you.

1) *How did you get the scar on your top lip?*

2) *Why do you want to be a doctor or a medical researcher instead of a fireman, even if never seriously considered it? I mean, Tom's a fireman. I think you could do it and isn't it every boy's dream to be a super-hero?*

3) *Do you miss living in Chicago?*

4) *Why do you want to know anything about me?*

5) *I've never seen you upset. Not even when I think you should be. What gets you upset?*

Bonus: If you could do anything, without any negative consequences, what would it be?

S.

Most of the rest of my Thursday was routine, except for a couple of things.

The first was that I had to have a discussion with Tom, since he was my legal guardian and all. I'd been kicking it around my head for a little bit and unfortunately, I needed his consent.

"Tom?" I asked, watching as he looked up. His knife stopped on the steak, mid-cut. "I want to get a job."

I needed money. Despite cooking and cleaning, Tom didn't give me an allowance, like other kids' parents. Helen never did either, so I wasn't upset about it, but I needed money.

"You want a job?" I nodded. I'd just said that. Tom looked like he was thinking, finally chewing that piece of steak. "Well, I know the Andersons. They own that fancy clothing store out on 27. I'm not sure if they need any help, but it *is* going into the holiday season."

"Anderson's as in Chris Anderson?"

"Yeah, he's a good kid. I've known his parents practically since birth. You know him from school?"

I sighed and then took a drink of my water. "Yeah. Does he work there?"

"I think he helps out."

Shaking my head, I continued, "I was thinking about the Breakfast Place." It was a little dive of a restaurant that served more than breakfast. Serving would give me cash in my pocket after every shift.

"No."

I looked up at him again, and saw his face was stiffly set. "But, Tom!" I whined, "why not?"

"That place gets a lot of truckers, drifters, and vagrants. A girl was assaulted there two years ago."

"But"

He cut me off. "No, Sophie."

I sighed. I could tell I wouldn't win. "Fine, what about the grocery store? Is that acceptable?"

"What's wrong with Anderson's?"

"I don't want to work there. It's a clothing store. Look at me, Tom. Do I look like I know about trendy clothes? Don't you think I'd be a tad out of my element standing there in my Walmart jeans trying to sell a rich kid expensive shit?"

He thought about it a moment. "I suppose the Quickshop's fine, but you have to keep your grades up. The judge said—"

Not wanting to hear about that asinine judge and his agreement, I didn't let him finish. "I can keep my grades up with or without a job." The academics at Damascus High left something to be desired, especially since Tom hadn't bothered to enroll me in the Honors or Advanced Placement programs, but I was kind of glad since that made it easy for me to pass without trying.

The second thing out of the ordinary was that after dinner I finally called Ian from Baltimore. The conversation consisted of him talking dirty to me and me pretending to care. I hung up about as unsatisfied as I was when I initiated the call.

❧ • ❧

On Friday, Elliott drove his own car to school. I'd been relatively stoned when I saw him pull up, but it later dawned on me that he'd driven to school alone so he could take me to the store to buy food for Saturday's dinner.

I was sort of nervous about being with him to be honest, but there was still a whole day to get through before that. Due to Homecoming, the day didn't even follow a routine and I had to listen to things like, "We are the Hornets, the mighty, mighty Hornets!" Rebecca, or as I now called her in my mind, "Barbie Wallace" and the rest of the cheerleaders chanted stuff like that as most of the high school cheered.

The gym was packed and I couldn't believe I wasn't out getting high during this, but I had no idea there would be a pep rally during Photography until the teacher told us to report to the gym.

I sat next to Pinny Dalton. I mean, *Jane* Dalton. I thought she'd be more into the school cheer thing, but she wasn't. She sat there rolling her eyes at the cheerleaders and only clapping when they introduced her brother David.

When she wasn't clapping, one of her hands was continually pressed to the wound on her stomach. I felt compelled to ask her why she cut herself because I wanted to understand since I had no clue why someone would hurt themselves intentionally.

I supposed if I'd had that self-injury urge when I lived with Helen, all I would've had to do was get in her way.

Shit. Why was I thinking so much about stuff like this?

I told myself to push it away; to not think about it. I needed something mindless to do, so I turned to Jane and asked, "Is Trent excited about the dance?" I looked around, wondering where he was.

She nodded. "He bought a green tie to wear."

I noticed she didn't answer the question, but I didn't push. "So what's he like?"

Her expression softened and she finally looked at me. "He's awesome," she answered in a soft voice. "He's really smart about a lot of things. He works really hard."

What she said was pretty simplistic and didn't give me much, so I decided just to go for it. If she got mad, it would be no big deal to me, but I figured people shared this kind of information all the time. "What happened the other day?"

Her expression fell again and she returned her gaze to the cheerleaders and jocks on the gym floor. "His dad's a jerk who moved across country and his mom ignores him, so sometimes he can be an ass."

"So the other day you hurt yourself because he was an ass?"

She whipped around to look at me. Her eyes were hard for a second, and then almost as if she'd been wearing it all day, a smile formed. "His tie matches my dress exactly!" I guessed we were done talking about cutting and boyfriends who were sometimes asses. "And he's going to get me an orchid corsage. It's white with little purple speckles. It doesn't really go with a green dress, but Trent knows my favorite color is purple. And Becca's going to wear…"

That was the point where I stopped listening. The cheering was getting loud and I didn't care about Homecoming at all. I didn't care about dresses. I didn't care about corsages, and I didn't care about any of these people.

Except for Elliott. I scanned the gym and couldn't find him anywhere. I guessed they didn't make him attend these assemblies because of his anxiety.

I met up with him outside after school. Jason had been a little put-out that I had plans for the evening that didn't include him. I reminded him that I wasn't his girlfriend, that I was *no one's* girlfriend, and going out with Elliott wasn't a date.

We were going grocery shopping. No romance going on inside of a grocery store, but it did give me a great opportunity to pick up an application.

"A-ar-are y-you getting a j-job?"

I looked at Elliott and gave him a smile. He had a sheepish look on his face. With an application in-hand, it was obvious that I was trying to get a job, but I wasn't going to give him a hard time. He tried harder to communicate and took more care in speaking with me than most people.

"Yeah. Less time at home, and more money in my pocket." Grabbing a cart, I grimaced. "Tom wanted me to get a job at Anderson's. How bad would *that* have sucked?"

Elliott smiled and the sight made me feel warm inside. "P-pretty bad." He laughed. I liked the sound.

I pulled out a list as we entered the Produce Department. "Here, will you look at this and let me know if you have any of this shit at home?"

Taking the paper, Elliott's eyes moved quickly down the list. "A-a-asparagus, b-b-beets, p-potato?" He looked at me again. "Ch-chicken and noodles has b-beets?"

I smiled at him and headed over to the green rack. "No. I changed my mind. I think I'm just going to roast a bunch of stuff. It's pretty easy and incredibly tasty."

"W-we have p-potatoes."

"What American family doesn't?"

"W-what kind of apples?"

I had toyed with the idea of making dessert because if I was going to be in charge of cooking, I was going to hook it up. Since Elliott's favorite fruit was apples, I decided on an apple crisp. It was quick and easy, and shouldn't garner too many questions about my diabetes. I was feeding a doctor after all, and the last thing I needed tomorrow was a goddamned lecture about carbs and sugar.

"Y-you like B-Brussels sprouts *and* b-b-beets? W-what kind of t-teenager are you?"

His joke made me smile and I shook my head. I liked all the weird vegetables that most people my age had never even heard of *and* I liked how funny Elliott was. It seemed sad that no one else seemed to know about his wit.

"W-w-why do you l-like to cook?"

I sighed heavily, my mood instantly turning to shit. I didn't like to cook. I *hated* cooking. I've never enjoyed it. I cooked because if I didn't, no one would.

"I *don't* like cooking, Elliott. I like eating. Eating requires cooking. If I don't fucking cook, I don't fucking eat." It came out harsher than what I had intended. I tried to choke it all back because I was *not* going to tell anyone about all the horrible things in my life. I wasn't going to tell him even if a small part of me thought it would feel good to let him in like that.

He inhaled quickly, and his brow knitted together as he looked at his feet. In an instant, guilt flooded me. I hadn't meant to snap at him, and I had no reasonable explanation as to why I had.

What I did know was that I wasn't high enough to discuss some shit about cooking. Yes, I cooked. Yes, I was good at it, but I didn't like it. Why the hell would I want to talk about the day Helen decided that I was responsible for all the cooking? Because at six-years-old, there wasn't much beyond dry processed cheese sandwiches that you could make without cutting or burning yourself.

Nope, I wasn't going there, and certainly not with Elliott in the middle of a grocery store.

I wanted to be high now, but he looked like a kicked puppy and I didn't want him to feel bad.

"I'm sorry, Elliott." I forced myself to pull my gaze away from the potatoes and look at him again. "I just…cook because I have to, not because I enjoy it or anything."

"D-d-didn't your m-mm-mmmmom cook?"

I pushed the rising anger down. "No. She didn't cook." He still looked confused and his hazel eyes burned me. "If I didn't cook, I didn't eat."

His mouth formed an "O" and his cheeks puffed out as he tried to say something. Between the shape of his mouth and the general sounds he was making, I imagined that he was trying to ask another question. Elliott's hands balled up and he hit himself in the thighs. I wondered if he even knew he did that shit.

"H-h-h-how old w-w-were y-you w-w-w-w…"

It wasn't hard to tell that he was nervous, or anxious or something, because he could barely get a word out without stuttering. He wasn't usually that bad. Again, guilt ate at me like acid from the inside. All he did was ask a question and then I kind of flipped out on him. Now he wanted to know how old I was when I had to fend for myself.

It was just a question. I'd asked him questions and he had trusted me enough to answer them. Even though I really, really, really didn't want to think about this shit, could I really just *not* answer him? If he'd typed that question into an e-mail, would I have answered it?

"She just stopped feeding me one day." Damn, he looked like he was going to try to ask it again. He was just going to keep on pushing. I didn't know why.

Fine. "I was six. Now can we buy some fucking beets or what?"

I wanted to catch another buzz, but I was with Elliott. I had gotten high around him in the past, but no matter how much I wanted to be stoned, I didn't want to do it around him anymore. It obviously bothered him.

Not that I didn't want to be high in his presence, I just didn't want to *get* high in his presence.

I huffed. Not at him, but the whole thing. Grabbing the list back from him, I started shopping in earnest. I would need to remember everything for tomorrow's dinner. I was going to make roasted vegetables with rosemary chicken.

And of course, apple crisp for dessert.

I found the apples and read the descriptions for which ones would cook the best. Reading them wasn't necessary, since I already knew, but the distraction was welcomed as my mind decided that thinking about apples meant I should be thinking about Elliott. In its usual sober attempt at pushing me to think about other things, my brain moved from thinking about Elliott, to thinking about his question about my mother and cooking.

Now I was thinking about Helen and the kitchen. I was thinking about the oven and the sharp implements. I thought about being burned and punctured. I thought about being hungry and having incredibly low blood sugar because Helen hadn't bothered to go shopping for us. I remembered having to stack up pots and pans on the upturned trash can so that I could stand on the counter and get into my mother's candy stash.

While I'd been happy that the sugar had made me feel better, I remembered how much trouble I'd gotten into when she found me shaking on the floor, a chocolate bar in my hand. Some parents grab the video camera and record their six-year-old covered in chocolate and send it into America's Funniest Videos.

Not Helen.

She grabbed me by my hair, pulled me back like a slingshot, and flung me against the wall. Afterward I…

"Shit," I whispered.

I turned to find Elliott just looking at me, and I excused myself to go to the bathroom. I didn't give a damn if someone walked in. I was getting stoned.

•

"That's nice," I said quietly as I sat in a chaise lounge, listening to Elliott play the piano.

It felt odd being alone with him in this great big house. It was usually bustling on Friday nights and it felt a little strange. We had planned to do something after grocery shopping, but my mood had gone south quickly and no amount of weed could help it.

We'd barely spoken since the exchange in the supermarket. I wasn't trying to be rude, and I hoped that he understood.

My high had started to fade. As far as coming down went, this one wasn't bad. The room was dimly-lit and the house was quiet except for the sound of Elliott's piano.

I had no idea what he was playing, but it was nice, calm, and soothing. He played a few things. I only knew that they were different by the change in tempo. He never stopped playing; just switched songs. I wondered how long he could sit there and play.

It was hours before my eyes fixed on the clock and I sighed. I was completely sober and the new melody that Elliott was playing further depressed me. It would be easy to dwell on everything I didn't want to think about. If I thought too much about it, I would come too close to telling him the truth about my life. I didn't want him to know. I didn't want him to look at me with pity. I didn't want what Helen did, or anything else, to define me like that.

Also, if I said it to him, it would be real. Not just the past, but my friendship with Elliott. It would be an acknowledgement that I'd let him in and that was scary. We would both know and then I would *really* allow myself to fall for him in a way that was completely unknown to me.

As exciting as it sounded to let this beautiful boy know me, *really* know me, I was scared.

It would hurt when he realized that I was too much; when he realized I was unlovable. I didn't want to be stuck loving someone who couldn't love someone like me who had become so messed up.

I wanted to get high or get laid. While we had this entire house to ourselves, I had no desire to make him feel uncomfortable. I figured both would have that effect.

"I think I should go, Elliott." His fingers stilled on the keys and he looked up at me. Tom had never given me a specific curfew, but I used the time as an excuse. "It's getting late."

Glancing at the clock, he looked surprised. "Ssssssorry, S-S-SSSophie. I-I-I didn't know it w-was sssso late."

I had no words to describe how his apology made me feel. I didn't want him to say that he was sorry because he lost track of time doing something he so obviously loved to do.

"It's okay, Elliott. I'm just tired."

He stood up when I did and crossed the room, his brow creased. "Ssssorry we didn't do anything b-b-but shop a-and sssit here."

We *had* done something. He had played music for me and I had listened. I could've stayed all night and fallen asleep to those peaceful sounds, but I had to go before it was too late. "I had a good time, Elliott," I replied in a whisper.

He was so… so damn decent it hurt.

Chapter 25

First Edition

Elliott

I knew Sophie had gotten high at the grocery store. It was evident when she returned, but I couldn't really be upset with her. I had pushed her into talking. While I wanted to know more and felt it was important, I never thought asking her about cooking would end the way it did.

I don't know why I assumed that just because she cooked, she liked it.

We didn't talk much after we got back to the house. I couldn't think of anything to say, and she seemed to withdraw into herself. I played the piano for her, knowing she had liked it when I played guitar for her that one day, and wanting to share something that soothed me. Sophie was in need of soothing and I doubted my hands in her hair would've had the same calming effect hers had on me.

She seemed so tired when she said she had to go. I stopped playing and I wondered why she seemed so small just sitting there. She was usually such a strong and powerful presence, but tonight she was different.

I drove her back to her house and we just sat in the car for a while. It was hard not to think about the last time I'd dropped her off and the mess I'd made of it all. Again tonight, I had my iPod plugged in, and the song playing was quiet. It was one I knew she'd like. The singer's voice was soft, like my favorite t-shirt felt as it brushed against the hardened skin of my back. The melody was lulling, but the words were engaging.

"Sorry about the store, Elliott." Sophie's voice surprised me. She'd been so quiet for so long.

I was confused. "W-what?"

"I didn't mean to snap at you like I did."

Looking into her piercing blue eyes, I realized that it was the first time I could see such bottomless sadness there. "I-it's okay."

She closed her eyes for a moment as she rested her head back. When she opened them again, our eyes connected and neither of us looked away.

It was only when I felt something touch my hand that had been resting on the center console that I finally looked away. Glancing down, I found it was Sophie with her hands on mine. My palm was up and she had one of her hands under it while the she stroked my palm with the other. The sensation of her touch was no less of a sharp chemical exchange than the last time.

I took a deep breath and willed myself not to start breathing hard. I willed my heart to regulate its pace.

She had turned her head just a little, and focused on something beyond my left ear. Again, I was struck by the magnitude of the sadness within her expressive blue eyes. I'd managed to steal many moments to look at Sophie, but in *this* moment we were very close. The skin of her cheek looked so soft, but the area around her eyes, which was probably just as soft, somehow looked harder with the pain she carried in them. She looked older than seventeen

I wanted to touch her face, just to see if it was truly as delicate as I thought it would be. Before I could tell my hand to stop, it floated upward, my fingers just brushing her cheek. It seemed to happen in slow motion, but then it gave way to a flurry of activity.

Instantaneously, the pleasant and slightly zinging sensation in my hand stopped and Sophie shifted her head away from my outstretched fingers. The peaceful calm that had settled over us seemed to shatter as she took her lip between her teeth.

Panic rushed through me. I shouldn't have touched her. She hadn't wanted me to and I did. I hadn't even been aware that I was actually going to do it until my hand was moving.

I had no idea how I screwed this up again.

I focused on her mouth as I tried not to freak out. My hands were tight fists in my lap. Her tongue came out to sweep across her lips. "Did you return my e-mail?"

Her voice was soft and quiet, but it was enough to pull me out of my spiral toward a panic attack. I had read hers this morning, but with David banging on the door and Jane shouting that she wasn't taking too long, I hadn't had time to reply.

"N-no, n-not yet."

Running her hands through her hair, she swallowed hard and licked her lips again. "Well," she began but never finished.

"S-Sophie," I said after a few moments.

She turned and gave me a smile; not a real one, but a smile nonetheless. Then she said, "See you tomorrow, Elliott."

I couldn't get out a goodbye for anything, even though I tried. She waited for a moment, but when I couldn't produce much more than random sounds, she opened the car door. "Bye," she said as she slipped out into the darkness.

I watched as she ran up the steps to her front door, sliding the key into the lock and then disappearing inside. As I sat there for a few minutes, I finally figured it all out. The central difference between Sophie Young and me.

I felt like I'd spent my whole life feeling every emotion and thinking about all the horrible moments I could remember, but Sophie had spent hers avoiding all that, and running from it all, using anything and everything she could to just…forget.

Even the few words she said, admitting something deep and painful, were huge. I knew this couldn't be easy for her, but something within me said it was necessary. Deep down, I knew there was a well of pain inside of her. I knew it because it looked so familiar.

It looked like my own.

It was suddenly more important than ever to get her to reveal more.

I wasted no time when I got home. I ignored all distractions and found myself moving as quickly as I could to my room to answer her e-mail.

Sophie,

I hope you're okay. You seemed so sad tonight. I'm sorry if I caused that. Since it's late and I'll get to see you tomorrow, I'll answer your questions right away.

I want to know things about you, probably for the same reason you want to know things about me.

I don't have many friends. It's interesting to know a new person. With David, it's like he's an open book. He hides nothing because he just doesn't see the point. With Jane, she doesn't remember anything much from before I met her, so I already know everything she knows, and everything she likes, since she discovered it in real-time while I was around. But you are like the book on the top shelf; the first edition not many people get to touch because it's way too precious.

I know there are things about you that I'll never know, and parts of you that everyone knows, but there's that area between those two extremes: the part you don't show everyone, but are willing to share. I want to know that part of you. Since I ask you to share, I will too. I don't usually do that.

I get upset, but it's usually on the inside and doesn't make its way to the outside, except in the form of panic attacks. I typically don't let it out, because there's no point. I get upset about a lot of things. One specific thing is being treated like an idiot because I have a stutter. I understand that it's a particularly bad stutter, but it's not like I do it in my mind. My intellect is intact, and just because it takes me a minute to say two words, doesn't mean that my brain function is any less than someone who can speak fluently.

There isn't much point in showing how upset I am to everyone. The jerks of the world like Chris would get far too much pleasure out of it, and the overly-helpful of the world, like Robin and Stephen, wouldn't be able to sleep until they cracked the code of why I was upset. I don't want to deal with any of that.

I don't really miss living in Chicago. It's a perfectly fine city and has most of the things that anyone could want in a hometown, but for me, too much happened there. To say I missed it would be like saying I missed everything that hurt me in the past.

Stephen likes to plan vacations and last year he suggested Chicago. He made it seem like he just wanted to take us to a big city, but it was fairly transparent that he thought it would be good for Jane and me to go back to see that it wasn't the city we didn't like, but our pasts. It didn't go over well. Even though she can't remember it, Jane knows something *happened there that she doesn't want to relive, and I have no desire to go there ever again.*

I don't think I could do the job of a fireman. David could, but not me. There's a lot of rushing into burning buildings, and while I could probably get over my human instinct of avoiding flames, I would not only have to work very closely with people, but save them too. I would have to touch them and talk to them. Generally, it's a "people" job. I need a job where I can just sit in a room by myself and find the cure for cancer or something. As a researcher, maybe I'd have to talk to five people, but it would be the same *five people, and I could grow comfortable with that. A fireman talks to the same people he works with everyday, but also has the potential to talk to lots of new people daily. That's not for me.*

The scar on my lip is from my teeth. For whatever reason, that skin is easy to tear.

As for the bonus, if I could do anything without negative consequences, I would ask you why you're so sad.

And now it's time for my questions and once again, I hope they don't upset you.

1) *Why did you volunteer to cook if you don't like it?*

2) *How did you fall onto a fork?*

3) *Have you ever had short hair?*

4) *How did you get the scar on your forehead?*

5) *You knew Otis Redding's music because your grandmother used to listen to him. Did you spend much time with your grandparents?*

Bonus: If we call Australia "Down Under," do people in Australia call us "Up Over"?

Goodnight, Sophie. I'll see you tomorrow. I don't really know how to cook, but I promise I'll help as much as I can.

Elliott.

Just like each and every time I sent an e-mail off to her, my chest tightened a little in anticipation of her reply. It was evident that we had moved past all the obvious questions about favorite this and favorite that. We were now firmly within the sphere of intensely personal questions. I knew they would make her uncomfortable, as hers did the same for me. But I also knew that both of us would answer them, some more in-depth than others.

Just as there was a story behind my teeth creating the scar on my lip, I knew there was more to her aversion to spicy food than it "can hurt," and I knew without a doubt that one doesn't just simply fall onto a fork.

I needed her to say it.

Sophie wasn't about to share those things easily. In the e-mail, I had compared her to a book. If she was a book, she'd be filled with poetry and only after constant study would I be able to understand her. She was abstract art; the picture in the clouds.

So I would continue to ask her the questions and be satisfied with every small crumb of information she dropped. Eventually the bread crumbs would lead me down the path to truly knowing who she was.

❧ • ❧

Saturday the house was a flood of activity. The Damascus Hornets won the Homecoming game the night before, and David had to recount it in the morning, play-by-play. I didn't mind; it was obviously important to him and I wanted to be a good brother, but I couldn't help but tune some of it out. Touchdowns were one thing, but quarterback sneaks and fifty-seven yard punt returns were things I cared little about.

Jane, despite her belly wound, was taking care of all the details of the day. She always took it upon herself to organize everyone she knew for big events like Homecoming and Prom. She not only had to supervise David's choice of suits, but also made sure his tie matched Rebecca's dress. After a half-hour of arguing, she finally convinced David that green, white, and gold striped socks, while being the school's colors, were *not* appropriate for the dance, especially if his date's dress was some shade of purple that even *I* couldn't identify.

Most of the day, I stayed on the outside of the action. I had no interest in the hair, the make-up, the ties, and the overall anxiety a dance like this caused in the Dalton house. Every once in a while, Jane would knock on my door and ask me if one hairstyle looked better than the last one. I always said yes, but really, they all looked the same. I didn't understand why she would ask me things like that, since I clearly had no clue, but it was important to her, so I played along.

After lunch and a little bit of guitar strumming, I checked my e-mail and was happy to see that Sophie had replied.

Elliott,

If you did ask me why I was so sad, I would tell you I'm not so sad and that you shouldn't waste your time wondering about things like that.

Here are your answers:

I volunteered to cook because it seemed like a good idea. If I'm forced to have dinner with Wallace, Dr. Dalton, and Tom, it might as well be tasty. I told you that I cook because I have to, and I decided a while back that if I had to cook, I might as well learn to be good at it. I like PB&J, but that's pretty much what I lived on for a few years, so sometimes it's nice to whip up a few days' worth of lasagna or put together a fruit salad.

I had short hair one time, and I didn't really care for how it looked. Besides, it didn't accomplish the reason I cut it in the first place, so I let it grow back.

The scar on my forehead is from the corner of a wall. Like the skin on the lips, the skin of the forehead is amazingly easy to rip open. And walls, especially the corners, are unforgiving.

I never knew Helen's parents, but I spent time at my Grandma Catherine's every summer when I visited Tom. His dad was never in the picture. Surprise, surprise. Like father, like son, I guess. Anyway, I usually got to spend a few days with her. I don't remember much about her, since she died a long time ago, but I do recall she used to let me eat windmill cookies and she loved strawberries.

Why do you have a fixation on the fork, Elliott? It's a meaningless scar that most people don't even notice. Forks are pointy. I am clumsy. It's been established that skin can give way rather easily.

> *Bonus: If we call Australia "Down Under", do people in Australia call us "Up Over"?*

You're entirely too funny to be locked away in some kind of medical research lab.

I'll be over in a few short hours, but I'll give you my questions.

1) Why do you want to know about the fork?

2) Do you know your grandparents?

3) *The news said it could snow this week. Do you like the snow?*

4) *Why do you like that picture in your art book? The* Flaming June *one.*

5) *Do you ever wish you could be someone else? If so, who would you be?*

Bonus: How are our baby Brussels sprouts?

I'll see you soon, Elliott.

S.

~•~

"Just cut them the same size as the potatoes," Sophie said, pointing to the vegetables on the cutting board with one hand and popping a piece of raw potato into her mouth with the other. She had shown me what she wanted with the potatoes. Now she would start preparing the chicken and leave me to my own devices.

Her father was in the living room with Robin and Stephen. They were having a discussion about football. Every so often, I saw Robin go into the dining room and peer around the wall. I was aware that she was looking in on us.

"Oh my God, that smells delicious!"

I looked up to see Jane enter the kitchen, pulling open the oven to get a better look at Sophie's apple crisp. She wore the long green dress she'd bought for Homecoming over two months ago. "Y-you look p-p-pretty, J-JJJJaaane."

Closing the oven, she beamed at me. "Thanks!"

Beets stain, so I went to wash my hands before continuing the cutting list. When I turned back around, Jane was at the cutting board, knife in hand. It was innocent. I knew that it was. On some level, I was aware she would not intentionally hurt herself today of all days, and especially not in front of people, but my lungs seized as I watched her eye the knife she held.

Sophie was busy rubbing the chicken with herbs and I was grateful that she was distracted. Very quietly and quickly, I moved back to the cutting board and carefully took the knife back from Jane.

She stepped to the side as her eyes stayed glued on me. It was clear that I had just hurt her feelings. As much as I hated when Jane's feelings were hurt, I would hate it more if she stained her pretty green dress by cutting herself, accidentally or not. The sight of her with a knife was just too much right now.

I looked back at her. There were tears in her eyes and I felt horrible. "D-don't, Jane," I whispered.

She sighed and then turned to Sophie. "I wish I could eat dinner here. It smells unbelievable."

"Thanks," Sophie replied.

"If I'd known you were going all "gourmet" on us, we wouldn't have made reservations."

Craning my neck, I saw Sophie give Jane a kind smile. "No worries. I'm sure there'll be leftovers, and I can cook for you another time." Despite being rough around the edges, Sophie was a good person. I wondered if she knew that about herself.

࿐ • ࿐

Sophie's meal was delicious, but I wished we hadn't had to eat it with Robin, Stephen and Mr. Young. She and I were mostly silent at the dinner table, both only responding when spoken to.

"This is an excellent meal, Sophie. Thank you for preparing it," Stephen commented.

"Yes, it's wonderful. Where did you learn to make it?"

Sophie looked at Robin and opened her mouth before closing it rather quickly. Her eyes flicked over to her father, then to Robin, then to me, and finally, they rested back on Robin. "The apple crisp is from a cookbook and the rest I just threw together."

Mr. Young's voice was full of pride. "She's a hell of a cook. She could go on one of those cooking contests on TV."

Sophie's brow creased as she looked down. Shuffling a potato piece around on her plate, she shook her head. "It's not that good," she said under her breath. She was obviously not comfortable with compliments.

The topic of conversation floated between humorous incidents at the hospital and the fire station, and the pros and cons of universal health care. Neither of us said a word. In fact, Sophie didn't look up from her food until Stephen said something about a study he'd read concerning teenagers and sleep. Her face remained neutral as her father mentioned something about Sophie sleeping until the afternoon today.

"I was tired," she mumbled before taking another bite of apple crisp.

"How has your blood sugar been, Sophie?" Stephen asked.

She sighed and carefully rested her fork across the top of the bowl before taking a sip of her water. "Fine," she answered, her voice sounding fairly tense.

"Fatigue is a sign of…"

"Yes, I know," she cut him off.

"A sign of what?" Robin asked.

While Sophie sighed again, turning her head to the side, her gaze fixing on some invisible spot on the wall, Stephen finished, "Diabetic ketoacidosis."

Her father, who was a trained paramedic, said, "It's a condition in diabetics in which the blood sugar is elevated to near-lethal levels."

Sophie's father flicked his eyes to her. It wasn't hard to see worry in them.

"Tom," Sophie said with yet another sigh, "I take my insulin, I monitor my blood sugar, and I'm fine."

"Do you know the symptoms?" Stephen asked an already irritated Sophie. I wish he'd just stop talking!

"Fatigue, vomiting, dehydration, excessive urination, and sometimes confusion, which can lead to a coma."

Sophie was silent and didn't talk until dinner was over and we had cleared the table. I told her that she didn't have to clean up, but she shrugged and did it anyway. "Boy, who knew eating dinner with a doctor and a "fire medic" could be so much fun?" she said as she plopped down onto my sofa. I guessed that "fire medic" was fire station shorthand for firemen who were also paramedics.

I smiled as I pushed play on my iPod.

"Talk of vomit and urination during dessert was incredibly appetizing. Does he do that shit a lot?"

Chuckling, I turned around to face her. Stephen was fairly limitless and oblivious to how many disgusting medical facts and stories he told. Thankfully, she hadn't had to endure the STD talk or the picture of the cancerous lung. "S-sssometimes."

I went to sit on my bed. She sighed and I looked at her quizzically, but she just shook her head. "W-w-what?"

"Can't you sit on your bed differently?"

The confusion intensified. I had no idea what she was asking. "W-what?" I asked again.

"Move back." I blinked at her, but immediately did as she asked, scooting back into the middle. "Now fold your legs." Again, I did as she said, and sat cross-legged. "Doesn't that feel better? You look like you own that bed now."

I smiled, still not really understanding her and even though I was going to sound like a complete idiot, I asked again, "W-what?"

"You always sit on the edge of your bed like it's going to bite you or something. Now you look… chill."

Something about her tone and the relaxed way she was looking at me made me nervous. I ran a hand through my hair and tried to think of something to talk about, even though I just wanted to ask her to run *her* hands through my hair.

"The s-sssprouts are doing w-w-w-w, g-good. Do you w-want to g-go sssee?"

Although she smiled widely, she shook her head. "Not now that you look so comfortable."

I had to close my eyes for a moment and concentrate on breathing slowly. I forced myself to mentally play a Chopin piece in my head to relax my tensing body. All the signs had been pointing to my having a *thing* for Sophie. Knowing this was the case, made me anxious.

"What's wrong?"

I looked up and swallowed hard. How had we both worn green today? She was wearing a t shirt with the word "Boo!" on it and I was wearing the shirt that had been too small for David.

"Elliott?"

"Y-y-yes?"

"I asked you what was wrong. For a minute there you looked like you just finished a marathon." Cocking her head, she added, "But you look okay now."

"I-I'm fine."

As I sat there looking at Sophie, I thought about something Robin had asked me a long time ago about what I would attempt if I knew I could not fail. At the time I had no clue how to answer, but today my answer would be to try to get closer to Sophie. The powerful feelings I had for her I'd never had for anyone else.

I had no clue *how* to "be closer" to Sophie, and the likelihood of failure was pretty high. I was nothing like the guys she seemed to like, and I had no idea what she really thought of me. I'd spent the majority of my life avoiding people in general. I was no student of human behavior, and was having a hard time figuring out if she really wanted anything to do with me or if she was just trying to make the best of being stuck with me in her involuntary quest to be less screwed-up.

Either way, I still felt compelled to wheedle more information from her. She carried so much on her shoulders and she steadfastly refused to let anyone help. She refused to even acknowledge the weight was there.

"S-Sophie?" She looked up at me and I looked away.

"Hmm?"

"W-why didn't you g-go to the dance?"

"I told you. They're not my thing."

Shaking my head, I refocused on her. Her eyes looked exceptionally big and bright. "B-but you were in g-g-gymnastics. I-isn't dancing almost the ssssame?"

Pulling her hair to the side, she exposed her neck and I caught sight of the small scars. It reminded me of her e-mail.

She had asked me why I was fixated on it. I truly didn't know, but I felt bound to ask; like I *needed* her to tell me. She was always so guarded, and even though she knew my life wasn't honeysuckle and roses, she still didn't share any more than she felt she had to. It bothered me.

I understood her silence, but I didn't like it.

It felt like if I knew that one piece of information about the fork, it would be a huge victory, and with that knowledge, we would finally realize we had something more with each other than just the verbally-acknowledged friendship.

"It's not the actual dancing that's not my thing."

I drew my thoughts back to the question I had asked before I got sidetracked by my internal musings about the fork. I said, "Then w-why didn't you g-go?"

"A room filled with a bunch of people I don't really like isn't all that appealing, Elliott. It's pointless. Stupid people subject themselves to rites and rituals they don't believe in. I don't want to go to a dance because everyone else does. I don't want to go to the dance as some sort of status booster."

I took a deep breath and moved once more to the edge of my bed. If I knew I wouldn't fail, I'd have gotten up off of this bed and sat next to her on the couch. It wouldn't be the first time we were sitting close together. We shared a table in the greenhouse. There wasn't anything different about that and sitting next to her on my couch. Absolutely nothing. So there wasn't anything to be worried, nervous, or anxious about.

A tingle in my chest told me otherwise, but my body rose off the bed anyway, even as my mind battled with itself. The couch wasn't far, but it seemed like a long distance for my feet to travel. When I was sitting next to her, I couldn't bring myself to look at her. I felt almost frozen in fear.

It was incredibly new to me to actually *want* to be physically close to someone. I wanted to touch her face like I had last night, and I wanted her to run her hand through my hair the way she had before. I wanted this closeness because the currents of energy that flowed between us when we were close like this, felt so good; so right.

When I finally looked at her, she had sunk into the couch a bit, her head lying back. Her eyes were closed and I wondered if she was tired, bored, or just comfortable. It seemed to be the latter because of what she said next.

"I love your room." Her voice was quiet.

Remembering that it was only last night when she took my hand in the car, I thought that if I had no fear of failure, *I* would touch *her* hand this time. Despite the racing of my heart, my hand moved closer to hers, my fingers just brushing against the backside at first.

Then they glided over her smooth skin, and I felt that same prickling feeling that made me shiver. Before I could let out a shaky breath just from the thought that I'd actually done something like that, my fingers curled around her hand.

It was small, much smaller than mine, just as a woman's hand usually is compared to a man's. But it felt so fragile, like if I squeezed too hard, it would fracture into a million tiny pieces. There would be no squeezing though, since it took so much energy to even be able to do what I was doing now.

It didn't go unnoticed that she hadn't protested my touch. Her eyes were still closed and I wondered if she'd even felt it. She nibbled on her lower lip as her chest rose and fell more rapidly than usual.

As the current song faded away, I knew the next one was practically made for moments like this. If I thought I couldn't fail, I would pull her up, bring her into my arms, and dance with her.

But only if I knew my attempt wouldn't fail.

Chapter 26

Heavily Guarded

Elliott

As Otis Redding's rich voice singing of lonely arms saturated the thick air of my room, I suddenly felt emboldened, as if I truly knew I couldn't fail. I was already holding her hand and she hadn't pushed me away. It was incredibly easy to stand up, my hand still attached to hers, and pull her up with me. Sophie's eyes popped open and for a moment, I saw a brief flash of something. That fear, panic, whatever it was, dissipated quickly as her eyes locked with mine.

I was nervous, near panicking, and yet it seemed incredibly right and natural to bring Sophie this close to me; as if bringing her *into* me.

She wobbled just a bit as I tugged her up, and she gripped my fingers. I stepped back just enough to pull her away from the couch and risked a look at her face. Her eyes widened and she licked her bottom lip. I heard her sharp intake of breath and I steeled myself for the rejection that was sure to come.

But it didn't.

Instead, she let out a long sigh and her expression changed. It looked as if she was confused.

One of my hands slid behind her as I wrapped my arm around her waist. I was amazed how well she seemed to fit in my arms, as if she'd been made to be there. I swallowed hard and mentally forced my body to behave; to *not* react to the sheer nearness of her. If I allowed it, panic could overwhelm me at any second.

She smelled so good.

Slowly and very, very carefully, I moved just a little, bringing her with me in a soft sway. For just a moment, her head was pressed into my chest and I wondered what she thought of my rapidly-beating heart.

"I can't really dance, Elliott," she whispered into my green button-down shirt.

"N-n-neither can I," I whispered back. I'd never done it before in my life.

So we swayed in the middle of my room to the music her grandmother used to listen to while her father, Stephen, and Robin were downstairs and everyone else was at the Homecoming dance.

I didn't have time to wonder how long she would let me hold her, because she was already out of my arms and across the room before the song was over, her hand gliding along my books as she liked to do. I suddenly felt very empty, as though I'd lost a bit of myself.

Rubbing my hands on the side of my pants, I watched her pretend to be interested in what was on my shelf.

"I was putting the dishes in the dishwasher."

I blinked when I heard her quiet voice, wondering what it had to do with anything at all.

"I'd been late coming home from school, so I didn't get dinner done in time and it was supposed to be some kind of 'special' dinner for her and her boyfriend. I served it late and undercooked." Sophie paused, taking a breath. "She waited until he left."

I had wanted her to look at me so I could see her, but now that I understood what she was talking about, I knew I wouldn't have been able to look at anyone either.

"I was trying to get finished. I had homework, and Helen's idiot cat had puked all over the floor and I had to clean it up. Usually I knew where she was at all times; it was safer that way, but I must have been thinking about something else, or maybe I was really high or whatever, because I had no idea she was in the kitchen with me." Sophie stopped speaking for a while, scratching at the wood of my bookshelf, and fingered a small green rock.

She let out a deep breath. "I didn't know she was there until I felt the pain in my jaw. She hit me from the side and I stumbled. My legs hit the door of the open dishwasher and I couldn't stop myself from falling. I hit my head on the edge of the counter, but the searing pain in my neck was too much. It was the last time I ever put forks or knives with the pointy sides sticking up."

"S-SSSSophie," I began as I took a step toward her. I stopped when she turned quickly.

"I have to go."

No. I didn't want her to leave. "D-don't." I took another step forward, but she pressed herself against the bookshelf. Her fingers wouldn't stop moving: curling, straightening, twisting. She was tapping her foot, but not to the beat of the music, and her shoulders shook a little. She looked like I felt during the onset of a panic attack.

I didn't want that for her.

"S-Sophie?" I took a step backward, knowing that any forward movement would just make her even more uncomfortable. "W-w-w-will you e-mail m-mm-mmme tomorrow?"

She swallowed hard and took a shaky breath before finally looking me in the eyes. She nodded. "But I have to go now." It was barely a whisper which let me know that she'd never told anyone this before; the newness of telling someone was probably more frightening for her than the night it actually happened. I knew how scary it was when people learned secrets which were never meant to be revealed.

I returned her nod and went back to my bed. By sitting down, I hoped that I was showing her she was free to leave and that she wasn't trapped. It took her a moment, but she surprised me by sitting down next to me. Suddenly she was in my arms again, her breath hitting my neck and sending shivers down my body. I didn't know what to do. I felt like it was vital that I do *something*.

I should've wrapped my arms around her and whispered that it would be okay, even if it wasn't going to be. I should've let her know I cared for her and I understood the pain she felt. I should've done a lot of things, but my chances were taken from me as she pulled back and then stood. Quickly, she ran her hands through her long hair and went to the door, muttering a goodbye as she left.

The feeling of her so very close to me was beautiful. Her short hug was an acknowledgement that something deep had now passed between us.

As painful as it was to watch and listen to her tell that story, I'd been right. It *did* feel like a victory.

ɞ • ɞ

I went downstairs as Mr. Young and Sophie were leaving because Stephen and Robin expected it. Sophie was quiet and wouldn't look at me. I didn't take it personally. While I'd only known her for a short time, it was easy to see that she wasn't rejecting me with her silence.

It was her nature to avoid thinking about things. She had just told me about being stabbed in the neck with a fork because her mother hit her. I understood her silence and that she felt helpless and exposed.

I retreated upstairs, to the only sanctuary I knew: My bedroom. I couldn't help but feel as though we had crossed some kind of invisible line in our relationship. These questions we asked had a purpose. She wouldn't answer mine if some part of her didn't want me to know these things about her. Again, that felt like a huge milestone.

Our dance was a dance for those who'd never been granted the right to be innocent. We'd barely moved and it was far too short, but I hadn't failed in my quest to be close with her. Afterward, she'd finally admitted out loud that something dark and terrible had happened to her.

If I hated Sophie's mother before based on pure speculation, I loathed her now. There was no funny, but scary story that accompanied the four little marks on her neck. Instead, it was *just* scary. There was only pain and confusion. It didn't matter how old Sophie had been when it happened, or what she did to deserve something like that, because no person, at any age, deserved to be hit. Thinking about how she could have died because sharp implements were so dangerously close to major arteries, made it that much more horrific.

For I moment, I felt paralyzed as I realized just how close to death she could have been. It must have been bloody. It must have hurt. Forks, while being sharp, were sort of blunt as well. Thank God there wasn't a knife to accompany it; otherwise Sophie probably would have died that night. I wondered if her mother took her to a doctor, or if it was just patched up at home to avoid all of the questions that would have surely come up if she'd gone to the Emergency room. I wondered if the dirty fork gave her an infection that her body had to fight off while it tried to heal itself.

I knew that kind of pain. I wanted to give her one of my heavily-guarded secrets like the one she had given me tonight, but my chest seized just thinking about it.

I wondered what the future would bring for us. She had a pattern of saying or doing something that was real, or at least that *felt* real, and then withdrawing. I wondered how much damage our pseudo-dance and her small but incredibly meaningful confession had caused, and whether she would even talk to me.

The next day I sent her a very short e-mail that was intended to let her know that I knew how scared she was.

Sophie,

I won't tell anyone. I realize that what you told me last night is a secret. I know that whether you meant to or not, you've entrusted me with its keeping. I won't betray that trust, I promise. I'm your friend, Sophie, and you're mine and that makes you the best thing in my life.

Thank you for giving that to me. I won't ever do anything to damage what you've given to me. I realize how special it is.

Thank you, Sophie.

Elliott

I typed her name three times and I liked how it felt doing it. I liked typing the word friend because I knew that we *were* friends. I felt warm and safe because whatever the future brought for the two of us, I would always have the comfort of knowing that she chose me, even if it was just for that brief moment in my room to the rich, soothing voice of Otis Redding.

While my siblings talked about the gym full of streamers and what songs were played, I thought again about my own dance with Sophie. It was short, probably not even a minute, but she'd let me hold her longer than I thought she would have. When she moved away from my arms, I knew that it wasn't about me. Then she'd given me a hug.

I wanted to hold her again, to feel her body close to mine. I wanted to feel that chemical exchange and the way her skin made mine tingle. I wanted to know if she felt a similar connection. I wanted to know her and I hoped that she still wanted to know me.

I wanted to make her happy; to see her smile like she had by the stream in the woods of flowers of fallen leaves, and in the book store. I wanted to take all those memories away from her that made her so sad.

I wondered if Sophie would ever let me dance with her again. I wanted her in my arms, pressed against me. I wanted to be so close to her that I could smell her. I wanted to be so close to her that she wouldn't have to share those heavily-guarded secrets, because they would just silently absorb into me.

I didn't just want to know her secrets. Surprisingly, I wanted her to know mine. There was so much I could tell her. There was so much about my real family that I'd never said to *anyone*. It would be painful, but at the end of the process, *someone* would know it all. *Someone* could help me carry *my* burden, but before I could allow that to happen, I needed to help her. I was *dedicated* to helping her as if it was my new mission in life.

Like speaking more fluently, understanding Sophie Young was a goal of mine.

Sophie was a puzzle, and she purposefully withheld some of the pieces. It was frustrating and baffling, wonderful and exciting.

These new pieces she handed me were bits of her; pieces of all the dark secrets she'd never given up. I understood why they were kept so secure. I understood the need to keep them safe, away from others. People judged. People hurt, and some things were never meant to be spoken of. There were memories locked within me that would take the Jaws of Life to pry the doors open, and yet some part of me desperately wanted to give them up freely to her.

With her admission, I could finally feel that we really were friends. Maybe now that she'd said it out loud, Sophie could learn to deal in another way. Maybe she'd stop spiraling toward self-destruction. If she never did, I was sure I'd still feel this way about her. Always. I was drawn to her. Despite it all, I was in love with Sophie Young and I wanted her to know all of me.

I just wasn't ready yet.

End of Book One

A preview of the next novel in the Old Wounds series

Little Battles

Coming from The Writer's Coffee Shop Publishing House in April 2011

~ • ~

It was after eleven when I finally opened the two e-mails from Elliott. The first was our usual question and answer. The second one asked just one question. *Are you okay?*

Why the hell couldn't he have just not cared like every other person? Why did he have to be so damned concerned and shit? Couldn't he just want to bang me like everyone else?

Hell, no. Elliott had to be all kind and caring with his puppy eyes and Otis Redding dances.

I probably should have just cut the whole thing off with Elliott, not even answering the questions and not letting him entertain the idea that it was a good idea to be my friend, but I had to acknowledge that there was something about him that made me want to truly be his friend. There was something about Elliott that made me *need* to be around him.

I was going to need to rein myself in just a little bit. I would allow myself to be his friend, but I wouldn't keep going the way we were. I had to remember how to keep it together. I certainly didn't need to continue to let myself get swept up into…

Who the hell was I kidding? I was in pretty deep with him already and I could never take back what I told him. He knew now and he would always know.

CPSIA information can be obtained at www.ICGtesting.com
Printed in the USA
LVOW080403221012

303854LV00001B/98/P